The Island Of Dreams

IMMORTAL DREAMERS

BOOK 1

JAYE VINER

I0772255

The Island of Dreams

The Island of Dreams
Copyright © 2025 by Jaye Viner

All Rights Reserved.

This book is a work of fiction. Any resemblance to actual persons, living or dead is entirely coincidental. This work, or any portion thereof, may not be reproduced in any form or by any means including information storage and retrieval systems, or used in any manner whatsoever without the author's express written permission. Thank you for buying an authorized copy of this book and supporting writers.

Developmental Editor: Kit Haggard
Copyeditor: Sarah McGuire
Cover Designer: Miblart
Interior Book Formatting by: Authortree | https://www.authortree.co/

ISBN: 979-8-9878525-8-3

MORTAL REALM
RUINS
JUNGLE
VILLAGE
CLOUD CITY
THE FALLS

FAE VILLAGE
CASTLE
TREE HOUSE
WINTER WOOD
G WOOD
SUMMER WOOD
MERMAIDS
CAVES
GREEN CITY

Other books by Jaye Viner

Jane of Battery Park

Elaborate Lives

Terrible Love

Casta Diva

Homme Fatale

The Afternoon Delight Shorts

Saucy Kaylee and her Stockbroker

Smart Jen and her Reality TV Star

Sweet Penny and her Tech Bro

Sour Marlee and her Sergeant

To All the Crips who've come before me for revealing the world for what it is, and for giving me the language to deconstruct the old to make something new.

Content warning

This book is in direct conversation with humanity's long tendency to associate disability with a lack of morality, and often, outright villainy. There are characters and moments in this book that reflect that ablest viewpoint on the way to understanding that there is absolutely no correlation between moral fiber and physical or mental ability.

Also note, the opening chapters of this book reflect a main character socialized with the racism and bigotry of nineteenth-century London and imperialism. It has been watered down for modern audiences but not erased.

CHAPTER 1
A Mythos

The Neverland knows when it is time for her children to swim the current of the world below, but even those who are ready to swim do not always arrive at the golden peaks of the Cloud City. Some are carried downstream to the Green Caves, where they spend eternity below the water. This is often no fault of their own, but rather the weight of what they've built up from their lives above. Sometimes what the Neverland offers is not enough to lift this weight. Some youthful souls, no matter what the island does, are never free enough to fly.

CHAPTER 2
All Hallows Eve

Oct 31st, 1898

Justine found Miss Barry in the morning as she went into the front room to stoke the fire. The asylum, being rather an ad hoc construction of rooms added on or amended as its needs grew, presented as more of a labyrinth. Justine had lugged her coal pail through the predawn dark up the stairs from the laundry, where she'd started the boiler fires, then down a nook hall to the kitchen. Then around the back way to Dr. and Mrs. Palmer's rooms and on around halls and up stairs and down stairs, ducking under this too-small door and that until finally she came into the front room through its side door. She wouldn't have noticed something amiss in the atrium if not for the whisper.

The ghosts have come early, thought Justine with a shudder. Spirits often brushed up against her, whispered their sad pleas to see their beloveds again. Always, always they came when she was alone, with no others to confirm her experience or keep her grounded to the stuff of the living world. Tonight, with the thinning of the veil between the realms making it easier for spirits to wander, she expected not a moment's peace unless she could keep herself in company.

The ghost's voice sounded like wind coming down the chimney. Justine hurried to light the fire in the hope it would banish the spirit. Thrice Justine attempted to light the hearth before the flame took. Each time it seemed the voice rushed down the bricks to snuff it out. Once the flame took, Justine still heard the voice, a hushed whine, not quite a moan, a staccato gasp of a breath going out. It caused her to look to her left, out the open doorway, to where she could see the corner of the reception desk on one side and the floor she'd washed the previous day shimmering in the moonshine.

No, thought Justine. It was a thought for the cleanliness of the floor, the deep dread that something had spilled, and she'd have to wash it again. Floors were the bane of her existence. She utterly loathed, despised, and all-out hated cleaning floors, even though Mrs. Palmer said it was unchristian to hate anything except the devil. What would Mrs. Palmer think if she knew Justine had seen a devil when she was a child? Not the Christian one, but one of the others, the Pan who stole children from death's door. Mrs. Palmer, who'd given herself the project of elevating Justine's morality with art and literature, so she might see for herself the path of the upright, didn't believe in haunting spirits, let alone the old gods.

Leaving her coal pail, Justine wiped her sooty hands on her apron, pushed herself up on protesting knees, and went to the doorway. Here, at the threshold, Justine paused. The air felt so much colder ahead of her than behind. There was a stillness that took up space, as though stepping forward would be a motion to press into something solid.

There was no need to test this boundary. Justine could clearly see the splayed form of Miss Barry draped elegantly down the center of the atrium. Her feet lay toward the asylum's front door, her head toward Justine. Her majestic mane of brown hair fanned out all around like a gaudy, baroque halo, her palms held open in supplication at her sides as though this presentation might salvage her soul's tarnished reputation; being a suicide begging at the gates of heaven.

Still, Justine stepped forward so she could more clearly see Miss Barry's face. If she had been marked by the Pan, something in her visage would have been transformed. "Is that why your spirit lingers?" she asked the still cold air as she tiptoed forward.

When she'd lived in the workhouse, she'd seen the Pan. He'd come to the bedside of the boy she'd loved as much as any child of six could love a child of ten who barely acknowledged her existence. Dietrich had been the most beautiful boy in the whole place, until he'd caught the fever. It had struck down dozens that winter, including both Justine and Dietrich's mothers, so there was no one at Dietrich's bedside when the death god came to claim him for that other place.

Justine had seen him across the sleeping room, a gangly, boyish figure who appeared human, yet hovered over Dietrich like a giant bird stripped of both feathers and wings. The demon had reached down to touch Dietrich's chest. In that moment, Justine knew all her prayers for Dietrich's recovery were going to be answered in the negative. She'd jumped up, running across sleeping bodies, waving her arms and screaming. But she'd been too late. The Pan laughed at her as he flew away. When she reached Dietrich's side, his face had already begun to take on the fixedness of death's shadow. That was the night she'd stopped believing in God and allowed herself to imagine other possibilities for her afterlife.

But still, she wasn't certain it was a better thing to be claimed by the Pan than Heaven. The fixed expression on Dietrich's face seemed wholly unknown to the stuff of the living; it had frightened her. Now, she was older and thought she'd look again and would be able to tell something about it.

The blood from Miss Barry's opened wrists had pooled on both sides of her, had seeped into her white nightgown and into the ends of her halo. It was a solid now, dark and sticky, and promised Justine a morning's worth of isolated labor. She was the most beautiful body Justine had ever seen. Miss Barry, looking like a painting, had claimed death as an act of power. She held nothing in concert with the workhouse deaths so common in Justine's childhood, the slow withering away, the hopelessness, the failure of yet another life to break the cycle of unpaid debts and empty opportunities.

For a long moment, Justine stood and looked down at the dead girl. She'd been a hysteric, prone to fits of dizziness and pains, of speaking about herself as though she was someone else. Once, Justine had chanced upon her standing very still, watching the younger children of the asylum playing in the gardens.

"Aren't they so like fairies?" she'd asked. "I wish I could fly away as they do." This seemed a strange thing to say. Justine saw only tragedy in the children sent to the asylum, but she kept quiet and let Miss Barry finish saying her piece. "They're so free. I never had the chance to be free like that."

In this last comment, Justine had understood some of what Miss Barry saw because it was something true for herself. She'd never thought of it before, that some children passed their early years in story worlds, playing at make believe adventures, and believing in fairies. They could do this because someone else gave them food and clothes, a home where they felt safe. Miss Barry was solidly middle class, so it seemed unlikely she'd wanted for any of those things, unless perhaps someone in her home had made her feel unsafe. Something inside of her had been broken because of it.

The spirit wind carried an uncanny breeze across the atrium. It touched Justine's face almost like a caress. She leaned into it for Miss Barry's sake and tried to think of this hint of ghostly touch as something precious.

"If you're taken to a magical place, will you come back and tell me next year?" asked Justine. "Even if it isn't heaven."

The wind withdrew, twirling in the air above Miss Barry's body, pulling at the ribbons on her nightgown, then shifting up toward the ceiling. "I hope He lets you in," said Justine to the drifting soul. "Or there's no hope for me."

She said this as though Mrs. Palmer might be listening, ready to punish her for any unholy thought. But in her mind, Justine wasn't so worried about making it to heaven. She dared to hope that she'd be allowed somewhere where floors cleaned themselves, food appeared from nowhere, and fairies held a party in the moonshine every night.

With a sigh that carried much more weight than a girl of eighteen years, Justine turned back and retrieved her coal pail. Four fires left, then she'd be needed downstairs to help Talia with the laundry. The most magic she could hope for from this life was dry kindling and, perhaps tonight, success at the All Hallows party she was attending without an invitation. At the night watch desk, she gently tapped the sleeping guard on the shoulder and told him Miss Barry had moved on to a new place. She didn't mention the restless spirit in the foyer.

TALIA, THE HEAD HOUSEKEEPER, HAD ALREADY STARTED THE FIRST load of Dr. and Mrs. Palmer's unmentionables when Justine arrived. "Happy Hallows morn," muttered Talia with dark irony. Justine returned the greeting with more enthusiasm. *Tonight, everything will change if only Sarah manages to steal the powder.*

"Plans for this unholy occasion?"

"Unholy plans should always be secret." Justine wiggled her eyebrows at Talia and resisted the impulse to tell. Talia wouldn't approve of Justine involving one of the patients from the children's ward in thievery. She'd approve of spellcasting even less.

Talia arched an eyebrow to cast doubt on the value of Justine's secrecy. "Superstitions get you nowhere good."

"Telling wishes before they come true ruins the wish."

Talia had always seemed impossibly old, but now, with thoughts of death on her mind, Justine saw Talia as not so removed from herself. She was maybe thirty, with the scars of pockmarks on her face and gray cracks in the skin of her hands where they'd dried out from doing all the washing in the damp of winter. As far as Justine knew, she'd never planned to do anything with her life besides someone else's cleaning. This was the message she carried in her body.

To Justine, a body was never just a body. It was a map, a collection of icons and markers that added up to one's fate. This was how the death gods knew who belonged to them. The icons and markers gave the possibility of diverging roads, of possibilities. Talia's body had always spoken to Justine of a single path, stretching out before her to the shadow land. To be younger and unmarked, as Miss Barry had been, meant infinite possibilities, if only she hadn't been ill. Thinking of Miss Barry made her wonder again if she'd been allowed into Heaven, or if she had been young enough to be marked by the death god, and if that was such a terrible thing.

Justine saw her road clogged with the markers steering her down Talia's same, narrow path. Each hour that passed erased forks in the road, possible alternatives vanishing with each backbreaking coal pail, with each unwieldy scalding linen pressed through the ringer. One could only live a life like this for so long before she forgot to dream.

"Did you hear the description of the Princess of Wales's dress from the ball?" asked Justine. "Crushed mauveine velvet!"

"I've touched crushed velvet once. Last year, I went to the

Circus of Dreams and sat on a bed of black crushed velvet while an acrobat spun through the stars above my head. Softest thing I've ever felt."

"I could die to wear a dress of crushed velvet."

Talia tsked steaming water at Justine. "Don't go talking of death today with the haunts so close. Crushed velvet anything won't be in our futures. Best not think of it." She gave a hard nod as though taking this thought into herself and resolving to hang on to it. In her own mind, Justine hung on to the opposite, the promise, a future where someone else would be doing the laundry. With any luck, it would begin that night.

Footsteps sounded on the stairs, running too fast.

"Slow down there!" called Talia.

The cook's boy crashed down the last two stairs, gasping and ashen. "Dr. Palmer says you're needed upstairs to clean the atrium floor."

"Nonsense. Justine just done it yesterday."

"There's been an accident." The boy swallowed hard. "A patient died there over the night."

With an oath, Talia reached under her apron to grasp the cross that hung around her neck. She pressed it to her lips. "Heaven save us."

"Heaven save us," echoed Justine because she knew this was the right thing to do. But she was just about to give up on waiting for heaven to save her. Tonight, she was going to make her own magic, ghosts or no ghosts.

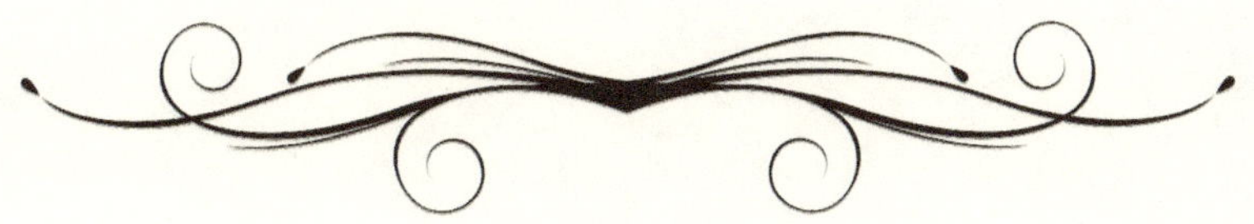

CHAPTER 3

A Mythos

For parents keeping vigil at their children's bedside, it is a sight bitter, sweet, and not a little strange to see the face of the Neverland's caretaker disturb the familiar features of their babies as he marks them for their divergent journey. The presence of the one they call the goat-footed god, the Pan, the Pied Piper, or more simply, Peter, the Lost Boy, means death has come, but hope is not lost. Their child will fall, not to the current of eternity, but to the way station of the island, where they will have every adventure and joy life did not see fit to grant them.

In those last moments of the child's life, the parents will see the Lost Boy come and go, leaving behind the crisp scent of dying leaves, a cloying sweetness at the edge of death's chill. Then their precious one will pass, a body emptied, as the spirit travels to that in between place. They become the child of another mother, who the island helps to be the best mother she can be.

CHAPTER 4

A Chestnut Spell

"Did you get it?" asked Justine when little Sarah crept into the privy that night.

Sarah handed over Mrs. Palmer's face powder.

Though Sarah hadn't spoken more than a word or two since she was three, (she was now almost eleven) she knew much more than people believed. She snuck around the asylum touching this door, that particular spot on the wall, moving a chair that wasn't where it should be back into its proper place. Any deviation from her routine triggered hysterics more deserving of someone catching Jack the Ripper in the midst of one of his bloody crimes than a young girl. The nurses had long ago given up trying to cure her, but because she was the darlingest of all, and seemingly harmless if left alone, she was sometimes allowed into Dr. and Mrs. Palmer's rooms. This was how she knew exactly where Mrs. Palmer kept her cosmetics.

In the light of a candle stub, Sarah watched Justine stand at the cracked mirror of the toilet table and whiten her face.

"Someday this could be you," said Justine. "Remember Hallows Eve. It's the best time for girls like us to make our mark. You don't want to live out your best years here, right?

And I certainly don't want to live out my best years here. So, we find a good house, we make like we belong, throw a chestnut in the fire with a name on it, eat the salt, make a wish, claim a well-stuffed husband by yuletide. Can't wait any longer or my looks will fade. As my mother used to say, 'An old maid is just a girl who didn't take hold of where she was going.'"

Justine paused her work to see that Sarah's attention had wandered to the cracks in the floor, tracing patterns as she so often did. The floor Justine had cleaned now already dirty, dirty, dirty as though the lino was a living thing that grew filth. She was so tired of doing so much work with so little to show.

Thinking this made her feel guilty. Mrs. Palmer was always praising Justine with fine ideas about the working girl growing the good of the world day by day through unmemorable acts. Apparently, these girls were valued even if they met their final rest in unvisited tombs, anonymous in their lifetimes of quiet service. Ideas written, no doubt, by one of those high-minded authors Mrs. Palmer was always reading, an author who hadn't started scrubbing washroom floors when she was eight.

In the mirror, Justine appraised the white mask she'd powdered over her face. It was so white it nearly matched the nightcap hiding her hair, but not as white as the excessively starched nightshift she'd stolen from the men's ward because it was long enough to hide her scuffed shoes. She wasn't quite the girl she wanted to be, not delicate and nymph-like as Sarah was, with her dainty, pointed chin and dewdrop eyes. Sarah, fast growing into the girl of men's dreams, and thus also the ideal of women's dreams. For what woman didn't want to be a perfect object of desire, if only for the breath of a moment? It was an ideal Justine would never match. Her bones were large and solid, rounded with stretched muscle and a solidness that sometimes made her feel like a rock when she wanted to be a bird.

It doesn't matter if I'm beautiful, she thought. *The spell will fix all that.*

"Wish me the stars and saints," said Justine as she kissed the top of Sarah's golden head goodbye. Quick as a lark, Justine flew down the dark halls of the asylum, tiptoes on the floors she'd polished, her ghostly reflection catching in the windows as she rushed to the women's ward. And then she was out the big front window, climbing down the ivy, and fleeing across the lawn to the side gate, her breath giving her away as a living being on this night when the dead rose up to mingle with the living.

I'll avoid the worst of them if I'm back by midnight, thought Justine with firm resolve. It was more a hope than a truth. Last year, she'd thought the same thing and still the spirits had found her. They'd been so thick they formed a cloud, passing through her body so she shivered and trembled. Their voices had been indistinct but insistent, pleading with her, though she couldn't imagine what help she could give. This year she was going to use the haunting night for her benefit. It was the only night of true magic that existed, and Justine was badly in need of a spell, or two, or five, to recast her fortunes. Spirits be damned.

Down Brompton Hill she went, past the dairy, around the bend of the postmaster's station, and into the houses of the glen with their old trees and stately brick facades. She passed several houses with their lights out before she found one that looked right. Jack-o'-lanterns lined the walk up to the porch where a figure draped in black stood sentry.

As Justine approached, she saw it was only a wooden statue with a sweet, mocking mouth and chains, not unlike those sometimes used in the asylum, locked around its wrists, then draped over the door. The door stood open, ready to receive visitors. She heard the chatter of voices within, though the entryway was dark. A circle of flame glowed in a dish of alcohol on the entry table, turned an eerie green by salt. Its light cast a whole chorus of gilded bric-a-brac—equestrian figurines, a bronze Herakles, portraits in miniature of Queen Victoria and Prince Albert—into haunts of a bountiful fairy wood wrapped up in the shadows of a tasseled runner made with the finest stitching.

She heard the pop of a fire, the startled yips of young women who'd probably been standing too close, then the deeper voices of the young men telling them it was just the fire, or was it? Nervous giggles. Justine wasn't ready to meet people. Rather than enter the party through the front room, she turned and went into the dining room where the lights were on. A servant was setting out candles carved from turnips and carrots between the brass candelabra.

"Need anything, miss?" asked the servant.

Justine shook her head. She pressed her lips tight together. Tonight, she'd play the mute ghost as Sarah did, so her service accent wouldn't give her away.

A small group had gathered in the library for a fortune reading. More circles of salted-alcohol flames burned green around the room, turning the lions and Januses of the furniture corners into gargoyles and demons. A curio full of paperweights and glass shells seemed to expand and shrink in the shadows. Indeed, the entire room pressed a weighted significance upon its occupants. This was a room of greatness, propped up with satin and rosewood and marble. And all along one wall, the spines of books, speaking not just of a life lived with the ability to understand such knowledge, but the time to pursue it. In the center of this great room sat five young people, who would, if not for the circumstances of their births, have been Justine's peers.

She could just make out the pointed hat of a witch, the

painted skirt of a queen of hearts, a two-sided clown, a fairy with paper wings, and there, at the head of the circle, turning the cards, a face that made her shiver with dread, the child-snatcher Pan, with wild hair, a twisted mouth, knobbed forehead, and slanted oriental eyebrows. The one who lured dying children away to his island lair so they couldn't rest in the grace of heaven.

Even as she recognized the costume, Justine felt the impulse to say it wasn't correct. The mask made the Pan look like a demon from the pit of hell that Mrs. Palmer was always going on about. But the Pan Justine had seen as a child was gentler, almost like he was doing the dead child a kindness stealing them away.

The boy wearing the mask was working very hard to be the kind of Pan they'd been taught to fear. Tossing his hair around like a lion, he read the tarot with a low, growling voice, turning the cards in slow, jerking movements, and leering this way and that into his friends' faces until one of them drew back, tittering nervously and said, "Come off it, Jack. Don't tempt that creature here."

Jack Woolf lifted the mask with a grin, his teeth green in the salt light. "Don't tell me you still believe that nursery story."

"It's real," said the queen of hearts. "I saw him in my baby brother. His face wasn't his own when he passed."

"Well, I don't believe it any more than I believe in ghosts." Jack looked past the circle right at Justine. "Come join us, ghost? Or are you haunting the halls this night?"

For a moment, she thought she might join them. Or at least she might speak. What would she say? Something impressive. *I've seen the real Pan.* Although they would all laugh at her when they learned she'd been so young. Who was she to say the Pan wasn't as demonic as the mask? All her life she'd been told what to fear and always somehow it had shown itself as a little less than she supposed.

I'll tell them the spirits are among us. Perhaps I could call one of them to me and we'll move the room around. But no. She couldn't be distracted from her purpose. This was her best chance; she couldn't waste it.

Justine stuck her arms out in front of her as though in a ghostly trance, leaned forward, then wavered back, turned and walked out. She returned to the front hall, then entered the front room where a group of girls clustered around the fire, winding chestnuts around sticks. Boys' voices could be heard in the kitchen shouting at each other.

"No, not that way."

"Don't let it get away!"

"Over here!"

The shattering of fine china was drowned out by the boys' laughter.

Justine cautiously approached the girls. She didn't have experience doing things like this, casual conversations, social graces, everyone knowing what was right to say and do. Most conversations she had with strangers, she had while bumming cigarettes and trying to keep warm while running errands for the asylum. Certainly, the men she met in the alley behind the smithy didn't expect polite conversation.

A girl waved Justine into the circle, but the others carried on without notice, chanting soft words as they wound their chestnut spells. Justine took up a stick and grasped a handful of chestnuts from the nearest bowl. She took up the chant as she began to wind.

May my marriage be my theme
To visit me in this night's dream
The image of my lover send
Let me see his name and face
And his occupation trace

One by one, the girls finished their chants and threw the sticks into the fire. They pressed together to watch for signs.

Justine pressed with them, feeling how much cleaner they were than her, the light scents of flowers on their clothes, their smooth-skinned hands. She watched her stick burn, the chestnuts sizzle and pop, then she closed her eyes and wished with all her might that she'd be one of those girls. She pressed the names of boys into her mind so the spirits walking the earth that night would draw them together.

Henry Dawson, the solicitor's apprentice.

Michael Shoemaker, who visited his brother in the asylum and was going to college next year.

Jack Woolf, wearer of the Lost Boy mask, Lord Mayor's son, bookkeeping apprentice, and nearly twenty-one, which meant he would shortly come into his inheritance and begin looking for a wife.

After the stick had burned to ash, Justine ate an orange—oh, sweet perfection—and watched to see if any of the boys had obviously fallen under enchantment. As the stroke of midnight drew near, the revelers prepared to burst from the house and run down the streets calling out the dead they'd never see. The boys declared themselves white knight protectors, arming themselves with torches and garlic-wrapped sticks to ward off spirits. Justine came out to the porch with the other girls, but no one offered his arm. She was left forgotten on the front porch as the couples dashed off into the night.

The spell just needs some time to work, thought Justine.

Still, she lingered, waiting just to see if perhaps the spell would bring her a savior, until the loneliness became unbearable.

THE ASYLUM SAT DARK AND SILENT ON ITS ALL-SEEING HILL, clutched in a suffocating skin of ivy, which held most of the windows shut fast and blocked most hope of light except on the brightest days. Justine trudged around through the shrubbery to the women's ward and the window she'd left open. Sarah might still be awake. She liked to stay awake at night because there was no one to bother her thoughts or press their presence on her mind.

They would sit together on Sarah's bed and Justine would whisper a story that was better than the stories Mrs. Palmer read aloud from her books. *It would be a love match story*, thought Justine, in honor of her hope that a young gentleman would soon come calling. Sarah's prospects were also looking up. A fine German doctor had come to the asylum to examine her and said he knew the kind of treatment she needed. At long last, both girls had a promise for brighter futures. Tonight, they'd celebrate.

Justine hoisted herself up over the sill and dropped into the sleeping ward. The room felt colder than outside, and she sensed again that thickness in the air as though it carried a weight. *Has Miss Barry's ghost wandered here?* thought Justine as she looked down the line of beds.

A figure stood over one of the beds at the far end. Sarah's bed. The figure appeared a stranger, and yet there was something familiar about him. Justine pulled off her shoes and crept silently down the aisle of beds until she came to Sarah's, to the boy standing over her sleeping body.

For a moment, Justine thought the boy was Jack Woolf, summoned by her spell to fall in love with her that very night. It would be Justine's luck that her future husband would be distracted by beautiful, golden-haired Sarah. But then she saw that this boy was younger than Jack. He still carried that uncomfortable posture of limbs he hadn't grown into. If she'd had any doubt, Justine noticed next that the boy's heels didn't touch the floor. He didn't so much stand as hover at the bedside. Jack Woolf, sensible, teasing, ambitious young man on the make, did not fly. Cold fear washed over Justine.

No. No. Not her.

The boy's wild hair glinted Irish-red in the moonlight. He wore a strange garment of rotting leaves stuck together. As he looked down at Sarah, his smile was like a wolf's bared teeth.

"You!" hissed Justine. "You're in the wrong room."

His head swiveled her direction, jutting forward as though to take a bite out of her. She stumbled back, bumping into the end of the bed on the other side of the aisle. The woman there stirred in her sleep. Both Justine and the boy froze. When Justine felt sure she would sleep on, she turned her gaze back to the boy and saw him in full moonlight. His skin, so perfectly smooth, glowing like an angel's, his finely etched features, an alabaster brow, strong nose and jawline. His beauty stunned her. She wanted to reach out and touch his face. But then, he turned back toward Sarah with that predatory hunger in his eyes and Justine remembered herself.

"Don't take her. She's not sick." Justine grabbed the boy's grimy arm to pull him back but immediately released him. Her fingers burned as though on fire.

He glared at her, then, as though belatedly realizing she could see him, his gaze softened into something like curiosity. His mouth moved as though he was speaking or trying to speak but couldn't make the sounds. The sounds came late, words scratching over his throat in a clawing rasp. "She's sick with age," he said, a cough. When he spoke the second time, the voice was clearer, more like a boy's. "Soon she'll grow up and be lost."

"Well yes, it's a hard thing growing up for some people. But we all do it."

"She won't." He turned his attention back to Sarah, reaching toward her.

Justine slapped his hand away with a quick, darting motion to avoid the worst of another burn. "You don't want her. She's quiet. A mute, actually. Didn't you see Miss Barry?"

"She'll be our new mother, heart of my island, girl eternal."

The way the boy said, *my island*, as though this new mother meant the world to him, made Justine's heart begin to pound with an unholy hope.

"Your island," she said. "Is it a magical place?"

"Hmm."

"Do fairies live there?"

"I suppose so."

Justine thought of beautiful Miss Barry, who saw all the cruelty in the world and dared to dream she could reach for something better. It seemed she'd made a good choice, much better than betting her future on a chestnut spell.

But he wants Sarah.

"Mother?" Justine held back bitter laughter. "She's just a girl. What you need is someone like me, who knows what you need. I would love to never grow up." She found herself slanting her hips, giving him her eyes the way she and the other girls sometimes did on Friday nights outside the dance hall, teasing the men on their way to the two-penny hop. "Or the spirit in the foyer, who I'm sure is calling to you." This last part she added because she felt sure this was what Miss Barry wanted. And now, Justine wanted it too.

The Lost Boy advanced on her, dark eyes keen but not with the interest she wanted. "How old are you?"

"Fifteen." She gave him Miss Barry's age.

"Do you tell stories?"

"The best stories there ever were told." Justine felt herself melting under the intensity of his gaze. Each answer seemed to draw him closer, which meant he was moving away from Sarah, but Justine hadn't meant to excite this degree of attention. He was young and boney, yet she knew, if he came at her, it would be almost impossible to defend herself.

"And what games do you like?" he asked.

"Games where dreams come true. Magic games."

He stopped advancing. A smile as bright and true as any innocent's spread across his face. "Alright. I promise not to take her if you can find the gateway."

"The what?"

"The gateway to the island. Only those with special sight ever find it. And since you can see me when I've been trying not to be seen, you must have it." The boy crossed his arms over his chest. "Or are you scared?"

Truth be told, Justine was a little scared. She didn't know what to make of this strange situation. She wasn't even sure what exactly was being offered. But she knew she didn't want to keep on living the life she had. And who was to say the Pan had really come for Miss Barry? Maybe he'd been ensnared by Justine's chestnut spell. Why couldn't the girl who saw spirits snare a god? Anyway, she wasn't going to waste her chance. "I'm not scared."

"Then let's find it."

The boy flew up over her head and landed on the sill of the open window. "Now?" she asked in a voice that seemed barely louder than a whisper. "The ghosts are out."

"So, you *are* scared!" he crowed.

"No, I—"

"Come on." He leaned into the room and extended a grimy hand to her.

The last thing Justine wanted to do was touch him again. She thought about pushing him out and slamming the window shut. But that would accomplish nothing. One step, then another, and she was with him at the sill. This time, the boy didn't burn her. His grip was as cold as an iron pipe in winter and so tight Justine wouldn't have been able to free herself from him even if she'd wanted. In that moment, his beautiful smile beaming at her and the impossible lightness of her feet lifting off the floor, Justine found herself offering a prayerful apology to Miss Barry's spirit.

"I'll take you to the park and give you one clue," said the Pan. "But then you either find it or you don't."

Justine nodded. All words had dropped from her mind as though they were the stuff of polished floors and coal pails, and here she was in the air, being pulled along like a child's balloon, up, up, and away.

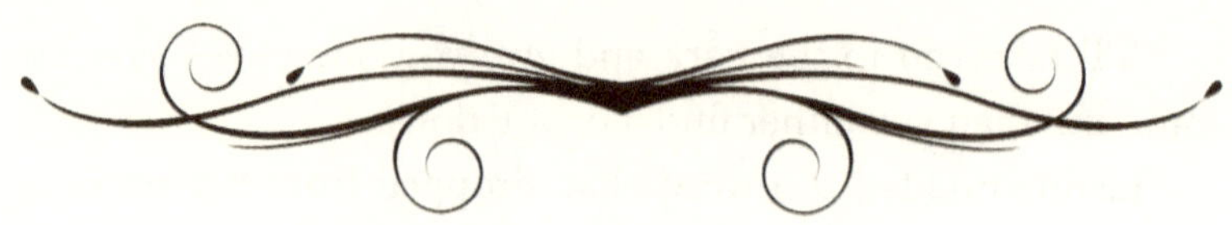

Kensington Gardens

They flew low across Brompton parish. The fields and pastures and clusters of buildings passed almost in the space of a breath. Not in her wildest imagination had Justine dreamed such a thing possible. To be weightless, to soar over the earth with more ease even than a bird. It made her want to laugh and cry at the same time.

This will surely ruin regular life forever. Justine stored up every moment, in the same way a bear stored up food for the winter, so when this fantasy inevitably ended, she would have enough to sustain her through the ordinary. *Magic is real.* The giddy thought burst out of her over and over in small explosions of joy in her lungs, behind her eyes. The air tasted like soot and still her mouth stayed open with an irrepressible smile.

Before Justine knew it, miles had passed beneath her, and they entered the heavy smog that cloaked the city of London. She sensed the Pan flying higher than before. Chimneys and roofs rose out of the soup with alarming frequency. The boy seemed to enjoy flying close to these semi-visible objects just to get a jump out of her. But then, as they crossed into a clearer part of the city, it was possible to see the bright, full moon and the buildings it shone down upon. He gave up his swerving and dipping and diving and steered them directly down the high street and into Kensington Gardens.

At such a late hour, the gates were locked and the gardens empty of the living, but this was no barrier to a demon and his captive playmate. He released her hand just before the ground so Justine fell the last foot and landed with a hard jolt to her ankles. She'd never been to these gardens, but she'd learned from Mrs. Palmer that the trees along the walk were a new addition, brought in to replace old trees that had died off in the fog. She also knew that these gardens were in a nice part of the city where mothers and nannies brought children to play. *What a thing it would be to play all day in a garden such as this,* thought Justine, which reminded her of Miss Barry. She quickly pushed her thoughts onward.

The moon shone silver light down through the trees making the rather ordinary gravel path appear spotted with pearlescent stones. The air here, though always tinged with coal soot, smelled of flowers and dead leaves, just as the Pan, she now realized, also smelled of dead leaves and something sweet.

"Are you ready for your clue?" he asked.

Justine remembered then why she'd been brought to this place, and a touch of the magic went out of it. She had to win his game, or he would take Sarah. Justine would be left alone, once again without prospects, hands reaching for empty dreams. "I suppose I'm ready."

"It's a place where sinking is better than swimming, for at the bottom is a world unknown."

"I hope you're not saying there's going to be swimming involved in this work." Justine began to walk down the path.

"It isn't work," said the boy. "It's an *adventure*."

"Well, I can't swim. This adventure had better go another way."

Small lights flickered in and out of the hedgerow beyond the line of trees on Justine's right. The streetlights in the gardens had all been turned down; she feared the moving lights were bouncing torches of ne'er-do-wells who'd broken into the garden.

"You're going to protect me against anyone we find here?" she asked.

"That wouldn't be much of a quest, would it?"

"I thought you said adventure," grumbled Justine as she ducked behind a tree trunk to spy on the lights. They didn't seem to be coming any closer, but they did seem aware of her. Or perhaps it was a trick of her imagination that made the lights' bouncing seem more cautious than they had been.

A cold breeze crept up Justine's neck. She turned with a start, expecting someone to be standing behind her, and saw only the gauzy filament of a spirit. It whispered what felt like an apology and made as though to hurry away, only to stop and drift so close to Justine she felt it on her arms, almost as though they were holding hands. Behind the spirit, she saw the solid form of the Pan watching with interest.

His ghost voice became a sigh in her mind and she understood that his name was Vistic, murdered at that place in 1207. It took her a moment to understand he wanted to know if she liked the lights.

"They're beautiful."

The Pan looked from her to Vistic, his expression shadowed. "You heard him?"

"Of course." The Pan's expression shadowed all the more and she felt a strange joy in confusing him. Seeing spirits had never been a boon and now, if only for a night, she enjoyed showing off. With a flounce, she turned again toward the hedge. As much as she strained her eyes, she could see no shadows of people holding the lights. Justine stepped off the path and began to walk toward them.

"Spirits like me," said Justine.

"Yes."

"And you, what are you? More than a ghost."

"Much, much more. Are we going to have a guessing game?"

"I'd rather you just tell me."

By now, Justine had crossed the square of lawn and was almost upon the hedgerow, though she seemed no closer to the lights.

"I don't spend much time in this where and when," said the boy. "I can't say what you'd call me."

"What do you call yourself then?" Justine was now walking along the hedgerow looking for an opening. Through gaps in the leaves, she could see the lights on the other side. They appeared to be dancing in prearranged patterns. Here and there, she caught sight of one closer than the others. She had the impression of wings and small heads.

Perhaps I am dreaming. It was a thought that gave her great comfort. If she was dreaming, it meant her imagination had conjured the boy, and Sarah wasn't in danger of death. Justine would wake up and tell Sarah a beautiful adventure story. And perhaps the Lord Mayor's son would be waiting with a pair of daisies, wanting to take her for a promenade.

If it's a dream, I don't want to wake up just yet.

She turned to the Pan and gave him a daring look. "Well?"

"I'm Makbal, caretaker of the Island of Dreams. But you can call me Lord Mak as the other children do."

"The Island of Dreams?" It sounded beautiful. And yet, Justine felt she was giving herself over too quickly. She needed to be sure she was going to a good place. "Is that what you call the place you trap innocent children so their souls cannot fly to heaven?"

"I save children from the current so they can have a childhood."

"That doesn't make any sense."

"Sense is as sense does," chirped the boy.

She'd found a gap in the hedge she could squeeze in. Thorns and sharp branches clawed at her as she pushed through. Then, because she'd focused on the getting through without thought to what was on the other side, Justine very nearly tumbled into a lake.

She caught herself on the mush of the embankment and scrambled back, crab-walking until she crunched up against the hedge. The lights she'd been following were now quite near. They flew about over the surface of the lake, swirling and pirouetting with trails of light beams flowing behind them like streamers that hung suspended for a moment before dissolving.

With the dancing lights came a faint music, as though each light contained a dozen choir boys trapped within it. Combined, the voices of the lights made a music unlike any Justine had ever heard. Not that she had much experience with fancy folk music, but this seemed something even beyond that. It was both spoken communication and song, both lilting on the air and hard lines of expression.

"The fae are dancing for you," whispered Makbal in her ear.

Fairies? Here?

Justine held her breath. Something so beautiful couldn't possibly be real. She'd never been given a moment in her life to decide whether or not she believed in fairies. Now they were before her, their lights so dazzling, she could just barely make out the shapes of their bodies, and this only proved how unlike the creatures of earth they were. Some had hands and feet, others only hands with trailing ribbons of light where their feet would have been. Some wore extravagant gowns and wigs and hats while others wore only their light. Some were as long as her forearm, others the size of her fist. Some glowed so brightly they hurt her eyes, others were as dim as fireflies.

One of them broke off from the dance and landed on Justine's knee. It wore a second skin of ribbons as though wrapped up in a rainbow of color. Its chime voice sounded like the tinkling of faraway bells. Justine couldn't see it clearly for the glow of its light, but she saw the silver dust that flecked off its wings as it tapped them together. She saw its delicate little hands gesturing to her, then pointing to the lake.

"Get away there," said Makbal to the fairy. "You're ruining the game."

Justine tore her eyes from the fairy to give the lake a closer look. It did all the ordinary lake things, with rushes half withered around its banks and a deepening of its dark texture toward the middle where it was deepest. But lily pads bloomed in its surface though it was almost November. And the darkness at the center of the lake wasn't the solid of threatening water that it should have been. As Justine watched, the darkness seemed to ebb and flow. And in the flowing, a dim glow peeked out. Just for a moment, Justine thought she saw the structures of an underwater city, golden pink and floating on clouds where there shouldn't have been anything but muddy sediment and a few weeds and rocks. *The Cloud City.*

"The lake is the gateway," whispered Justine.

Makbal flopped back on the grass beside her and waved his arms and legs as though swimming through it. "It isn't fair," he cried. "You had help."

"Hardly."

Somewhere in the back of her mind, Justine knew she'd achieved her end. If the word of the Pan could be trusted, he was a god after all, Sarah was safe from death. But this triumph felt irrelevant as she strained her eyes to see down into the lake to catch another glimpse of the hidden city.

"Is it true you give children a life they wouldn't otherwise have?"

"I only lie to my friends." Makbal's eyes remained bright with the promise of adventure, but a sheen of calculation shaded them. He had decided something about her, and Justine wasn't sure she was going to like it.

"I'll take you instead of the girl in the bed."

"To have my lost childhood?"

"No, silly. To be our mother. The island needs a mother, or it doesn't work like it should."

Justine had never thought of herself as a mother. She'd experienced great relief multiple times when her late menses had finally arrived. This didn't necessarily mean she was opposed to children. But it had always seemed a distant thing, something she'd explore after she'd procured a promising husband and a life where someone else woke up at four in the morning to start the fires.

"What happened to your last mother?"

"Eaten," said Makbal with a grin that had lost none of its boyishness and gained only a fraction of the demon he hid beneath his beautiful, white face.

"Well, I don't think that's a life for me just yet." Justine stood up.

"It clearly is," said Makbal as he also got to his feet and stood between her and the gap in the hedge. Justine was taller than him by almost a head, but again she felt the power seething within. She wouldn't be able to push past him.

"Why don't we meet here again tomorrow, and I'll give you my answer?"

"I'll be gone tomorrow." His eyes narrowed. "A new mother would be just the thing."

A quiet panic began to grow at the back of Justine's mind. What had she been thinking?

Magic exists.

And now she knew it existed, she would live differently, better. It was enough to have seen it. "I like my life here, thanks very much. I'm going to marry the Lord Mayor's son and have children of my own, by the by."

Makbal stepped toward her, more menacing now. Justine stepped back.

"That sounds so terribly boring."

Another step forward. Another step back for Justine, but this time, her foot found no solid ground to land on. She fell backward into the lake. True panic gripped her as the water closed in around her head. Her thrashing arms got her upright, so her head cracked the surface, but almost as soon as she'd gasped air, she fell below again.

Kick your feet, called a voice.

Justine kicked against the clinging net of her stolen night-shift. Again, her head broke the surface of the lake, but she opened her mouth too early and water filled it. Coughing and sputtering as her arms stirred up a storm of water, she saw Makbal on the bank watching her. His expression of interest, the curiosity in his eyes, was one of an audience member at a magic show trying to puzzle out how it all worked.

"Help me," she gasped.

"You wish the process to go faster?"

"No, I—" Her head dipped under the water again. Each time, her body seemed heavier, her limbs less effective at propelling her upward. What she really needed was to move toward the bank, but for all her thrashing, she'd been unable to gain any traction on the water. She remained almost exactly where she'd started, close enough Makbal could have reached out and grasped her flailing fingers, but not near enough for her feet to touch the shallows.

"Soon you'll face the current," said Makbal. "Unless you wish to come with me to the island."

"Yes, please. I'll do it. Just don't let me die here."

Makbal smiled. "Fantastic. I'm so excited." He flew out over the surface of the lake and pressed the palm of his hand against her forehead. Justine felt a momentary heat, a hint of something new in her mind, though she had no idea what, then Makbal pressed down so suddenly, Justine's mouth was open as she went under. He held her head below water as she coughed, then coughed no more.

Justine didn't know when she stopped struggling or when the burning in her lungs faded away. She sank into the darkness of the lake. Down. Down. Somewhere around the time she found herself extremely disappointed that the golden city in the pond had been an illusion, Justine had stopped sinking and was instead falling through unending darkness.

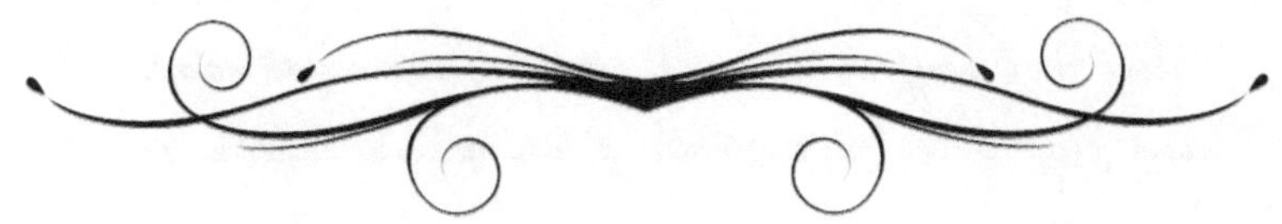

CHAPTER 6

The Neverland Fae: A Chronicle

Notation from the Author

We fae used to be a delightfully frivolous people, always frolicking to and fro wherever we pleased, riding the breezes, tormenting the lesser creatures of the earth, of which humans were the chief object. Perhaps in other realms, this remains our primary occupation, I cannot tell, cut off as we are here on the island. As a result, we've become a transactional people, surviving by our wits, ever in the crosshairs of the warring brothers.

This record assigns blame where it correctly belongs, lest anyone think we chose this path. For the story of our journey into trade and negotiation, there are other texts taken down by Posietta. They may be used for others who wish to follow in our newfound ways. As with all else, we must adapt our flights to the currents if we are to survive.

Tassi the Scribe

The Brothers Who Broke the Rules

What are rules to gods? Polite niceties. But those niceties are the things that hold the world together. They prevent war, foster collaboration, maintain the hierarchy. This last is a preeminent value to the gods because most of them believe in a law of diminishing returns. Each subsequent generation created is innately lesser than those that came before, and none will ever be as godlike as the First Ones.

The brothers created by the goddesses Coleodal and Apismal, are over a dozen generations removed from the inception of godhood, thus nothing was expected of them. One might say they suffered from a lack of supervision. One might also say they were a cut above what should have been possible for their generation.

The first rule they broke: They created a new realm without permission. This isn't to say that a god cannot create a realm. But, until the brothers, realms existed wholly in the eternal and served the interests of gods and other eternal beings such as myself.

The Neverland was carved out of a space between the realms, a space that didn't exist before the brothers made it. The first of many things that shouldn't have been possible for these lesser gods.

The second rule they broke: They began to mark the spirits of children with a map to this place. No one else could find it except those children. In doing this, they were stealing souls from other death gods and their eternal realms.

The third rule broken was not one of godhood, but brotherhood. In his desire to love the girl Osuana, the brother known as Arandasal, and later the Voyager, and the Black Hook, broke this perfect place and invited the passage of time to exist on one side of the island, giving the souls living there the second chance at a human lifetime. This crime betrayed not only the brothers' purpose of giving children a childhood unblemished by the passage of time, it also broke the island itself. Its place in the realms was further thrust into uncertainty. Its place in the cosmos, hazy at best, had become impossible to define.

After he invited Time, the passage of eternal beings to and from the island became impossible. Those of us there at the moment of the severing, remained there. Even the brothers were trapped in the Neverland a good while before the fae managed to solve the problem of coming and going. And as the Neverland worked to try and heal what had broken, it became something unto itself. More powerful than this undefined place made from lesser gods ever had a right to be. It began to look for help.

CHAPTER 7

The Island

S till falling.

Justine lost her nightcap. She couldn't say where. The falling wasn't darkness anymore. Nor was it light. She couldn't tell if she was awake or asleep. Sometimes she felt cold, other times hot.

Gradually there was a brightening, then she felt herself in a space, which became a blue sky, and she could see below patches of water and spots of land through the clouds. The patches of water grew until it seemed there was only a small bit of land compared to an endless sea. A brilliant sun, too orange to be the sun she rarely saw in London, beamed down light that danced on the water.

Passing through the clouds made her eyes water, but then everything below became bright and vibrant, as though painted in oils. Below her, a lush island, like something out of adventurers' expedition tales. And another island, shrouded and gray. A good many rocks, both in the water and out, were arranged as though to make a fence around the green island. In the distance, a wall of mountains all crowded together grew out of the sea. And there in the mist, a village of huts. And there, far out from any land, a ship with white sails churned up the smooth surface of the sea behind it.

Justine began to wonder how she was going to land. The possibility of hitting the water filled her with dread. She'd just drowned in a lake. And now she'd come to a land of water. A flock of sea birds scattered as she crashed through them. The water was coming up larger and larger now. She thought to cry out for a rescue from Makbal and realized he was nowhere in sight.

The ship grew larger quite fast. A great deal of movement had begun on deck, apparently in response to her arrival. She heard a pop and a bang, and suddenly a large round ball came speeding toward her. It blew into little pieces just above her head, sending out a rush of air that pushed her down even faster. For a moment, the smoke set Justine coughing and wiping her running eyes. When she could see again, the air was filled with objects all flying at her.

Bullets, she realized with surprise. The people on the ship were shooting at her.

One landed hard in her chest with enough force she flew sideways. She was no longer falling toward the water but toward the green island. This good fortune seemed nothing compared to the burning fire in her chest. *I've been shot. Perhaps I'm dying a second time.*

The air seemed to gather speed and close in around her. Or perhaps she was expanding to take up too much space against the air. The force of the blow had turned her around and she struggled to turn again so she might see ahead. Before she could make that happen, the feeling of the air narrowing itself to a point, and she landed on the beach as soft as a wounded feather.

The orange sun shone bright overhead; she closed her eyes

to it. Just at the moment when she'd been promised to be eternally young, she was dying. Wasn't that just how it always went? Bleeding on a pristine paradise island was better than drowning in a dark lake, but Justine still regretted her adventure had come to such an abrupt end. She wondered if it was still possible she'd wake up in her bed on the asylum's kitchen floor.

Shadows blocked the sunlight. Justine opened one eye. A circle of heads hovered over her, all boys as grimy as chimney sweeps and dressed in leaves, their skin colors an astounding variety. They stood without any apparent awareness of their differences and whispered to each other. One voice rose above the others. "Go call Tassi. They'll know what to do."

Running footsteps crashed through underbrush at the edge of the beach. Justine closed her eyes again. The sun's light had turned cold. She managed to lift her arm to her chest and felt the hot wet seeping out of her. "You have to stop the blood," she whispered. Could anyone hear her? They all seemed very far away, these boys. "Press down." She tried to show them with a bunch of the nightshift in her fist, but her hand had grown too heavy.

This must be my punishment for trying to make out better than my station. Mrs. Palmer had promised hard work was the pathway to heaven, but Justine had never been good at appreciating her own supposed virtue when it came with so little benefit.

At her back, the sand seemed to move beneath her. Justine felt she was sinking and jerked with a start, the way she sometimes did just after drifting to sleep and having a falling dream. But this was different. The sand seemed alive. It curled itself around her shoulders, crawled all around her, the grains of tiny footsteps danced on her chest. She managed to peel one eye open enough to see a bright red shell with a great many jointed legs extending outward from a soft body hidden beneath. Through the film of her eyelashes, she saw there were dozens of these—crabs that were also perhaps spiders or very, very small turtle-like creatures. A herd of them had gathered on her chest and seemed to be pushing her down into the sand.

Some part of Justine knew this should be a frightening thing, but she didn't feel afraid. One creature crept up almost to her chin. She saw it had only two eyes. *Not a spider then.*

"What do you want?" it asked.

A wonderful question, delicious with possibilities. But Justine didn't know how to reply. Her usual answer, to snatch a husband with a good income who would keep her from working for five shillings a day until she shriveled into a stooped old maid, no longer seemed relevant.

Justine felt something come free inside her, as though she'd carried this tremendous weight her entire life and now it had been cut away and left behind. She had flown over a city and watched fairies dance. She had died and yet somehow—though her position seemed tenuous—was still alive. She had come to this place. A magical place. All that remained was the possibility of everything.

"Everything," she said, for want of something more specific. She didn't want to limit herself if this really was the heaven of her just reward. "I want everything beautiful, and bright, and soft, and warm, and easy."

The sand footsteps retreated. Justine saw a small, bright light flickering ahead of her. When she tried to reach for it, she felt a sharp pain on the end of her finger.

"Sarah," she said, "I believe a fairy just bit me."

JUSTINE WOKE IN PAIN. PAIN WORSE THAN ANY SHE'D HAD AFTER A long day's work. Pain worse than that time she'd nearly been run over by a buggy. Pain in places of her body she hadn't known existed. At first, she thought she must have taken a wrong turn coming from Makbal's island and gone down to the fiery pit instead of up to the pearly gates. But the pain didn't feel like burning. In fact, she felt quite comfortable in temperature. And the pain had already begun to fade. In its place she became aware of a faint humming, and the mossy scent of wet soil as though it had just rained.

A lovely smell. It reminded her of the early months of her work at the asylum, when she'd been excited to make enough money for a rooming house, before she'd realized she'd never make enough for a rooming house. She'd catch Sarah sitting at the window on rainy days, always alone, and happy with her aloneness in a way Justine envied. It was on such a rainy day that Sarah had spoken her first and only word in Justine's presence.

"Petrichor."

When Justine had asked what it meant, Sarah had pointed to the wet ground and repeated the word. "Petrichor."

Later, Justine had asked a nurse to look it up. Petrichor was the word to describe the smell of soil after rain. How had Sarah known such a strange word? No one could say.

Justine opened her eyes. She lay on a bed of leaves and grass all tied together with woven rope. The bed was one of many such beds spread out on a platform of logs tied together. Tree branches made a roof over her head. On the lowest branch, a red bird stood at attention watching her. Beside the bird sat a fairy twittering its lace wings and emitting bursts of chimes as though in response to the bird's chirps. Justine had the distinct impression they were talking about her.

The fairy appeared quite unlike the creatures she'd seen in storybooks, yet also somehow different than those at the lake, mostly because its features were clear to her. It had arms, but no legs. Its garments appeared so thin, she could have folded them in half and half again and they still would have been no thicker than a sheet of paper. Its features were fine and delicate, its wings the near exact appearance of a dragonfly. For all its beauty, it frowned at her with the darkest gaze as though it knew all her secrets and disapproved.

It took some doing, but Justine managed to turn her head so she didn't have to look at the fairy. She saw several boys who were perhaps the ones from the beach. They seemed intent on ignoring her and were sitting together clapping the hollow shells of many different sizes of cups painted to look like peasant women. Beyond them, at the edge of the platform, Makbal sat swinging his legs. When he heard the chime of the fairy, he turned and saw Justine was awake.

The Lost Boy had lost much of his angelic appearance, though he didn't seem as hideous as the demon mask Jack Woolf had worn. He was something in between. A demon who could be an angel, if only he washed up and resisted his naughty instincts.

The other boys noticed her as well. "She lives! She lives! The pirates failed again."

They left their wooden cups and gathered around.

"Am I dead?"

"You were going that way," said Makbal, leaping up and coming to her side. "But Tassi saved you."

By the direction of his eyes, Justine decided Tassi was the name of the fairy. She blew it a kiss. "Thank you for saving me, Tassi."

A chime that sounded more angry than anything else came back as an answer.

"They'll get used to you," said one of the other boys, a pale-skinned, scrawny thing who couldn't have been more than six or seven.

"It's good not to trust too much in a fae, they're always doing what they want," said Makbal with a smirk. The words sounded like they were meant more for Tassi than Justine.

"And you, don't you always do what you want?"

"I suppose we do." He grinned.

"Are you our new mother?" asked the scrawny boy.

"I'm Justine."

"But you can call her Mother," Makbal added quickly.

"You're older than our last one," said another boy whose skin was the brown of the platform's wood planking.

The one who was eaten, thought Justine with a spike of fear. But as she instinctively glanced around for signs of danger, the thought vanished from her head. All around were sun-dappled trees and a rabbit's warren of platforms and child-sized nests and rope bridges and bird song and the distant laughter of boys at play. She seemed to have dropped into the middle of the Robinson family tree house come to life.

Justine looked down at her blood-covered nightshift and the hole where the bullet had gone through. Beneath it, her chest was smooth. No bandage, not even a mark. Tassi chimed some message to Makbal as Justine looked to her right at the boy of seven or eight. His left eye had gone cloudy from some old injury which had left a scar through his eyebrow. Many of the boys had injuries. This wasn't a place where wounds healed without a trace. And yet she had been.

"Tassi says the island likes you," said Makbal. "Maybe you'll be the best mother ever."

"Hurrah for the best mother!" cried a boy.

Justine blushed as the other boys on the platform took up the call. Even more voices called back from the surrounding platforms until the whole forest seemed to echo with their shouts. For such enthusiasm, Justine supposed she could pretend to be their mother. In accepting this role, Justine chose not to ask her two most pressing questions: How exactly did your last mother die? And how did you come to be here? Instead, she asked, "What are all your names?"

A chorus of answers fought to drown each other out. Justine laughed. "One at a time." She pointed to the scrawny one.

"Jakob."

And then to the boy beside him.

"Ian." Red hair and milk-white skin marred by freckles, a gaunt body and shadowed cheeks as though he'd died of a wasting disease or starvation, and that swagger of the drunkard Irish. Justine shuddered but kept her smile on her face.

"Olewendo," said a boy with dark skin. The only boy who wore cloth, though its remnants were tattered beyond recognition. *He's an African*, thought Justine, resisting the urge to reach out and touch him. She'd never seen one before. "Where are you from?"

Olewendo frowned. "Here," he said, "I've always been here."

"The past is another land," said Makbal. "We live only in the present we create."

Puzzled, but determined to be polite, Justine moved on down the line.

"Ling." A Chinese boy who appeared to be fifteen or sixteen and had a scar along his forearm. In contrast to Ian, he carried more than his share of flesh on his long body. *He died suddenly of an accident*, thought Justine.

"Pah." Also from the Asian continent, but not Chinese, even more mysterious in appearance to Justine than the African boy.

"This is Delldell," said the boy with the cloudy eye as he pointed his thumb at his chest. Justine smiled. Here, though the boy's features implied a mixed race, she felt familiar ground. More than one asylum patient had spoken the way the boy did, with a thickness in his tongue, and referencing himself as though he were another person.

"Qassim." An Arabian boy, also flesh heavy.

Justine didn't even have time to stare at these exotic faces because more kept appearing and startling her. They dropped down from the trees. They climbed up ladders and leapt in front of her wearing their strange leaf clothes, grimy, and smelling of old sweat and the forest, chests puffed out, hair spilling out around their faces. The names went on and on with not a one appearing older than sixteen.

"Why do you only take boys?" Justine asked Makbal.

"Girls are silly," said Pah.

"They don't know how to have adventures," said another boy.

Ian looked uncertain. "I've never seen a girl before."

"I'm a girl," said Justine.

"You're a mother," he said. "That's different."

Justine looked to Makbal, who still hadn't answered her question.

"This is how it has always been," he said. "So it will always be."

The tone of his voice was so serious, so different in character than she'd become used to that Justine immediately wondered if he was lying. Before Justine had time to consider this possibility and what it might mean, Makbal broke into a grin. "What shall we do today, Mother?"

Justine stared at him. Surely she wasn't to be in charge of—

"Do we need to prepare for new boys?" asked Ling, who seemed responsible beyond his evident years.

"Indeed!" said Makbal. "Four new boys are coming."

"And shouldn't we avenge Mother?" suggested someone else.

Makbal's eyes glinted with dark passion as he nodded. "Strike now while they're still reorganizing. They'll need to go to town for supplies."

"We'll get the Black Hook when he least expects!" cried Delldell.

Justine had heard enough adventure stories to understand

this Black Hook was the captain of the pirate ship that had shot her. "I'd like a turn at him," she said with a laugh. "But I wonder, is it possible to have a bath first?"

"Bath?" echoed several of the boys. Their faces brightened with interest.

"I don't suppose you have some soap around here?"

"Is that something you wish for?" asked Makbal.

"To wish for soap?" Justine laughed. "I suppose I do. And some new clothes." She looked doubtfully at the leaves he wore.

"Clothes are here for you." Makbal motioned toward a steamer trunk on the far end of the platform that looked quite out of place in the rustic tree house. "We'll go down to Coral Falls and see if the island grants your wish for soap."

"Hurrah for soap!" cried Pah, jumping up. Then all the boys were dashing away into the trees, swinging from branch to branch until they disappeared among the leaves. Justine knee-walked to the trunk. When she unlocked the latch, the lid fairly sprang open from the pressure of the garments stuffed inside. She began to lay the clothes out for sorting. This proved an unnecessary project. They were all nightgowns.

Some styles she recognized. Others were impossibly extravagant, stitched with elaborate designs and bright colors. Others were made from cloths she'd never seen, light, gauzy things, and fabric that shimmered as though with tiny jewels or golden thread. Some were not gowns, but pants and a bodice in one. One even had the picture of a girl printed on it, oversized eyes, a perfect elfin chin, blue dress in the style of Tennyson's Lady, long, white hair braided and held over her shoulder so thick it seemed impossible a girl so small could support such a mane.

As she looked for something that would fit her, Justine noticed some gowns had small tears in them. Some had been patched. Others were stained. One was so worn out the ribbon that had once woven through the collar had been replaced with a dried, leafy thing Justine supposed was seaweed. It seemed clear that the girls who'd worn these gowns had lived hard and now no longer needed them.

Justine didn't want to think about that. She found a night-gown that looked fit for Princess Louise, tucked it under her arm and looked expectantly at Makbal. "Shall we?"

"We shall." He leapt from foot to foot as he led her across a bridge to another platform where he lowered a rope ladder to climb down. They walked side by side through the forest. Tassi followed them at a distance like an oversized insect.

"Is there something I can do to thank Tassi for saving my life?"

"If the fae want something, they make it known," said Makbal. "They're good to have around even though they're small. Never know when you'll need one."

Justine nodded. As she did, she caught sight of the blood staining her chest. Her nightshift had been marked with violence just as so many of the other nightgowns were.

"Do pirates often attack you?"

"All the time. They're blackhearts, you know. All they want is to destroy beautiful things." Fire sparked across Makbal's expression. "I won't let them hurt you again."

He spoke with such fierceness, his voice pitched down, momentarily becoming something not just deeper but darker. He didn't seem up to the task of being her protector, or at least he didn't fit the fantasy she imagined in her head, but she still drew on that fantasy when she joked, "I've always wanted a chivalrous protector. Shall I be Guinevere to your Green Knight? It's a much more exciting game than Mother and children."

"We shall play both."

They ducked off the path they'd been on, pushed through a thicket of lilacs just on the edge of bloom, and entered a golden clearing of dazzling fall colors and gloaming sunbeams filtering down through the canopy. In the center of the clearing was a lake the color of an emerald with a rock face rising on one side and water flowing down from a series of channels that fed two great falls, one on top of the other. The mist from the falls caught the sunlight and made rainbows so solid, Justine thought she could reach out and touch them.

"Coral Falls Lake," said Makbal, obviously proud. "Do you like it?"

"I do!"

"Good, because I made it just for you."

Justine laughed. What beautiful flattery. She knew it couldn't be true. This boy had wanted Sarah, not her, and he'd been meant for Miss Barry who summoned him with her death. But Justine didn't give voice to her doubt. *Let it be true,* she thought, as she ran to the water's edge and dipped her toes in the perfectly warm water. *Let it be mine.*

"The soap has come." Ling dropped down from a tree and suddenly stood before her holding a brick of carbolic soap just the same as the ones used in the asylum. It seemed almost disappointing having such ordinary soap in such an extraordinary place. Justine realized the island had given her exactly what she'd imagined soap to be. If she had thought of Windsor soap, or the soaps in the windows of Pear's, would they have come to her?

Again, she laughed, giddy with the possibility.

The boys were now dropping down from the trees like monkeys, none of them cautious or gentle in their movements. Some flung themselves toward the ground. Others simply dropped without fear. Jakob and a boy whose name Justine couldn't remember leapt from the trees and flew out over the lake where they plummeted like dirty, leaf-covered rocks into the water.

She found a place where the shrubbery came right up to the edge of the water. Here she left her new nightgown on top of a hedge, where she could have some privacy changing after her bath, and waded into the shallows wearing her stolen nightshift. Petrichor scent lingered in her nostrils, seeming to cast everything in a languid peace. She wanted to float across the water even though she had no idea how. Indeed, it seemed impossible she could be standing in water so soon after drowning and not be afraid.

"Who's first for washing, Mother?" asked Jacob, bobbing toward her.

Here I am in paradise, washing up.

"Can't you wash yourself?" she teased.

"Is that Mother's wish?" asked Makbal.

"I'm sure every mother has wished that since the beginning of time." She laughed and threw her arms out against the water. "I wish for you all to be clean."

There was a great deal of splashing, the boys frolicking in the water so that some moments passed before it became evident that the wish had somehow been granted. When the boys started to wade out of the water, she saw that, in all the various skin tones, they shone as perfectly clean as a babe's smooth cheek.

I think I shall like it here.

"Shall you all get dressed?" she asked.

"We like to dry off first," said Qassim. "The leaves stick better that way."

"But what about your real clothes?"

Makbal grinned at her. "Does Mother wish to dress us now?" He seemed just as delighted as her that she had this power. The power of wishing.

"Are you doing it?" she asked.

"It's the power of the island," he said. "She likes you. Or is it something more?" He gazed at her with a child's adoration that was also somehow more knowing.

Justine decided she'd do better with her imagination than

she'd done wishing for the soap. She looked at each boy in turn, sizing them up, grouping them in ages, and imagining them as the younger brothers of Jack Woolf, even though many of them would have been turned out of his house for the barest hint of familiarity.

Makbal seemed to run his island as though all the boys were equal in intellect, ability, and morality, so Justine resolved to act the same. This wasn't London. And it seemed Makbal believed, or at least selected, boys who didn't represent the typical failings of their races. Indeed, as Justine looked them over, once she attempted to focus on other things than their variety, she noticed how very similar they were, especially the older boys. Not in all of London would she have found a group so alike in their beauty. Like a collection of Greek sculptures, all without pockmark or pustule, with strong bones in their faces, and a shared physical presence that was both grace and power.

A whisper sounded through the trees. Bunches of leaves began to fall in a bright rain of reds, yellows, and oranges. Jakob gave a shout and leaped up, scaling a tree in nothing but his skin. A moment later, he called down, "I got one!" Then he reappeared, crawling down the tree dressed in short pants, undershirt, vest, and jacket.

"There's another!" Qassim pointed to a bundle falling toward the lake. He swam out to catch it.

Soon, all the boys were occupied chasing down the bundles. They seemed only to see the bundle intended for them, for each set of clothes fit perfectly. In no time, Justine was walking down the line straightening collars and fixing buttons. The little boys wore sailor outfits, the older boys wore vests and jackets. No shoes had come for any of them.

Olewendo frowned down at his trousers, plucked at them with the tips of his fingers.

"Something the matter with your clothes?" asked Justine.

"I prefer girl's clothes."

"Whyever would you want that?"

Olewendo shrugged. "I have a spare dunyasha from Mother. But it ripped. If you could mend it, I'd be glad to wear it."

The mother who was eaten.

"Yes, of course." Justine continued down the line, hiding her confusion in activity. Makbal stood at the end in a men's waistcoat. He pulled uncomfortably at his necktie.

"This is a new game," he said, then laughed. "Am I to be Father today?"

"You look lovely," said Justine. "Will you take everyone back home? I'll change and be along in a moment."

"You don't even know where home is."

Justine realized Makbal was right, but also not right. "The island will guide me," she said. As soon as she spoke, Justine knew the strange words were true.

Makbal gave a sharp whistle through his teeth and the boys bunched together, shoving and laughing as they headed off. Justine weaseled herself between the bushes, taking care not to snag her new nightgown as she passed through. She found herself on a secluded part of the lakeshore. It was connected by a channel of shallow water to the main lake with shrubbery all around so no one on the land side could see.

The voices of the boys faded, replaced by the chorus of birds, as though their presence was an imposition on the natural way of things, but hers was not. Justine yanked the nightshift over her head, glad to be rid of it. Her toes scrunched the sandy soil of her new secret space. She ran her hand over the branches of the shrubs, which seemed the same kind she knew from her world and an entirely different kind altogether.

"This is real," she whispered as she gathered the soft material of her new nightgown and slid her arms through. She lifted it and let the rest drop over her head and slide down her body. Such a delicate caress as she had never known from any piece of cloth. Indeed, she didn't know of any garment so brightly colored nor so finely woven.

"I'm like a queen of my own island," she said to herself.

The island seemed to confirm this as she weaseled her way back out of the shrubbery as it didn't once snag the fragile gown.

Justine started off walking in the direction she knew the boys had gone. But the prospect of story time sounded so positively mundane that she couldn't help but divert to a new path. She walked through the woods and found they formed distinct sections of the seasons and weather. There was a grove of budding springtime blossoms, and a grove that hummed with the business of high summer insectile productivity. She worried about being stung until she saw a bird with gold and red feathers but the head and chest of a woman. The bird woman smiled as though she'd been waiting years for Justine's arrival. This wasn't a place one need be afraid of insect bites. It was a place of wonder.

With each step, Justine felt a pulse in her feet go down into the island. It answered her with a pulse of its own, a light tingling in her toes, an energy that caused her heels to spring up, leaping easily as though she was just a step away from flying. She tried to fly as she and Makbal had flown over London. When that failed, she wished to fly, but the island stayed silent.

Branches reached out to caress her cheeks as she passed. Vines rose up from the ground and created a bower over her head, showering her with flower petals. Everything whispered to her of desire, as though paradise had been sitting alone for eternity, waiting for her to arrive and give it purpose. She wished for a blanket of crushed velvet like Talia had felt at the circus and it came down to her in a shimmering ripple as though made from the sky.

Wearing the velvet as a cape, Justine came to a grove of

stark, dark branches covered in snow. Within it, a pond cloaked in mist. Here, the trees were so dense as to nearly make a roof from the snow-burdened canopy. The sun shone through in dim, patchy light, but she could see clearly enough by the light of a single lamppost that stood in a clear area to one side of the pond. Justine planted her foot on the base of the lamppost and twirled herself around it, free arm out, hair flying free above the ripple of velvet cloth. Her laugh echoed off the dense, silent snow. She became neither terribly cold nor terribly wet, and yet the grove had all the sense of being what it appeared to be. Without a thought, Justine wished for a bridge to span the pond, and a bridge appeared. As she skipped across, she wished for a tall, handsome stranger to walk through the mist toward her.

This wish didn't come true, so she carried on to the next grove, damp as though just from a rain shower, but without the lovely smell of petrichor. Here, she cried out as she encountered a giant creature with horns and human arms and legs and teeth extending from its face in a gorilla's snout. This ogre had been in the midst of picking mushrooms and only gave her the slightest head nod of interest as she ran from it.

What a strange and wonderful place.

As she carried on, Justine expected to eventually come to the beach of the great sea where the pirate ship lurked. Or a sea with another island on the horizon. She was sure the island couldn't be so big that she could walk this far without reaching its edge. But the more Justine walked, the larger the island seemed. She saw a small hut with a hunched, Slavic peasant woman bent over a cooking fire. She found a bear wearing a ribboned collar and a hat as though it had escaped from a circus. Neither peasant nor bear seemed surprised to see Justine.

Presently, the woods retreated, and Justine found herself climbing a pleasant grassy rise. For no reason she could explain, besides her pure joy in being in such a place, she began to run and run and run until she crested the hill and swung herself in a circle, arms flung out, swirling the air. Only when she ran out of breath did she stop, bent in half, and gasped with laughter.

"How can I be dead when I have never felt so alive?"

She straightened and saw the hill she'd climbed was a high point of the island. At her back rose a ridge of mountains. To her right, the woods she'd just walked through stretched to the edge of her vision, ahead of her and all around to the left side, an open grassland empty except for a thin river and what looked like a collection of dollhouses. *A fae village*, she thought. Beyond it, over the tops of a smaller, thinner forest, there was the sea and only the sea until, at the horizon, she could make out a range of pink mountains shrouded by clouds.

Not far from them, a jagged barrier of dark rocks tinged green. And between them, so strange she couldn't trust her eyes, speckled fall of a rain shower taking up all of the space of the sky. Confused by what she saw, Justine pulled her gaze back to the near shore. She looked all around trying to locate the other island she'd seen from the air, the one cloaked in mist. She also couldn't help looking for the puffy, white rectangles of the pirate ship. She didn't know how pirates could come to be in such a perfect place, but she was determined to forget them. Now that she'd arrived, they couldn't hurt her. Nothing could.

A light humming sounded behind her. Justine turned. Straining her eyes, she could just see the fairy Tassi spying on her from a distance.

Now that I have made myself island queen, some changes need to take place. Disguising her purpose with a light, dancing step, she walked up to Tassi.

"I'm so thankful you saved my life. But I don't think I'll need you anymore. As you can see, I'm quite in charge now."

The fairy fitzed one direction, then another. Its wings

buzzed as though brushing too hard against each other. A staccato chime burst out of its tiny mouth.

Justine waved her hand. "Off with you now. Go bother someone else. I'll not be supervised."

After a moment, when it seemed her command wouldn't work, Tassi emitted another sharp musical burst, then flew away. In this, Justine felt a triumph. She'd forgotten what Makbal had said about fairies: You wanted them on your side even when you didn't seem to need them.

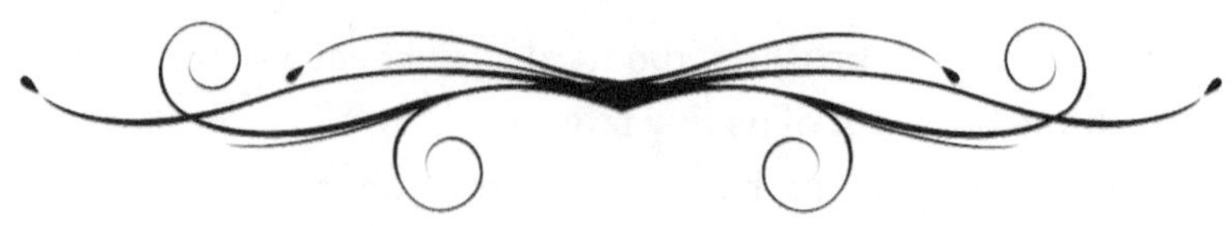

CHAPTER 8

The First Story

The boys' shouts ran through the treetops as Justine walked up to the grove of especially tall trees at the center of the island called the Canopy. They were playing a game of catch, tossing not one, but two balls through the air from tree to tree, using vines and branches to swing and catch and throw. When Justine arrived, some boys dropped down to the ground around her, their new clothes all in tatters.

"Story now, Mother?" asked Delldell, the boy who spoke of himself as a stranger. Justine could easily imagine how such a child had died through neglect or misunderstanding, perhaps even the brutality of a world that would've tried to make him fit better with its own expectations. She thought how wonderful it was Delldell had been taken by Makbal to have a life on the island.

"Well, I don't know," she said. "You've all gone and ruined your clothes. You don't deserve a story, do you?"

Delldell frowned as though he didn't understand. Olewendo shoved his way through the other boys. "But it's your first day. You have to tell a story on your first day. Mothers always do." He spoke with such confidence, Justine realized he'd known multiple mothers. *How many and what happened to them?*

From the edge of the circled boys, Makbal found her gaze, laughter in his eyes as though they shared a secret joke. What could be done with demanding children except indulge them this once? Justine found herself laughing. "Alright, one story. And you all will promise to be better with your clothes tomorrow."

Some boys climbed up to the platform in the trees where she'd awoken from her second death. Others opened doors hidden in the trunks of the trees that appeared to be hollow. These boys each took to his tree with a particular style. Pah, scrunched in butt first, grabbed his ankles and pulled them over his head. Ian dove headfirst. Qassim had carved notches inside his and used them to climb down.

Makbal led her to the largest of all the trees where a smaller tree grew right beside it. Justine's hand brushed the smaller tree and found it quite warm to the touch.

"Our chimney." Makbal twisted an iron crank so the top turned itself from a point directed to the sky to an open cone. "This way everyone above will be able to hear you."

He pressed against what looked like solid bark on the bigger tree. The bark popped open as though on a spring, revealing the narrowest set of stairs. "Don't be scared now." Makbal motioned for her to follow as he led the way down. Justine found the substance of her body made the stairs a tight fit. Her shoulders grazed both sides of the tree at once and she had to walk sideways in some places where Makbal didn't.

The door in the tree slid closed, locking them in complete darkness. Justine pressed her hand against the tree, reaching out for the island presence that had kept her company on her walk, but it didn't answer her.

"Mak," she whispered. "Where are we going?"

"Home," he answered. "Trust me."

Trust me. Justine had never thought much about those words. It wasn't a promise people gave her very often. In fact, the way of her world most often taught her the opposite. Trust was something rich people did because they could believe in good things coming from the world. Not much good had ever come for Justine until now, which of course made it all the more reasonable to expect something to go wrong.

Finally, light shone down below. The stairs ended in an archway that opened into a cavern carved out of the ground. A cooking fire had been lit in a stone-walled hearth. Little alcoves pockmarked the walls of the room where some of the boys had built nests out of the materials each liked best: leaves and grasses, woven or not, feathers, and pillows within pillows. One corner had been set up with a table and a painting of what looked like Catholic Mary with a gold halo over her head. Red and white embroidered linens framed the painting. An incense chalice and loaf of bread sat before it with the loaf slowly being carried away by an army of ants.

A throw rug covered the center of the room. A high-back chair draped in a tiger's fur sat like a throne beside it. At the opposite end of the rug from the chair was a lumpy mattress, worn and patched and stained, with two pillows in a similar state and a neatly folded quilt at its foot.

The boys who'd descended through the entrances of hollow trees had all gathered on the rug except for Jacob, who'd taken a tin from a shelf and was studiously stuffing a wooden pipe with dried leaf. He presented the stuffed pipe to Makbal. "Here you are, Father."

Makbal took the pipe and splayed himself sideways across the arms of the high-back chair. Pah ran to the fire, lit a twig from the wood pile, and carried it over. "Your light, Father."

Justine watched this ceremony with a smile frozen on her

face. It seemed both strange and quaint; this make-believe game they played was more than a game.

"Mother?"

Justine turned and found Qassim behind her, holding out the quilt.

"This is your place." He motioned to the end of the mattress.

She sat down, careful not to wrinkle her nightgown, and draped her velvet cape around her shoulders. Qassim draped the quilt across her knees. The two smallest boys, Delldell and Pah, crawled over from the rug and squeezed themselves up on either side of her legs. Pah began to pet the velvet.

Ling and Olewendo emerged from behind a curtain carrying trays of very small cups filled with a pungent lavender liquid. Each of the boys took one, but when Justine reached for one, Makbal said, "Mother must wait for her tea." As the boys drank their tea, she noticed that though Olewendo held a cup, he hadn't drunk a portion with everyone else.

When all the empty cups had been collected, Makbal clapped his hands. "Now our minds are tidied up and ready for new stories. Mother, if you please."

"Well," Justine said as she blushed. "This is interesting. I don't think I've ever told a story to so many" — she paused — "children." But this didn't seem like the correct word. The boys gave every appearance of being children, but their presence spoke of something uncanny. What did one call a boy who'd been a boy longer than his father had been alive? But this wasn't even enough to fully grasp it. Unending childhood. Could a boy still be five, or ten, or fourteen, when he'd experienced eternity? Was it merely the body that remained young?

"Mother, you look sad," said a boy whose name she didn't remember.

"I'm just thinking of all of you and how happy I am to be here."

"We're happy you're here," said Ian with a wide grin. He didn't seem to harbor any of the distrust toward her being British that she felt with him being Irish. She smiled back, resolving to think only good things about him until she had true cause to think otherwise, even though Mrs. Palmer had always said that God gave some races better blessings than others, according to their ability and moral quality.

It was strange to think of Mrs. Palmer who, Justine realized, had believed Justine was poor because she deserved it. For all the good Justine believed Mrs. Palmer had done, she wouldn't make the same mistake of looking at a person and judging them through preconceived ideas.

"Will you tell us a story now?"

So many questions swirled in Justine's head, it seemed an odd time for a story. But she pushed back her desire to understand and settled on playing her role until the boys had gone to bed. Then, if this was a true-to-life game, she'd be alone with Makbal, and she could ask her questions.

"What kinds of stories do you like?"

"Baba Yaga stories!"

"Rusalka stories!" said Ling. "Did you know we have some here? Tomorrow we can go meet them."

"How long is tomorrow?" asked Pah.

"A half a nacel," said Ian.

"A what?" laughed Justine.

"A nacel," said Ian. "It's a silly thing. Nacel is a boy who rarely speaks. So we count time by him."

"One nacel is about a quarter of a day on the sun," said Qassim. "Which is about the number of words he speaks in that amount of time."

Olewendo glanced around. "Where is Nacel?"

"Who cares?" said Ian. "He's happier alone."

Makbal gave Ling a stern look. "They're not rusalka anymore. Mother will name them for herself."

"I'll be excited to meet all of your friends and the island creatures," said Justine. "But I'm afraid I don't know those kinds of stories."

"An adventure story then," said Ling.

"With nothing that's sad or ugly," added Qassim. "Ling and I are going to swim the current soon, so we need the best stories."

Justine arched a curious eyebrow, but rather than ask for an explanation, she put this question away for after the boys went to bed. "Alright. Well, how about the story of the King of the Golden River?"

Heads nodded with enthusiasm. All around her, bright, excited eyes with anticipation the likes of which Mrs. Palmer had never seen when she'd read stories to the asylum patients. Justine thought she should warn them that she was probably not the best storyteller, but this stalling would've only made her more nervous, so she simply started in on the story of the three brothers, two of whom were evil and beat the youngest brother when he didn't do what they said. She told of how they met the king of the Golden River disguised as a traveler and how the older, wicked brothers turned him out only to need his help later when their business went bad.

The river king offered a great treasure to anyone who could bring at least three drops of holy water to the source of a great river. This would turn the river to gold. The two wicked brothers both tried and failed to claim the water. They became two giant black stones in the river. But the youngest brother, being very good, with a kind heart, passed the tests of his journey, sharing his precious water with thirsty people along his path, so that he had none left when he arrived at the source of the river. This was what the river king had wanted, for only the worthy could claim his treasure. The river changed its course and began to flow into a valley where it turned the land into lush green farms that did indeed produce gold for the younger brother and his entire village.

The boys' eyes became heavy lidded before the youngest brother set out on his journey. They began to pick themselves up from the rug and stagger to their nests. Delldell fell asleep on the quilt by Justine's feet. Pah crawled into her lap.

"I should like to find real gold before I leave the island," said Ling with a yawn. "It's here somewhere."

"Maybe the next golden key will lead us to it," said Ian.

"One thing we know is that brothers can never be trusted to do the right thing," said Makbal with surprising vehemence. He hadn't seemed to enjoy the story at all. When he came to the mattress to carry Delldell to his bed, he didn't look at Justine.

With all the boys asleep, Justine and Makbal were alone. The two of them came together by the fire. Makbal knelt to tamp down the logs to low-burning embers. Justine watched the flames flicker and die down to glowing coal. If she kept her eyes tight on the embers alone, she could see the fires in the stoves at the asylum, sooty, and never warm enough.

"This is a beautiful place you've built."

He grinned. "Now that you're here, it will be even better."

"I'm not sure how I'll be able to help you. Are the pirates so terrible?"

"They won't be now that you're here."

"Yes, but—"

"Don't worry. You'll see."

Makbal turned and skipped across the room to an empty alcove and tucked himself in. Justine turned away to hide her irritation. There was nothing else to do but go to bed. She studied the worn mattress, a bed not much different than the stained thing she'd slept on at the asylum. And yet, it seemed so out of place here. When she lay down, she smelled old sweat, and earth, and the slightest hint of hair oil or something like it.

Who had been the girl lying here before? What stories had she told? And how had she been eaten? The questions circled as Justine fell asleep. She needed answers so she could protect herself. She had no intention of becoming an empty nightgown in a trunk. No matter what, she would find a way to survive better than those who'd come before.

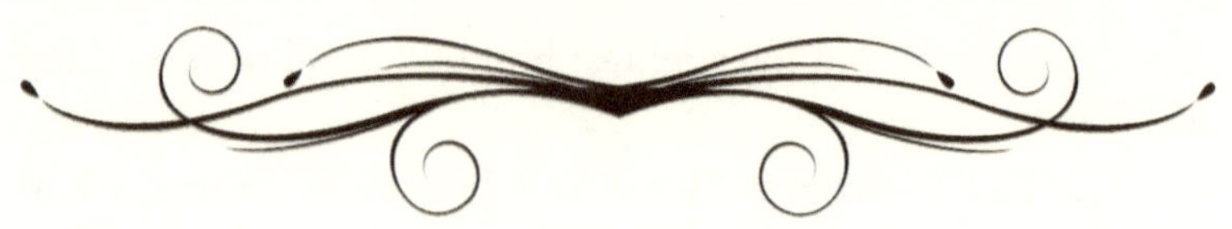

CHAPTER 9

Time and the Prophecy of Mending

When the third mother perished, the island said to me, This is intolerable.

I wished to clarify because sometimes the voice of the island could be confused in translation. "What exactly does the island find intolerable?"

All of it.

The brothers, said the island. One doesn't hear me. The other hears only what serves his fears. They are haunted by Osuana.

On that, I couldn't agree more. Who would have thought such an obnoxious little girl could have caused such a ruckus? I fear in my emotion, I said impulsively, "What if she could be brought back?"

And the island immediately latched on to the

idea. Osvana could mend them. She can mend me, said the island.

Of course, as soon as that suggestion had left my mind, I regretted it. I'd not thought through all the implications. We weren't in the business of bringing souls back from death even if it was only halfway.

As I remember it, we left that conversation unfinished. I told myself the island forgot, as islands can be distractable. New children had just arrived, and the island was investigating them to see how it might mold itself to their joy.

But that must have been about the time the call started going out. Later, when I realized the island had been calling to Osvana for quite some time, I tried to create a caveat. This was where the prophecy came from.

"Another worthy soul," I suggested. "What if there was someone else who might do the mending you need? Give them a pathway."

The island also liked this idea. And then went a little overboard with it, creating not just a new pathway to mending the island, but a pathway to godhood. Did I feel it was important to point out that only gods could create new gods? Not so much. What I'd learned about the rules of gods was they were mostly a collection of hearsay and precedents.

Someone did something once, so therefore that was the way it would always be.

The island was created from pieces of the brothers, and it had grown quite a lot on its own since then. I thought, Why not tell the story and see if it comes true? Even untrue stories have power.

From The Reflections of Archivist Posietta

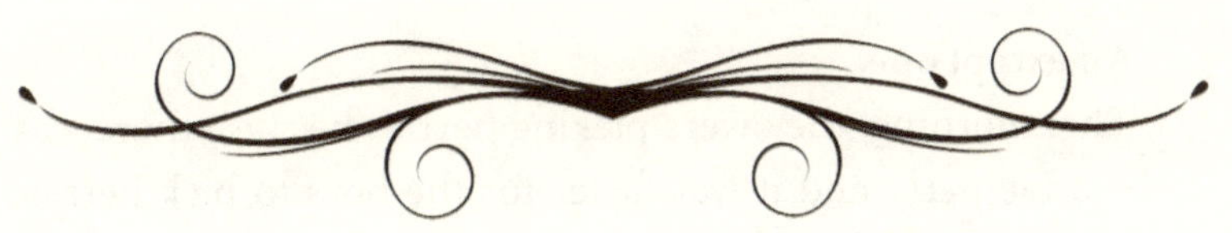

CHAPTER 10

Even Magic Requires Planning

Justine asked three boys how the last mother had died. They'd all appeared confused by her question. She'd also asked them about where they'd come from. It seemed such an unusual thing to have this variety of boys all together and she thought it would be a way to collect experiences. Or at least prepare herself for how she was going to relate to them. If she should prepare barbed replies to the Irish boy's impending comments about English girls, if she should expect the Chinese boy to want to eat strange foods, or the African boy to—well, she wasn't sure exactly. But something unexpected.

Only, none of them remembered where they'd come from. It was as if they were just boys from nowhere. It gave her the most uncomfortable feeling; she'd never thought about how much of a person came from the language they spoke, the people they knew, the ways they lived. And if a person came from nowhere, how was she supposed to treat them? What conversations could they have? These boys, all they wanted to do was roam around the island on adventures. They cared only for monsters and pirates and swimming and fishing.

All except one.

That morning, they were picking berries because there was to be a fae party and it was faster for the boys to pick berries than the fae. Mak had caught her asking the boy Sven her questions and had given her a strange look, which made it useful to just sit quietly and watch the boys with the berries. By that time, many of the older boys were growing restless and were making sounds about being off to do something else.

Across the berry patch, Olewendo, who preferred to wear girl's clothes, was also quiet. He was the one who hadn't drunk the tea. And she saw, every so often when he looked up from berry picking and their eyes met, that he knew where he'd come from.

"Let's go up the mountains and have a fight," said Sven.

"Bravo," said Ian.

"Will there be knights to kill?" suggested another.

"There will if we go now," said Mak, just as enthusiastic as the others.

Justine started up. "You're leaving?"

"You'll be fine."

"Will I?"

She thought, *I don't even know what danger to watch for.* More desperately, she thought, *I don't want to be eaten.*

"Watch out for pirates," said Mak. "And any shimmer in the air. Don't touch it."

"Or monsters or dragons or ogres," said Qassim gleefully as the boys began to run off.

There were six or seven young boys who remained picking berries, none more than seven years old. They busily plucked berries and gathered them in buckets set out on a platform. When a bucket was full, a trio of fairies spirited the bucket away.

Olewendo was the only one of the older boys who remained. Did he know how to fight off a creature that might eat her? Justine thought her chances were better with him than the young boys, so she came to sit on his side of the bushes.

"How long have you been here?"

"That's not a relevant question," said Olewendo. "Time only exists in pirate space."

This was an interesting piece of information, but Justine refused to be distracted by it. "How many mothers do you remember?"

"Three."

"And what happened to them?"

"I don't think you should—"

"Just tell me. Was it horrible?"

One of the boys ran up and snuggled against her. "Mother, Delldell is helping the fae with their berries so we can have pie tonight."

"What's your favorite kind of pie?"

"Allberry pie," said Pah, coming up beside Delldell.

"Delldell likes that one too." He set his full bucket on the platform and retrieved an empty one. As he dropped his first berry in, he tilted his head, listening for the plop. Then, as though making up a song, he dropped two more in, one right after another.

"Ymmmmmm," hummed Delldell.

Pah clapped his palm against the side of his bucket. In response, a boy in a tree slapped his palm against the tree trunk, then the pattern repeated. A single berry, then two in succession, a clap, a thump. Other boys took up the pattern, adding their own hums as it went around. Even the fairies added a chime as they came and went. Pah put words to the pattern as he sang, "What is better than allberry berries? An allberry pie in my tum-tum-tummy."

To Olewendo, she said quietly, "Why is it a secret? No one remembers them."

"Pirates," said Olewendo finally. "They come onto the island to take mothers."

"Only mothers?"

"Boys also, but they kill mothers."

"Why did Mak say the last one was eaten?"

"The Black Hook fed her to the mer in the lagoon."

Justine shivered.

"Actually, the one before died just there." Olewendo pointed into the trees. "We had a battle. She was protecting us, and the Black Hook ran her through."

"But why?"

"It's said that someday, one of the mothers will be powerful enough to put the island together. The pirates don't want that to happen. Then they won't be able to grow up anymore."

"The pirates are boys who have grown up?"

"And girls. A long time ago, there were girls here, not just a mother. I don't remember that, I just hear things. The creatures talk sometimes." He gave her a sidelong glance. "Don't tell Mak I know all that. He'll be so mad, and you don't want him to be mad."

Justine nodded, her mind spinning.

As the bushes and trees around the platform were picked over, the boys moved farther afield, spreading out and sometimes wandering off on their own. She could only see two heads bobbing up and down among the bushes. *If the pirates came now, what would I do?*

Almost as if her thought had called catastrophe down on her head, Justine heard rustling in the bushes. She told herself it was one of the clumsier boys reaching for berries. As the rustling behind her got louder, then was followed by the huff of a large animal snorting, she thought, *This must be a game they're playing.*

But beside her Olewendo had gone still, alert.

Justine stood, then took a step backward to shift to a new

bush. Her first heel came down on the ground as expected, but her second heel tripped over something hard. She turned and saw a long tail edged with spikes along its top and covered in brown-red scales that glinted in the sunlight. The tail retracted under the bushes, apparently irritated at being stepped on, but Justine stood frozen, staring at the place where it'd disappeared.

Slowly and with great effort, the impossible word came to her mind.

Dragon.

You just stepped on a dragon's tail.

The grunting and huffing she'd heard now took on a new meaning. She straightened to her tallest height. Off to her right, a section of bushes was pulled sharply over, then released to snap back into its upright position. This was repeated as Justine's mind so, so slowly made meaning from it. *The dragon is eating berries.*

This is a good place, she told herself. *This is a good place.*

But to Justine's horror, she spotted Delldell, Momoaro, and two other boys making a line of attack. They each carried a short knife in one hand. In the other, they carried a stick or empty bucket. On tiptoes, they advanced toward the dragon.

No! No! Don't—

Olewendo grabbed Justine just as she would have run forward. The boys rushed the dragon with cries of, "Die, Red Zmaj!" and "Give up your treasure!"

The dragon's head appeared above the bushes, startled and as wide-eyed as a child. It recovered its shock and blew out a puff of putrid breath. There was a slash of crushed foliage, the rush of air disturbed as the dragon swung its tail toward its attackers.

Pah cried out. His head disappeared beneath the bushes.

This would have been enough for normal boys to give up. But Delldell and Momoaro pressed on. They ducked and slashed against the swinging tail. The dragon emitted more festering clouds of its poisonous breath. When Momoaro was knocked hard against a tree trunk, the fight should have been over. But Delldell used the distraction of the fallen boy to circle around and mount the dragon's spined back. He wrapped his arm around its neck and hung on as the dragon tried to throw him off.

"Dastardly Zmaj of the Dark Woods, Delldell demands his treasure or he'll cut you from stem to stern."

If Justine wasn't so frightened, she might have laughed at the nonsense of this strongly spoken threat. Then she thought that perhaps the words themselves didn't mean so much as the tone with which they were uttered. For, at Delldell's voice, the dragon stilled. The knife Delldell held at its throat was unlikely to be much use against the layers of scales. And the boy himself surely could strike no other form of mortal blow. But this didn't matter. He believed in the fact of his conquest, and this fact of believing made it so.

With a roar that shook leaves from the trees, the dragon disappeared in a puff of smoke. Delldell fell to the ground and a moment later, his arm appeared above the shrubbery, holding a silver key. "Delldell has got it!" cried the boy.

A cheer went up.

"Hurrah, we're adventuring today!" said Pah.

"Mother, do you see my key?" asked Delldell, running up to Justine. "Now we must find its lock so I'll know the path to the country from which the shadows fall." He swallowed heavily as if drawing down a tight bundle of fear, his small face crunching together in response to some dark thought Justine couldn't guess at. "You're coming with us, right?"

"Of course," said Justine, though she was sure she had no idea what was going on. It seemed a marvelous thing to be led on an adventure by young boys who knew no fear, or at least not fear as she knew it.

A shrill whistle burst through the woods. The boys paused to listen. The first whistle was followed by two short whistles.

"Lord Mak is coming to join us," said Pah.

"Now we'll have to share," grumbled Momoaro. "The big boys always get all the best treasure."

They set off almost immediately. No bags were packed, no provisions collected, the berry collecting was abandoned and apparently forgotten. The older boys flowed in here and there along the path through the woods. Justine didn't see Mak, but no one seemed particularly nervous or wary of danger so she told herself it was safe.

We're playing a game.

Presently, someone shouted, "I found something." Everyone rushed to that spot. There was a golden coin in the nook of a tree. In the next tree, a shiny gem buried under moss, like the glittering bounty hidden in storybooks. Justine thought that the island must be a place wholly created from imagined things taken from stories. She'd walked alone the previous day without a hint of treasure. But now, because this purpose of a treasure hunt had been suggested, it seemed every ten steps revealed some new prize.

The trail of treasure guided them through the woods, then along the edge of the cliffs that led into the mountains. Justine had not yet been to this part of the island. Turning, she could look out over the woods and see in the far distance the roofs of the tree house, which appeared on the far side of the island. She could also see the coast, or what Olewendo had referred to as the lagoon, a strip of water marked with boundary rocks that was slowly eaten away by a growing mist. And in that mist, the other island. Or, as she thought she understood now, a broken off part of her island. It appeared to be a dense, hilly jungle. But there, just the barest outline of what looked like a castle ruin. And even farther, the pinpricks of torches and thatch wooden houses.

An entire village over there.

She realized the boys had moved on without her and she was in danger of being lost. As she scrabbled to come down from the cliff, she found Olewendo standing to the side of the path, waiting for her.

"Stop there," he said, holding up his hand.

She stopped and saw that he was guarding part of the path. It appeared in shadow, the air shimmering in a defined space from the ground up to the sky.

"What is it?"

"A runnel in time." He motioned for her to step carefully around it. "The pirates make them when they come onto the island. You touch it, you change."

"Change." She swallowed a hard lump rising in her throat.

"One of the mothers died this way. Her soul aged a lifetime in moments, and she passed on to the current."

Justine's knees knocked together as she followed Olewendo's instructions to step around the runnel. "That's horrible. Can't Mak fix them?"

"When you bond with him, yes. But not now."

"A bond, like marriage?"

Olewendo laughed. "Much more than marriage." He grew quiet for a moment, seeming to listen to something, then he said, "It's hard for me to remember, but I think you're the best that's come."

"Best?"

"Mak was so happy with the soap, remember?"

Justine found herself struggling to remember anything with soap, then it came to her, the first day, washing in the lake, the power of her wishes.

"Not all the mothers have been able to do what you do."

"What if I don't want to be bonded to Mak?"

Olewendo shrugged and started down the path. "It's not a good thing when he's angry."

They found the rest of the group stopped at a rushing river so wide and fast they could not safely cross it on foot.

"Aw, no. We're stuck," said Pah.

Ian waded in to test the water and would've been swept downstream if Makbal hadn't been there to pull him to shore.

"Can we make a bridge?" asked Ling.

"No time for that," said Makbal, pointing up to the descending sun.

Delldell walked thoughtfully along the edge of the river. There was a duck sitting on a rock in the sun. When Delldell approached, it flapped its wings in greeting.

"Are you Ryaba the golden egg hen?"

"Squawk!" the duck answered.

"Do you think you might carry me on your back across the river?"

"Squawk!" The duck waddled to the edge of the water. Silver key in hand, Delldell carefully climbed onto the duck's back. To Justine's astonishment, the duck swam out into the water, not at all bothered by the current. It didn't sink under Delldell's weight even though he wiggled terribly and kept turning around to wave.

"The key," called Ian.

"Yes, the key," echoed Delldell. He leaned dangerously forward over the duck's shoulders and dipped the key in the water. It trailed along with him all the way across. When Delldell and the duck waddled up onto the far shore, the silver key had turned gold.

"Where's the keyhole?" called Makbal, a bright joyous grin on his face. For a moment, he seemed more proud parent than boy.

Delldell slid off the duck and looked all around. The duck was about to start off on its return journey when it was startled by the sudden arrival of a large, speckled thrush, which landed on its back and began to peck at its feathers.

"Dear thrush," said Delldell. "Have you hidden a keyhole for Delldell?"

"Not today, to-day," chirped the thrush. "But for the fae." Then it flew away.

Delldell's face fell. "Delldell isn't to find the country from which the shadows fall after all." He might have begun to cry except a golden gazebo had appeared in the river, diverting it into two streams quite easy to cross. The gazebo was lined with shelves of all the most wondrous things. While Justine stood still and stared at it, the boys rushed forward. Fairies flew around with them, taking the treasures the boys had collected during their adventure in exchange for magic wands, rings, roses, mirrors, a fishbone polished to look like pearl, an invisible jacket, a miniature flying horse, and swords that extended as long as the bearer wished.

Makbal was quick to choose a sword for himself, then went off alone to speak in low tones with one of the fairies. This one had legs, long hair, and breasts, which they covered in a shimmering dress. The tones of their chime language seemed different than Tassi's, who Justine felt was perpetually disgruntled. Justine strained her ears to hear Makbal answering in word language, but he spoke his answers to the fairy's chime so softly, she could only hear mumbles.

Their arms full of treasures, the boys marched back to the Canopy, where they found a stew dinner set out in an assortment of clay and wood bowls. It smelled amazing, but Justine's appetite couldn't be summoned. Her thoughts unquiet with too many of them competing for her attention. Most of all, she was thinking, *I cannot marry Mak. He's a child.*

And the answering thought, *He's also a god.*

In her mind, a dim impression of Jack Woolf in his Pan mask, looking more and more mature and respectable as she thought of him. A boy who could give a girl what she needed. It didn't matter that in the realm of the living she'd never truly had a chance to make him hers. *I'll never see him again.*

She looked around the table. For as long as she survived here, her only options were these boys.

When everyone was done eating, Makbal clapped his hands and flew to the edge of the sand pit. "We have new initiates today, friends. Where are Eloy, Wapasha, and Walter?"

Three boys detached themselves from the tables and came forward. Walter had the hooked nose and corked teeth Justine had seen every day in London. He wore a wrinkled nightshift slightly gray with coal dust.

The other two boys seemed wholly alien. Eloy wore only a cloth around his waist and Wapasha wore an animal skin tunic and pants with parts of his hair braided to keep it out of his face. Justine noticed that Wapasha, who was the oldest of the three, had those fine, high cheekbones and athletic grace Makbal cherished in all his older boys, except perhaps Wapasha was a little older than usual. *He could be seventeen or eighteen,* thought Justine. She wondered what it would be like to bed such a boy who, in the world above, probably came from a tribal people in the Americas and didn't speak English or know about any of the things she knew about.

But sex is sex, thought Justine. *And I can't carry on here for very long without it.*

All three boys moved clumsily as though half awake, but once they stood before Makbal, their posture straightened, and they became alert to his attention.

"You have come now to the land between, a special place that makes all your dreams come true." Makbal held out a golden cup to Wapasha. "Drink and let your old lives be washed away. Here you bring nothing with you but what your mind can conjure."

Wapasha took a sip from the cup and handed it back to Makbal who gave it to Walter.

"You'll go on many adventures. You'll fight beside each other in great battles. You'll face challenges that now seem beyond you, but with time they will become yours." Makbal passed the cup to Eloy. "And when you're ready, the island will grant you a final quest, a key that you must first turn to gold. Then you'll find the keyhole that will unlock for you and you alone, the path to the land where shadows are made."

Justine sucked in a breath, but no one seemed alarmed. Ling and Qassim were passing around the same mind-tidying tea from the night before. Those who had already drunk their portion looked at Makbal with half-lidded eyes, dreamy and glowing with the possibility of adventure.

Justine searched for Delldell, who was now on his final journey toward leaving the island and found Olewendo watching her from across the sandpit where he sat at the far table. He held his empty cup in his hand.

Makbal led the new boys over to Justine. "This is your mother," he said. "When you're afraid or uncertain, she'll comfort you. She tells us a story every night. You'll now go with Smear who knows the best places to set up beds so you can see the stars."

As though on cue, Smear stood up from his seat at the table. "If ya'll follow me. We'll get to collecting your bedding."

Like mindless creatures, the three boys followed Smear away from the circle of torchlight that rimmed the Canopy. The rest of the boys began breaking off from the tables. Some climbed up to their own beds. Others began to lay out the things brought from the fairy gazebo and divide them into smaller packages. The tables were left empty of boys but filled with dirty stew bowls.

"I suppose I do the cleaning." Justine began to collect the bowls, but Makbal had climbed up on a table and stood in her way.

"Cleaning?" he cackled. "We've never heard of it." The

cackle died on his lips when he saw her face, which she was sure resembled some kind of resentful shock and far too adult irritation. Of course someone had to clean the dishes.

"But if some gallant young man might think of a solution in which no one must do the dishes, I'll grant him a gold coin I had left over from my purchase today."

Ling and Qassim looked at each other. Ian appeared thoughtful. One of the little boys scrunched up his face to ponder. Finally, Delldell held up the magic wand he'd purchased at the gazebo. "I have an idea!" He stood up on a table, knocking bowls with his dirty feet as he walked to the center, raised both hands high over his head, and said, "Dishes, wash!"

One by one, the bowls rose into the air, formed a line, and began to move into the stairwell tree and down to the cave. Jakob got up from the table and followed them. In short order, he called out, "They're washing themselves in the pantry!"

"Wonderful," said Makbal. "I suppose its bedtime for you little ones."

"Not yet," said Pah. "Look!"

A flame had shot out from one of the torches and flown all the way across the sandpit to the table where Delldell stood. It landed just short of his feet.

"Oh no, the table," cried Justine. But then she saw the fire had burned only a key-shaped hole in the wood, then gone out. Delldell knelt and fitted his golden key into the hole. It clicked once, twice, then a golden light grew out of it. It suddenly seemed very familiar, this story of golden keys and the search for a distant land. Justine remembered Mrs. Palmer reading the asylum children such a story.

"Did you create this rite?" she asked Makbal as they watched Delldell gaze into the light.

"It was a story told by my Wendy, the first mother. I liked it, so I kept it."

"Delldell sees it," said Delldell. "Delldell knows the way."

"You're ahead of us then," said Ling, clapping the boy on the back.

"We'll go to the current after sleep," said Makbal. "You can pick your final adventure."

"Can't we go now?" Delldell looked like sleep was the last thing he could do at that moment. But Makbal picked him up, held him in the crook of one arm, and set his free palm on Delldell's forehead. In a moment, Delldell's body relaxed into Makbal's, cuddling against his chest with heavy lids. Makbal joined the line of dishes making its way down to the cave so he could put Delldell to bed.

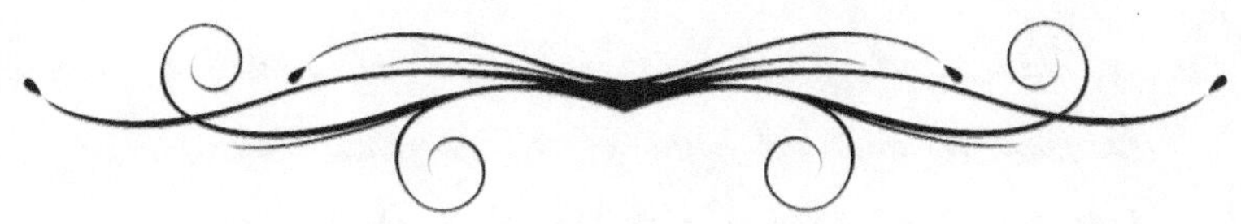

CHAPTER 11

The Voyager Becomes a Pirate

Of all the troubles brought to the island when the Voyager brought half of it into time, the merfolk suffered the most. Mer are eternal beings that aren't gods because they don't have the power to impose their wills on mortals, even though, like the first gods, they were created from the imaginations of mortals. There's a fine history on the mythologies of gods and creation written by Posietta, which includes a lengthy passage on the categories of immortals if you wish to know more. For our purposes, it's enough to know that the mer existed in pockets of magic and superstition in the mortal realm, and the brothers invited them to summer in the island, a place they could be assured of a friendly reception from the children, which was certainly not the case in the realms of the living.

The island, as it was envisioned, allowed for the free coming and going of all immortal beings. Like the mer, us fae also took to making the journey for routine vacations from the nonsense of mortals. It was a delightful thing to leave behind the rage and fear that dominated so much of human life and instead frolic in the purest sunshine with children. We would stage the best parties and go on moon hunts and cut designs on the ice of the winter pond.

Then, thanks to the Voyager, it all ended.

By creating a pocket of time in an immortal realm, the Voyager had cast the island's identity into a nether sphere. Those traveling to the island couldn't find it without a map, a condition nearly irrelevant by comparison to the fact that without a fixed position in a determined realm, no one could find a path to leave. The children couldn't graduate to their eternities in the lower realms. The brothers couldn't journey uprealm to claim more children's souls. And those of us, mer and fae who'd been on the island at the time of its division, were trapped.

There were only five of us fae present at the time. With the children's joyous laughter, we quickly multiplied. Before any of us knew it, we had established a village for ourselves. It was our researchers who thought to use fae dust as an amplifier to navigate a path to mortal stars. We also helped the island develop the key system, tokens wrought from fae dust that gave children a map to their eternity when they were deemed worthy of it. In this way, we adjusted. It wasn't easy, but we've made ourselves useful in this world, and that is more than many beings can say.

The mer were less lucky.

The barrier of time was not immediately visible underwater. The mer were often caught in runnels of disjointed time, their bodies contorted. They are naturally elegant creatures, picky over their cleanliness, attentive to their appearance. With these disturbances, all their natural habits became impossible. They morphed into monsters with overgrown nails, carrying debris from the sea on their bodies without notice, allowing disease to fester and tarnish their scales.

Too quickly, they forgot who they were. Cut off from their stories, and the humans who wove their mythos, they created one for themselves as vicious demons of the deep. As their bodies festered so too did their hearts. They stored up great bitterness against the Voyager. When his brother came to them with his plan, they were more than willing.

We, Lord Mak, and the fae council had come to believe that if the Voyager wouldn't heal the island, he could be removed from the equation. And if he was removed, either Mak would have the power to mend the island himself, or he could bring a replacement to the island who might channel the Voyager's half of the island's power. He called this figure the Mother, after the mortal role of some women to be caretakers to their children, guiding them through earlier life and being a source of strength and comfort.

Given what happened with Osuana, Lord Mak was reluctant to take this path of finding a mother. So our first step was to remove the Voyager. In what by then had become a robust tradition of independent decisions, Mak didn't consult friendly gods on the matter, nor did he consult the fates and their records of eternity to see if any precedent had been established. The island has always been a unique situation, and it was unlikely reasonable advice would have been found if it had been sought.

Two children were chosen to take a small boat out into the lagoon and toy with the mer. The Voyager had built a ship in the fashion of a nineteenth-century French schooner so he might harry the shores of the island from a distance. In particular, he had begun to scoop up boys who were swimming with nets, then keep them in his hold until they were too old to play.

These two boys who acted as bait had been armed with nets themselves and ropes with hooks made from fae dust on the ends. These hooks would fly true and snag the thick clothing the Voyager and his people wore, pulling them into the water where the mer waited.

As expected, the Voyager came around the cove in his ship and stopped at the edge of time, which was now a visible veil of mist we'd created for our protection. The ship broke through the veil in a cacophony of groaning wood and flapping sails, sounds the boys had learned to dread. But they held their position, and when they saw the Voyager standing on deck preparing to supervise their abduction, they threw their hooks, which flew so silently, the Voyager's crew didn't know he was snared until they heard the crash of him hitting the water.

They scrambled to assemble a rescue. It was the quick thinking and sharp mind of his head boy who dove in after him and fought off the converging mer that saved him. Instead of the gruesome ending his brother had envisioned, the Voyager survived the encounter with some gashed skin and the loss of one hand, which made a delightful meal for the prince of the mer, an old favorite of the girl Osuana who'd been lost.

Since the hand had been taken in a space where time existed, it couldn't be imagined back into place as it would have been on the other side of the veil. We knew this was how it would be from past skirmishes where other injuries hadn't solved themselves in time as they did without. This was why the mer pulled the Voyager back across the veil once they had him in the water. If they'd managed to devour him into nonexistence, much would have been different.

Instead, the ship bartered for a fae blessing of dust and sailed uprealm. When they returned, the voyager had obtained a collection of prosthetics, including a stainless-steel hook, which he never spared an opportunity to use in battle. Until this point, the deaths of children on both sides had been accidental, part of the hazards of conflict. After the Voyager lost his hand, death became common on the island. I don't remember who first called him the Black Hook, but it was a name earned in every way.

We believed he had passed beyond all redemption. In his desperation, the brother was convinced to bring the first mother to the island.

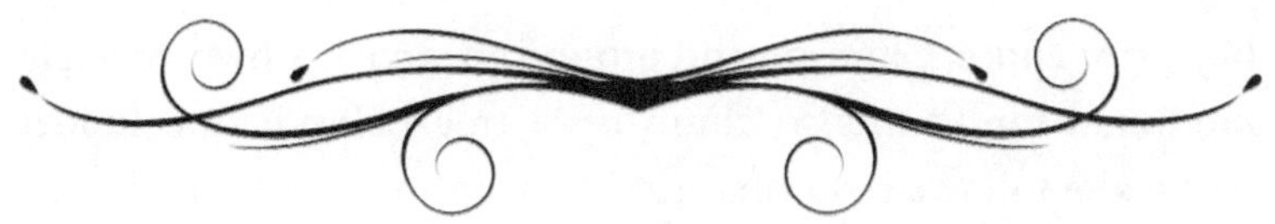

CHAPTER 12

Delldell Swims the Current

For his last adventure on the island, Delldell asked to visit the mer.

"This is a good choice," said Makbal. "Mother hasn't met them yet."

"But what if they eat us?" asked Pah.

"The great moon hasn't risen," said Qassim. "We'll be safe."

"Whooeeeeh!" cried Makbal, grabbing Delldell's hands and swinging him in a circle. "Here we go adventuring, adventuring, adventuring. What will we find? What will we do?"

"First one to the water gets the first shot," said Qassim.

The boys whooped and yelled as they raced away from the Canopy. Justine followed at a more dignified pace carrying Momoaro even though he squirmed to get down and run with the others. She needed the reassuring presence of his body to ground her in this waking dream. She didn't want to be forgetful like them. She didn't want to be the pill in the honey that asked if this was safe, and hadn't the mer eaten a mother? She clung to what Qassim had said about the moon. Perhaps mer were only hungry at certain times.

Makbal flew back to her, gently detached Momoaro from

her grip, and set him on the ground to find his own way. He motioned for Justine to climb up a tree behind him. Reluctantly she followed, putting her hands in the rough handholds where he'd put his hands, her bare feet scraping the bark in a dull pain that somehow made her feel better.

Up in the tree, Makbal showed her how to find a path along the largest branches. It took some doing because Justine wasn't at all in the mood for games, or even this new challenge of walking across trees as though walking on the ground. But by the time they crossed the beach, Justine's heart felt lighter. And when she saw the strip of brilliant, white sand fading into clear azure water, it was impossible to hold dark thoughts in her mind.

She had never seen such a beautiful place. The water was so clear she could look down to the white sand on the bottom until it dropped away into the dark, deep water. All along the western side of the cove the cliffs cut up into the sky. She saw now that the mist wasn't a natural mist but a veil that divided the two islands. It wasn't as thick as it had seemed when she'd looked at it from high up on the cliffs. Justine could more clearly see the jungled hills of the island across the water as they rose from a rocky shore. She saw the dark maws of several caves in those rocks and, up high where the jungle gave way to white-capped mountains, she saw the ruins.

An island where grown men live. Justine felt a tight warmth spread over her belly. Trying to ignore it, she bent over to pick out a seashell glinting blue and silver. "How beautiful." She looked at Makbal. "Shall we go hunting for seashells?"

"That sounds terribly romantic."

"It is."

Makbal shook his head. "Search yourself if you like. Just don't go past the rock line." He pointed out to the water where a scattering of rocks seemed to create a boundary just in front of the mist.

Pah raced by them, his pockets stuffed with acorns. Ian was right beside him, feet pounding the ground, sand flying, as they rushed to beat the others to the water. Ian dove in first. He seemed to skim all the way down to the sandy bottom before coming back to the surface, already halfway to the rock boundary. He made a cawing sound as he mounted a rock. "Vile creatures of the depths, come get me if you can."

It's just a game.

More boys burst out of the woods and ran for the water. Soon the lagoon was full of them splashing and shoving each other to claim their places on the best rocks. Makbal dove in with them, swimming as easily as a fish. Justine waded out almost to the nearest rock, then thrust forward, her fingers scrabbling to grasp the rock and pull herself up. From there, she could walk from rock to rock until she found a large flat one with plenty of space so she wouldn't be likely to fall into the water. Ling came and sat beside her. He offered her a few of his acorns. "These are your weapons," he said with great seriousness. "Don't let the fish pull you in."

Justine looked at the water around her rock. On the island side, the sandy bottom only showed the occasional minnow. On the other side, below the mist, the water became deep. She saw only a thickening darkness. If she strained her eyes, she thought perhaps she saw the outlines of drowned rocks or perhaps caves, but nothing else.

A shadow passed over her vision. Justine looked up and gasped as the pirates' three-masted brig came around the point of the opposite side of the cove. It glided through the water with hardly a sound. Only when it was so close that the water of its wake made small waves against the rocks, did Justine hear the creaking of its wooden body, the groaning of its rigging. And there they were. Full grown men. Almost a dozen of them walked its decks and climbed to the crow's nest. As the boat glided past, Justine thought she saw one of them wave, but such a friendly gesture seemed unlikely for a pirate.

"The Black Hook is off again," said Qassim.

"He'll never find what he's looking for," said Makbal with a surprising amount of bitterness.

"I hope he's gone for a long time," said Pah. "That way, he won't be able to steal me."

"No one's going to steal you," said Justine.

The ship appeared to be moving toward the gap between the island cliffs and the mountains, but then it turned toward the mountains, apparently steering itself into walls of solid rock.

Justine's hand went to her mouth. "Are they?" But no. As she watched, the front of the ship began to dip forward and slowly sink beneath the waves. The rest of the ship followed until all that was left to see above water was the name printed across the stern. Justine knew her letters, but she wasn't good at reading. It took her all the time of the ship's sinking to read them.

"Osuana," she said, as the ship disappeared with a quiet whoosh and a gurgle as though it had been swallowed for the lagoon's dinner.

"Shh," whispered Qassim, his eyes cutting to Makbal. "That name isn't spoken."

"Where did she go?"

"Downrealm to the green caves," said Ian. He didn't seem to understand that it was unusual for ships to intentionally sink beneath the water.

Justine strained her eyes at the deep water where the ship had disappeared. She saw no trace of it. But, as she watched, the water seemed to move. Pieces of shadow detached themselves from the mass of darkness, became long swimming shapes.

"They're coming!" cried Pah. "Are you ready, boys?"

The boys seemed to be anticipating a new game, and yet

Justine felt afraid. The rock she'd chosen suddenly didn't seem large enough to protect her from whatever was coming. She moved three acorns around in her palm like worry stones. They clicked against each other, *tick, tap, tack.* Their clicking became the only sound around. Not a bird called overhead. Not an insect swarmed on shore. Even the lapping of the waves fell silent. Then the water rose up all around them in a great rush. Not water, Justine realized, but the shadowed shapes she'd seen in the deep. In the fury of splashing, long, gray-green arms reached out to snatch the boys from their rocks. Hands with horrible, hooked claws tore at the boys' feet as they valiantly, and futility, pelted their attackers with acorns.

One by one they were dragged in. Some went by those hideously clawed hands, others were knocked over by huge fish tails that slapped them from their rocks. When the claws took hold of Ling, Justine tried to grab him, but he disappeared over the edge of the rock so quickly the acorns he'd aimed to throw dropped to the empty rock in his place.

"Mak, do something. Do something!" shouted Justine. She looked toward the rock where Makbal had stood but couldn't see it through the furious splashing.

Just as quickly, the water quieted once more. Justine found herself alone with empty rocks all around. And there, in the water, the shadows circled. Around and around. She could see snatches of color that were the boys' clothes among them.

"What the bloody fuck is going on here?"

One shadow broke free and slithered to the surface. A head popped up at the edge of Justine's rock. The creature's face was pitted with scars, but Justine barely saw them. She'd become trapped by the gaze of the creature's red eyes. The ridged gills along its neck seethed open and closed as it hissed, "A new one."

Another creature bobbed to the surface to Justine's right so she couldn't keep both in her sight at the same time. They had seaweed for hair and smelled of rotten salt grime.

"Return the boys," she said, though the tremor in her voice undermined her command.

"So old," hissed the second creature. "They haven't bonded yet."

"Because he knows she'll be difficult for him."

A clawed hand crept up on the rock and stopped just before touching Justine's knee. "What's your name, child?"

"I'm Justine."

"Justine," hissed one. "So old."

"But not old enough to be the one he's waiting for."

He who? But the boys had been taken so she said, "Make up your minds. Am I too old or too young?"

"Come with us, precious girl. We have a better place for you."

"As your lunch?"

The creatures cackled joyless laughter. "Aha, she thinks she knows. But what can she really know?"

Justine hadn't been able to stop staring at the first creature's eyes. She found herself leaning forward almost against her will, drawn to them by some magical power. "I want to know everything."

For a moment, confusion crossed the first creature's face. It blinked. With this blink, it lost Justine's gaze. But it was too late, Justine was already falling into the water.

Falling again.

The water was pleasantly warm. She saw the creatures swimming around her, churning up the water with their fish tails, which ruined her view. She very much wanted to see if the pirate ship was somewhere down here.

Clawed hands reached out from the masses of flowing hair and grabbed her. She jerked away, angry that they'd coaxed her down and now were getting in her way. She reached out to swim toward the darkness of the deeper water, kicking her legs against the net that had become her nightgown. She only made it a little way before she came up against a barrier she couldn't see. When her hand went out, it pressed against something solid, like a glass window.

A creature rushed at her, pulling her arm. "Don't break through!"

This command only made Justine more determined. She shoved the creature away and managed to put her hand back against the barrier. *It's not the wall I think it is,* she thought, then pushed with all her might. Her arm burst through. The water on the other side was just a little colder, but otherwise it seemed the same. She pulled the rest of her body through, ignoring the pack of creatures hissing and spitting their fury behind her. It seemed they couldn't follow and this made her triumphant. She had thwarted their game.

Justine turned in a circle to orient herself in the world she'd seen above the surface. She found that breathing wasn't a problem. Though her lungs strained for air, and this feeling frightened her, it wasn't sufficiently frightening to be a problem. She didn't need to breathe; she was no longer living. Behind her, she looked up and saw the line of rocks. Everywhere else, empty water.

Not empty, she realized. As she sunk down to where the sun didn't reach, the darkness took on forms. More shadows moved. Not the shadows of the creatures who had attacked her, but others, some much larger. She turned the direction she thought the *Osuana* had gone and saw what looked to be a deeper darkness. *A cave?*

As she tried to move that direction, a rush of warm water came from the side. She turned and saw a giant shadow emerge from the darkness. Red eyes the size of her fists shone through the water. A giant mouth opened to reveal four rows of teeth lining a long snout.

Justine screamed. She covered her head with her arms and kicked her legs as hard as she could. Her nightgown, previously a nuisance, became a trap. She kicked and kicked. But the giant fish only grew larger. Just at the moment she thought its teeth would come down on her, claws latched around her arm and jerked her away, back through the barrier and up, up, up to the surface.

She collapsed on the beach coughing up water she didn't remember swallowing.

"Hurrah," cried the boys. "She's alive!" Half of them were doubled over with laughter or rolling in the sand. Their supposed drowning at the hands of the mer had all been a game. Only Makbal was silent, not laughing. He didn't even look at her.

"Why didn't you save me?" sputtered Justine.

The boys fell silent, waiting for Makbal's reply.

"I told you not to cross the veil."

Justine opened her mouth to argue, then realized she had no argument, though it still seemed unfair. If he cared for her, he should have saved her.

Movement at Justine's side drew her attention away from Makbal. The creature who *had* saved her had come up on the beach. Justine saw it clearly for the first time, a human torso attached to the body of a fish, complete with glittering scales and a flipper at the end. It smelled rotten. Justine saw that in some places the scales had chipped off. In others, they appeared covered with white mold, which was also on its skin and in its hair.

"Dangerous creatures on the other side. Time has made them cruel and hungry." The mer sniffed. "You're also hungry." Its eyes widened, became glowing orbs with black tunnels in their centers. "We can help you. Have you heard the legends of our genitals?"

One of the boys chortled and was quickly hushed.

The creature stretched out a scaled, festering arm. "As long as—"

"Is that what happened to the last mother?" asked Justine.

"What's she talking about?" whispered Pah.

"When I crossed the first time," began Ian. "A snake wrapped itself around my leg and—"

"That's nothing. Last time I crossed, this glowing thing tried to—"

Makbal's hand shot up into the air. The boys fell silent.

For a moment, it wasn't clear why he'd signaled for quiet, but then Justine heard the gathering rush of water. She followed Makbal's gaze. Out on the cove, a whirlpool had begun to swirl and spit foam. It spun faster and faster, until, carried on a geyser of water, the *Osuana* shot up from the depths and became once again an ordinary brig on the surface of the sea. It drifted forward, just short of the veil, and settled directly opposite them. Men lined the railing, looking out at the beach. On the upper deck, a lone figure, all in black, raised a spyglass.

"Pirate eyes!" screeched the creature. With a swish and a puff of putrid air, it slid back into the water.

"Happy now?" snapped Makbal. "You've summoned them. They think one of us is trying to join up. They'll invade, just you watch."

Justine's mouth dropped open to protest but, at the same time, she thought the idea of joining the pirates wasn't as terrible as it should be. *Adults,* thought Justine. *If only I could convince them not to kill me.* But the thought passed, replaced by a sinking feeling that churned through her gut. She'd never seen Makbal so angry. His face was nearly red, the tops of his ears burning. Around them, the boys fell silent.

"You're plotting to betray me."

"No."

"I can see you. I know everything about you. You think you want him."

The boys were cowering, but Justine couldn't help but see only a spoiled little boy throwing a fit. Part of her knew she should be more frightened, but she'd just been almost eaten by a giant fish.

"Can you actually read my mind?" she asked, it seemed like a useful thing to know.

"If you can't be mine, you'll be no one's."

Has this happened before? She looked to Olewendo and thought for the first time perhaps he hadn't been honest with her about the past. Watching Makbal fume, imagining if she was Sarah, the girl he'd wanted, how easy it would have been for him to overstep. For an accident to happen. For him to discard her.

Justine shivered and summoned something that looked like love. "I'm your mother," she said. "I would never do anything to hurt you or the boys." Then, if only to diffuse the situation, she looked around for Delldell. "Is it time? Perhaps he'd like to stay here a while longer?"

Makbal suddenly laughed. It was a truly unnerving sound given how he'd been just a moment before. "How very strange you are today, Mother. Don't come along if you don't want. But I know he wants you there."

Very well, thought Justine. *We'll pretend nothing happened.* She thought if she pretended long enough, the quavering in her chest would still. *This isn't a good place.*

Ling and Qassim led the way around the lagoon to an outcropping where a dinghy was anchored. It only held a few people so most of the boys stood on the shore and waved goodbye as the boat was rowed through the narrow channel of cliffs between the two islands out to the point around the far side of the mountains. Delldell stood at the front of the boat not the least fearful of his approaching fate.

They'd just gone far enough that the details of the trees of the island had become muddled. Here the water went from perfectly smooth to a festering boil of rapids in just a moment. Delldell pointed into the center of the rapids, where a whirlpool had begun to form. "There it is. Dive, dive, dive!"

Justine screamed as the dinghy dipped forward, pitching Delldell and the prow of the boat straight into the center of the whirlpool. The scream ended as Justine's mouth filled with water. She tried to claw to the surface but found herself cemented to her seat by the force of the water pressing down on her. The boat continued to sink, nose first, into the depths. Great hulking shadows of unnamable creatures passed by. Bright, glowing eyes. The flickering of giant fins. Her mouth was still open in its trapped scream, her arms flailed as she tried to protect the boys. But there was no need. None of the creatures swam close to them. And presently, the dinghy came through to the surface of a rushing river that seemed as wide as a sea.

It took a moment of coughing and crying and wanting to scream out, *What the bloody fucking hell?* But then Justine cleared her eyes of the stinging salt and looked around.

"Lads and lassie," said Makbal. "Welcome to the lower-realm. We'll be spending as little time here as possible to avoid notice."

"And also to save our arms," gasped Qassim as both he and Ling strained to keep the dinghy in place.

They'd breached the water between two clusters of mountains, one range golden pink, the other jagged and green-tinged black. Justine had seen them from the island, but now the obscuring clouds were in the sky and the mountains appeared as the edges of whole continents. Justine twisted around in her seat and saw that what she'd thought was a constant rain falling between them was actually people. They were falling, as she had fallen, from the sky into the water between the two land masses.

Her heart leapt in her chest. The people were far away, but she could see their heads bobbing in the water, being rapidly carried toward the dark shards of mountains downstream. Precious few made progress swimming against the current toward the golden peaks.

"Are you ready for your next great adventure, Delldell?" asked Makbal.

Delldell only had eyes for the golden peaks. "Delldell can see it in his head. First, he swims, then he climbs a long time."

Justine gasped. *Surely he wasn't going to swim for the—*

Momoaro crawled into her lap. "Mother, I'm scared."

She wrapped her arms around him, pressing all her fear into his small, round body as Makbal palmed the top of Delldell's head. "Swim hard, swim fast, for the path to the country of shadows remains long before you. There's no return from that yet undiscovered country. Don't think of what you leave behind. Know only that you go to a far better place than here, and you'll touch far more than you can imagine."

Then, without pause or kiss goodbye, Makbal pushed Delldell into the water.

Justine watched, fingernails dug into poor Momoaro's flabby sides as Delldell came up to the surface and began to swim. At first, he appeared to make no progress against the current. But then, as though propelled forward by a sudden surge of power, he moved away from them toward the golden land.

"Has he made it?" asked Qassim.

"He better," said Ling, "I can't keep this up much longer."

"Return to the Mouth of the Ocean," said Makbal. "Delldell's beyond what good our sight can do for him."

"But how do we know if he found the golden city?" asked Pah. "It's so very far."

"Far to land," said Ling. "And then he'll have to climb through the mountains."

Tears filled Pah's eyes. "I hope I never find a key. I don't want to go." If he hadn't been crying, Justine would have cried for him, for them all. She wanted to see it as beautiful. To reach out to final death with such confidence was indeed beautiful. But now the boys would live their lives without one of their own. The absence would be deeply felt.

Makbal used the tiller to turn the dinghy. Once again, they pushed into the whirlpool. But this time, instead of descending, Justine had a strong sense of being drawn upward even though it didn't at all make sense to climb upward through an ocean.

No one spoke as they reemerged in the midrealm and rowed back to the island. Pah had stopped crying, but he leaned against Justine's side for comfort. Ling and Qassim exchanged messages with their eyes that Justine couldn't interpret.

What do they know that they don't speak?
I cannot stay here.

CHAPTER 13

Allberry Pie

I t used to be that the fae lived in the nooks of trees along with squirrels and owls and insects. These other creatures, being so different from the fae, often got in the way of fae activities. One of the previous mothers—one from the Orient, Justine thought—had built little homes for them and mounted the homes on sticks almost like they were floating in the air.

So it was when Justine came to the clearing in the spring woods for her first fae party, she saw clusters and clusters of what appeared to be oriental-style dollhouses with rounded roofs and latticed windows and brightly painted walls. Some stood as high as her knees, others above her head. Between the houses, platforms had been built with little tables (the fae didn't need chairs) or little gathering stations filled with a network of troughs and pullies for transporting nuts and seeds to various storage areas around the village. Though fae could fly, they were like any other creature in not wanting to go farther than needed for their food. They had developed quite a complex system for moving their crops from the terraced fields in the cliffs at the edge of the forest and the paddy fields on the plain in the shadow of the cliffs, so that they could retrieve what they needed for cooking without moving far from their front doors.

Each cluster of houses was supplied with a bathhouse surrounded by spider webs. In these bathhouses, fae did the precious work of cleaning their wings, in the process, shedding the magical pixie dust that was prized above gold and silver and all precious gems.

Get through this, then make your own way, Justine promised herself. Not that it seemed the fae party would be a terrible burden or a place where she was in danger. After all, that was the problem. She couldn't tell what was dangerous or not.

Thousands of chime voices called welcome from all sides of the village. Some fae flew up to Justine and the boys as they walked through. They lit their bodies with a soft glow that made her skin look as creamy white and beautiful as Makbal's. Having lived her entire life bereft of beauty, she couldn't claim to be immune to its lures, and even as she hung tight to her plan for what would come after the party, she felt herself drawn to dreams of a life she might live here with a fantasy Makbal and the boys. She enjoyed feeling beautiful.

They were escorted to a clearing where human-sized cushions had been set out among hundreds of small open platforms of fae tables all laid with sweet smelling food. Birds had been invited to sing. For once the boys seemed to be using their manners. They sat very quiet and still around the platforms, though their eyes were bright with a delicious merriment as though they knew a bounty of secrets and couldn't wait to share them.

"What do you think of my new dress?" she asked. "I'm playing a queen today."

Makbal nodded, the corners of his lips twitched as though suppressing a tease. "Yes, very nice. We should find you a crown."

"I wouldn't mind a crown. And perhaps a castle? Queens usually have at least one."

"Perhaps."

This was her plan. To be everything Makbal wanted her to be and more just for tonight. Then, when he was lulled into the comfort of believing she was his, she would leave. Since they'd taken Delldell to the current, she knew where to find a boat. She didn't know a thing about rowing a boat, but she'd figure it out. She would cross the veil and hop over to the other island and just see if life over there was better than life with the boy king who had captured her.

It seemed like a strong word, captured. But the more she'd thought about it, the more it felt true. Besides that, today she'd woken up and couldn't remember the name of the person who had worked with her at the asylum. She'd had the picture of the woman's face, how much she would have loved wishing for things to be clean instead of cleaning them, but she couldn't remember her name.

And it had terrified her.

The moons had risen to full, glowing disks on their bed of shining stars. The fae lanterns made the woods around them glow so that Justine felt as beautiful as she had ever been, and Makbal exceptionally so. She struggled not to stare at him, part of her hoping she could still salvage some dream.

The chime of fae conversation rose a pitch as the council of the village announced the party officially begun. The boys dipped their fingers into their small plates. A pair of fae carried a pitcher around the platforms, pouring golden liquid into child-sized cups. Tassi came and stood at the platform opposite Makbal and Justine. Their body vibrated with unusually good cheer and what seemed like a toast as they raised their cup with both hands. Everyone around the platform also lifted their cups. Tassi took a sip. Everyone took a sip. Then, with a wicked smile, Tassi flung the cup across the platform. It sailed through the air and hit Makbal in the chin, splashing his face with drink.

In turn, Makbal scooped a finger of pink pudding from his plate and flung it at Tassi. It hit not just Tassi, but three adjacent fae. They flew into action grabbing food and flinging it at Makbal and Momoaro who sat beside him.

"Avast you dastardly pirates!" cried Momoaro as he flung fistfuls of corn through the air.

A chorus of chimes answered him in turn.

A slab of something green slapped against Justine's neck. She hadn't seen who'd thrown it. But soon it didn't matter because everyone was throwing and flinging, and it seemed best to join in. Justine flung her bowl of soup at Ian. He paused to lick some of it off his face before grabbing a fistful of berries, pelting them at her, then everyone down the line of the table as he ran, ducking and leaping over other boys. Someone's head was shoved into an allberry pie. A roast flew up into the air and became pinioned on Ling's sword. He only managed a bite before another boy ran down the table, crashing dishes, stepping on hands, disturbing fairy flight paths as he seized the roast and ran away with it.

On and on it went, the antics both spontaneous and planned as the best food was stolen from the table only to be stolen again by new culprits. When the fight was over, the revelers lay in the grass and licked themselves clean. Fresh drinks were poured and passed around. The edges of Justine's vision became hazy and golden. Makbal lay beside her, their boys all around.

"You're far away," said Makbal. His voice teased, but his eyes searched hers.

"Sometimes I feel the island trying to tell me something."

"A story about two brothers?" He sounded suspiciously eager.

This was a new idea to Justine, she felt certain. But then,

almost as soon as he said it, the story felt familiar to her. She realized it was an old story, the one she'd told to the boys her first night on the island. Dickens, the brothers who became rocks, and the third who passed the tests and saved his country. Funny how everything that happened on the island had an echo.

SHE LEFT THE PARTY IN THE MIDST OF THE BOYS ALSO BREAKING off to go back to their games. Makbal said he would go night fishing with some of the older boys and perhaps look for a treasure tree. So he'd be occupied, not thinking of her as she made her escape.

The island pulsed beneath her bare feet as she walked now familiar paths through the hills and into the woods, all the way to the lagoon and the alcove where she knew the dinghy was stored. With every step, her heart pounded in her chest, every part of her straining to hear if someone was following her, if there was a creature stalking her. All wishful thinking. If either were true, she wouldn't have heard them except from the grace of the island.

She came out of the woods at the cliffs and paused to let her doubts take her. There in the mist, the shadow of the other island, the far lights of the village. Down below, the reef glowed with starfish and incandescent seaweed flowed like hair trapped between the rocks. Tears sparked her eyes as she thought how unfair it was to be brought to such a beautiful place, every moment being pulled toward a dream, and if not for her wits, or perhaps her dissatisfied cooch, she could have given herself over to it and forgotten the dangers, forgotten the apparent curse on all the mothers who'd come before.

I want to live. It was almost a prayer. Beneath her feet the island was a beating heart. *I want to be loved.* This second, felt like a trespass. As if paradise wasn't enough, Justine, the servant girl, only wanted to share it with certain people.

There has to be something else.

To Justine's surprise, a voice she could hear only in her mind seemed to answer her, *Climb the path to the archive.*

"What?" She spoke this aloud and was suddenly aware of her voice breaking the silence of the night that she'd guarded so carefully. She turned her attention back to listening, straining the darkness. Movement, almost directly below her. Two boys walking to the alcove on exactly the path she'd planned to take to the dinghy.

But there was also another sound. The soft, rhythmic lapping of the waves against something solid. When she turned her eyes outward, she saw it, a shadow cut out of the mist, another dinghy with three figures rowing stealthily toward the island.

"It'll be fine, come on," said a voice below. She recognized it as Qassim's. The voice that answered was Ling's.

"We don't even know if they'll let us stay. What if we just wait a little longer? The island will give me a keyhole."

"We've waited," said Qassim. "What happens when I get my last quest? I'm not swimming without you."

They spoke with only a mild hush, entirely unaware of the boat approaching down the shore. The boys would be mortified if she revealed herself. But if she didn't warn them, it would be so much worse. Her eyes shot back up to the boat. It was in the shallows now, almost at the beach. Justine began to climb down the path. It was a narrow, rocky thing, difficult to find sure footing, to say nothing of the night. She slipped once and caught herself. The second time her foot gave out, she crashed down on her bottom and slid painfully over several bumps and turns before coming to a stop.

A breathless silence. There was no way the people in the

boat hadn't heard her fall. They'd certainly heard her all too feminine gasp at the force of it.

The two boys had retreated against the shadows of the cliffs, hiding. But now, Qassim crept out. "Mother? What are you doing?"

She thought ruefully that a better raised boy might first ask if she was alright, but that didn't really matter now. "The same thing you were apparently. But there's no time for that. There's another—"

Before she could say it, Ling hissed from the darkness, "Pirates!"

And a moment later, a dark, vile voice slithered through the night. "Hello, chitlins, we know you're in there. Come out and we won't make a mess of it."

Qassim grabbed Justine and dragged her around the end of the path into the shadows of the cliffs where Ling was hiding.

"What do we do now?"

"Take the boat and try to outrun them?"

"They'll catch us for sure then."

"Wasn't it what we wanted, to meet them?" asked Ling. "Maybe."

"But they can't find Mother."

"You're sure they'll—"

"I'm not sure about anything," said Qassim. The whites of his eyes showed as he looked at Justine. "I'm sorry, Mother. We don't mean to betray you."

"You're a couple," she said. "And you want to swim the current together." She said this as a way to explain to herself what was very new knowledge. Qassim suddenly seemed much older. She couldn't imagine what it'd cost him to take on the responsibility of this decision, to think that life with the pirates was better than life with Mak. Of course it was true for her, but the boys had seemed so happy. Perhaps to them, she seemed happy.

"Let's not play games," said the pirate, much closer now.

"Good luck," she whispered.

Qassim grabbed Ling's hand and the two of them stepped out of the shadows. "We surrender."

The jagged edges of rock dug into her back as Justine pressed herself even farther into hiding. The rock wall came around in a curve so she couldn't see the boys or the pirates, but she could hear the susurrating of sand disturbed by footsteps.

"Where's the girl?"

"There aren't any girls here."

A second voice, not as vile as the first. "The one you kids call Mother. We know there's a new one."

"The one you shot out of the sky?" said Ling.

A collision sounded, flesh against flesh, then a soft *thump* of something big landing in the sand.

"Tell us where she is."

"We want to go to the village," said Qassim, voice quavering, more scared than he could hide now.

The pirates laughed. "Sure, you can go to the village. If you take us to the Mother. Has Mak set any booby traps since the last time?"

"Yes," said Qassim. "More than you'll ever find."

The second collision was harder, followed by the whoosh of air rushing out of strained lungs.

"We'll take them back to the ship and make them talk," said the first pirate.

"The Hook isn't going to be happy."

"He's never happy, and I'm tired of playing nice."

She heard shuffling, then a disturbance of the water. When Justine dared to look out around the curve of the wall, the pirate's boat was already rushing away from shore, the two boys captives in the middle with the man not rowing pointing a gun down at their heads.

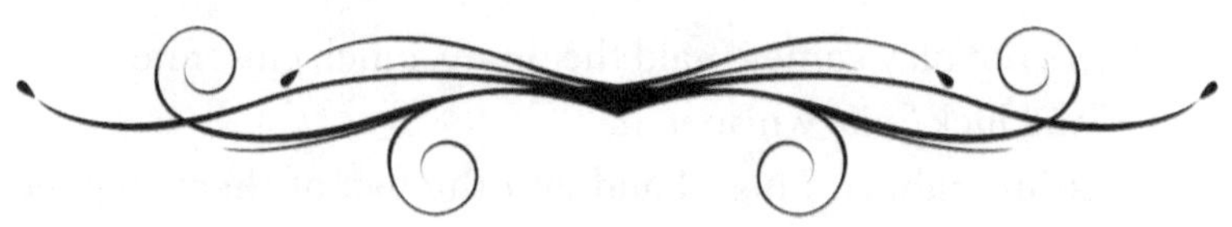

CHAPTER 14

A Beginning that is Also a middle

The god who would become a pirate was once a boy. As much as any god can be a boy. Which is to say, he took on the mantel of boyhood and filled himself with the confidence of invincibility, of restless power, and did not conceive what he might thoughtlessly destroy.

The making of new gods is often ill-considered. After permission is granted from one of the Firsts, it is simply a matter of gathered energy and recipe making. All made gods come with flaws intended to prevent them from becoming more powerful than their elders. And all gods experience a period of youth where they are educated both by their elders and by the world. In this particular case, the boy who would become a pirate liked best to wander the mortal realm collecting experiences from all its creatures, especially humans, which he found the most interesting of all.

Why this interest? It is a fatal flaw particular to gods that they desire love above all else. And what better place to receive it than from mortals? To be a god walking the mortal realm is to easily snare the attention of everyone. The weakest minds catch a glimpse of the divine on earth and can think of nothing else. Even the strongest minds experience a pull, an ache in their deepest marrow to please that god and be allowed to bask in their presence.

This is what our voyager boy god was doing on that fateful night. He'd escaped some trouble in his realm that had left him feeling decidedly unloved, so he traveled to visit the more welcoming, less critical mortals. In fact, he crashed the wedding of two people who would later think of him with great fondness and never wonder how they knew him.

A wedding is a delightful setting for the collecting of love. Guests of all ages look with envy upon the happy couple and wonder if they might snatch a bit of that feeling for themselves. In this way, the Voyager made his way through the reception like a spotlight, eyes turning to him as he passed. When his gaze landed on a subject of interest, that person experienced the greatest delight to be the one, or the first or second, his arms filled. Or perhaps sitting, both sides of his lap filled with this giddy enchantment. The kisses he bestowed were compliments that would burn half a mortal's lifetime. His whispered temptations, the words by which all future partners would be measured and found wanting.

He had been at this seduction an hour or more, leaving small ruptures of love-struck chaos in his wake and feeling quite pleased with himself, when he saw her. The goddess was on the dance floor with one man, then another, a whole herd of them cutting in to steal a few moments in her arms. Or rather one arm and a prosthetic appendage in the place of the second.

This seeming imperfection was the second thing the Voyager noticed after her beauty. She did not appear to him as other gods he'd met. The ones he'd come up with in school, with whom he was most familiar, seemed ordinary by comparison. And when he saw that her body was augmented in a way that a god's body need never be augmented, his curiosity grew his attraction.

He stood by the dessert table. This was where she found him. Rather, when she failed to notice him the way a mortal would, he insinuated himself into her perception with a comment about the food. Then she was staring at him, which was a new experience. The effect of divinity on mortals meant they rarely truly looked. What they saw of a god was a simulacrum of their true selves, which were too bright to ever be seen. But this woman, she not only saw, she knew.

"I've been looking for you," she said.

"For me?" He was flattered.

"Across the stars."

"That's quite a ways." He moved down the table so it would no longer be between them. At the end, she tripped, also an unusual thing for a god to do. When he reached out to catch her, she drew back as though afraid of him.

"We can't touch," she said, but then she gave him her prosthetic hand. "This is safe."

He found her caution mesmerizing. After a diet of easily gained human affection, here was a challenge, a woman putting up barriers for him to summit. Of course he had learned about the hazards of god bonds in school. Every god carried the ability to bond, and some were predisposed to certain types of bonds over others. They were most commonly used for controlling mortals, enacting large building projects, sharing mental space, reorienting the fates, etc., etc.

The mysterious woman refused to tell him about her bond and, in the end, they found ways around it. He touched only her garments and the prosthetic and found himself quite proud of how he respected her wishes. This respect earned him an invitation back to her home where he made it clear that such a magical night must end in a magical way, though he was already thinking of how it might never end.

She said her name was Thessaly. She had made a life for herself among the mortals, was passing herself off as one of them. He thought she could have him as a partner. He would leave behind the difficulties of his home realm and stay with her until something else claimed his attention, though that seemed impossible. The woman gazed at him with a love he suspected he had not earned, but this did not bother him. It felt larger than whatever affection he could gain from a hundred mortals. To be in her presence was to be truly seen, loved even, perhaps for the first time. He did not wonder why she looked at him with love, or how she seemed to know so much about him. These details could be excavated later, after he'd explored her body's strange mixture of mortal and divine.

She drank a potion that protected her against accidental bonding. With that barrier dismantled, she came to him, and he gave his body to her as he had never given it to anyone. Afterward, he found himself content to lay in her arms. He told her of his life on the island he'd created with his brother to give mortal children the childhood of their dreams, boastful of his accomplishments because he wanted her to be impressed with him. He had recently divided the island in two and given one part the gift of passing time so that some of the children could grow up.

Somewhere in his storytelling, Thessaly turned sour. She seemed to think him irresponsible for leaving the island children, who were growing up without him. At first, he found this idea amusing. Growing up was a preoccupation of mortals. It meant nothing to him. But she kept after him, implied he was insensitive. And the bombshell. She revealed that she had once been human. Her godliness had not come through the usual way. And when he did not respond well to her suggestion that all gods would benefit from experiencing aging as mortals did, she asked him to leave. Even more shocking, she threatened to banish him if he did not leave willingly.

This was a wound to his ego. He was not a god people banished, certainly not by a mortal who had tricked the fates into changing her. She used her magic to force him from her bed. She summoned his clothes back to his body against his will. A thing that should not have been possible.

And in this moment, as he reeled from the insult and the surprise of her power, she gave him the strangest parting message.

"Later, when you think of me, remember I made this choice. I chose not to change you or do anything that would alter what happens for you next because I love you the way you are. I'll be there waiting for you."

She spoke a command and he was propelled from her presence, across space and time, a whirlwind journey made all the more disordered by the mess of his thoughts crashing within his mind.

As soon as his feet touched down on the island of his home, he made ready to leave again to find her. He did not pause to think about her displeasure or the children he was leaving behind to grow up alone.

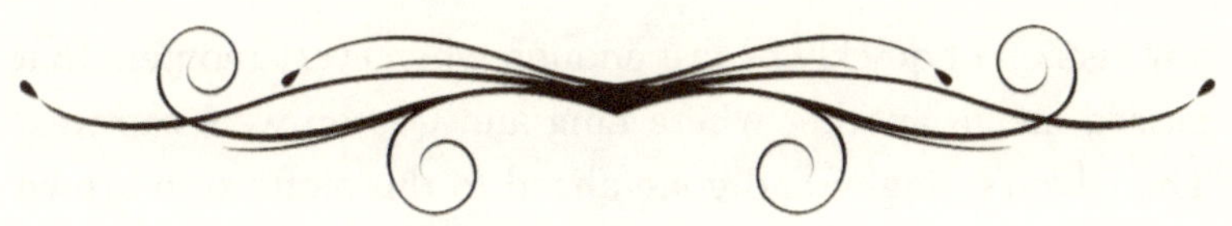

CHAPTER 15

Pirates Don't like Little Boys

Sven had painted blue stripes under both his eyes and tied his hair back from his forehead with a strip of cloth. He'd already made it clear to Makbal that he didn't think Justine should be with them. And now that the attack group had split into those going in the dinghy and those who would be flying, he tried again.

"What's she going to do when we land?" he asked. "The pirates will be on us in a wink."

This time, Makbal didn't bother to answer him. The other boy who was flying with them, Cal-Li, said, "Any adventure with Mother is the best kind of adventure."

"She's wearing a dress. Who can fight in a dress?"

"Actually, there's many traditions of warriors in skirts and what you'd call dresses," said Justine, thinking of a particularly frightening version of King Arthur she'd once heard a woman tell in the workhouse.

"Well, I'm not flying with her," said Sven. "She'll get scared and wiggle and make me drop her. Or she'll drop me."

The plan had come together quickly. But then, who was to say what quickly meant in a place without time? And would any version of quickly be fast enough when every moment that passed meant another where Ling and Qassim were captives? The island's dinghy had gone ahead to the pirate ship armed with eight boys and various supplies Makbal already had on hand for some reason. Meanwhile, Makbal was going to use his flying power to carry Sven, Cal-Li, and Justine through the air to the ship and attack from above.

"Everyone have what they need?" whispered Makbal.

There was no one else anywhere nearby to hear, but his whispering fed the energy thrumming along her spine.

The other two boys did an inventory of the various belongings they'd strapped to their bodies.

"I don't have a weapon," said Justine.

"What would you do with one anyway?" asked Sven.

"Take my vengeance." She looked at Makbal. "You have two swords now because you got one from the fairies. Give me the one you like less."

Without a word, Makbal pulled a sword from the belt around his waist and handed it to her. "The Black Hook is mine."

"You can have him if you get to him first."

Fire lit Makbal's eyes. He took Cal-Li's hand in his left and Sven's hand in his right. Cal-Li took Justine's hand. They lifted off just as naturally as birds. Justine's stomach flip-flopped as the ground dropped away and there became nothing down below except the deep water. This flight wasn't as magical as the one over London. The wind on her face tasted of wildflowers and salt. In it she smelled the voyages of Captain Cook, the dread pirates Flint and Silver, the promise of vacations on the seashore, haunted lighthouses. But she could only distantly absorb it. All she could think of was rescuing Ling and Qassim. They'd been taken because they'd been protecting her. If they were hurt, she would never forgive herself.

The air changed when they passed through the veil of mist;

it was hard to say how exactly. Justine felt no shift in temperature, but rather the substance of the air felt thicker. Flying seemed just a little more work than it had before, which was to say, before it had felt like nothing and now she became aware of holding herself stretched out, of the need to keep her hand clasped around Cal-Li's. A shiver went through her body that felt the way spirits felt when they passed through her. She very nearly lost Cal-Li's hand because of it.

They flew over the dinghy filled with boys and were coming up now on the pirate ship. Justine sucked in a breath and tried to quiet her thoughts. They landed lightly on the upper crossbeam of the tallest mast. Makbal of course had no trouble balancing, but Sven quickly dropped to the crow's nest basket just below. Justine, with Cal-Li's help, followed. A moment more trying to balance on that narrow length of wood and she surely would have plummeted down to the deck or at least crashed into the rigging. Even safely behind the railing of the crow's nest, Justine pressed her back up against the mast to steady herself.

"We wait here for the signal," whispered Makbal as he splayed himself out, laying on his belly along the crossbeam as though he was lounging on solid ground and not midair.

"What's the signal?" Cal-Li whispered to Sven.

"Shh." Sven pointed down to the deck where a man had emerged from the cabin on the quarter deck. For a moment, as the door stood open, the sound of many deep voices in half-drunken conversation could be heard. And among them, someone higher pitched but still throaty, a woman's laughter.

A whole ship full of adults. It had never occurred to her that one of them was a woman. Justine tracked the progress of the man who'd left the cabin. He had an uneven gait and his feet sounded differently on the decking, one shoe and one wooden leg.

Justine shuddered as though his false leg told her the

horrors the man had perpetrated in the name of his innate evil. He had to be one of the villains who captured her boys. But then, as she studied him, besides the fact of his missing limb, she had to admit, the man was quite neatly dressed in breeches, a loose blouse of billowing sleeves as had been the fashion in England in the previous century, and a formal brocade vest with silver buttons. He kept a neat beard and had his hair tied back in a ribbon.

Clean hair, thought Justine. *Clean clothes, clean deck, clean everything.* She was suddenly aware of her nightgown. It had been fine and beautiful but was now stained with allberry juice and caked with dust and mud and smelled of her unwashed body. The boys on either side of her smelled worse.

It was in this moment, as Justine realized she surely looked and smelled like a beggar, that the smoke began to seep out from the portholes. With it came the worst smell Justine had ever smelled, worse than burning tar, worse even than the highsmith tannery at peak hours. A hatch at the center of the deck popped open and a pirate ran up from below shouting, "We're under attack! Sound to quarters!" A river of smoke was close behind him, obscuring any glimpse below deck.

The pirate in the brocade vest ran to the far side of the deck and began to ring a large bell that hung from the overhanging roof of the quarter deck. As it rang, several more pirates burst up from belowdecks, coughing and wheezing, holding wet cloths over their mouths. From the stories, Justine always imagined pirates as uniformly grizzled and ugly, with patched clothes and sun-weathered tattoos. But these men were not like that at all. In fact, what most surprised her was the variety of their ages, from a wrinkled old man to a boy of twelve who possessed those fine cheekbones and athletic grace of Makbal's boys. These pirates weren't as well dressed as the one who'd left the cabin. Some of them wore only trousers, some only shirts.

The bodies, despite Justine's focus on rescuing her boys, were distracting.

Someone shouted, "There's rats. I saw rats!"

The door to the cabin slammed open. Justine turned her gaze and saw a single figure in a long, black coat, his silhouette cut out by the cabin light behind him. The shadow of the deck overhang hid his face, but she was sure his hair and beard were as black as his coat. He stood quite tall and wide in the shoulders, a nice figure, though Justine quickly dismissed this thought when she saw the glint of the silver hook that stood in replacement of his right hand.

Someone rushed up and handed the man a wide-brimmed hat with several feathers. Captain Black Hook slammed it on his head as he shouted with all the vehemence of his black heart, "What the fuck is that smell?"

"Burning swamp grass, Captain. Mak's boys—"

"Are they onboard?"

The pirates looked at each other. "No, Captain. Just the burning weeds shoved through the portholes."

"And rats."

"And this thing tried to take my other eye out." A pirate with a patch over his left eye held a kitten by the scruff of its neck. The poor thing had raised its fur, so it appeared nearly double in size as it hissed and clawed at its captor.

Captain Black Hook snatched the kitten. It appeared he was going to stab his hook through the kitten's neck. Justine screamed, "NO!" The captain's head swiveled upward. For a split second, she saw his face, a blazing red mask of murderous rage. Then Makbal whistled. The boys from the dinghy leaped over the railing to charge the startled pirates. Ca-Li grabbed Justine's hand and they were flying downwards, a near nosedive into the deck with Makbal in the lead, holding Sven's hand, and Sven holding Ca-Li.

The boys had their weapons out and were dashing toward

the pirates as soon as their feet touched the deck, but Justine stumbled. She'd gone from very high in the air to standing on the deck of a floating ship. She could barely keep her feet beneath her. All around, boys shouted and cheered, whooped and screamed. Metal clanged against metal. Beams of colored light cast from magic wands flew through the air, snapping rigging that then fell from the sky. She failed to move as the rigging fell, and it felled her.

Someone kicked her as she lay tangled beneath the rope. Someone else knocked her to one side where she slid into a puddle of mud that had been carried in the dinghy and was now being spread across the ship's no longer pristine deck. The rigging lifted away and Justine was pulled to her feet by an iron grip on her arm. She was then held upright by that same grip as her feet slid and sloshed in the mud. A boy ran by shouting gleefully, "Make it green!" A beam from the magic wand fizzled over Justine transforming her nightgown green, which wasn't as wholly remarkable as it sounded since Justine was covered in mud.

A pirate crashed into the railing behind her, pursued by two mudslinging boys. Justine barely stepped out of reach of his saber as it stabbed the air. The iron grip pulled her into the corner where the cabin wall met the railing. The pirate who'd rescued her blocked her so her back was pressed up against the wall. *A woman, not a pirate,* thought Justine as she took in the satin, off-shoulder outfit that seemed to be a blouse and trousers, though they were more tightly fitted than any clothes Justine had ever seen.

Can a woman be a pirate?

"You're the new mother?" The woman studied Justine with hard eyes. She had brown skin with a red undertone almost the same as the new boy, Wapasha. Her black hair was done up on top of her head with a flower tucked into it, the same deep maroon as her lips.

"Are you a pirate?" asked Justine.

"I'm the Tigress to anyone on the other side." She leaned closer, peering at Justine as though in recognition. Justine lurched back, afraid of this strange woman who bared her shoulders in public and painted her face like a prostitute. "Have you bonded yet?"

Behind her, a boy ran up the stairs to the top deck flinging magic from his wand left and right. "Make it red. Make it red. Make it red." Then a pirate came up and slapped him across the face, knocking him down to the deck.

Justine stepped forward to help, but found her way blocked by more than just the woman. Men and boys chased each other around the deck, slipping and sliding, calling each other names. She saw a pirate with rabbit ears and another with hoofs for hands. Half the cloth on the ship had been turned green and the other half red, though what was one color seemed to constantly change to the other. It had all the appearance of a game, yet blood mingled with the mud on the deck. A kitten ran through Justine's legs and cowered against the wall behind her.

"Where's Mak right now?"

"Where are Ling and Qassim?"

The woman glared at her so fiercely Justine felt herself cower. "I don't know where he is."

"Good." The Tigress once again seized Justine's arm, pulled her into the cabin and shut the door behind her. "Don't move."

"Are you capturing me?"

"Do you want to be captured?"

Justine looked around the cabin. The remains of an abandoned card game lay on a table. There was a bench around one side of the cabin interrupted by a cannon in its casings. On the other side, a feather bed neatly made with several pillows and blankets folded at its foot. There were books in a railed shelf beneath it and a door through the windows at the stern that led out to a private deck. Everything was neat and clean and far more comfortable than what Justine had on the island.

"What's your name, girl?" The Tigress was rummaging through a bag stowed beneath the table.

"Justine."

The rummaging stopped. "Justine? You're sure?"

"Of course I am." Justine felt her face growing hot, the woman stared at her with such intensity. "What's it to you?"

"Maybe it isn't you Aranda's looking for." The Tigress frowned. "I thought she'd be older."

Justine coughed out a bitter laugh. "I'm apparently the oldest mother that ever was."

Something slammed against the door making Justine start and jerking the Tigress out of her surprise. She pulled a pair of leather gloves from the purse. "Put these on."

"Whatever for?"

"To protect you."

Another slam against the door, this time so hard it shuddered in its frame.

"Open up in there!" called a boy's voice. "Open up so I can ruin you, you filthy pirate!"

The Tigress sent the door a weary look. "Put the gloves on. We'll come for you. Are you sure you haven't had another name?"

Outside, as though it sounded from far away, Justine heard Makbal whistle. She wheeled back as the Tigress reached for Justine's hand. "I don't want to be killed like the others." Justine felt herself unraveling. This was the same day she'd laid in the grass at the fae village and dreamed of an adult conversation, and now, now it felt like she'd made such a terrible mistake and this was her punishment.

"Or else, I guess you can kill me, but let the boys go."

The woman was starting at her. "What the hells are you talking about?"

The door smashed open. Four boys armed with a cage of rats and a bag of mud began a rampage around the cabin. Justine ran out. On the deck, the boys were retreating over the ship's railings. There were Qassim and Ling being sheltered by some of the older boys. They looked shaken but okay. *They're fine.*

Or mostly fine. The bell had summoned pirates from shore and now the boys were badly outnumbered. Justine spotted Olewendo sparring mightily with a man twice his size. Just when it seemed the pirate would strike a deadly blow, Olewendo ducked down and rolled through the man's legs, then kicked him in the crotch. Not the queen's fighting, but effective, nonetheless.

He saw her watching and grinned. "Time to escape, Mother." He pointed to a section of the railing. "Ladder there."

Justine ran to him and together they ducked and fought their way through the chaos.

"Make it green."

"Make it red."

"You fucking brat!"

"Eat this, you pirate!"

"You'll be sorry."

Just as Justine had gotten herself over the railing and was about to start climbing down, she saw Makbal flying over the fight, headed for the prow quarter deck where the Black Hook stood fighting off Sven and Wapasha.

"Time to meet your maker, Black Hook!"

The pirate captain shoved Sven away and kicked Wapasha so he fell back down the stairs. Even from a distance, Justine could see his dark eyes glint with fire under the shadow of his hat. Their swords rang out as Makbal summersaulted through the air and fought from high ground balancing on the deck railing. This didn't give him as much advantage as it would have otherwise since the Black Hook was much taller. Indeed, he seemed monstrously large compared to Makbal, who sprinted and dipped and dived to avoid the pirate's sword thrusts.

Much of the other fighting had stopped even though a few boys remained on deck. Everyone watched Makbal fight the captain. When Makbal's sword sliced a button off that fine black coat, the boys cheered. And when the captain beheaded a section of Makbal's new leaf tunic, the pirates cheered.

When someone, Justine thought she recognized Ian's voice, exclaimed quite loudly, "Darby, is that you?" Makbal turned his head to look. In that moment of distraction, the Black Hook brought his silver hook down upon Makbal's arm and sliced it clean open. With a cry, Makbal leaped into the air. Blood trailed him as he flew across the deck. He collected a boy from amid the pirates. The two of them flew over Justine and dropped down to the waiting dinghy. Two overheated drops of blood landed on Justine as she scrambled to climb down the ladder. When she got close enough, someone pulled her backward, causing her to fall the last few feet into the dinghy. Even as she landed, it seemed to be pulling away. Two splashes sounded in the darkness, then the even strokes of fast swimming. A safe distance away from the ship, the dinghy stopped and Ian and another boy were pulled up out of the water. Someone giggle-whispered, "We did it!"

For a moment, they all sat still, breathing hard with their exertions and exhilaration. The boys sitting nearest Justine thrummed with energy, a heady mixture of conquest and relief, even though all she had done was lose Makbal's sword in the crow's nest and nearly be captured by a pirate woman who had somehow, mysteriously, known her.

Justine shook her head. *It was a trick. She was trying to trap me in time. What does it mean to be in time?*

The Black Hook came to the railing. His silhouette cut a stark line against the ship's torchlight as he called out, "You're failing them, Mak. Come in peacefully and we can discuss a ceasefire."

"Never," muttered Makbal under his breath.

Justine felt the boy on her right shift to twist around. She realized it was Ling and he was counting. "Lord Mak," he whispered. "We're missing someone. We're twelve with Darby, which means—"

"Who?"

"No surrender?" The captain's harsh voice rang out over the water. "Very well then. Accept this latest casualty of your war. He preferred to die for you than live with me."

Two pirates carried something to the railing and pushed it over. *A body,* thought Justine as the splash reverberated in her ears. *They actually killed one of the—Father in heaven, save him.*

"Make ready the cannons!" called the Black Hook.

His call was repeated by someone else, then someone else again as the ship came to life with the grinding and rolling of cannons in their braces.

"Row," hissed Makbal. "Row if you want to live."

No one spoke as the dinghy cut through the dark water. Justine realized that the moons had sunk below the horizon. She wondered if that meant it was nearly dawn or if moons worked differently this side of the veil. It didn't seem to matter. Her thoughts scattered across her awareness like leaves pushed by the wind, fleeting and inconsequential compared to the weight in her stomach. She barely noticed when cannon shot exploded geysers of water to the left of the dinghy, then right behind it. Water sloshed over the sides, soaking all of them.

"What happens if you die and the island hasn't given you a map?" she asked.

When no one answered she said it again, hardly able to sit still. "What will happen to him?"

When they passed through the veil of mist back to their island, it barely registered. She saw only dimly that here there was more light. The two moons had returned in the exact position as they had been before. And below the boat, as though playing a duel of beauty with those brilliant silver crescents, hundreds of starfish glowed on the rocks below the waterline. Makbal leaned over and plucked one which he set over his wounded arm like a bandage.

"You can slow down," he said. "The ship's at anchor, he can't follow us tonight. Go around to the point. We'll say our goodbye there."

Justine looked around the dinghy. Sven was the one missing.

"The current will take him," said Makbal. "He has no chance of swimming against it to reach the golden city. If he's lucky, he'll catch the rocks and find a path to the Green City."

"And if he's not?"

Makbal didn't answer. A heavy silence descended over the boat as the boys thought their own thoughts. Then one of them began to cry. "I don't want to ever be kilt by pirates."

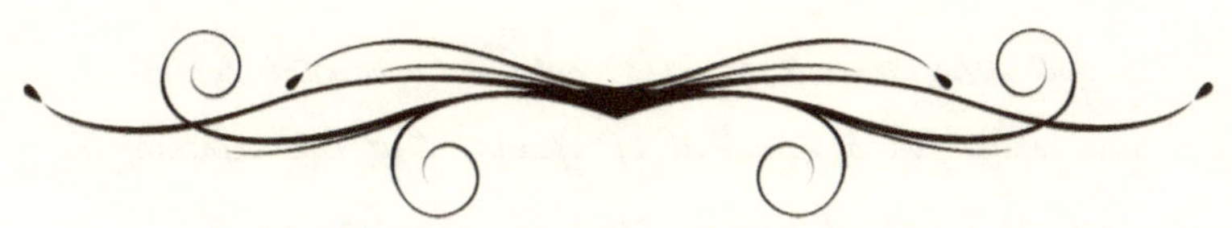

CHAPTER 16

The Voyager's Travels

He searched time for the god known as Thessaly. She existed before their meeting, but only three mortal years. After their meeting, nothing, as though the record had been wiped clean when she banished him from her presence. In the immortal realms, she was entirely unknown. One elder dared to say he'd birthed the woman from his imagination, and she existed only for him. An insult that resulted in a duel where several hundred mortals lost their lives, the first of many casualties in this ill-fated romance.

Undeterred, the Voyager crossed eons to meet every being in recorded memory with her name, but none of them were her. In the past, he would have asked his brother for help. They might have bent their heads together and tried to solve the riddle of a god who seemed to exist only in a mortal realm and only for a handful of years. But the relationship had turned putrid since the dividing of the island between time and eternity.

They took to launching raids on each other. The Voyager's aging children went across Mermaid Lagoon to try and snatch away the brother's children. Likewise, the brother led his children on raids of their own to hound and taunt and prank those within time as mortal children did to adults who had forgotten what it was to have fun. The aging children built a village. The brother's children burned it to the ground. They went adventuring in the mountains and found themselves ambushed. And on it went. Fun and games disguised as a piecemeal disintegration of both the island and the bond between brothers.

Having been made at the same time, some might say as two halves of one whole idea from their mothers, the brothers had come up through their godly lessons together. As such, they were occasionally called back to refresh their knowledge. These sessions were also seen as important for the fellowship and good relations between gods, which in turn facilitated harmony in the cosmos.

On one such meeting, the animosity between the brothers became so palpable, the elder sent them from class and said they would have to learn on their own the right behavior of gods because she couldn't teach them. This lesson, on the nature of bonds across time and space and the godly responsibility of good care for mortals, would have been a valuable thing for them to have fresh in their minds. Both brothers would walk paths altered by bonds that didn't conform to the rules.

Who is to say if staying in their lesson would have changed anything? That is neither here nor there.

This moment is important because the brothers, unable to go home before the session ended, sulked in respective corners of the realm. One brother went to plaster palace windows with honey to discover what could be snared. The Voyager went to the library. Rather, he walked through the library on his way to the drinking hall, where he was joined by Ankou, who mortals called Servant of Death. Though Ankou was quite old, one of the first gods made by the Firsts, he'd become familiar to the Voyager. He often negotiated to reclaim souls Ankou had collected and take them to the island.

Really, Ankou thought it rather cute what the brothers were doing. It was a break in tradition to separate the souls of children from the River of the Dead and allow them a chance to have the experiences mortal life had denied them. Perhaps he thought the brothers a little soft in their choice of pastimes. But when he saw the look on the Voyager's face, he ordered him a flagon of the strongest drink and invited him to express his troubles.

If not for Ankou's bias against the children and the island, the Voyager might have spoken of the brothers' rift. Perhaps he might have admitted that bringing time on to the island had been an idea not fully formed. And now he didn't know how to fix the problem he'd created. Instead, the Voyager spoke of the woman who still occupied his mind.

As he listened, Ankou was blessed with an idea. He'd recently been in conflict with the Prince of Shadows, who was in an expansionist mood, claiming mortal graveyards for himself and his many wives. Ankou, lazy by nature, wanted to keep his graveyards without a fuss. Something the Voyager had said struck a chord of significance with the Prince of Shadows problem. By the time the story finished, Ankou remembered it.

"I don't know a god by the name of Thessaly," he said. "But there's a rumor of an unknown god causing trouble with the Prince of Shadows. She's claimed one of his wives as her own. Last I heard, he was coming for them both."

"She's in trouble?" The Voyager forgot his

drink, forgot his troubles with his brother, and the promises he'd made to the children growing up on his side of the island. "Where? When?"

Ankou laughed at the young god's eagerness. "It probably isn't her," he said. "There are so many gods running around now. Every eon it seems a new one causes a stir."

"Tell me how to find her," said the Voyager.

When Ankou gave him the time and place, the Voyager flew there as fast as he could go, heedless of all else except the one thought that the woman he loved, who had said she also loved him, was in danger from one of the most dangerous, most unscrupulous gods there ever was.

Here, I, Tassi, scribe of the Neverland archive, must confess that the full story of what the Voyager found when he went off on that ill-considered rescue cannot be related because I do not know it. The island has blocked this information from my awareness. I mention it only because it seems a catalyzing event for what followed, the events of which are my main purpose for writing this manuscript.

The Voyager returned to the island a different

being. He extended the proverbial olive branch to his brother. But their peace accords were sabotaged by his aging children, who did not want to go back to endless adventures and the aimlessness of childhood. They'd grown too old to understand its joys or be transformed by its lessons. They wanted to grow old in the village they'd built and pass on to the underworld as adults. Their leader was a girl, Osuana, almost woman by then, with such a powerful imagination that the island responded to her will in ways it did not respond to the other children. Sometimes, what it allowed her to do, it was almost as though she'd become a god herself.

When his brother said there could be peace between them if the girl was banished from the island and sent to her afterlife, the Voyager did everything he could to protect her. He even sent other children onward to afterlives they were not ready for, a direct violation of the island's purpose.

So, it was then, when the brother had finally found a way to send the girl to her everlasting, that her absence solved nothing. The brothers' ossified, as immovable as two solid boulders. The island, growing ever weaker by the ongoing war, created a secret path to its broken heart. If ever another child with the imagination of the girl who had been lost came to the island, she would be offered the chance to mend what had been broken.

The only problem was that by then, the brother was only bringing boys to the island. He shaped them into warriors and taught them how to cross the barrier into time. He taught them the things that most bothered the Voyager so that war consumed him.

CHAPTER 17

The Baba Yaga

Justine couldn't sleep. Every time she closed her eyes, she saw the black shadow of Sven falling from the ship into the water.

Could Mak have stopped it? Was it fair to blame Makbal just because he seemed as cavalier with true danger as he was with any other adventure? Even worse, the dread feeling in her gut having to do with how she'd been hoping the pirates might give her an alternative home. And now it was quite clear that was impossible. She was stuck on the island with Makbal and his boys for however long she managed to survive.

At some point, Justine got out of bed and went above ground. Though it felt she'd been in bed for hours, there was no hint of dawn in the sky. The torches had all been put out. Everything was still and beautiful and quiet. But then, far up in the trees, she heard a sniffle, then, even more distant, the thin voice of a young boy singing.

Justine followed a winding ramp up into the treetops. She walked as quietly as she could so as not to wake the boys with bed rolls laid out on the large platforms or nests in branches.

When she saw boys' eyes watching her, she stopped to tuck them in and kiss their foreheads.

Gradually, the ramp led to a rope bridge that went up to a watchtower platform built at the very top of a tall tree. *A ceibas*, she thought. *Tree of the gods*. This information, that she had no reason to know, didn't strike her as strange, but innately familiar, as though she had always known this towering tree, the bite of its bark, the pebbles of its seeds, the soft velvet of its leaves. Ian sat with Pah in his lap, their faces turned up to the moons as Pah sang a song about the beautiful moon who was always looking out for all her children.

Ian's gaunt face was swollen and his skin splotchy around his eyes from crying. When he saw Justine's head poke up over the edge of the platform, he scooted over and made space for her. Together they listened to Pah's plaintive song. His voice was so thin, the light wind that rustled the treetops seemed to pick it up and carry it away. When the song ended and the silence returned, they heard the faint echo of what seemed the same song being sung on the other side of the island.

"Oh, hello, Mother. Did you like seeing the pirates?"

Justine opened her mouth but before she could formulate an answer, the boy was wiggling past her and down the bridge.

"Can't sleep either?" asked Ian.

"Wild night."

Ian nodded. "I used to like pirate raids better. Tonight felt, I dunno, wrong."

"Because of Sven?"

"Naw, Sven was a right arsehole. I hope he rots in the caves. It was more seeing Darby," said Ian. "We used to be good mates, him and I. Then the Black Hook got 'im. Now he's almost grown up and it seems okay for him."

"He was a boy here?"

"They all were. Except for the captain. He steals boys away

and locks them in his ship until they get too old to have adventures. Then they become pirates with him."

"Horrible."

If the pirates all used to be Mak's boys, where did that woman come from?

"What about your past mothers? Did the pirates take them also?"

Ian's eyebrows drew together in confusion. "What other mothers?"

"Remember the other day, when I asked you what happened to the other mothers?"

"Sorry, I don't. What day?"

"Before I was here, there was a Russian girl, I think. And there were others before her."

"I can't recall others. But whoever they were, I think you're the best one."

Justine laughed to hide her disquiet. "I think I'll take a walk." She eased herself off the platform and down to the bridge. "Try and sleep a little, okay?"

"Yes, Mother."

Instead of taking the ramp to wind around back to the Canopy, Justine used the first ladder she saw to climb directly down to the ground. As soon as her feet touched down, she felt the quiet thrum of the island welcoming her. A moment later, almost without Justine realizing it, she was following its currents on an invisible path through the woods.

Why doesn't Mak want the boys to remember? It's one thing to push away their past lives, but why forget what they've experienced here? Isn't that the point?

She angrily reached out and yanked a leaf off a tree branch. A sharp pain sparked against her heels. She yelped in surprise. "I'm sorry. I just—" Justine let the leaf drop. "I'm sorry."

Then she shook her head. Did she really think the island could hear her?

That woman pirate had been so insistent about those gloves. Why? And she'd recognized me. Someone she knew has been waiting for me? Justine laughed. None of it made any sense. But hadn't the mer also said someone was looking for her?

Another echo of the island.

Light shone through the trees ahead. The island had guided her to the peasant's hut. Justine would have continued walking, dismissing her arrival as coincidence, except she saw the woman was awake, sitting outside in a rocking chair smoking a pipe and looking like she expected company.

Why not? She stepped into the clearing around the hut. The woman continued smoking. Her only acknowledgement of Justine's arrival was a slight nod of her gnarled head. Justine knew nothing about Russian stories, but the woman was recognizable enough as the witch/old crone character who brewed potions and gave out advice or perhaps attempted to cook small children in her oven. She had a hooked nose and a wart with two sprouted hairs above her right eyebrow. Her three teeth clinked against her pipe when she removed it from her mouth to croak, "So you've come at last."

"Have you been waiting for me?"

"A new mother always has questions."

Justine settled herself on the stump of a tree trunk. "I feel like a very old mother."

"Hmm."

"I think I'm too much a grown-up to be here."

"You can take the night potion and forget," offered the woman. "But then what stories would you tell, I wonder?"

"I don't want to forget where I came from."

"Then I guess you'll have to teach yourself something new. What you see when you look at a person isn't the person at all."

Justine nodded. She thought she was becoming better at not trying to place the boys in her time, trying to think of them as just boys. But in doing that it made her afraid she was losing part of herself. In this strange world, all she could hang on to was what she knew about who she'd been and where she'd come from.

"The island wishes me to tell you about bonding."

The bonding. A sour taste welled up Justine's throat. "The Tigress wanted me to wear gloves to protect myself." Justine looked down at her hands as though they were suddenly going to betray her. "Olewendo said it was more powerful than marriage."

"There are many magical bonds in the eternal realms. When a caretaker marks a dying child with the map to this island, that is a bond of awareness. Some gods, when they are restless will bond with humans or spirits which is both a bond of awareness and control. Some bonds are partial controls, some turn the less powerful bonded one into a shell for the will of the other."

You should've taken those gloves, Justine.

"And here the mother can become bonded to the island."

"I think that's already happened."

The peasant woman shook her head. "It's a bond you take by accepting the great quest. It's an adventure available only to mothers."

"And there's a bond that involves my hands?"

"You may bond with Makbal in defense of the island."

"That sounds . . . useful."

"Very useful. Very powerful. This is the way he made to replace his brother."

"Brother?"

"The island was created between them using pieces of their hearts. It's incomplete without both. So a mother comes. If she's powerful, she can be a substitute and the island is sometimes satisfied."

"What kind of bond is it?"

"Hmm?"

"So far there's awareness and degrees of control. What kind of bond is the one to protect the island?"

The woman studied Justine through a cloud of exhaled smoke. "That depends on many things."

"Well, I certainly don't want to be a shell for Mak to control." Though Justine did want to protect the island.

"You won't defend the island then. He can't force you."

Justine wasn't sure whether to be relieved or irritated. The woman's answers weren't enough. She needed more, something that felt true and real, which was a silly thing to think since the woman herself wasn't real.

What's real in this place?

You're thinking like an adult, Justine.

I watched a boy die before his time tonight. Someone needs to be the adult here.

"Do you know someone named Aranda?" As Justine spoke the name, the trees rustled as though with a collective shiver down their trunks. A breeze rushed into the clearing and seemed to echo a whisper of the name. The peasant woman drew off her pipe and rocked back and forth entirely unaware that the island seemed to have been disturbed.

"Island?" called Justine, trying not to feel silly. "Island? Is there someone here who knows me?"

"To speak to the island that way, you'll need to be someone else." The woman's eyes widened with mischief. "Something more."

Justine jumped to her feet and turned in a circle around the clearing. "Island, tell me what I'm doing here!"

In answer, new voices sounded on the wind.

"Mother."

"Mother!"

"Mother, where are you?"

Justine sank down to the stump again. She hadn't noticed the sun encroaching on her solitude.

"Have you anything else for me?" she asked the woman.

"What the stories teach you about who is good and who is evil, or smart and foolish, are never true to life. The path of reseeing also involves expanding yourself beyond what has been taught."

Not ready to face her duties as mother, Justine hid from the boys in the woods and took a circular path back around to the Canopy, which she expected to be empty by then as the boys rushed off to their adventures. She was surprised, and perhaps also not surprised, to find three of them waiting for her in the cave. Olewendo, Ling, and Qassim.

"Good morning," she said.

"Do you need help with anything?" asked Olewendo.

Justine looked around the room on the pretense of finding a task even though she knew why they were really there. The cave was dusty and cluttered with leaves that had fallen off the boys' clothes. She thought that today or tomorrow might be a good day for another bath and a second attempt at dressing the boys in real clothes. Thinking of clothes reminded her that she had not mended the dress Olewendo said he wanted to wear.

"I was going to do some mending." She pointed to the overflowing basket where she'd collected the least tattered remnants of the boys' clothes. "If you bring that dress, I'll look at it."

Olewendo went to his sleeping cubby and came back with a brightly colored Russian folk dress with a rip through one side of the skirt. Justine sat on a low, three-legged stool. Olewendo sat at her feet. The other two stood, waiting.

Who's going to start this conversation? she wondered. Then, since she was meant to be the adult, she said, "I'm glad you're safe."

"Yes, Mother," said Ling. Qassim only looked at the floor, the fierce expression on his face half hidden by his hair falling forward.

"I've been wondering something." Justine focused on Olewendo, which seemed easiest.

He looked up at her, patient, waiting.

"Why don't you drink the nightly drink?" Since the two of them had already discussed it, she thought this might be a way to draw the other boys in. Demonstrate that they could trust her.

"We want to remember," said Olewendo.

"Your life before?"

He nodded.

"Makbal hasn't noticed?"

Olewendo shrugged. "He doesn't watch me. I'm not what he wanted." He glanced at the other two. After a pause, Ling said, "It's been the same for us since we've been together. His attention moves beyond."

"And there's a problem with your key, right Ling? The island hasn't given you its key hole yet?"

"Maybe it doesn't like that I remember," said Ling.

"But why would we want to travel to the shadowlands not knowing who we are?" huffed Qassim.

"You asked before where I'm from and I lied to you," said Olewendo. "I'm from Boston."

"Boston in America?" asked Justine in disbelief.

"I was going to be a race car driver."

"Race car?"

He laughed. "What time are you from? Race car, like—" He held up his hands to pantomime turning a steering wheel.

"A motorcar driver?"

"When I'm from, it's a job. To win races."

"I would've liked to see a motor race." She had so many questions for him, a boy from the future.

"I remember my parents. They owned a grocery store. One day I was out running their errands and the police stopped me. I ran from them."

"You ran from the police?" Justine frowned.

"It's hard to explain how it was—is—there. I was scared. And they—" His hand went to his side, pressing against his ribs as though injured there. Blood began to seep out between his pressed fingers.

Justine stared down at the blood. Instinct told her to make a compress, but Olewendo was so calm. She held still until her mind could understand it. The island was a place of imagination, and memory was part of it.

"Don't do this to yourself." She threw aside the dress and knelt beside him.

"It's alright," said Ling, coming to kneel beside her. "This comes for all of us sometimes. The pain of the true self."

"It happened a long time ago." Olewendo's voice dipped as he struggled to breathe. "I like to remember, even the pain. It makes me feel like I'm still alive."

"Yes, but—" Justine stopped, afraid of saying the wrong thing. There were so many things and none of them seemed right. That a child would intentionally relive his death, that the island would allow him to experience it so vividly. She wanted to grab him and take it all away, make him new again. *No wonder Makbal gives them that drink,* she thought as she pushed back tears.

"And the two of you? Where and when are you from?"

"China," said Ling, "The twenty-second century. You wouldn't believe the things that were normal for me if you're from horse and gaslight days."

Justine wondered if he meant the new invention of electricity had caught on, but then Qassim said rather forcefully, "And I'm from Babylon during the reign of the great Sumu-la-

El. But that doesn't matter. You're running out of time. Once you take the bond, you'll lose yourself."

"I don't think that's going to happen."

"Because you're leaving?" asked Ling.

Justine wished for all the world they hadn't caught her trying for the dinghy that night. How could she explain? Yes, she had wanted to leave. But now, everything felt different. Nothing was safe.

"Our last mother made beautiful food," said Olewendo. "Her father had been a baker, so she knew special things like that. Before that, Mother grew flowers."

"Flowers?" asked Justine. "I like that idea."

"I'll show you the spot." Olewendo pushed himself to his feet and led her up the stairs with the other two trailing behind. By the time they exited the tree into the outside, Olewendo had recovered. He led her several paces through the woods to an area beyond the edge of the tree house. Here a circle of land had been cleared, the dirt turned up, rocks removed. It was a space that was both out in the open and somehow also private.

"Mother asked the fae for seeds and magic water to grow them," said Olewendo. "I think the fae have seeds for whatever kind of plants you want."

Justine considered this. It seemed a difficult and long process to grow plants from seeds. Besides, any interaction with the fae probably meant an interaction with Tassi, and she didn't like them in the least. A thought came to her, not quite her own voice, *Why bother with seeds?* Justine walked to the edge of the dirt, knelt, and placed her palm in it. A pulse stroked her skin. Justine dug her fingers into the ground, then pulled her hand up. As she pulled, green leaves followed her out of the ground, up and up, until her palm cupped the crown of a bush.

"Fuck me," muttered Olewendo. "It's a motherfucking rose bush."

As Justine sat back on her heels, she saw he was right. She

had conjured a rose bush from the ground. It sat in the dirt as though it had always been there, fully grown, with plump buds ready to bloom amid the leaves.

"Did you make a wish?" asked Ling.

"No, I just—" Justine shook her head. "I made it." She stood up and walked into the dirt patch. At first it took a great deal of concentration, then it took none at all; she didn't even need to use her hands. Each place one of her feet landed, a plant rose in its absence. There were roses and herbs and thistles. She'd no sooner finished than the clearing became busy with the hum of insects rushing to investigate the new plants, the first of which had already started to bloom.

"That's something," muttered Olewendo.

"Past mothers never did anything like this?"

Olewendo shook his head. "All the mothers I've known used wishes. But wishes made them tired, so they'd have us cut down trees, harvest reeds, and stuff. You're different, huh?"

"I guess I am." She stood up, feeling refreshed, even renewed, as though the island had fed her something remarkable. "So, we must convince the island to give Ling his keyhole. And you." She looked to Qassim. "You need both key and hole, am I correct?"

Qassim nodded, still looking at her like he was suspicious.

"We need to create some adventures for you that'll test your mettle."

"Mettle?" asked Ling.

"Prove you're ready for your final quest."

"Why do you want to help us?"

"I'm your mother," she said. "I want you to get what you want even when the world doesn't give it to you."

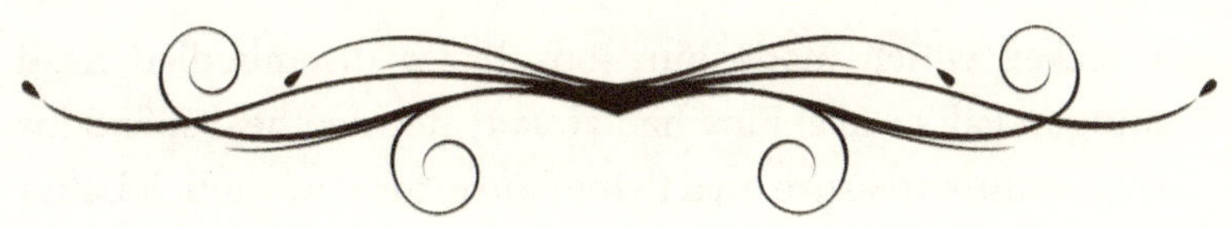

CHAPTER 18

Invasions

That night for story time, Justine chose a story that might produce key-worthy acts of bravery. She told about the boy Wart, who pulled a sword from a magical stone that made him king of all the land. In the morning, the boys went out in search of the sword in the stone determined to pull it themselves. Justine decided to go with them.

"Keep Tassi with you for protection," said Makbal, who'd convinced, cajoled, and perhaps bribed Ling, Ian, and Qassim to go fishing with him instead.

"I don't need a babysitter," she said, when what she'd meant to say was she didn't need a spy.

"Think of them as a guide then. You'd be surprised what they know."

Justine squinted at him. Ever since the raid on the pirate ship, Mak had been strung a little tighter than normal, but she also felt she might just be anxious and looking for trouble where it didn't exist. She started off through the woods with Pah, Jakob, Momoaro, and the new boy Eloy, who seemed to have already forgotten he was new. Jakob rode the flying pony he'd purchased from the fae gazebo. Momoaro wore his invisible jacket, which made him look like a disembodied head floating in Pah's wake. Eloy had already decided he'd spend his first adventure treasure on a flying horse, for it was much better to fly than be invisible.

Tassi joined them as they crossed the summer woods. Their chime seemed as irritated to be with her as she was to be with them.

"Wait for me," cried Jakob. "I want to catch the butterfly."

"The sword waits for no one," said Pah.

"Doesn't it wait for the one who's worthy?" asked Eloy, who took up the butterfly chase with Jakob.

A warm summer wind blustered Justine's face like a greeting. It picked up her hair and arranged it on her head in ornate braids. Tassi looked at her hair, then at Justine, then back at her hair. Their little mouth pursed in a thoughtful moue Justine couldn't begin to interpret.

"The island likes to do my hair." She shrugged as though this happened all the time. "And look here, we grow things together." Justine sent awareness into her feet and, in the wake of her footsteps, new wildflowers sprang up, already in bloom.

Tassi chimed a chorus of notes that sounded unimpressed. Yet the look on their face said something else, something calculated.

"Do you know where the sword is?" she asked. "I'd like to find it before anyone else. See if this time it might let a woman be queen of the Britons."

Tassi flicked their wings with disapproval.

Island, can we send Tassi away? She didn't exactly expect an answer, but the stroke of energy against her heels felt like a secret between the two of them. She looked ahead to see Qassim had taken the lead on the adventure. Closer to her, the younger boys had become lost to butterfly chasing. And there, the mysterious and perpetually absent Nacel sat on the low branch of a nearby tree watching the other boys.

"Do you want to come play with us?" called Justine.

Nacel didn't turn his head or give any indication he'd heard her. This was the first time she'd seen him in what seemed quite some time. Had it been yesterday, the picnic? Or the day before? *How long have I been here?* He seemed an ordinary boy, if rendered a little strange by his silence, and by the studied narrowness of his gaze that seemed to see only one thing at a time. She became so lost in watching him that she didn't notice when the other little boys moved on.

When Nacel climbed down from the tree and began to wade through the flowers, Justine followed him with Tassi flitting along behind her left shoulder. They crossed through the winter grove and the spring grove. At the fall grove, Justine paused to take in the leaves. No matter how many times she saw it, the spray of autumn foliage felt new and even more vibrant every time. Justine told herself the island was imaginary and not true nature, but it still felt like some part of the true thing. The crisp, dry crackle in the air hinted at a winter that would perpetually remain trapped in the adjacent grove. The crunch of leaves underfoot was every autumn of spiced apples and rum apple pie she'd never been able to afford.

But today, perhaps because she was moving according to Nacel's interest rather than her own, Justine noticed a blemish in the perfect fall scene. A group of trees in the grove was losing their leaves. Before her eyes, they seemed to turn from brilliant red to brown, then they began to fall.

"Tassi, what does it mean?"

The fae swiveled right and left, sputtering harsh shards of sound that meant nothing good. When Justine tried to walk closer to the trees, Tassi flew into her face and flashed their body a luminescent green.

"Fine then. But we should at least check on the lake." It was a short walk to Coral Falls. Nacel, despite appearing disinterested, followed her. As she walked, Justine quieted her worry by listening to the island. It didn't seem bothered or alarmed by the dying trees. Such a powerful island would be in control of this—whatever was happening.

The lake was as it'd been when she'd first arrived, a brilliant canopy of color around a circle of emerald water, misty rainbows rising from the throats of the falls, the vine-covered cliffs disappearing into the clouds.

But there, on the far side of the water, a bobbing head marred the glassy surface. Justine blinked and it disappeared. Another blink and it appeared again. A head attached to a person, who lay on their back and swam.

As she watched, the person finished swimming and emerged from the water. Like the boys, he wore no clothes for swimming. This was a more significant thing because he was so much older than the boys. Even from that distance, Justine felt the size of him, a complete person. An adult. *A man.* She couldn't help but evaluate the size of his knob. *I could make use of that.*

Heat burning her face, she whispered, "Who is he?" as she prayed there existed some new group of adults that wasn't murderous pirates.

Tassi crossed their arms, a pouting silence.

The man had passed out of her view. Justine twisted and turned to try to see where he'd gone but found the shrubbery blocking her way. *He could help me.*

Behind her, a gargled screech sent chills running down her spine. She jumped up and ran, then almost tripped over Nacel squatting on the ground not far behind her.

"Are you alright?"

The boy wiggled his hips and tapped a pattern with his toes against the ground, perfectly fine.

Justine looked back at the lake, but the mysterious man was gone, and the older boys were shouting from the woods at the other side of the lake. Qassim's voice rang out above the rest.

"I'm Arthur, King of the Britons! Today, we unite the realm! Come forth to be knighted." She couldn't see the boys, but she sensed the island telling her that Qassim had been granted his key. Now at least, he and Ling were at equal stages of their journeys.

Whoever he was. If he's been here, he'll be back, she thought. *He has to come back. Next time, I'll be ready.* Ready for what? Somehow she would claim him, or convince him to trust her, or something. Anything, so she wasn't alone anymore.

Nacel squirmed up out of the hole and shook the dust from his face. In each hand he held a tiny, fuzzy ball. He dumped one of the balls into Justine's cupped palms. It wiggled and unrolled itself, revealing a distinctly round body with fur the blue-purple color of a bruise, a head, and two oversized ears. *A baby rabbit,* thought Justine, perfectly formed with a pink button nose and itty-bitty paws.

"Is this a pet?" she asked Nacel.

The boy stood up and trotted off, carrying his ball in front of him. Justine followed until Nacel came to the place in the grove where all the trees had lost their leaves. Tassi emitted their same warning sounds but didn't stop Nacel as the boy walked up to the trees.

Justine felt a ripple run through the pulse of the island. Different energy. Or perhaps energy going away. She felt the breath sucked out of her. When she could breathe again, Nacel stood before her somehow different. She couldn't quite tell why she felt he'd changed. Perhaps he had grown taller. The scar on the right side of his chin didn't seem so distinct. In his arms, instead of an infant rabbit, was a much larger creature with the same oversized ears, the same rabbit-like paws and nub of a tail, but its eyes were much too large, and its head was round instead of elongated.

It wiggled in Nacel's arms until he released it. They watched together as it scampered into the forest. Nacel held out his hand. Justine reluctantly handed over the other baby ball of fur. Another rush of energy, Justine gasping at the shock of it, then Nacel returned to her side. This time she was sure he'd grown taller. The substance of his face seemed a little older, perhaps more a child of seven than six.

The creature he returned with leaped from his arms up onto Justine's shoulder. It was a little too large to perch there comfortably, so it draped itself around the back of her neck like a lady's fox fur. It gave a small cough, then a squeak, as it began to purr.

Nacel squinted up at the creature as though it had betrayed him.

"Is this what you do?" she asked as her brain slowly provided the words *time runnel*, and the memory of Olewendo saying one of the old mothers had died by aging into death in one of them. Then she wondered if the man she'd seen had been a boy caught in a runnel. And she prayed not. She couldn't bear it if her one hope for salvation was just an older version of one of her boys.

Nacel blinked at her, looking past her instead of at her. Then he pressed a finger to his lips.

"You want me to keep it a secret?"

His eyes became wider. He pressed his finger to his mouth over and over until he was hitting himself, and Justine reached out to stop him. But then she heard it. Footsteps crushing leaves. Many footsteps, all moving together. The giant ears of her new pet stood straight up and twitched. Tassi fluttered up into the tree branches and hid behind a leaf, not at all the protective guardian Makbal said they'd be.

Justine gathered Nacel to her and turned in a slow circle. All she saw were woods in every direction, then a flicker of something. Eyes, the glint of sunlight on metal, a weapon. It was happening. The pirates had come for their vengeance. *He was a pirate after all.* She didn't have time to mourn her loss.

Island, which way do we run? she asked. But the island didn't answer.

Behind her, a twig snapped. Justine whirled only to find her vision blocked by a burlap sack pulled down over her head and all the way to her knees. A stout rope pinned her arms to her sides, trapping the rabbit-not-rabbit creature inside. It hissed and fitzed, an agent of scampering, scratching chaos as Justine was hefted over someone's shoulder

A woman's voice cried, "To the ship!" Then they were off running, Justine bouncing painfully this way and that. She tried to scream for help, but it was impossible to breathe, let alone scream, in such a condition. The creature dug its claws into Justine's chest. Its panting filled her ear with overheated air. All Justine wanted was for the person carrying her to slow down. To maybe let her walk. Yes, she would cooperate if they just let her walk and promised not to kill her.

And then, with a woosh, she was flying through the air, crashing horribly to the ground. *My captor tripped.* But it was more than that. The air came alive with shouts from above. Justine's heart leaped. Her boys had come to rescue her. She heard the sharp whistle of Makbal giving wordless orders. Branches cracked and leaves rained down. Justine's would-be captors found themselves in a surprise fight.

The woman shouted, "Don't let them touch!"

Then Justine was being lifted and carried again. Not as fast this time. Her captor had been injured and was limping. She did her best to make things difficult, wiggling this way and that, shoving her knees into his chest until again she fell. The rope came loose. She threw off the bag and found herself in the middle of a battle. Adults in rough, woven clothing fought her boys. These weren't pirates, so she assumed they were Delts, the people of the village. They were mostly men, but Justine also spotted at least two women. The Delts carried knives and axes. The boys carried swords and wands and poisoned apples that exploded and burned skin. Jakob rode his flying horse and Momoaro blended into the trees with his invisible jacket, stabbing adults in the legs by surprise. She spotted the Tigress fending off Ian's furious sword thrusts.

"Stop!" she cried. "Please, stop!"

No one listened to her. Two men noticed Justine was free and came running toward her. Justine held up her hands. "Please, I just want to talk."

Fighting pressed in on all sides, but there, just a few trees away, she saw Makbal making his way toward her. "Take my hand," he shouted over the fray.

"What?"

"Take my hand and send them away!"

Justine tried to move toward him, but one of the men had lunged forward and grabbed hold of the edge of her nightgown. It ripped as she struggled to get away. Eloy and Pah had mounted one of the attacking men and were stabbing him over and over with their child-sized knives. The man stumbled into her, knocking her free of the other man, but also tearing off most of her nightgown skirt. She tumbled into Makbal's arms. He seized her hands in his, fingers interlaced. There was blood on his hands.

"Wish them away," he said again.

"What? No. Can't we just talk?"

The creature continued to breathe into her ear, sounding like a dying cat in its terror. More adults had broken free of the boys and were running toward her with such expressions of hatred in their eyes; they appeared willing to do anything to catch her.

Beneath her feet, the island rumbled.

"Wish it fast before they can steal the boys," said Makbal. She saw in his eyes the fear that sparked anew in her own heart, a naked, starving fear that everything could be lost.

"Yes," gasped Justine as she took his hand. "Send them

away." Energy coursed out of her like a tide rushing toward an unseen shore. As it rippled through the woods, the cries of more than a dozen people rose up all at once and were just as quickly snuffed out. The fighting stopped; there was no one left to fight. The adults had disappeared. Only Justine, Makbal, and the boys remained.

"What happened?"

"Nothing," said Makbal, beaming at her. "And everything. My queen." He knelt before her. "You were perfect." He gazed up at her with such love Justine thought she might melt into a puddle for the joy of it. As he rose to his feet, Makbal looked ready to kiss her.

But he's just a boy.

As he leaned toward her, Makbal's eyes turned white and fluttered closed. Justine caught him as he fell. She cradled him in her arms, panic surging through her veins.

"Somebody help! What's wrong with him? Mak? Mak!"

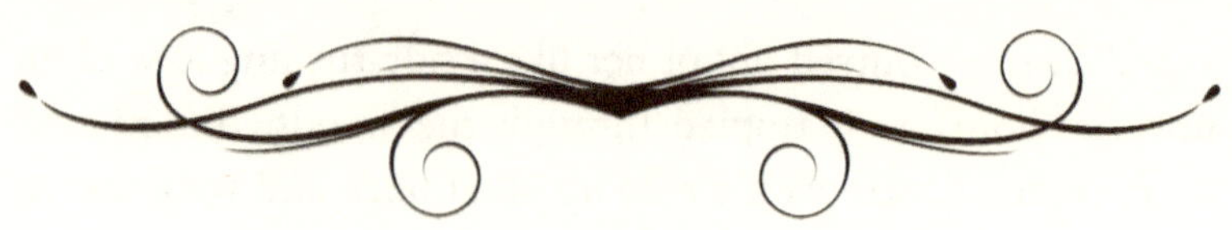

Time and the Prophecy of Mending

The fact that I can sometimes interpret the voice of the island does not mean I am always privy to its thoughts and schemes, as I clearly was not in the case of her calling to Osuana, then also making the secondary call that resulted in the myth of the rising goddess.

When did I know the girl Justine was special?

Not until the end. There was no sense of her being more than just another mother. The island must have known; they were having all these special moments creating plants out of nothing, but it wasn't shared with me.

If I had known, would I have attempted to prevent the bonding given how it had gone in the past? Probably not. I always feel sorry for those girls, but the plain fact is that when Aranda did what he did, the island was wrecked, and anytime there isn't a mother available for Mak to tap into that extra power, life on the island does not go well. And I for one, prefer to be trapped on an island that is going well as opposed to the other.

From The Reflections of Archivist Posietta

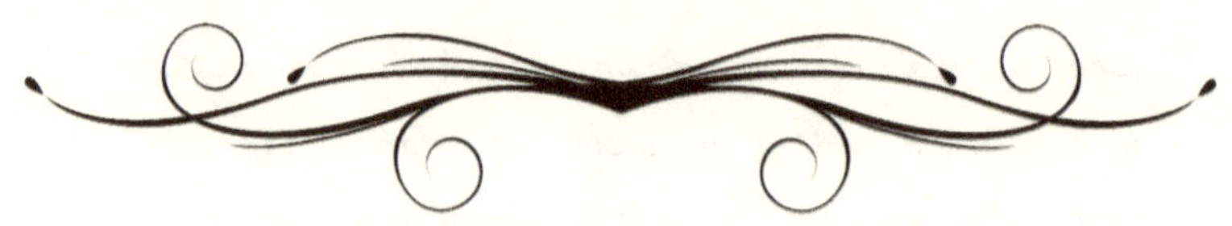

CHAPTER 20

A Promise Made

The island, as you've probably already understood, was not divided equally when the Voyager pulled part of it into time. The heart of the island remained outside of time, along with all its awareness. Thus, the island within time was amputated flesh severed from its body. Sometimes that body still felt it, could reach out and have a sense of it, but it had no power over what went on in its own core.

Any magic—the appearance of imagined creatures, the building of houses from thin air, procreation—came from the Voyager. This meant that if he found himself in a foul mood, the weather likewise became foul, and if he was distracted or disinterested in releasing the power to make the inhabitants' dreams come true, there was no remainder to fulfill them instead.

This was not so different from the body of the island, except that the Lost Boy's moods came and went with the tides; he did everything in excess, but his attention spanned the length of a fly's wings, and the island could moderate him to some extent. Not so his brother. The Voyager's first major dark period created a torrent of rain and lightning, which started a fire that burned even the soaking wet jungle to its roots. The second caused a mudslide that buried the Delt village. Afterward, they had to start over in new dwellings on a different side of the mountains.

No one said it, but as the war with the Lost Boy dragged on, the worse the weather went, the more it became clear something needed to be done.

"Bond with me," said Osuana, who still believed that if she could find a way to pin down her god, everyone would be happier.

"I wouldn't do that to you. You'd be like my slave in body and mind."

"I already am." She thought this was a sexy thing to say. There were quite a lot of things the Lost Girl said that weren't quite right; she came from a hard place of hard people who had become accustomed to a certain way of living. The way her world had imprinted on her was one of the reasons the Lost Boy had asked us to help with tidying his children's minds, so they could be fully free of their past lives. If only we'd had the right tea for the Lost Girl, she might have ended better.

As it was, she was close to the breaking point herself. Twice more, the Voyager refused to bond with her. Each time pushed her further toward the path she would take to her ending. She never knew how close the Voyager came to agreeing to her request. He had become a desperate man, unable to think clearly. Everything he'd attempted to accomplish or correct or change had failed. He saw his failure reflected back to him every day in the eyes of the Delts, in the carnage, in the rage that festered beneath his skin and the moments when it burst out of him beyond his control.

On the day he had finally made up his mind that he would take the Lost Girl fully as his own, creating an immortal bond so she would always belong to him—perhaps he thought this would erase his memories of Thessaly—he went alone back to the body of the island.

You've returned.

The leap of hope he felt seep up from the ground was enough to break his heart once again.

"I want to bond," he said.

The island's hope faded. It is rather smart for an island, so it knew without him saying what he must want.

I will not help you with this.

"She is no longer yours to protect. Release her to me."

You do not need my permission, said the island.

But the Voyager wanted it. Or perhaps he wanted to be talked out of what was obviously a bad idea, or at least an ethical line that made all the past unethical lines he'd crossed pale by comparison.

"I cannot go on like this," said the Voyager.

The island had been waiting for this moment. It had long ago surpassed the feeling of not being able to continue, but continue it had, resolved to keep everything running until one of the brothers gave himself up. The Voyager's confession was as close as a god came to admitting death was preferable to immortal life.

"If you do not help me, I will find myself an ending. I swear to you."

Help you, how? asked the island. It was not going to choose sides.

"To end it."

The island appreciated the strategic vagueness. *There's a future for you,* said the island. *If you can find a way to make your peace.*

"Is that a fae prophecy or a promise?"

It's a promise. I have made a way. Two

hearts as one, larger than time itself.

"How can I believe that?"

Your alternative is more destruction. Take hold, believe in it, redirect your path.

The Voyager did not fully believe the island's promise, but he did feel a little better, at least a little less self-destructive. There was an interlude of pleasant life on the amputated limb of the island. The sun shone. The Lost Girl lay in his arms and teased him with her hard jokes and her sly eyes. Neither of them knew that until then, the girl had been protected by her bond with the island. Neither of them knew that after the Voyager's meeting with the island, it released that bond and finally allowed the Lost Girl to walk down the path of her fate.

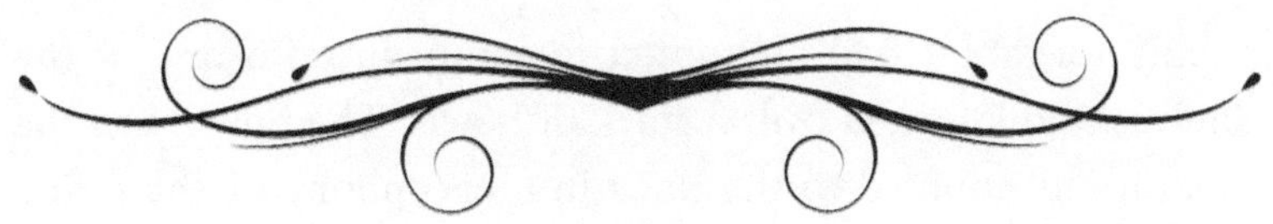

The Bonding

Ling and Qassim helped Justine carry Makbal to the Canopy and down the narrow stairs into the cave where they laid him on her mattress.

"What's happened to him?" she asked.

"It drains him to do that," said Eloy. "Anytime he and a mother send invaders away, he sleeps like this."

Justine pulled back Makbal's eyelid. It was still all white underneath. She had seen seizures at the asylum where a patient's eyes had been white, but not for this long, and not without the violence of tremors. She ran to the pantry to see if there was anything that would be of use. The rabbit-not-rabbit creature hopped off her shoulder and began to prowl around.

"Can someone find Tassi? They were with me in the fall grove before—" Justine stilled. "Nacel! He was left behind. I must—" Again, she stilled, her words and her body a full stop of motion. Every inch of her said she should remain with Makbal; he would want her when he woke up. But beneath that urgent insistence was a smaller, more familiar voice telling her to go find Nacel.

A crash sounded, startling her out of her stillness. The

rabbit-not-rabbit had attempted to jump up onto one of the shelves and knocked over a stack of bowls. The bowls and the creature all toppled to the floor in a cacophony of shattering pottery. The creature's ears flattened as it bolted to Justine, scaled her ruined nightgown and took shelter around her neck.

"Those things are pests," said Ling. "Do you want me to kill it for you?"

"Absolutely not. We're friends."

She was startled to hear, as though from a person unseen behind her, a raspy little voice echo, "Absolutely not." The creature could speak. Or perhaps was learning to speak. "Friends," it said.

On the mattress, Makbal stirred. Justine poured water from the jug that refilled itself each morning and brought it to his side.

"This is a bad one," said Ling.

"He said she's more powerful," said Qassim, speaking about Justine as though she couldn't hear him.

Momoaro crawled up on the bed and lay down beside Makbal. He began to make cooing noises. The rabbit-not-rabbit came to investigate, decided this was an interesting activity, and began to mimic the cooing, flattening its ears against its head and thrusting its chin forward with each sound.

"I need some of you to go to the fall grove and find Nacel. I'm sure he was very frightened. He might be having a spell of his own." Justine's eyes searched the room and landed on Olewendo who was hanging back against the wall, watching.

"He's better alone," said Qassim. "If he's upset, being around us doesn't help."

"But surely he wants to know I'm safe." Justine looked to Olewendo. With a nod, he pulled himself up into his tree and disappeared. With the problem of Nacel addressed, Justine felt free to give Makbal her full attention. She leaned over and stroked his forehead. He felt cold to her touch, pristine, like a statue cut from alabaster. His angelic face seemed to glow with light from within, yet he barely breathed.

And there was a new thing. He wasn't even conscious, yet he felt more present with her than he'd ever been. He was like a seed glowing warm in the corner of her chest. It felt a little bit like love and a little bit like something else.

"Justine?" Makbal whispered.

"I'm here."

"Is everyone safe?"

"Yes."

Makbal struggled to open his eyes, but when he did, they were his clear, dark eyes again. He gazed up at her as though seeing her for the first time. "I'm so very tired."

"You needn't do anything except rest. I have water."

"Can you come closer? It will help."

This puzzled Justine; she was already right up against him. But then, she had the idea of moving herself onto the mattress where she pulled the quilt onto her lap, then pulled him onto it so his head rested in the corner of her waist. Makbal closed his eyes in deep contentment. He reached for her hand and held it. As he did so, Justine suddenly felt very tired herself.

Her small voice shouted warnings she didn't hear. It felt so, so good to be close to him. This wasn't the pleasure she'd been missing from late-night rendezvous in London alleys, but something simpler, and older. She sank into it, this comfort of a time beyond time. Everything she didn't understand melted away. She leaned herself over him, making a cocoon of her body so she might touch as much of him as possible, skin on skin, hearts beating in time. She fell asleep that way, bent in half, her head on his chest, their fingers entwined.

WHEN JUSTINE WOKE, MAKBAL WAS GONE. SHE JUMPED TO HER feet, frantic to find him, then calmed as her senses reached out and located him above ground. He was happy. Justine didn't question how she knew. It was enough to realize that nothing was wrong with him. At first, the power of this desire for Makbal to be happy and safe seemed natural. But as she came fully awake and realized how difficult it was to think of anything else, Justine shivered.

This is the bond, a voice whispered.

The day passed in a haze. Justine played with the boys. She wandered her rose garden, but it didn't seem as beautiful as it had before. When her feet touched the ground, she felt only the thinnest answering stroke of the island. She remembered that the Russian peasant woman had never actually told her what kind of bond would exist after she and Makbal defended the island.

You should have gone with the Delts, whispered the voice. *You've lost yourself.*

"This is who I am," said Justine without confidence. "I choose to be Mak's heart of the island. I'm a queen."

Did you?

Pain zigzagged through the side of Justine's temple. She couldn't remember. There had been that conversation in the asylum. Makbal had told her how important a mother was for the island. She'd said she would do it, hadn't she? But hadn't there been another person involved? Someone silent, but beautiful.

The pain moved from her head to her hands. Justine looked down to find she had plunged them into the thorns of the roses. Pinpricks of blood had bubbled up all over her fingers and palms. In the pain, she felt her haze retreat. *Take a boat, escape to the other island. The Tigress will help you.*

"The Tigress is with the pirates."

"Are you alright, Mother?"

Justine looked up and saw Olewendo watching her. Beside him, just on the verge of wandering off, stood Nacel. *Am I alright?*

"Of course. I've just taken a spill here." She laughed. "Lost my balance."

"Qassim has his key now. Ling is worried the island has forgotten him."

"Yes, I've thought about that." She paused and felt the answers coming to her like trickles of a stream all converging in her mind. All of them bright and clean and so, so powerful. "Mak has promised me a crown worthy of a queen. Ling and Qassim will claim it for me. This will be enough to earn their keyholes. I'm certain of it."

She turned and began to walk, she wasn't sure where, then, as though she'd never had the thought, her plan to create a quest for a crown vanished from her head.

CHAPTER 22
The Realm Below

"Now we're off." Qassim jabbed his sword in the air. "What foes will we conquer in glorious battle?"

"Wait," said Makbal, "I'm not knighted."

"No time today, Lord Mak." Qassim charged into the woods, his knights charging after him.

Makbal kicked at the ground. Justine felt the tremor of his frustration in her chest and immediately went to comfort him. "There's always tomorrow." She rubbed his back. To do this gave her great satisfaction; her touch soothed his spirit and allowed him to tidy his mind.

"I didn't want to be a knight to that imposter king anyway. Anyone can pull a sword out of a stone. If I'd found it first, it would've been mine."

Clashing swords and violent shouting sounded from deep in the woods. Makbal cocked his ear to listen. Justine understood from the way her body responded to his moods that Makbal sensed the presence of all the boys because he'd bonded with them when he gave them a map to the island as they died.

"They've found some kind of monster."

"We should go see it." Justine reached for his hand. "They might need your help."

Together they walked through the woods. It was one of the most beautiful days she'd had on the island. The sun shone bright but not too hot overhead and streamed through the trees like the golden beams of a thousand electric lights. Birds chorused and fairies flew here and there in their busy enterprise.

A great roar sounded from a creature followed by a cheer from the boys. Just as quickly the cheer died out. Justine was wondering over the abrupt end of the sound when Makbal dropped her hand and began to run. At the base of the cliffs, the game had ended. Qassim and his knights had killed a giant boar, but something was wrong. As Justine rushed up behind Makbal, it wasn't immediately clear what.

The dead thing had disappeared. All that remained was the pool of its blood. In the center of the pool, a keyhole glowed. But Qassim didn't approach it. Indeed, the boys stood in a jagged half circle around the space watching the shadows of clouds pass over one particular section of rocks.

Justine squinted up at the sky, cloudless except for one very small section cut out of the blue expanse. Even stranger, an unseen sun seemed to move across this patch of sky. The rocks that had shone as clear as day moments earlier were now turning orange and pink in the glow of an invisible sunset. She felt Makbal roiling, a rage building up inside him that made her tremble.

"Don't go in," said Ling to Qassim. "The keyhole will stay until the runnel passes."

"It's part of the quest," said Qassim. He adjusted his grip on the sword as though the weapon would help him conquer this new challenge.

Ling pulled at Qassim's arm. "Nothing is hurt by waiting."

Full night had descended in the runnel. Wapasha stepped

forward, extending his hand toward the darkness. "What demon does this magic?"

Ian grabbed his hand and pulled it back. "Don't," he said.

"We can fix this," said Justine, wanting things to be better as quickly as possible. She reached for Makbal's hand. "Set it right with me and Qassim can claim his map."

But Makbal's hand was clenched in a fist and pinched against his chest. "This shouldn't still be happening. You're here. We're bonded."

Makbal was giving her a hundred signals of *everything is wrong,* and Justine didn't know what to do. Nor was it clear why this runnel was somehow different than the ones that had come before.

"Mak," whispered Justine. "Talk to me."

"It's getting worse," he said through a clenched jaw.

Beyond the shouting coming down the bond, she sensed the boys had decided to act. Qassim and Ling shared a kiss goodbye. In Justine's peripheral vision, she saw Qassim sucking in deep breaths, preparing to plunge into the runnel. How fast was it passing? Justine didn't remember how time worked, but she knew she didn't want Qassim to risk aging into an adult before their eyes.

"Mak, heal the island with me." She wrapped her fingers around his clenched hand.

"We're losing. You're not powerful enough."

"But we're enough together," said Justine, an idea she knew Makbal often held in his mind. He used it to comfort himself in times of uncertainty. But this had gone beyond that. "Come on." She uncurled his fingers, interlaced them with her own.

Still, he resisted. Justine pushed back a flush of frustration. "Mak, come on! Wish it away with me."

With a dramatic sigh, Makbal exhaled his tension. Just as Qassim was about to cross over, he sent his will into Justine, who channeled it through her own connection to the island. A wave of energy pushed through her heels. It traveled through the ground, then rose around the edges of the runnel, swallowing it whole. As Qassim stepped toward the cliffs, he stepped in continuous timelessness.

Several of the boys whooped and cheered. Ling rushed forward to be at Qassim's side as he inserted his key in the glowing keyhole.

Justine put her arm around Makbal's waist and squeezed him tight. "It's gone. We're fine."

"I don't understand why they're still appearing. You should be stronger than he is."

"He who?"

Makbal shrugged. She felt his awareness drift away from her to focus on the boys. A wistful longing filled him as he watched them. "Qassim won't leave without Ling," he said softly.

"You can't just tell the island to give Ling a quest to find his keyhole?"

"It doesn't work like that."

"Can we create one for him ourselves? They should be able to swim together." And then, a thought came to her, slowly unfurling like an arthritic flower. "Didn't you promise your queen a crown?"

Makbal suddenly brightened. "That's an idea." He stepped into the circle of boys. "Well done, Qassim. You've united the realm. But this reminds me. We promised Mother we'd play kings and queens, but we never got her a proper crown."

"Shall we make one?" asked Pah.

"I was thinking of something more dangerous." Makbal arched a deviant eyebrow. "Pirate's booty."

"Hurrah!" they shouted.

"We're going downrealm." Makbal paused to let this sink in.

"I can only take a few of you with me. The boat's small, and we need space for our loot." He pointed to Qassim and Ling, then to Ian and Wapasha. "The rest of you, divide yourselves into scout groups and search the island. When I return, I want to know about every runnel we've never seen."

The four selected boys walked down to the dinghy anchored by the cliffs. Though Justine couldn't remember the day passing, the sun had set. She could see nothing through the veil except the gray shadow within the shadow of the opposite island.

Smear climbed down from the lookout shelf and helped Ian ready the dinghy, then he held it steady while they climbed aboard. "All ready?" Smear pushed the dinghy off. "Journey well, and plunder better!"

The moons were hiding their faces from the sky, so they traveled in nearly complete darkness, ears straining for sounds of movement. No one dared whisper. Even breathing seemed too loud. They crossed the lagoon with Ling and Qassim at the oars, stealthy with the precision of their movements. Ian took the prow and Wapasha took the stern as lookouts. "What are we looking for?" whispered Wapasha.

"Pirates," said Makbal.

"Or hungry creatures," said Ian.

Justine felt only a gentle shiver as they crossed the veil. On the other side, the moons were thin crescent slivers that did nothing to penetrate the darkness. Ling and Qassim left behind caution for speed. They rowed as fast as they could for the far cliffs and the tunnel beneath them that led to the lowerrealm. Justine felt Makbal's excitement, so she also felt excitement instead of the fear that seemed much more natural. It was one thing to live halfway between the living and the dead on a magical island. It was quite another thing to purposefully dare full death by going downrealm for an adventure.

Are we going to heaven or hell? she wondered, then realized she couldn't remember which was the good place and which the bad.

"Hear that?" whispered Wapasha. He lay against the side of the boat, his hand trailing in the water. "The rhythm has changed."

"What rhythm?" asked Ian. "I don't feel anything."

"We're almost there," whispered Makbal.

Even in the darkness, Justine saw his eyes glowing with a righteous excitement. She felt the kind of defiance she'd known in children of the asylum when they prepared to stake their wills against the doctors and nurses. Makbal trained his eyes ahead of the dinghy's course. They were headed down to the depths. Justine could just make out the mountains growing closer by the way they blocked the stars from the sky.

"Can't you feel it?" asked Wapasha, forgetting to whisper. "The current's disturbed."

"For god's sake, get your hand out of it then," said Ian. He was about to lunge over and grab Wapasha's hand when Makbal stilled. "She's here," he whispered.

Justine strained her eyes so hard she started seeing spots. Then she felt it, a presence ahead of them in the dark, the huge weight of it pressing down in the water. And within that weight, something familiar she'd long ago forgotten, a person she'd once known. No, she corrected herself, a person Makbal had once known.

Up ahead, a man's voice shouted a call. Another answered. A flash of flame lit what had seemed empty sky ahead of them. Then came another flame and another, and an outline of the *Osuana's* deck became visible, glowing as though on fire itself. Torches came to life along the deck, illuminating pirates standing ready with grappling ropes and fire arrows.

"Surrender and you'll not be worse harmed than you aught," called a deep voice. It lingered in Justine's ears, reverberating, sinking deep, so familiar. *I hate that voice.* And yet, a small part of her wanted to reach out, wanted more of it.

"Faster!" hissed Makbal.

The *Osuana* was maneuvering to block their path. The figures raised their grappling ropes. One was thrown and splashed down in the water beside Ian. Another landed at the boat's front and Makbal scrambled to unhook it and throw it away.

"We're here," whispered Ling and Qassim almost at the same time. They stopped rowing as the dinghy took on speed.

A shout sounded above. "They've made the rapids."

"Catch them!"

More hooks, a dozen of them all at once flew through the air, but they were not fast enough.

The dinghy dipped forward and began to fill with water.

"Heads down!" cried Makbal.

The side of the *Osuana* came up nearly on top of them. Justine, who sat the tallest, would have lost her head if she hadn't thrown herself down in time. Water closed in. She tried to breathe normally as she listened to the groaning of the *Osuana* above them fade, then disappear. With it she felt as though she had left something important behind. Or at least, that was how Makbal felt.

The feeling didn't last long. They were diving quite fast now through complete darkness. Justine gripped the side of the dinghy with one hand and the back of Makbal's leaf tunic with another. Water became like a sharp, cold wind blowing her hair back as they flew through the darkness, dipping, then turning, rising to one side like the turn of the most terrifying toboggan trough, then drifting back to center. Her stomach flipped and spun and threatened to unleash its contents in her mouth. Shapes formed themselves out of the darkness. Walls perhaps, or animals. Justine didn't dare consider what.

Finally, a green light began to shine ahead. It grew brighter and brighter until she saw an illuminated archway. The dinghy slowed down. They passed through and tilted upward for an ascent.

"Let's do that again," laughed Ian.

"Quiet," said Makbal. "This isn't the world above. Everyone here can see us and hear us."

"And if they see us or hear us, they can capture us and send us over the falls to our end," added Qassim.

Ian sobered. "Then perhaps we can turn around and ride the current back home now?"

"We're here to find a crown for Mother," said Ling. "We can't go back yet."

"And Ling's keyhole," added Wapasha.

Ian turned accusing eyes on Ling as though this unexpected danger to their adventure was his fault.

They floated past houses carved from cliffs on both sides of the water. No stars shone overhead; Justine thought they might be in an underwater cavern. The roar of rushing water sounded on the right side and above them, falls hidden behind rock.

In places where a path ran along the water connecting clusters of houses to each other, torches lit the way. Then the river turned a bend and the houses passed less frequently. Tunnel entrances hinted at life even deeper within the caverns. Laughter could sometimes be heard, but more often the sound that split the shadows was the crack of a gunshot or someone screaming.

Another bend revealed a series of open courtyards in what Justine thought might be called the French style with walls painted pastel colors and buildings of white-railing balconies and archways. A crowd of revelers overflowed from a pub. Some of them looked no older than Pah. They were tossed about by the adults like toys.

Two men dressed in the tatters of long, blue coats chased each other up stairs and along a balcony before they disappeared behind a door. A woman screamed as a man lunged for her with malicious eyes. Two other women watched from the shadow of another doorway. Gunshots peppered the air seemingly at random. A calliope sounded from far away and echoed off the walls of the cliffs. The cavern opened to reveal layers upon layers of buildings cut out of rock towering up to unseen heights.

"This is the Green City," whispered Makbal. "Eternal realm of my mother, Coleodal, the Goddess of the Falls Eternal."

"I don't think she's doing a good job with her mothering," whispered Ian.

He pressed up against Justine. "Are you sure you want a crown?"

Justine wasn't so sure. The city was stunning in its size. The debauchery looked on par for London on a payday if the constabulary all happened to be down with the pox.

The roar of the falls grew louder.

"So, this is the true afterlife?" asked Wapasha.

"Only if you fail to reach the Cloud City," said Ling.

"It doesn't seem so bad here," said Ian.

The dinghy turned another corner into a cavern with only a few houses. A long stretch passed with empty cliffs cut with paths leading to dark tunnels.

"We're coming up on it now," said Makbal. "Remember, they can see us and hear us. So move fast. Don't be greedy." He fixed his eyes significantly on Qassim, who shrugged away the warning.

"It was just that once," he whispered.

Around another corner, they drifted in darkness, then light appeared dim and distant down the mouth of a tunnel. Ling and Qassim steered the dinghy to the shore. Everyone but Ian hopped out to help pull the boat out of the water.

"I could stay here," he said.

Justine reached for his hand. When he took it, she gave him a reassuring squeeze. "I'm scared too. But we'll be fine if we're together."

Makbal took the lead, walking on tiptoe but as brazen as

though he lived in the city. Ling and Qassim followed, then Justine with Wapasha and Ian.

They walked for what seemed a long way before the tunnel opened into an immense cavern filled with riches. It seemed very much like a pirate's hoard. Gold bullion and chests overflowed with jewels and strings of pearls, fine carpets, and candelabra. Beside the chests, statues of gods and goddesses, religious icons, and paintings.

The reflection of torchlight along the walls illuminated an eternity's worth of wealth all stolen from the living. Tunnels led from the main cavern to other caverns, which led to other caverns. Justine found one room of clothes and immediately lost all desire to look for anything else. There were clothes from all over the world, clothes from her time, and clothes from times before and after. She studied the ones she liked so she might picture them in her mind and wish the island to create them in the future. Justine took only small articles as her booty: a painted silk scarf and a necklace of glass beads.

"Mother, over here," called Ian from an adjacent cavern.

Justine followed his voice to a narrow room lined with shelves. Neatly ordered on these shelves was row after row of hats. Tucked back in the corner sat five jeweled crowns. Justine touched each one in turn. They were all gold except for one which was wood and painted a golden color. To her great surprise, Justine realized she didn't like any of them.

"These aren't what I want."

They moved to another cavern, then another where Wapasha had found a collection of soldier figurines all lined up on a plate of bicolored squares. Ling and Qassim could be heard nearby, their laughter punctuated by the tinkle of cascading coins.

Justine stowed a few coins away in her pockets. One never knew when a few coins would be useful. She imagined saving the day when one of her boys wanted to purchase something from the fairy gazebo toy shop but didn't have enough treasures to trade.

"What about this?" Makbal emerged from behind a pile of trunks holding a diadem pinched between two fingers as though it might burn him. His feelings were a strange mixture of excitement and uncertainty, as though he worried Justine wouldn't be pleased.

Justine took the crown gently in her hands. It was a fragile thing, wrought of fine metal and woven together in a vine pattern. The metal had been shaped into leaves with veins etched in precise lines. Seed pearls of purple and white and pink clustered together reminiscent of dewdrops trapped on the leaves.

"It's perfect." Justine whirled around in search of a mirror, spotted one in the adjacent cavern, and ran to it. Her hair was a sopping mess from the ride through the current, but she set the diadem on her head anyway. It rested as light as air, but full of weight. She suddenly felt years older but in a good way. Justine straightened her spine, pulled back her shoulders.

"I'm now Queen," she whispered.

She managed to hold her somber pose a few moments before she dissolved into giggles. "What did I do to earn this life?"

"You made a deal with a damn hot demon," a woman's voice answered.

Justine turned and saw the speaker, a woman wearing pants, *green* pants no less, and a matching green shirt, with a blue coat over them that reached down to the elaborate ankle buckles of her boots. Her face was partially covered in shadow by a wide-brimmed hat the size of a serving platter. On a chain around her neck, Justine saw a gold key exactly like the ones the island gave the boys.

"You're here stealing from me, I suppose? Have you come alone?"

Justine looked around and realized she was alone. The only other people were the two constabulary-looking figures behind the woman. They wore the same green and blue clothes she wore, but no hats.

They've left me, thought Justine, but then she quieted this thought. If Makbal had fled for the dinghy, she would feel his absence. Instead, she sensed him quite close, almost as if he were right by her side.

And then he was. "How are you, Guine? The old hoard looks like its compounding interest nicely."

The barest ghost of a smile pressed the woman's lips. "Lord Mak. You haven't aged a day. So the island still holds. I'd heard otherwise."

"Yes, well. I'm sorry to say, we're on a tight schedule. Have to run."

He hates her.

And something else.

The hate was so overwhelming, Justine wanted to rush at the girl and start ripping through her with her bare hands.

"You know she's calling to me?"

Makbal stopped short. "I haven't the faintest—"

"The island. She's made an offer to anyone who can find their way up to her."

It hardly seemed possible, but Makbal seemed to go even stiller as though her words had struck him to stone. Justine felt nothing from him but the dimmest spark of consideration. And somehow, with the absence of the passion that'd been there moments before, this dim spark of consideration was even more frightening. She felt him trying to hide it from her.

Guine's eyes flicked to Justine, seeing her as though for the first time. "Your new savior seems a little old for you."

"As I said, nice seeing you." Makbal clenched his fingers against Justine's arm, pulling her backward. The added power of their connection through physical touch shocked Justine.

Makbal was a ball of nerves, screaming, rioting, making her feel the same.

"I can't allow you to take what I have earned." Guine appeared calm, even delighted to have caught Makbal stealing from her, while he was terrified, furious, and so many things Justine couldn't sort out. Her head ached, her vision swam.

"Earned is an idea we should discuss sometime." Makbal kept backing up. Justine couldn't feel her feet on the ground as she struggled to follow Makbal's retreat. She wished he'd hold her hand instead of steer her with her arm. She had so little control. If she stumbled and—

The passion returned in a rush, exactly as before.

He hates her.

And something else.

In this moment, Justine's foot caught on a statue. She fell backward with a yelp, pulling Makbal down on top of her.

"Get them!" yelled Guine in a voice that seemed only halfway serious, as though she too played life like a game.

Justine barely knew what was what as Makbal hauled her up and they began to run through the caverns. With her free hand, Justine held the diadem on her head. Not for all the gold in the world did such a woman as Guine deserve a beautiful crown. It was hers now.

In one cavern, they met up with Ian and Wapasha. In the next, Ling and Qassim emerged disheveled from behind a collection of weapons. As though to prove they'd been plundering, they seized some of the weapons and fell in at the rear of the group. Shouts sounded behind them. They passed one cavern intersection and nearly ran into more people in green and blue. These people carried guns. For a moment, they were just as surprised to find the invaders as the invaders were to find them. But that moment quickly passed. The guns were drawn, waved threateningly in the air.

"Stop or we'll shoot."

Makbal didn't stop. He steered Justine around to a side cavern, grabbing a particularly nice-looking carpet roll on his way. Justine saw the tunnel up ahead and felt her heart leap with hope.

Shots rang out.

A cry sounded. Justine would've stopped, but Makbal still had hold of her arm.

They were out of the tunnel. She nearly fell on the soft dirt of the bank as they stumbled, then tumbled over the side of the dinghy. Ian was right behind her, but he was the only one. She looked to Makbal in panic. He leapt back onto the landing and began to run toward the tunnel. Qassim and Ling were just coming out. Qassim had Ling's arm around his neck and was dragging him along, a trail of blood behind them. Wapasha covered their retreat, brandishing two spears. Makbal took one of them. He stepped past Wapasha and planted his feet at the tunnel entrance. With expert form that seemed impossible given the proportion of the spear compared to his small size, Makbal threw the spear into the tunnel. Shouts and curses sounded.

"Until next time, Guinnie!" Makbal ducked a bullet and sprinted back to the dinghy, nearly shoving Qassim and Ling over the side as he and Wapasha pushed off.

More gunshots. Justine huddled in the bottom of the boat. She felt the current catch and begin to pull them along. The gunshots faded until the only sound was Ling's pain-filled breathing echoing off empty cliff walls and the roar of the unseen falls rushing far above their heads.

They floated by more sections of the city, its residents going about their lives. No one noticed them until bells began to sound the alarm. People in green and blue poured out of the drinking houses and launched themselves into little boats tied up at docks. Makbal took the oars and began to row with the current. The rest of the city passed in a blur of movement and shouting and the horrible pepper of gunfire pockmarking the air, splintering pieces off the dinghy.

Justine held as still as she could, not breathing, praying to the god who she'd been taught heard prayers, and all the rest she'd been taught were evil pagan idols. Only when the dinghy began to tilt down into the water did she draw a full breath. Even then, it felt difficult. Carrying her portion of Makbal's feelings—he was still so very upset, so frightened—she couldn't find relief.

Not fear over Ling, thought Justine. *Or perhaps partially that.*

Who was that woman?

What were they to each other?

The thrill of the current passed almost without notice. Being underwater amplified the sound of Ling's staccato breathing. It grew quieter and quieter. Even before the dinghy fully resurfaced, Makbal began to row toward the island.

The gray light of morning cast the shadows of the mountains across the cove. The mer bobbed along the veil like a reception committee. Their red eyes tracked the dinghy to shore, their heads moved without a sound as though they were animated statues, soulless and dreadful.

As the sun crested the mountains, Justine could see that Ling had been shot in the leg. During the time they spent outside of eternal space—which was just the current's tunnel and the time it took to cross that side of the cove—the wound had healed over the bullet, leaving a small lump in the plane of his thigh. But it was the change in Ling's face that most shocked Justine. He seemed to have grown years in minutes. Justine had supposed him fifteen or sixteen, but now he appeared at least eighteen, with stubble on his chin.

"To heal the wound, time claimed more from him than us," said Makbal.

"Will he be able to swim the current?" asked Qassim.

"Doesn't matter," said Ling. "My keyhole's still missing. Probably won't ever reveal itself now."

"Don't say that," said Justine. "It will still come." She had no idea if any confidence came across in her voice. With Makbal still a pent-up ball of warring emotions, she had trouble placing herself in reality.

They beached the dinghy. Everyone else climbed out first, then stood around watching as Ling pulled himself to standing and gingerly stepped over the side of the boat. He walked a few steps, then grimaced.

The heads of the other boys swiveled toward Makbal, silent questions in their eyes.

"I don't know," he said. "We'll wait and see."

"Wait and see what?" asked Justine to no one in particular. The healing seemed miraculous. When they'd been in the current, Justine had thought he was dying. They should all be celebrating instead of acting like he'd been cursed.

A mer lounging in the shallows answered Justine's question. "Was the crown worth it, girlie? That poor boy's path has changed now."

"It wasn't my fault. We were—"

"You're Mother. Everything's your fault. That's how it works."

Justine kicked sand toward the mer. "That's just silly."

"He won't be able to swim against the current. When he passes on, he'll have to risk the falls. And he'll have to pass sooner now. Lord Mak won't want him to stay."

"I don't understand." Even as she spoke, Justine felt something new in Makbal's troubled spirit, something darker even than his fear. He was putting up a wall, pushing Ling away; the fact of him so undermined Makbal's idea of an island boy, he could think of no way to help him.

The mer flopped back on its back in the sand, twirling its

seaweed hair. "He really didn't tell you anything, did he? Don't you notice all the perfect boys?"

Justine thought immediately of Nacel, who wasn't like the others. She was about to hold him up as a counterexample, but then she stopped. That was exactly what the mer meant. Nacel wasn't like the others. Makbal had made a mistake with him somehow, and he didn't fit within the rules of the island. Makbal took almost no notice of Nacel, allowed him to live as an outcast. *Would Ling end up the same?*

"But this is all magic," said Justine. "There's no reason he can't swim as well as anyone else."

The mer shrugged. "An injury like that, the pain. It will undermine his faith. Plus, the road will be harder without a map."

"But there must be another way."

"There is." The mer untangled its finger from its hair and pointed. There, just coming around the western edge of the mountain island, was the *Osuana*.

New Stories

"I must away," said Makbal one night as he passed around the mind-tidying tea that helped the boys forget. A restless impatience rolled off him in waves. It'd been getting worse each day, but Justine had thought he was just in need of a good adventure to cancel out the memory of the last one.

"Now?" asked Justine, stabbing her finger with her mending needle. She was attempting to patch the holes in one of the past mother's nightgowns.

"I can't put it off any longer."

"But you're a god," said Jakob. "You can do whatever you want."

"Everyone has to be responsible sometimes." Makbal placed a hand on Jakob's head. "You're responsible to sleep sometimes, yeah?"

"And when we find ways to do impossible things," said Pah.

"When we must sharpen our knives," said Wapasha.

"So I must go above and watch for boys who should come to us," said Makbal. "While I'm gone, Justine will look after you, and you'll look after her." Makbal's gaze strayed to Ling and said, "By the time I get back, you'll be walking with full strength again."

The energy in his body told Justine this was a false sentiment. Makbal didn't expect Ling to walk well again. He was going to the world of the living for new children because he was expecting to lose one, though she couldn't tell how.

When Makbal went above ground to receive the fae dust blessing that would allow him to fly up through the clouds, Justine followed him. The night lay clear and smooth, a seamless blanket of stars over them, the moons in their half circles. The view never failed to make Justine's head swim with desire for a stroll along the water, her arm pressed into the strong crook of a gentleman's elbow.

She glanced at Makbal, certain he could read her thoughts and about to laugh at her. Instead, he smiled. "You'll be fine."

"What do we do if there's an invasion?"

"Hide in my cave. Tassi knows where it is."

"I don't trust Tassi."

"Good. You shouldn't. The fae pick no favorites except the givers of the best gifts."

A light blinked through the trees, first one, then two, then three.

"I could come with you." Justine edged closer to him, a flutter in her chest at the thought of being without him.

"Make up a new game while I'm gone."

"Will you bring me a girl?"

"I want only you."

"Yes, but . . . " Justine didn't know how to say what she was thinking. Didn't he feel her the same way she felt him? Couldn't he just understand her without needing a complicated explanation this once? The lights were almost on them. Justine was running out of time. She linked her elbow through Makbal's arm even though it hung straight at his side, disinterested.

Everything will go wrong if you leave. She closed her eyes and beamed this thought into him so he would realize how much she needed him, then she sent her wish to the island. *Make him stay.*

Silence.

Do this for me, and I'll be whatever you want me to be.

Still silence. Justine opened her eyes and saw the lights had come to a stop and hovered in the air before them so bright Justine had to squint to make out the bodies within the glow. Tassi carried a glass vial of dust. The fae next to them sang out a chime of high, cheerful notes.

In response, Makbal reached into his pocket and pulled out one of the gold coins stolen from the Green City. He also pulled out a strip of metal, flattened into a sheet like paper, then rolled. The fae chimed their thanks with what sounded like excitement. The two fae flew away with the gifts. Tassi flew up above Makbal's head and emitted one of those grating, staccato chimes that made Justine hate them.

"You're standing too close." Makbal pushed her away. "If you need it, Tassi will give you some tonic. But I don't think you'll need it." He beamed a boy's rogue grin at her as Tassi enveloped his head in shimmering dust.

At such a moment, Justine wanted to say, *I love you*, but the words felt wrong in her mouth. She didn't love him, not truly. And yet, she felt this preparation for separation like the sundering of the heavens at the Revelations. Her mind scrambled for a reason to make him stay even as she fought down bitterness that she wasn't enough. As the dust covered him, her anxiety and her bitterness became blanketed with an ebullient joy, a rushing of anticipation, as though she were about to fly away on an adventure herself.

So beautiful.

Makbal took a couple test jumps, each one lasting longer and taking him higher until he hovered off the ground. He set his hand on Justine's shoulder, the same way he did with the boys. "Remember, I expect a new game when I return."

Then he was off, a human shadow shrinking and blending into the dark sky. Justine watched him pass across the moon and the stars nearest to it, then she could no longer see him. Her gaze returned to the ground. Tassi remained hovering, seeming expectant.

"You stay away from me," said Justine. "I'll stay away from you."

Tassi flashed a bright light from their body that might have been agreement or irritation. They flew off, leaving her alone in the dark night. Justine drifted into her garden, taking deep calming breaths of the blossoms' perfumes to counteract the feeling that the very substance of her soul was draining away as Makbal flew from her. She sank her hand down on the bushes and let the thorns prick her skin. What relief! Over and over, she stabbed her hand until it was covered in sticky, pulsing dots of blood. Then, as quickly as flicking a switch, Makbal's presence was gone. She was alone in what felt like the first time in a lifetime. As she crossed the garden, she felt the island rise to greet her, vibrant and pulsing as though welcoming her from a long absence.

She laughed for the joy of it and twirled around with her arms thrust to the sky. It was evident now that Makbal's mind wasn't one of childlike freedom and innocence. He possessed lifetimes of adult experiences within him and kept them hidden if only for the possibility of pretending to be young and free. She wished, though only for a moment, she could call Makbal back and tell him she understood, that they were both walking paths trying to claim things they wanted but hadn't been allowed to have. But having him back would have returned his presence to her mind and Justine didn't wish that for anything. The world felt new and bright and incandescently full of possibility.

That afternoon, she took the younger boys on a twirling adventure through the meadows where they spun like tops, then crashed into each other and made boy-shaped silhouettes in the crushed grass. That night, when the boys gathered for story time, Justine declared herself on vacation from story-telling. "I simply cannot do it tonight. My head's empty of stories. One of you lot will have to do it for me, or else we shall have to go to bed with our minds empty."

"But I don't want to do anything bad," said Pah. "Or I won't get my key."

"It isn't going to hurt you," said Ling.

"What about our drink?" asked Jakob.

In her excitement, Justine had forgotten all about the potion. Ian was in the pantry preparing it and she didn't want to discourage his effort at being helpful, so she said, "You may drink as you wish, but you don't have to take it."

"Lord Mak says we have bad dreams without it," said Momoaro.

"If you have a bad dream, you can come find me in bed." Justine sat down on the mattress and patted it. Momoaro plopped down beside her.

"I can tell the story tonight," said Olewendo.

"Sit here," said Qassim. "Or they won't hear you above." He dragged Makbal's armchair close to the fire so Olewendo's story would travel up the chimney.

Olewendo sat, then looked around the circle of expectant faces. A hush fell over the group. Even Jakob, who'd been walking around with the tea, went still in anticipation of the first word.

"This is the story about a princess who lost her hair, and the boy named Muoma who found it for her after a long and dangerous adventure." Olewendo paused, then added, "My grandmother used to tell me this story."

"What's a grandmother?"

"Shh!"

As Olewendo told about the princess with beautiful hair who refused to give a small bit of it to a bird for its nest and thus lost her hair as a result, Justine felt a new layer of magic descend on the island. She'd always been the storyteller, with her mind focused on the events of the story, of animating her voice to bring characters to life. Because of this, she'd never been able to notice the effect her work had in the moment. She felt the change in the air, a stirring of nature as the island took up Olewendo's story and wove it into the larger world.

The next morning, the boys set out to replicate Muoma's quest to find the tree that grew hair and the magic seeds that grew it. They called to each other the poem of the bird:

I am he who knows, knows,

That the wind blows, blows,

That the water flows, flows;

Here the tree of hair grows, grows,

I am he who knows, knows.[1]

That day, Justine took a walk alone. The island guided her to the coast, then down along the cliffs. She strained her eyes as though to peel back the veil and see that other world, the adult world full of things she knew, but no longer felt, were real: growing older, keeping time, a schedule. She tried to imagine what it would be like to be among them, the Delt villagers, adults with adult sensibilities and desires. *I could take the dinghy and cross over. Just a visit. I could be back in time for supper.*

An image flashed across her mind, a man's body, dripping as he emerged from the lake in the golden sunlight, the power of those thick, muscled limbs.

"You're a silly girl to think there's someone over there to love you, Justine."

---

1. From, *The King's Daughter Who Lost Her Hair*. African Folktales, Ed Roger D. Abrahams. Pantheon

The island thrummed beneath her feet, an answer Justine couldn't interpret. What did the island know of life beyond the veil anyway?

THAT NIGHT, AS SHE ENTERED THE SLEEPING CAVE, JUSTINE startled a heated conversation among the boys into sudden, suspicious silence.

"What's all this then?" she asked, searching their faces for the one who looked the most guilty, as he would surely be the one to reveal their secret. Jakob looked the most guilty, but he ran away to the kitchen to pour the tea.

"Mother, we've thought of a game," said Ian.

"I want to say it," said Pah.

"Alright, say it."

The little boy threw open his arms. "We're going to build you a castle!"

Justine laughed as she gathered him in her arms and they rolled together on the mattress. "A castle?"

"'Every queen needs a castle.' That's what you said."

"Tonight, I'm telling the story," said Ling, his eyes dark with purpose.

"And tomorrow, you should wish the island to give you a book of the story with pictographs so we can see what it looks like," said Qassim.

"Oh, I think that's taking storytelling a bit too far," said Justine. "You're meant to be moving forward without the weights of the adult world."

"It can be allowed for a good reason," said Ling. "This is a good reason." He limped over to Justine's mattress and sat where she always sat. With surprising authority, he waved her toward Makbal's chair.

Justine hesitated, alarmed by the conflict that had arisen

within her. She felt the echo of Makbal telling her this wasn't a good thing. And yet, some truer, older part of her rejoiced at the boys' plan.

Ling cleared his throat and sat up tall. "This is the story of Kuan Yin, whose name means 'one who hears the cries of the world.' And she was a princess both beautiful and wise."

It was a gorgeous story, not just in its meaning, but in Ling's telling. Justine supposed after listening to so many stories, he'd made a study of how one told a good one. She thought perhaps he'd done this many times with different mothers, keeping his past alive every time Makbal went on a journey. *Is that why the island has refused to reveal his keyhole?*

Then an errant thought, *Have I ruined Makbal's perfect island?* Justine shook her head. She couldn't feel guilt for this. It felt right. If the stories meant the boys remained on the island longer than they would have otherwise, she didn't regret that either.

In the morning, as the boys had instructed her, Justine went out to the bright dawn and wished for a Kuan Yin storybook with pictures. The boys raced each other to catch it as it fell from the sky. They spent a nacel looking at the pictures of the king's palace, which was unlike anything Justine had seen before, with layers of golden roofs stacked on top of each other like squashed squares, their corners pulled upward in lopsided smiles.

It was Nacel himself, emerging from the woods, who drew their attention to the strange clouds that had formed over the grasslands. Some were white, as clouds should be, but others appeared in pastel shades of blues and pinks and yellows, and they moved like balls bouncing on the ends of strings.

A boy named Matteo was in a particularly adventurous mood. When a cloud happened to fall close to the ground, he leaped upon it and found, to everyone's surprise, that he could stand upon it and, as long as he moved quickly to another cloud, he didn't sink. Soon, many boys were playing this new game of cloud hopping, laughing and shoving each other as though gravity was no longer something to be feared. Tassi buzzed out of the woods like an angry hornet to investigate. When they saw what was going on, they gave Justine such a look of ire, she felt her skin burning.

THE NEXT NIGHT, QASSIM TOLD THE STORY OF PRINCESS Scheherazade, who was a storyteller herself. He regretted that he didn't remember as many of her stories as he knew there had been. But he knew enough of them that the night was half over and the youngest boys had fallen asleep by the time his words were spent.

When Justine wished for a picture book the next morning, a giant tome fell from the sky, its pictures brilliantly rendered in bright colors with silver and gold around their edges like framed paintings.

On the fourth night, Ian said he would share a story, but not a princess story. Instead, he told of kings and wars and their stone fortresses. Justine forgave him for all the passion he used to describe the killing of English soldiers. But she couldn't help but laugh the next night when Matteo announced he would share the story of Robin Hood, which turned out to be the story of a red fox that walked on its back legs and sang a cheerful song; Matteo taught it to the whole group.

The nights went on in this way. The storybooks became a stack beside the mending basket, until finally, Nacel announced it was his turn. He walked to the end of her mattress and sat down. Beside him sat the rabbit-not-rabbit creature the boys had named Rogue. Its long ears hung down the side of its face like a hound, but its posture matched Nacel's, stiff with performed importance.

The other boys all took up their listening posts, not quite sure what to expect. Nacel was so easily a forgotten part of them, a shadow perpetually lurking in their footsteps, until something scared him and he made such noise that nothing could be thought of except his agony. But as Justine considered it, she realized he'd been around more than usual. She'd awoken once or twice in the middle of the night to find him in the cave, not sleeping, but wandering, making patterns between the furniture, studying the walls. He never seemed to sleep.

Nacel set his hand on a spot of discolored fur on Rogue's back. Rogue opened its mouth and said, "My real name is Fetu, but I don't care if you call me Nacel. My mother was the queen of an island. Her castle was a hut bigger than this room with walls and a roof made from palm leaves. There are no storybooks about her life or mine even though I guess I was a prince. If I had lived, I would've been married off to the princess of another tribe. But some people on our island didn't want me to live because I was strange to them. So I did not live. And now I'm here, which is better. But sometimes I miss my true mother."

A heavy silence filled the cave. Fetu lifted his hand off Rogue, who promptly curled up, clapped its ears over its eyes and went to sleep. A sob sounded somewhere behind Justine. Then, over by the pantry, another.

"I miss my mother too," said Momoaro. "Why can't we go home?"

This is why Makbal doesn't let them think of their old lives, thought Justine. *It makes what they've lost too present.*

"This is our home," said Qassim. "We can't go back. Only forward." He stood up and walked over to Momoaro, took him firmly by the shoulders the way Makbal did. "Don't fall apart on me little brother. We're building a castle, remember? That's why we've given our stories."

"And hey, we should celebrate," said Ian. "Nacel—I mean Fetu—has found a way to talk."

"I bet Rogue's an alien," said Matteo. "Remember that movie?"

"I think I do," said Jakob. His story about the princess of Ergetz had given some of the boys nightmares and he had been trying to make amends by being agreeable.

Ian took the stack of storybooks and spread them out on the floor. The boys gathered around and began to flip through them frowning, considering, twisting their heads this way and that.

"The castle should have a moat like Nottingham's," said Jakob. "So we can escape the towers when they're on fire and swim to safety."

"And tall, golden spires," said Ian.

"With flags?" asked Momoaro, still sniffling.

They looked to Justine.

"Flags would be great."

"And what else?" asked Ling.

"An orange grove," said Qassim with longing.

Justine's eyes traced the open pages of the books. From each picture of a castle or palace, she took a piece and put it together with other pieces in her mind until she had a complete building on the outside. Then she tried to imagine what it would be like inside. She pictured a huge space that was also cozy, a hard stone place filled with growing things and cushions and windows to let the breezes through.

Before she had really thought through what she was doing, Justine moved from imagining to wishing. She felt a small drop as though her heart fell from her chest, down through the packed earth floor, down into the island. She fell back against the support of Makbal's chair, suddenly so very tired.

Above them and very far away a thump sounded, then a

splash, like the sloshing of a giant tub of bathwater. The ground beneath their feet shook.

"Is it here?" asked Jakob. "Can we go see?"

Justine leaned her head against the side of the chair, barely able to keep her eyes open. "You go on and look. I can't right now. I'm so . . ."

Then she was asleep. Not just an ordinary sleep of course, but the sleep demanded of a body after a great amount of work had been done. Even on a magic island, one couldn't expect to wish a brand-new castle into being and not pay a price for it.

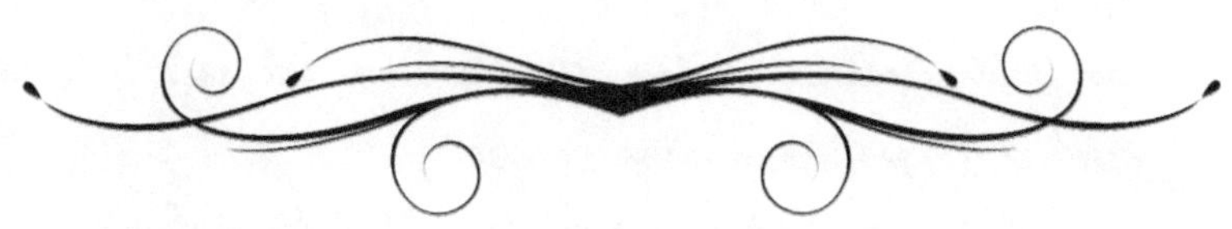

CHAPTER 24

One Man's Past, One Girl's Future

The boy god who became a voyager, then a pirate, allowed time and its companion, disappointment, to corrupt him, just as the mer were corrupted, so he no longer remembered who he had once been. He oscillated between extremes of rage and apathy. In one state, violence unmeasurable. In the other, a stillness so complete life seemed to have left him.

Before the mer ate his hand, he had carried in him only one reason for living. It was the promise of the woman he loved. Those few words spoken to his bruised ego which promised the fates had written them a future.

I chose not to change you or do anything that would alter what happens for you next, Thessaly had said. Because I love you the way you are. And I'll be there waiting for you.

But he had failed to find her. And the future she'd promised seemed out of his grasp. A woman like that could never love the man he had become. He had made himself unworthy of her, and because he could not find a way back, he pressed his existence around a new purpose, to destroy his brother and everything he loved.

What the brother loved most was himself. What he loved second was to play. In this way, when he began to bring mothers to the island, he wanted them to be the kind who blended in as quickly as possible, the kind who did not ask too many questions. But these traits were hard to find in girls who were also self-possessed enough they could tap into the power of the island and keep the pirates away.

The first Wendy was a test case. Before he found her, we weren't even sure the idea of replacing the Black Hook with a girl would work. The brother was sloppy, creating the bond because he'd never made one of that kind before. But somehow it worked. The next time the pirates crossed the veil, the combined power of her with the brother banished them back to time. There was a period of peace during Wendy's reign. No matter what the Black Hook tried, his efforts were rebuffed. If Wendy had not been filled with a sense of obligation to her dead parents, much might have been different. But the brother was foolish enough to let her go, believing her to be easily replaced. We had no way of knowing a fae defector would go to the Black Hook and tell him about the Mother plan.

The next three mothers were lost to the pirates before a bond could be made. Others failed to be powerful enough to fit the Mother role. Several more were too old and set in their ways to be the malleable character the brother needed. Of course, the ghost of the lost girl haunted him. Unable to bear the possibility that a girl would betray him again, the brother took to killing any mother he believed was unfaithful. And so, the cycle continued until the last mother came.

Here, I will go back and say some things about the village the pirates called home. Not all the children who lived in time thought of themselves as pirates. They called themselves Delts. In the time of mothers, only a few Delts who had been children when the island divided remained. Of them, the woman known as the Tigress, was one of the few who had managed to gain the Black Hook's confidence. As he descended into the violence that earned him his name, she became the voice of opposition. First, she attempted to broker peace between the brothers. Then she attempted to sway the Black Hook from outright murder. And then, when the deaths of mothers began to rise, she split herself from the pirate crew and formed her own group of Delts who made it their mission to steal the mothers away from the island before either brother could harm them.

The Tigress did not do this because she possessed a soft heart or any particular compassion toward girls. She did it because one night, when the Black Hook was just a voyager with a desperate heart and wounded pride and whatever else he experienced when the devious god Ankou sent him off on that rescue mission, he'd told her an impossible story to explain the impossible existence of Thessaly the god who had once been a mortal.

"They told us the island wouldn't work," he said. "It hadn't ever been done before. They said it was cheating to create a holding place for souls, to train them how to be worthy of the afterlife they wanted. But we did it."

"Of course you did." She laughed. Maybe then she was a little in love with him. His sadness makes him a better person, she thought. In those early days there had been an opening when he might have made himself better for his experiences. Instead, he became something else, which was harder to love.

"It must not be a coincidence that I met an impossible god," he said. "What if . . . " He trailed off, his hand absently tracing the line of wood flooring in the small, stone house where he'd made a home with the lost girl. "What if the island made a god?"

"Then you'd know about it."

"Would I?"

"How would it work?"

He shook his head. "Thessaly knew me. And since I didn't know her, I have to think that means she met me as a mortal. Then she became a god."

"But she didn't tell you when you met on her side?"

"She was damnably careful with what she said. But I'm sure she knew everything about me, the island, our problems." His face contorted as he inhaled the memory of his beloved Thessaly, root of all their troubles. "She smelled like the island."

"So, eventually she will come here as a mortal, and you will meet her for the second time, but it will be new to her."

"Maybe." He laughed. "I'm losing my mind, aren't I?"

They'd laughed about it. He seemed to forget the idea. Or perhaps, as he descended into bloody vengeance, he began to hope his idea was wrong.

But the Tigress did not forget. When a new boy captured from the island told the story of the Black Brothers and the girl who made them human again, the Tigress listened with interest. She felt a glimmer of possibility that perhaps both pirate and island might be saved.

Only half believing her foolish dream, she stole a photo from the Black Hook's cabin. The caption at the bottom of the photo described a woman named Thessaly Green, founder of the nonprofit The Necessary Limb, which provided medical care and equipment to amputees who otherwise couldn't afford it. The woman in the photo did not match the Tigress's idea of a goddess. But hope was thin, and even if all she had to hope for was the woman in that photo, it was more than nothing.

On a dark night, when the lost boys once again attacked the pirate ship, the Tigress found herself staring into the face of that woman. Except she was still a girl. And both her arms were made of flesh.

"I've found her," she told him when the dust of the fight had settled. "She's here."

"Who?"

"Thessaly. She's the new mother."

The Tigress did not anticipate the agony that burned across the Black Hook's face as the truth sank in. There was a first blush of it, then a deeper flame of despair as the next level of under-standing took hold. At last, their paths had crossed, but she was not the woman who had entranced him. Even worse, she belonged to his brother, a fate no girl had yet to survive.

"It isn't her," he said.

End of conversation.

deeper flame of despair as the next level of under-standing took hold. At last, their paths had crossed, but she was not the woman who had entranced him. Even worse, she belonged to his brother, a fate no girl had yet to survive.

CHAPTER 25
Once Upon a Dream

J ustine's sleep was deeper than true sleep. She fell so far down within it that she stepped outside of herself and saw the castle she had made: its moat and tall spires, the oriental stacked roofs and lattices, and the island huts in the courtyard for banquets, the white columns of Rome, the wrought metal gates of Buckingham, and the orange grove.

It was an easy thing for her mind to walk through the grand foyer with its double staircase, its round, vaulted ceiling with the chandelier, the library full of books she couldn't read, the kitchen and pantry, and all the bedrooms, which Justine had wished would each be decorated to represent the past life of one person who lived on the island, the way the Great Exhibition had represented all parts of the empire.

She found herself in a room much like a picture she'd seen once of Princess Louise's bedroom, an elegant vanity, a dollhouse in the window seat, a four-poster bed lined with gauzy curtains. In the bed, with her hair all spread around her on the pillow, Justine lay sleeping with her stolen diadem of pearls perched on her head.

I'm dreaming.

Somewhere in the recesses of her mind, she wondered about the boys, where they were, what they were doing. But mostly she admired her castle. Perhaps she did this for a good, long while.

Vines grew up the castle walls and came in through the windows. Dust gathered on the dollhouse and the unused pots in the kitchen.

I think I've slept long enough, Justine decided. She tried to open her eyes and return to her body but found she couldn't. This didn't bother her as it should have. The vines sprouted flowers and seed pods. At night, fae came and fertilized them. Justine didn't see Tassi among them.

When it seemed the castle would be swallowed up in vines, a man came up to the gate. He cut through the vines holding it shut and walked in like it was his castle instead of hers. Justine followed along behind him, admiring the strong cut of his clothes, the line of his broad shoulders, the confidence in his stride as he climbed the staircase two steps at a time and hacked his way down the corridor to her room.

As Justine followed, she no longer felt certain this was her life she was watching. No man lived on the island. And there was something familiar about this story, which made it not her own.

Real or not, Justine enjoyed watching the stranger work so hard to reach her room. She saw the curly black hairs at the back of his neck turn slick with sweat. She felt the corded muscles straining beneath his clothes.

At the moment of his triumph, she rushed ahead to the bedroom so she might get in front of him and see his face. But when she arrived, he was already there, bending over the Justine in the bed, resting his lips on hers. They touched. Rather than withdraw, he pressed closer, drawn down as the Justine in the bed threw her arms around him, then her legs.

Justine woke with a start. Her face was wet. When she touched it, she found blood. She'd bitten her lip in her sleep. She was also damp all over, as though she'd been the one hacking through a castle full of overgrown vines.

"How long have I been asleep?" she asked.

Something moved in her peripheral vision, and she turned to see Rogue at the foot of the bed blinking at her with that irritated expression of being awoken too early.

The room appeared just as it had in her dream, a Princess Louise bedroom, except her window was open to the breeze. She could see the forest and, beyond it, the rocky beach of the island shore. Justine blinked sleep-drenched eyes. Something about her view wasn't quite right. The trees there were too tall, and where had their leaves gone?

Perhaps a spot of time has come to the island like before. She was too sleepy to worry over what it meant that time was on the island. The thought passed through her mind slowly, clouded with the fog of sleep. But then it sharpened and became a thing she could understand.

What she saw on the shore of the island were not dead trees, but the masts of a ship.

"Pirates!"

Justine sprang out of bed only to have her feet collapse beneath her. She picked herself up, slapped her palms against her thighs to get the blood moving, then stumbled toward the door.

Nacel met her just on the other side. He was clapping his hands together looking all around to try to understand why she was upset.

"Nacel." She hugged him in relief. "I mean, Fetu. The pirates are here."

The boy seemed to calm down. If pirates were the only problem, it was one that didn't bother him.

"Where are the others?"

Justine didn't wait for an answer but prepared to go out at once. How long had she been asleep? Did asking how long even matter in this place?

Thinking came in clumps of clarity stuffed into boxes of dull dreamscape.

The castle was beautiful.

The castle was perfect.

And around every turn she expected to find the man who had dared to kiss her. She could taste him on her lips. If he was here, she didn't want to meet him in her nightgown, so she imagined a dress of rough, woven fabric suitable for heavy use. It flew in through the library window as she passed. The wind came with it and arranged her hair so when she entered the kitchen she appeared as presentable and as adult as she could possibly be.

The boys were making a gleeful mess as two fae flew around trying to teach them how to cook.

"Mother!" cried Ian when he spotted her in the doorway. "We're learning breakfast."

"Pirates," gasped Justine. A question or an announcement?

"They've been here two days, I think," said Ian. "Or maybe three. They came up to the gate, but the gate wouldn't let them in. Now they're down at the lake. Qassim and Ling are watching them."

Justine smacked the palm of her hand against the side of her head a few times as though this would clear the cobwebs. "So, you're all safe."

"I burned my finger." Jakob held up his forefinger for Justine to kiss and make better. She put on a smile even though she still wasn't quite sure she was awake, that everything was fine. Something.

Something.

"*Who* is watching the pirates?"

"Ling and Qassim."

The something clicked into place. "Oh no. No, no."

"What's wrong, Mother?"

"I need to go. You all stay here. Don't anyone leave the castle."

If she had been asked, Justine couldn't have explained the thought that drove her out the castle gates, down the grassy slope of the hill where it stood, and into the woods. It was more a feeling than a thought. The work of the island had been soured for Ling. He no longer believed in its purpose. And somewhere, buried deep in her swamp of a mind, Justine knew when belief was lost something must always replace it.

Justine's headlong run came to an abrupt halt just past the edge of the forest. The trees around her weren't the trees she knew. In fact, they were the same, but much older, with gnarled bark and trunks so wide she couldn't wrap her arms around them. Their canopies towered over the other trees. Without realizing it, Justine had entered a runnel of time.

She began to run again. The runnel of old trees seemed to go on and on, but eventually she felt a small pop in her chest, as though breaking through the surface of water, and the trees were once again the trees she knew. Coral Falls Lake was just ahead. She slowed down to calm herself, to prepare for what she might find.

"Makbal will be very upset if I get myself captured."

The idea of being captured didn't seem entirely terrible, but she didn't want to be separated from her boys. They needed her.

She sent her awareness into the heels of her feet, felt how the island reached up to touch her back, a reassuring caress that swept over Justine like a warm blanket. Without Makbal's dominating presence, the old Justine strode forth, determined, angry. She, who was queen of an island and belonged to no one, would banish the pirates on her own and protect her boys before they could do the foolish thing they'd attempted before. It seemed so long ago now, almost as though it had never happened.

A rustle in the shrubbery—voices. Wind whipped leaves on the ground, pointing her way forward. Each step seemed a confirmation of her path, the island wouldn't fail her.

"I am Queen Justine. This is my island. And I don't want you here."

She repeated this quietly to herself with each step until she could hear the voices clearly. Deep baritones mixing with tenors, calling to each other, laughing even.

Taking a few steps to her left, Justine found herself in the bushes at the edge of the lake where she'd first exchanged her stolen asylum nightshift for the nightgown of a princess. She knelt and poked her head through. Bobbing in the sun-sparkled water, she counted eleven pirates, the island's supposed terrifying invaders, splashing around like the children they'd once been.

She pulled her head back from the shrubbery, circled it, and crept in again for a different view. On the bank of the lake, the pirates had laid out their clothes with surprising order. Each man had folded his leggings and tunic, set his belt on top along with his weapons. Everything out in the open and easy to steal. If Makbal were with her, he could have defeated his most dreaded enemies in a few moments.

Most of the clothes piles also contained extra items which marked them as doers of dark deeds. Justine found a sling, two eye patches, a wooden leg, and there, at the end, shining even brighter than the sun on the water, was a metal hook attached to a wooden cup, to which was attached a series of straps to hold the cup in place.

Not daring to breathe, Justine crept even closer. The clothes folded below the hook were lined with little loops of thread, all finely stitched, though a little strange to look at. She wondered about those little loops and their purpose on such a fine garment. The jacket was dyed the richest black with silver trim and lined with matching buttons. Below it lay black trousers and a crisp white shirt.

The clothes of the Black Hook, thought Justine with a shiver.

A rush of disturbed water. She looked up to find a swath of skin almost upon her, dripping, dazzling in a way Justine had never thought skin might be in sunlight. Before, she would have sought a label for him that fit with the races of her time, but she could no longer remember them. Her brain could summon only a single word for the brown sheath of the pirate emerging from the lake—beautiful.

Of course his skin was marred with nicks and scars, the legacy of a long life of violence. But these small things Justine noticed only in passing, for the overall effect of this giant person, a full adult, shaking water from his head, brushing it from his beard, stretching long, powerful muscles, left her mind empty of everything else. The glare of the sun kept her from seeing his face, but when he turned back toward the water and began to dress, she knew him.

The man from her dream.

The kiss she could still taste.

Beneath her palm the island pulsed toward her, a series of small beats, the jitter of fallen leaves.

The man tilted his head as though he also felt the island. He twisted around toward the shrubbery and raised his arm to part them. Where his hand would have been there was only a smooth curve of skin. Just as this moment, when Justine might finally have seen his face, she ducked back out of sight, crawled a short distance, then jumped up and ran.

Tears streamed down her face. She didn't feel them until

she reached her rose garden. Here the spirit of the island was strongest. Here there was no mistaking its intent.

"Island," she gasped, then she screamed, "Are you out of your ever-loving mind?" She drove both her hands into the thorns and thrashed them around until her skin was a masticated mess of bloody tissue. The blood looked real, but the pain made it more so.

She understood now, the still small voice that had been telling her something was wrong. That voice was the island. Selfish, stupid island, that had decided she couldn't be happy with Makbal. The island didn't want Makbal on the island at all. It wanted him. The Black Hook. Murdering, kidnapping, pirate. And it would give her no peace until she claimed him.

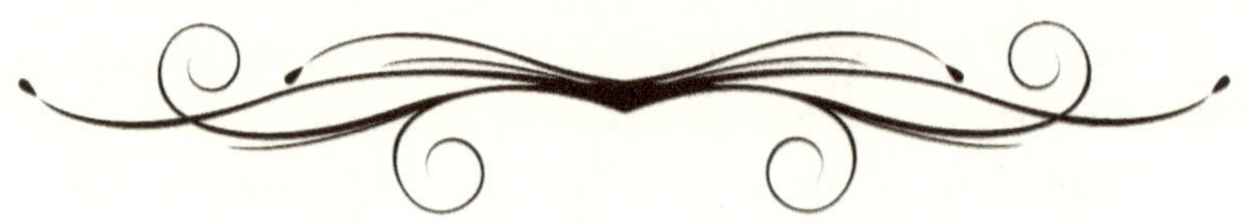

CHAPTER 26

Family Meeting

L ing and Qassim found her there in the garden, her hair in disarray, her skin splotched, and hands bloodied. They didn't ask what had upset her. Perhaps they already knew, had always known. Perhaps this was how it had happened over and over, an innocent girl trapped in an ageless battle between good and evil. Except she was far from innocent and barely a girl.

By the looks on their faces, she knew what they'd come to say.

"They said we can set up in town if we like."

You can't trust their promises, thought Justine. But she said nothing because it felt like a thought from somewhere else.

"You can always come back," she said, even though she didn't know if that was true.

"Do you want to come with us?"

This offer was unexpected. It rang through Justine like a bell falling from its tower, shocking at first in its clanging, then slowly fading away into the place lost thoughts fell.

"I'm needed here."

"We'll try to convince them not to invade for a while," said

Qassim. "There are four runnels in the forest. As soon as Lord Mak returns, you'll make sure and heal them, right?"

Justine nodded. She reached for each of their free hands and squeezed them tight in her bloody hands. "I hope the life you build is as wonderful as what we've had here."

"I hope you also find something wonderful," said Ling. For a moment, it looked like he would say more, perhaps to warn her of something, but Qassim was pulling his hand. Together, they walked into the forest.

It took a great deal of effort for Justine to rise to her feet and even more strength she didn't know she had to climb up to the tree house's central platform where she'd left the trunk of nightgowns.

One by one, Justine laid out each gown until she sat in an expanding circle of cloth. Twenty-four nightgowns for twenty-four past mothers. Before, she'd thought the pirates had killed them. But now it seemed possible the island itself had played a role. Makbal's deep fears of betrayal no longer felt irrational. She lay on the gowns and curled into a ball. She listened and listened. But the island was silent.

WHEN JUSTINE WOKE, THE THIN LIGHT OF A NEW MORNING warmed her face, and bodies were falling from the sky. Three of them, careening and tumbling madly through the air. Far in the distance she heard the shouts of her boys running out to meet the new arrivals.

Justine pounded stiff limbs into submission to climb up to the top platform, which allowed her a view over all but the tallest trees. The *Osuana* was anchored far out to sea. It didn't fire cannon or musket at the new boys.

"So he returns."

An image came unbidden to her mind, a line of flesh dappled with water droplets sparkling in the sunlight.

The wrong he. *Island, enough. Stop the nonsense.*

"Talking to yourself now?"

Justine whirled in surprise. Makbal hovered beside the platform railing, hands on hips, grinning his rogue's grin. Her heart leapt out to him, so very pleased. And yet. Justine felt it was not a true reaction. The bond had taught her to want him and always consider his needs above her own. Now it yearned for her to reach out and touch him. She dug both hands into the railing, holding on as though braced against a gale force wind. "The island doesn't want me with you."

Makbal suddenly dropped below the railing, his flying power sputtering as the fae pixie dust faded. He pulled himself over the railing.

"What's happened?"

"I've been having dreams of someone I don't know. And sometimes when I walk, the island suggests things."

For a long moment, Makbal stared at her without moving, not even blinking. It was clear from his gaze that he wasn't truly seeing her, but rather the object of his gaze existed in his mind, and Justine was only a background fixture. Suddenly Makbal dropped to his knees. He pitched himself forward and pounded his fists into the platform with an agonized scream as though the life had been torn from his bones.

Over and over, Makbal pounded his fists into the platform as he released one cry after another. He might have been an ancient pagan, kneeling before an altar, begging his god for mercy or justice or, perhaps in this case, revenge.

How does one take revenge on an island they created?

The platform began to splinter. Justine jumped back to avoid the flying shards. She'd known since the Green City that Makbal was stronger than his slight body suggested. But this was much more than she'd imagined. Before her eyes, the logs of the platform dented, then cracked open under his blows. If he carried on for much longer, the platform would collapse and they would fall a good, long way to the ground.

Justine knelt, tried to get her arms around him. "Mak. Mak, tell me what can be done. What does it mean?"

He threw himself down into the platform twice more before her words seemed to reach him.

"I must speak to the mothers," he said. "This time, they'll see reason and let me kill him."

"I don't understand. Would you just bloody talk to me for once? I'm not a child."

"Yes," he said. "I know that now. I was a fool to think this time would be any different than the last."

He stood up and walked off the edge of the platform. Justine heard him land on the ground with a gentle thump, then he was off, running toward the cliffs. Justine looked up at the peaks that made a wall around one side of the island. Dark storm clouds gathered. She realized it had never rained on the island. These clouds and what they portended weren't the same as what she'd known in her old world. As the sky grew darker and darker, Justine dragged herself back to the castle. Ian met her at the gate.

"The fae say Qassim and Ling left the island."

"Yes."

"Am I the new first boy then?"

The question came with just enough uncertainty that it brought Justine's racing brain to a halt and redirected her focus. She met Ian's gaze and held it. "I suppose you are."

He swallowed and she couldn't tell if the new responsibility excited him or scared him. Maybe it was both. Being Makbal's second-in-command wasn't an easy job. "I've gathered the three new boys in a bedroom," said Ian. "I thought, now that we have a castle, they'd be more comfortable here than in the Canopy. What do you want to tell them while we wait for Lord Mak?"

They had reached the castle doors and passed through to the grand entrance. Justine sank down on the first step of the right staircase.

"Tell them?" she asked.

"About how they've come here."

"Mak didn't explain that to them when he chose them?"

Ian tilted his head to one side, puzzled. "When new boys arrive, he gives them a speech, remember? But it appears he's going to be busy for a while." Ian looked out the window where rain had begun to fall in a great silver sheet that cloaked the view with an impenetrable downpour.

"How many mothers do you remember, Ian?"

"I'm not sure, I—two, I suppose."

"And what happened to the last one?"

"Eaten by sea creatures when she crossed the veil."

"Had she done anything to upset Makbal before that happened?"

The boy's mouth worked like he was deciding how best to form the lie he already knew how to tell. Justine slapped him on the knee. "Come now. This isn't hard. The pirates claimed her?"

"No."

"The Delts from town then?"

Ian shook his head. He paced down the length of the entryway, tapped his feet against the stone floor, turned, and walked back to her. "She was killed in the Green City on an adventure."

"Why is that such a big secret?"

"We left her behind." Tears filled Ian's eyes. His face crunched in on itself in the effort to hold them back. "We could've saved her, but Lord Mak made us run. He said nothing could be done." Ian's hands made fists that he brought to either side of his head, as though wanting to crush out the memory.

"Did Mak go up to meet with his mothers before that happened?"

"I don't remember. Maybe. There aren't many meetings. Only when something big is wrong."

When Mak and the island aren't in agreement, he calls in reinforcements.

Sloppy, padding footsteps sounded on the stone. Fetu emerged from the doorway beneath the left stairs. Rogue walked beside him. "We know the way up the cliffs," they said.

"You read my mind," said Justine. "Who wants to go adventuring?"

THEY HAD NO CLOTHES TO WEAR AGAINST THE RAIN BECAUSE IT never rained on the island, so they simply started out the castle door. Fetu took the lead with Rogue, who scrunched up its eyes and hissed in protest before stepping out into the deluge with Justine and Ian behind them. They crossed the grassy hills and descended into the forest.

Here, the trees blocked some of the force of the rain, but the noise of it pounding the leaves above made Justine feel like she was trapped in a giant cage being swallowed by a flood. Water filled the low ground revealing gullies and rivulets that hadn't been visible in the island's perpetually fair weather. By the time they reached the base of the cliffs, the forest floor had become a series of streams, some of them so wide and rushing they carried their own currents. Fetu was nearly washed away as he stepped into one without realizing its power.

Many paths ascended the cliffs. Indeed, as Justine began the slow climb up the path Fetu chose, a veritable labyrinth of possible other paths presented themselves as streams. Justine had to concentrate to stay close so as not to lose sight of Fetu. One wrong turn would surely have led her into a wilderness of caves and aimless wandering.

Staying close enough to keep Fetu in sight became more

and more difficult the higher they climbed. Without the shelter of the trees, the rain poured down on them so thick it felt more solid than liquid, as though Justine was walking through an endless wall. She struggled for breath. She struggled to see even the hand she held out in front of her face to help feel her way. Water ran down the path over her feet making the rocks slippery. In some places, small rivers of rocks rushed down the path and needed to be avoided.

By the time Fetu held up his hand to signal they had reached the summit, Justine was so tired she had no idea how she would climb back down after their adventure was over. Despite her exhaustion, Justine felt a familiar longing in her chest. Makbal was nearby. This presented a problem she hadn't considered. If she could sense him, he could probably sense her. This visit wouldn't be secret. But then, she reminded herself, they hadn't renewed the bond since his return. Her awareness of him remained shallow, a dim itch at the back of her mind she could easily ignore. She hoped, as Makbal was in such a state, he wouldn't notice her.

Fetu led them into a cave with a circular tunnel that wrapped around the summit. Though the echo of the rain outside made quite a din, it was still possible to hear voices made indistinct by the storm. When Fetu stopped where the cave opened into an outcropping and looked down on a platform of smooth rock sheltered all around by other rocks, the voices became clear.

The three of them wiggled to the edge of the outcropping and peered down. It was easy to see because, though the rain fell all around, it didn't fall within the platform, which appeared completely dry. A silver coffee set encrusted with jewels sat on a stone table between two giant stone chairs. Two giant women filled those chairs, sipping steaming drinks.

Perhaps it wasn't quite true to call them women. They seemed both human, with the regular human parts, but also not human, because of their size and because a set of gray-blue wings extended from the back of one, and the other had the tentacles of an octopus instead of two legs, dark blue on top with soft, emerald-green flesh between the suction cups. It was this contrast of blue and green in such specific shades that told Justine this octopus woman was Coleodal, Goddess of the Falls Eternal. Thus, the one with wings was surely Goddess of the Mountain. Together they ruled the realms of eternity. Or at least, they ruled this eternity.

But now they sat as mothers listening while Makbal paced before them shouting with such a rage Justine had never imagined he carried inside him.

"He's ruining everything. I finally have a heart strong enough to hold back time, and he corrupts her. I'm gone for one adventure, and I return to four anomalies. The trees aging, plants dying. My boys' faces unfamiliar."

"The island hasn't forgotten him," observed the winged goddess.

"Lift your protection," said Makbal. "Let me kill him."

"What will the island be then?" asked Coleodal.

"The result is unpredictable," said the winged goddess. "It could be lost, changed."

"Then I'll start again," said Makbal. "A new island farther upstream."

The goddesses exchanged looks, their doubt evident.

"Give me something! Will you always favor him over me?"

Coleodal's tentacles spasmed as though in pain. "Our love is always for you both, Makbal. Undivided, unchanging."

"Yet you allow him to destroy everything I love."

Justine blinked. It seemed such a strange thought, for Makbal to love. She knew he loved her in a way. But she had also felt a coldness from him that the trance of their bond disguised. As though his idea of love had also been given to him by something outside of himself.

He loves the boys, she thought. *He loves his work with them. He loves to play and laugh and roam the forest.* What was being threatened was Makbal's very purpose in the world: to never grow up, to be forever outside of time, and keep the most vulnerable innocents of earth safe. Justine clenched her fists in silent fury at his mothers, who sat so complacent in the face of their son's despair. Did they not see how he suffered? As his mothers, did they not yearn to give him everything he wanted?

"We'll see what your brother will say," said the winged goddess. "This has gone on too long."

As though he had been an actor waiting in the wings for his cue, the Black Hook emerged from a split in the rocks and stepped forward. He walked from deep in his hips, a strut that appeared as a careless sashay. It captured Justine's eyes so she couldn't look away. When he kissed the winged goddess on her cheek, Justine blushed. She could almost feel those lips on her skin, the scratch of his beard. And when he leaned forward to be wrapped in Coleodal's upper body tentacles in a tender embrace, Justine imagined herself likewise enveloped by his strong arms. Weren't they so like the sword-wielding arms of the man from her dream?

Justine's breath caught. She looked from the Black Hook to Makbal and back. "Brothers," she whispered. Of course they were. Even with their bond faded, Justine felt Makbal's emotions spike, a confused mixture of rage and hurt, longing, and contempt. All of it so large, so old, it momentarily overwhelmed her awareness, then she pushed it away.

Brothers.

She looked to Ian for a confirmation of what seemed completely impossible, yet somehow obvious, but he studiously looked ahead as though he hadn't noticed her gaze. Fetu had become distracted digging muck out between the cracks of the rocks with his fingernails.

"Arandasal, my love, our family is at war with itself," said the winged goddess. "Aren't you so very tired of it?"

"I thought the war ended when the sacrifice was made. We remembered the Shadows of Mortality. Or am I mistaken?" The Black Hook turned in a dramatic circle, looking around as though searching for an unseen culprit. He paused with his gaze in Justine's direction.

Heat tightened like a banked coal in her gut. The man from her dreams had a name and a face. It wasn't a knight-errant's face full of holy purpose, and it wasn't Makbal's smooth, angelic youth. Justine wasn't even sure she could call Arandasal's visage handsome, with the lines of the forehead hardened by dark brows, the sharp cut of the beard along a strong, stubborn jaw. A slightly bulbous nose was his worst feature if one could ignore the arrogance, the complete disregard for his brother's feelings, the fact of his criminal nature, etc., etc.

Indeed, if she couldn't go so far as handsome, she at least could admit, he appeared distinguished. She thought he carried a presence that wasn't just the magic of the island manipulating her interest. In her old life, Justine would have noticed him on a London street, found a way to make herself known to him, then run for her life when she spotted his hook.

"You brought time into this eternal place," said Coleodal. "And you continue to hold it captive here where it doesn't belong."

"My brother has been whining again." A sad smile creased the Black Hook's lips as he looked toward Makbal. "Have you come to take another piece of me, brother?"

Makbal's voice filled with scorn. "Your aging body is only good as fish food."

"It isn't just Makbal who speaks his concern," said Coleodal. "The island has been calling into the eternal realms. There are those who want to answer her."

"No one from below is allowed to come here," said the

Black Hook. He looked to Makbal. "It doesn't have to be this way."

"I assure you, it does."

"Why don't we both just admit the past cost us a great deal and—"

"You're destroying the island!" screamed Makbal.

"I came for a swim. It's your fault you can't keep it together."

"I wouldn't need to keep it together if you weren't always attacking it."

"A bath is hardly a—"

"You know what I meant." The force of Makbal's words nearly carried him off his feet. Justine felt him wanting to reach for the fae sword in his belt.

"Perhaps if we could pause here and clarify exactly this iteration of the problem?" suggested Coleodal. "It occurs to me that we've done this before and whatever the result—I can't remember, can you remember, my love?"

The winged goddess shook her head.

"Whatever the result, it clearly didn't solve the larger problem."

"The problem," said Makbal through gritted teeth. "Is that he hates the idea that I can do our work without him. Now that I have a heart stronger than he ever was, he's pushing time against us."

"Stronger than I?" The Black Hook's laugh rang out, rich and dark and deep and full of derision. He waved his hook in the air. "You're speaking of the past of course. If you still thought of me as that strength, I could come back to your side."

"You're too far gone for that to ever be possible."

"So instead, you enslave innocent girls to your will and exploit their power. Brilliant."

"You were in her dreams!"

The Black Hook arched a mild eyebrow. His eyes shifted

ever so slightly toward the outcropping where Justine hid. He tilted his head as she had seen him do at the lake, listening.

"Is this true, Arandasal?" asked the winged goddess.

"If that has happened, it's no fault of mine. The island has its ways. Perhaps it's part of this call you mentioned. For myself, I want nothing to do with Mak's girls."

"Unless she's the one, " mused the winged goddess.

"The Tigress thinks she is," said Coleodal.

Both mothers looked to Makbal. "She's mine," he barked. "We're bonded and you're trying to steal her."

Justine flinched against the force of his feelings reverberating through her mind. She both loved and hated the idea of belonging to Makbal.

"I haven't so much as laid eyes on your new mother," said Arandasal. "Nor do I want to."

A vibration, like far distant thunder, rose from the island. Loose rocks rattled.

"As I said, the island has her own ways," said Arandasal.

Makbal looked to his parents, desperate now. "If he were dead, the island would forget."

"It would be incomplete in its foundation."

"It's already incomplete. He left. He betrayed us and he left to live in time. He *deserves* to die."

"Perhaps we'll speak with the island?" asked the winged goddess. Before she'd finished speaking, Coleodal was shaking her head.

"I don't think we're there yet. Inviting an island for a conversation never ends well. Besides, I'm so busy with this rebellion at the falls. I might have to start over, push some bad eggs into the foam."

"I'm also quite busy," said the winged goddess, her eyebrows drawn together with concern. "The water dancer showcase comes with the next full moon. And there's an apparent shortage of pixie dust. We can't have the showcase without it."

"Yes, what's going on with that?" asked Coleodal. "I've heard rumors of fae stockpiling because they've foreseen some catastrophe."

"I heard some of the bathhouses were stolen."

One of Coleodal's tentacles clutched her throat in astonishment. "Perhaps they foresee the destruction of the island because one of its creators no longer lives." She cast a meaningful glance at Makbal.

"I'm leaving," declared Makbal. "You're no help at all." But Makbal didn't move. His small chest heaved with boyish fury that might have been comical if it didn't also seem so dangerous. "Stay away from the island, Hook. Don't cross the barrier or I *will* kill you."

Makbal and the Black Hook looked to their mothers. The mothers looked at each other. A long moment passed until finally the winged goddess drew a deep sigh. "I believe this is a reasonable request. Thus, violation of the request should require some actionable consequences."

"Banishment would be better suited than true death," said Coleodal. "Death is so unnatural for a god."

"They may fight to injury," said the winged goddess.

"Perhaps they should fight now, the exercise might help work out some of the—"

"I have no wish to fight," said the Black Hook. "Let this be the end of it, brother. I banish myself as I did once before. And I won't allow the island to call me home." His voice dipped slightly as though he struggled over the word "home."

"It isn't enough," said Makbal. "He comes to her dreams. I have no defense."

"Let the girl fight him then," said Coleodal. "It's her will that hangs in the balance after all."

"Perhaps then we'll see if she's the one he's been waiting for."

The mothers exchanged glances. "A romantic idea, isn't it?" said Coleodal.

"But troubling to have to deal with her."

"Maybe it'll give her more choices than the others," said Coleodal. "Makbal, you do have to admit, your plan to replace your brother with mothers hasn't gone as splendidly as we'd hoped."

"She's different."

"We shall see, won't we?" The winged goddess poured more steaming brew into her cup, again she studied it as though searching for answers. "Have we been very bad mothers?"

Coleodal set a tentacle on her wife's nearest wing. "After a certain point, a grown child makes their own way."

"And yet the one who grew up seems to be the source of our troubles."

A pff of disbelieving air escaped the Black Hook's fine mouth.

"Makbal's new heart of the island has the power to kill if she sees it right." Coleodal brought a tentacle down against the arm of her chair with finality. "Let us hope this spares her Guine's madness."

At the mention of Guine's name, Justine felt Makbal stiffen like a robber caught in the act by a police torch. She felt him waiting for more, a judgement, a verdict, something punishing that might alleviate his guilt.

The winged goddess smiled at her sons. "We love you both so much. I hate that it's come to this. We used to be so happy together."

"If one of us were capable of compromise, we might be happy again," said the Black Hook. A second time, Justine heard that tremor, as though he was barely holding himself together. He bowed and strode quickly toward his exit.

Makbal called after him, "You betrayed me first! You ruined us!"

"Well, I suppose we'll be moving on," said Coleodal. "Makbal, will you and the boys join us for the showcase?"

"Perhaps." Makbal was still, looking at the slit in the rock through which his brother had disappeared. A hard line of tension ridged Makbal's back from neck to heels. Then Justine felt Makbal's emotions fading, their complexity smoothing out as he put them away in the places he hid them and put on the guise of his boyhood.

"I have work to do," he said.

"Of course we understand. Give us a kiss, sweet boy, and we'll leave you to your island's troubles."

The show over, Fetu and Ian began to wiggle backward toward the tunnel. But Justine lingered, watching Makbal's rage melt away under his mothers' touch. They each held him for what seemed like a long time. As they did, Justine felt his joy, as though all of him were taken up and soothed by their touch. It unnerved her how powerful these feelings came. Even more unnerving, how he was taken up with their opposites just a few minutes later.

As expected, walking down the rain-drenched cliffs proved much harder than climbing them. The rain had dissipated, but it left behind a treacherous path of loosened gravel and mud, striped with rushing streams. Somehow, Fetu led the way just as confidently as before. If Justine had followed him as closely as she had on their ascent, everything might have been different. But her mind was too full of other things to keep on Fetu's heels, stepping where he stepped, moving from one side of the path to the other to avoid the worst places.

What Justine had seen on the clifftop changed everything

she understood about the island. It was run by a family at war, with Justine at the center, so important, but also only a pawn to be moved. The Black Hook wasn't just a dastardly pirate, but a son, a brother, who'd committed some terrible act and now so much was wrong because of it.

I'm both pawn and the most powerful, thought Justine. *I'm the glue that mends the rift. I'm the savior who's been kept ignorant so she'll be malleable.*

"Look!" cried Ian.

Up ahead, a single fairy light danced on the breeze. In its hands a silver key.

Ian blanched. "Has it come for me?" he whispered.

But no, the fae stopped at Fetu, hovering until the boy held out his hand. The fae dropped the key into it and flitted away without the chime of a single note.

Fetu turned the key over and over in his hand, then he put it in his pocket with all the other interesting things that lived there and continued down the hill.

He'll be leaving me soon. A gnawing darkness began to creep into her mind. *Always alone.* She shifted her focus to Makbal. His presence ebbed and flowed in her mind. Near then far, near then far again as he flew around the other side of the cliffs.

She was trying to summon Makbal to her side when she lost her footing. She stumbled forward, bumping and crashing against the rocks along the path. This was a steep part of the path, so her stumble gathered momentum. She couldn't pull herself up onto her feet and she couldn't see through the blur of movement to grab on to something solid.

At the turn where the path wrapped around the cliffside, Justine didn't turn. She felt herself weightless for quite a long moment as she flew without the aid of pixie dust away from the cliffs. She remembered that flying without pixie dust was just the same as falling in her old world. Never a good idea.

Falling.

Falling.

"Makbal!"

Falling.

Her body turned in the air and she could see, rising up with astounding speed, the base of the cliffs below.

She called out again both in spirit and voice. This time she felt Makbal come to her. She waited for his arms to reach out and snatch her from the air.

No arms came. She closed her eyes and thought of arms, tried so hard to imagine large, strong arms taking her in, pressing her close. Not Makbal at all.

Arandasal.

The name sounded like music.

As she fell, Justine thought, *Do I think of him because of the island? Do I think of him simply because I know of no one else who might finally love me as I want to be loved?*

An absurd thought. Justine's mind shook itself to reason.

He had said he wanted nothing to do with her.

And Makbal's mothers had promised Justine's next contact with the Black Hook would be as the instrument of his death.

But not now, thought Justine, *because here I am dying again. Maybe it will reset the scales. I'd like to start over. I think I would do some things differently.*

Her last thought before she hit the rocks came too quickly to be a full thought. In the dread of knowing what was about to happen, it was impossible to be calm or clear about anything. But she was almost sure Makbal was near enough that he was watching her. She felt his distrust, a position so deeply entrenched in his mind he experienced it as though she had already betrayed him. He was willing to let her die for the hope of a new, more loyal, mother.

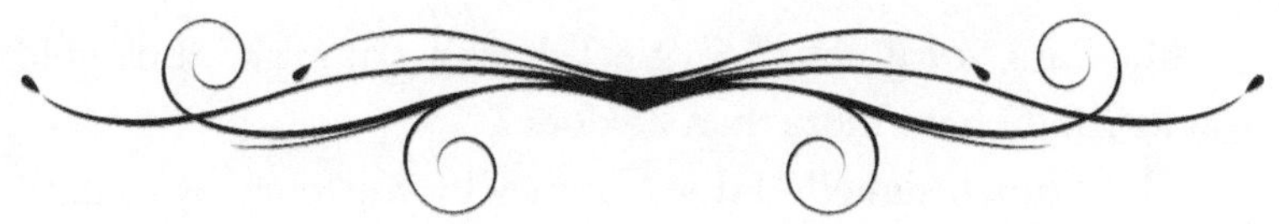

CHAPTER 27

Amputee

He fears a powerful mother just as much as he needs her.

This was Justine's first thought. She wasn't quite awake. Rather, she might have been awake but not present in the world of other people or the world of her body. The thought filled her awareness. Others grew from it. Makbal needed her to keep the island whole because his brother no longer helped him. But because the island was trying to use Justine to bring Arandasal back, Makbal distrusted her.

Because he doesn't want to lose control.

Because they have all watched this happen before.

Or at least something like it.

Justine's thoughts lost their path forward. She became aware of voices around her full of animation, words spoken on the knife blades of teeth and clenched jaws. One of them was a woman's voice. Justine thought she recognized it.

"Your duplicity has reached a new low, Mak. When Zeinab is done with her, we're charging double. I don't want anyone saying I've come to your side on this. I promised Aranda."

Makbal's voice sounded gleeful with triumph. "But gold spends, and I have more than he does."

The woman sighed. "I don't know why you're trying so hard to save someone who's doomed. If you'd let us snatch her when she first got here—"

"The island wants her."

The woman spoke with more force than what seemed necessary when she said, "The island's failing. First the time runnels, now the pixie dust is missing. And who knows what else hasn't been noticed?"

"The dust is a fae problem."

"You're naïve if you think the island isn't linked to the fae."

"Well, it wasn't made that way, so ha. Anyway, I'm taking care of it."

"Taking care of it how?"

Justine felt someone poking around her body, bringing pain alive in her side, her back, her hips. And then, a terrible, bright heat shot through her left arm. She opened her eyes and saw the Tigress sitting in a chair on the other side of Justine's Princess Louise bedroom, legs crossed, arms crossed, defiant, wearing trousers.

More poking. Justine tried to turn her head to see who or what was poking her, but her body hadn't yet come back to itself. She lay in two parts, body separate from her now very aware mind. She focused on the Tigress.

Trousers.

Boots made from tiger skin wrapped not just her feet, but half of her astoundingly exposed legs.

A hatchet balanced on her lap.

Her hair braided, though some had been shaved from the side of her head.

A blouse like a man might wear.

The Tigress twirled the handle of her hatchet, all the while holding Makbal's gaze. He stood restless against the wall parallel with the foot of the bed. For a man with the heart of his island on her deathbed, he looked remarkably cheerful.

"I'll triple your fee if you have her up and walking by the new moon. The boys are restless now that I've erased all their stories and the creatures that invaded with them."

"You missed the water dragon. I saw it in the lagoon this morning."

"No, I sent that out to you to keep you busy. It's Ling's dragon after all, and he's defected to your camp. You're welcome. What I'm missing is the books she conjured. They've been hidden from me in some plot."

"I thought only fae could erase creatures."

"Not anymore."

The woman frowned. "The last time you went dealmaking with the fae—"

Makbal shrugged as though unconcerned. "When Justine wakes, we'll be able to put everything back to order. You know she can banish time just by touching me? It happens in an instant."

"How nice for you."

"It *is* nice."

Another sour look crossed the woman's face. "I'm quite happy where I am, aren't I, Zeinab?"

A voice spoke from Justine's left side where the pain in her arm continued to flame. "Very happy, Tigress."

"I believe you." Makbal smirked. "So, we're all happy. If you'd just stop raiding the island—"

"You should let Aranda meet her. Then you'll know for sure, and we can all calm down."

Just then, an especially sharp pain spasmed through Justine's arm and she couldn't keep back a cry.

"Ah," said the Tigress. "Awake at an opportune moment? Or has she been eavesdropping?"

Makbal came to the side of the bed, his face filling Justine's vision. "How are you feeling, Mother? We've missed you." He took her hand. A rush of tender feeling mixed with something bitter flowed into Justine's mind. She instinctually returned his touch, sending comfort and warmth to try to soothe the bitterness. It felt so good, so right to be close to him again.

Justine opened her mouth but found her throat too dry to speak. A water pitcher sat half full on the table beside the bed. A more considerate boy would have offered her a glass, held it tenderly to her lips, perhaps cupped her head with his free hand. A *man* like the one she'd seen at the lake would have—Justine banished the thought.

With another impatient sigh, the Tigress pushed Makbal aside. She poured the water, sat down on the bed, and held the glass to Justine's lips. She used her free hand to lift Justine's head, a practiced motion. Of course it was. She'd been a mother here.

"Tigress, pirate," whispered Justine.

"I'm hardly a pirate," said the Tigress. "Now we're going to know each other better, you may call me by my given name. I'm Lily Flatwater of the Omaha." As she spoke, Lily cast a sly glance toward Makbal. "When he gets ornery, just remind him that you remember where you came from. As soon as he washes it out of you, he wins."

"You tried to kidnap me," whispered Justine through her cracked lips.

"I'm sorry we weren't successful. Now you'll be stuck with this pudge." Lily gave Makbal a playful sock in the arm. "You should take better care of her. I think she's a keeper."

"Don't listen to Lily, Mother. She wants to turn you pirate." Makbal shuddered and Justine felt that he couldn't think of anything worse, so she couldn't either.

"It wouldn't be like that," said Lily.

"Well, the Hook's not coming back to the island, so I don't see what else it would be like."

Justine gasped, first at the rush of Makbal's determination that his brother never live on the island, then as a fresh burst of pain vibrated through her arm. This time, she managed to turn her head and see Zeinab, a dark-skinned woman wearing clothes similar to Lily's but with an apron over her front spotted with blood and gristle like a butcher. Where had all that blood come from? Justine looked down and saw her arm was no longer a complete arm. Indeed, it was only half an arm, with the elbow and all else below it gone. While she'd been coming back to the world, Zeinab had been cleaning and bandaging the stump that hung down from her shoulder.

"Oh, bloody hell."

"Cleaned out the infection," said Zeinab. "But I'm afraid you're going to be stuck in this bed a while. Got to let those ribs heal up, eh?"

Justine stared at her, then at her missing arm. "What have you done? Where's my—" She tried to push herself up. The body that had been dormant, now came to life in a frightful wave of screaming warnings. Everything everywhere was wrong. She looked down and saw a rudimentary cast made from sticks holding her right leg straight. Bandages on both legs and her right arm, which was still intact, though her thumb was purple and twice the size of her other fingers. Her chest felt locked in a broken corset and her neck shook with strain when she tried to hold her head up.

"What's happened? Why am I like this?"

As soon as she asked the question, Justine knew. Her slip off the cliffs, falling, falling. And Makbal nearby, not rushing in to save her. If she'd struggled to believe it before, she felt it now, a pure and potent guilt, pulsing into her awareness like she'd been the one to commit the crime against him. Makbal turned away from her. "I'll go tell the boys they can come in. You've kept them waiting so long."

Zeinab began to pack up her supplies. "Tassi is going to

look after you now, but you can always send for me if you need something." *Tassi.* Justine fought down panic. Tassi was the last person she wanted looking after her in this state.

Who will want to bed a girl with one arm?

"But my arm," said Justine, barely aware of her words as her blood began to race. "What happened to it?"

"Crushed in the fall," said Lily gently. "There was an infection."

"So you cut it off? I'm ruined. You've ruined me!"

Zeinab stepped back from the bed with a bow. "You might not feel like it now, but you're lucky." She retreated across the room to the door.

Justine shouted after her, "You're not even a doctor. You have no right to tell me what I am!" The tears came, hot and furious. They brought new pain as her throat came back to life and her chest heaved. All the while, Lily sat on the bed, watching.

When Justine had marshalled herself enough she could speak through her tears, she said, "What do you keep looking at? Has my face been ruined as well?"

"The swelling will go down and I think you'll be much the same as you were before in that way." Lily glanced at the door to make sure Makbal hadn't returned. "If you would like me to rescue you, this might be your only chance to tell me. Moving you will be difficult. But I'm willing to try."

"You're so sure I need to be rescued."

"I'm sure no one can be what Mak wants."

"I *am* what he wants."

"But you can also challenge him. You're like Osuana."

"The ship?"

"One of the last girls who lived on the island." To Justine's blinking incomprehension, Lily added, "This wasn't always just a place for lost boys. The brothers brought girls here as well and everyone in between. But when they decided Osuana was ready to swim the current, she refused. Instead, she convinced Arandasal to build her a new island where they would grow old together, raise a family. She wanted to be a mother."

As Lily spoke Arandasal's name, the ground beneath the castle shook, sending a shiver up through the stone and through Justine's bedposts. The two women sat still, listening to the reverberation die away.

"I like your castle," said Lily. "Would have been fun when I was here. Are there secret passages?"

Justine had no idea about passages, nor did she particularly care if there were. "You aren't a past mother then?"

"I was brought here as a saved child, the same as Osuana."

Justine squinted at Lily, trying to judge but also not judge her age. "You must have been so young."

"I wasn't even ten when I died from a wasting sickness brought by the men who came in the big ships. So many died. When I go uprealm for haunting, the place I remember is gone, as though the sickness consumed everyone. Last time, I stayed here. Makbal is right about the way remembering ties you to the past. It's easier sometimes, to pretend it never existed."

"He doesn't seem able to take his own advice."

Lily smiled sadly. "I've always thought it must be different for him, or he surely would've changed by now. But time is even less relevant to them than it is to us. The brothers each gave part of their selves to form this island. They cared so much about the kids being lost over the falls, they made themselves lesser gods. Then one decides Osuana, and her second chance at a normal human lifespan, was more important than this thing they'd built together. For Mak, it probably feels as if it happened yesterday."

Pounding feet sounded in the hall outside Justine's room.

"Last chance to agree to a kidnapping," said Lily. "Nothing gets easier after this."

The boys were calling to each other. Makbal was among

them, a carefree boy with a roiling ball of adult feelings buried inside.

Mak was ready to let you die.

Justine lay back and closed her eyes. She reached for Lily's hand, felt the rough skin around her knuckles, the smooth underside of her palm. With this touch, Justine probed for the true edges of her desire. Not what the island wanted, nor the bond that drew her toward Makbal, but the edge of the Justine who'd once upon a time hoped to catch a husband with a hexed string of chestnuts so she'd never be an old maid, who had always made her own way even when her dreams felt impossible. She held her breath as a brace against the gnawing thoughts that told her being alone was the worst thing to be. They came in a rush of dread but still she pushed her awareness further, grounded it in the touch of Lily's hand. *This is me and only me.* Then she opened her eyes.

"Did other mothers dream of him?" she asked.

"Mak? I don't know. The girls I've met didn't have any space for dreams after the bonding. You're the first to have retained so much of yourself."

The doorknob rattled, and Justine wondered how the door had become locked when Makbal and Zeinab had easily passed through it. *I'm doing it,* she thought, though she didn't know how or how long it would hold.

"Not dreaming of Mak." Justine couldn't speak the other name aloud.

New understanding washed over Lily's expression. "Interesting." Justine watched the inflections of meaningless meaning flit across Lily's face. When she didn't immediately say anything else, Justine prompted her, "You're sure I'm the one he's looking for. So is the island."

Lily nodded.

"Why does he want me?"

"He's—" Lily pressed her lips together. "I'd rather you come meet him. Let me rescue you."

The idea of needing rescue sparked such revulsion in Justine that it took great effort not to shout as she said, "I appreciate your offer. I'll rescue myself if need be."

Lily nodded a kind of resigned acceptance, as though she believed Justine spoke from the parts of her that weren't truly herself. She'd probably seen this before. She'd learned that a mother was a bound thing who could never speak for her own self-interest.

What do I know is true? wondered Justine. *That I have a purpose here. And I'm the first to have a chance at making good. I can teach Mak to trust me. I will be good.*

A chime sounded at the window as Tassi and another fae buzzed in, carrying small purses on their backs. Tassi landed on the bloody towel where Justine's left arm should have lain. They chimed a series of long notes. The other fairy unpacked Tassi's purse and flitted up to Justine's head where it perched beside the pillow and presented Justine with a vial of the tonic.

"Be careful with that," said Lily as she stood to leave. "You'll find it easy to lose yourself. And there's no one here to pull you back."

Justine nodded her acceptance if only so the woman would leave. With it, the door burst open and the boys rushed in. Jakob and Pah in the lead, Ian, Olewendo, Matteo, and others behind. The vial was clearly a healing remedy, something to help with the pain. Whatever Lily's suspicions of it, Justine didn't care. She pinched the vial in her right hand, pulled the stopper off with her teeth, and downed the contents in one gulp. A gentle river of warmth washed over her. The pain vanished like so much dirt in a hard rain.

"It smells like petrichor," said Justine. For a moment Lily's face became a different face, the round cheeks, the elfin chin, a world of secret knowledge wrapped up under the packaging of simpleness. "Forgive me," she whispered. But Sarah had turned and was walking away, vanishing like the phantom she was as the boys circled the bed.

Justine felt herself smiling at them, accepting the small gifts they'd made. She found herself telling them she wasn't so badly hurt, that they had all been very good while she'd been away, that soon they'd continue on as they had before. She didn't feel pain when they jostled the bed, or when one of the very young new boys jumped upon her broken leg. She didn't feel anything at all except the warmth of wet dirt after a rain.

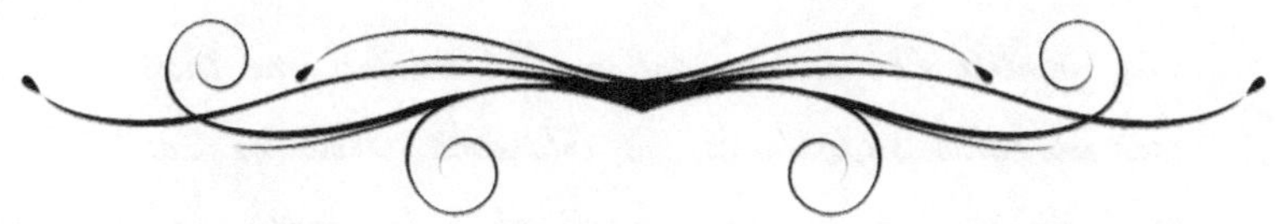

CHAPTER 28

In Dreams Found

At the first opportunity, the Black Hook stole onto his brother's side of the island. He did this even though he knew his presence created runnels of time. It did not matter to him that he was destroying the sanctuary of childhood he'd made. He needed to see the new mother. He could not believe the Tigress was correct, that she was the girlhood version of his Thessaly. And yet he could not ignore the possibility.

As soon as he stepped foot on the island, it greeted him. A warm embrace of wind, a presence so much stronger than on his side. He closed his eyes and stepped back to that previous version of himself who believed in better things. It seemed now the faith of his youth that had led him to create the island had not been a complete faith. He had wanted for an occupation and created one that seemed most suitable to his interests. Now he saw he had acted more for himself than the mortal souls he was saving.

"Take me to her," he said.

She is mine. You cannot steal her.

"I just want to see."

The island guided him up from the coast, secreted him past the brother's sentries, into the woods all the way to the mountains on the far side. There, a group of boys hunted through the tide pools that dotted the inlet. Perched on a rock some distance away, a girl stared out at the sea. No, he corrected himself, she was looking at the veil of time and the gauzy Delt village just visible behind it. In her eyes, a dreamy look, her body soft with fantasy.

Was it Thessaly? He stepped closer to see her more clearly.

No, the island warned.

"Let me take her. She'll be safer with me. She's meant to be older." He said this even though he still wasn't sure it was her. Nothing in her manner spoke of familiarity. The Thessaly he knew set her foot upon the world with authority. This girl, though she carried the same heaviness in her bones, the same substance of body, seemed a lost soul, empty in the spaces where Thessaly had seemed so enticingly full.

She's mine. The island blew him backward, pushing him back the way he'd come. He surrendered to her will with a laugh. It felt good to duel wills with the island. He'd forgotten this love. The warmth under his feet, the way the bark of the trees reached out with a comfort he did not deserve.

Come back sometime, said the island. Swim in the lake.

"I'm sorry," said the Black Hook. The invitation, which he did not deserve, had left him overwhelmed with things he had not allowed himself to feel for a long time.

There is a path to follow, said the island.

It should be here noted, in my opinion, the island is not an accurate source of prophecy, and it is unlikely she spoke from prescience. Rather, she had a vision of how she might achieve her own ends, and this was the beginning of those machinations.

The Black Hook later returned with some of his crew and enjoyed the pleasures of Coral Lake. An episode that struck wounds in the skin of the island, dashing her through with parasitic time that pulled so much out of balance. Still, it was what she wanted. And she made sure the mother came to see the visitors. More importantly, she saw the

Black Hook and she was not as afraid of him as the brother said she should be. Quite the opposite in fact.

Black Hook and she was not as afraid of him as the brother said she should be. Quite the opposite in fact.

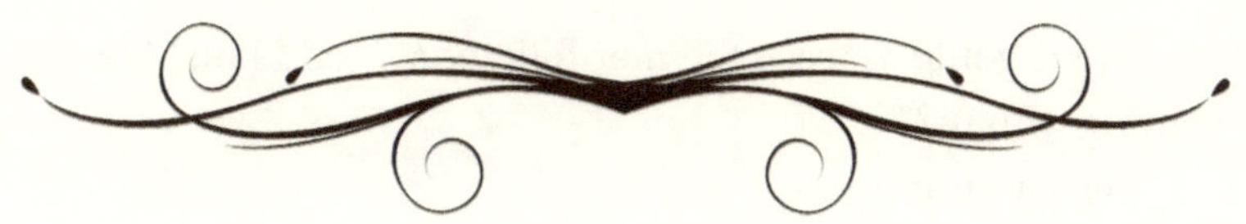

CHAPTER 29

An Archive's Riddle

As soon as she was well enough, Makbal and the boys moved Justine back to her old bed in the cave at the Canopy, and the castle was abandoned. "You'll be stronger here," he said. He took her hand and together they pushed time out of the island and past the boundary rocks. The magic took much more from her than when they'd joined before. Afterward, Makbal looked like a skeleton version of his usual self with his face all sunken in and dark bruises around his joints. They slept bundled together like puppies. Justine didn't dream.

When Justine awoke, much of the visible wounds of her body had faded. She couldn't find a mirror in the cave, but when she touched her face, it felt familiar. The broken corset around her chest turned out to be a brace, which she removed. Whatever it had been healing had solved itself. Her thumb was no longer swollen. Her broken leg could hold her weight, but its stiffness and the quiet ache that came with movement didn't go away. Her severed arm didn't grow back when she wished for it.

"We're going to tease the mer folk today," said Ian. "Are you coming with us?"

"Perhaps tomorrow."

And the next day, Jakob, wanting to be helpful. "I've collected up all the mending for you, Mother."

And sometime after that, Makbal in his chair with his pipe by the fire frowning as one of the new boys read the evening story from one of the picture books he couldn't erase. There had been no deliveries of night tea from the fae. Apparently, all production was behind because of the pixie dust shortage. So the boys, both old and new, remembered where they'd come from. Justine was hardly aware of his darkening mood as she stared into the fire until finally, the pipe came flying toward her.

Justine ducked out of the way. The pipe hit the stone hearth and bounced into the fire.

The boy stopped reading. Justine couldn't remember his name.

"What are you thinking about?" asked Makbal.

"Nothing," said Justine, which was mostly true.

"I demand the truth."

Justine wearily turned toward him. "What version of soiled truth will bring us back to that fragile beginning? Even then you didn't trust me."

"How can I? You've brought the world above into the island." Makbal snatched the picture book from the boy's hands and threw it into the fire. "How am I supposed to help these boys prepare for the current when you undermine me at every turn?"

"Perhaps if you had explained more, I might have understood better when I was doing wrong."

"If you gave yourself over to me, you would never do anything wrong."

There was probably a truth in this. But Justine wondered

even then if it would have been enough. Lily had seemed to think no one ever truly satisfied Makbal.

"So, we shall burn the books?" she asked.

Several of the boys cried out, "NO!"

Fetu jumped up and began to run around, batting his arms in the air, not caring if he ricocheted off the walls.

Makbal started back in alarm. He turned in a circle like a trapped thing, staring first at Fetu, then at the rest of the boys. Only Olewendo dared meet his eyes. The others all looked away, shuffling their feet, picking at the holes in their clothes. Jakob began to cry.

This, Justine thought, *is the beginning of the true end. The more he tries to control them, the more he'll lose them. One by one, they'll fail when they take the current or refuse to even try. I can save him or watch him destroy it all with his fear.*

"Father didn't mean that, children," she said quickly. "Remember, the stories were only for building the castle. It was a game we would only play once. Now, the books can go away. I'll put them on the shelves in the castle library where they'll look very pretty. Remember, in this place, we tell stories to each other instead of read them," she said. "It's a special game we play. It's just that I've been unwell. Perhaps tonight, Father can tell us a story."

Makbal glared. "Fathers don't tell stories."

Justine held her smile on her face. "Alright, I will tell you a story."

"Hurrah!" cried Pah. "You'll like this," he promised a new boy sitting beside him. "Mother tells the best stories."

Justine took a quilt over to Fetu and wrapped it around his shoulders. When he was quiet, she took Jakob on her lap and began the story of King Arthur and Guinevere. She'd only just mentioned their names when Makbal waved his hand and barked, "I hate this story."

Thankfully, because they'd already had most of a story from

the picture book, it was quite late, and when Justine said perhaps they should all just go to bed, no one complained.

"And we might talk a little before bed?" She felt Makbal bristle against her.

"Talk like grown-ups? About what?"

"Your jealousy perhaps? The island trying to undermine us? Or anything else you're thinking about. I'd like to know so I can plan for the future. You have a plan for the call of the island?"

"There is no future here, Justine. There is only now."

"You believe that even less than I do. Your entire life is spent looking back at the past, waiting for it to happen again."

"You know nothing."

"Exactly! You keep me in ignorance because you can't imagine that I'd want to stay here. This has become my home as much as it's yours."

He blinked at her, a long sideways glance, searching for the lie in her words. Finally, he said, "I don't know how to have a mother who's always doubting me. That isn't how it's supposed to be."

"Could we agree that it might be a useful thing to have a mother who's a woman instead of a mother who's a child?"

"Perhaps."

There, a concession, but Justine struggled to articulate her thoughts further. More than anything she wanted to help him feel safe with her. It wasn't fair that he had suffered so much, all of it arguably because of his brother.

"What if there was a way to remove time completely? Then this middle space between realms would be as it was when you made it?"

Makbal's eyes glimmered in the firelight. "You mean to kill the Black Hook."

"Well, no, actually. I thought there might be another—"

"The only way is to kill him and start again. If you truly want the island as it was made to be, that's how to do it."

"I've never killed someone," said Justine, then, to try to ease Makbal's dark look, she added, "And it's a strange thing to consider, killing a god when I'm not even alive myself."

"It won't be hard for you. Not after you know what he has done."

She felt him softening toward her, sinking into the possibility of shared revelations. Finally, she was making progress. Makbal would tell her the full story of the dread pirate, turncoat brother. *Man of my dreams?* Justine pushed the thought away. Her rebellious mind replaced it with a flash of a moment from Coral Falls Lake. Arandasal rising out of the water, such a figure of strength and—

Justine stopped herself before she thought of his knob, which seemed more than up for doing the job. She ached to be filled, to be wrapped up in another's body, so she lay back on her mattress and crooked her finger at her only option. "Come to my bed, Lord Mak. Tell me a dark story."

He came to her as a boy to a mother, eager to be held and coddled and convinced that everything would be fine. Even if his touch didn't awaken the same heat as the mere thought of the other did, she made herself content.

It wasn't a particularly good story. Makbal had no sense of narrative drama. He simply spouted off the first things that came to his mind, then, as he remembered things he missed, he went back and started over with the new things added. And after all that, much of the interesting parts of the story were lost in tangential wanderings about families and trust and how the worst thing someone can do to someone else is leave them. He paused to bury his head in Justine's shoulder as though he couldn't face his own memories. Justine held him as tightly as she could with her one arm as though her touch could reach back through time and protect him from the ruined dream of his childhood.

Lily Flatwater had already given Justine most of the basics, but what Makbal added was a larger sense of destruction. The way the sky turned black and the island, which had once been much larger, broke into pieces. Time became a space around his brother and Osuana so that everywhere they went, everything they touched became subjects of it. Creatures that had once been beautiful and perfect, majestic and mysterious, became evil and dangerous like the fish that swam the depths and the merfolk trapped between time and eternity, both ageless and subject to age, so that they became contorted and hideous.

He told of innocent children forced to choose sides and how the ones who went with the rebels died so quickly, so uselessly, in battles or claimed by the falls or by growing old and feeble and, in Makbal's mind, useless, because they could no longer play. He spoke of war. Each brother building up an army of followers and training them in violence. A war that went on and on until Osuana went to her true death and Arandasal built his memorial ship and sailed away to find her soul in the eternal realms.

Though Makbal didn't intend it as such, the story was one of the most tragically romantic stories Justine had ever heard. How wonderful to be the woman a man loved so much that he would burn down the world to give her what she wanted.

THE NEXT DAY, JUSTINE WOKE TO FIND AN ENTIRE WOODEN CASE of healing vials set out on the floor of the pantry. She thought she would drink a vial and go back to bed, but then she surveyed the cave. Every surface, including the floor, was practically buried in debris—dishes, cast-off clothes, leaves and branches and whatnot brought in from outside—and the air stank of stale flesh.

"How long since their last bath?" wondered Justine, not

thinking that perhaps the smell might be hers. It seemed a monstrously large task to corral the boys from their morning activities and get them down to the lake. Then she'd have to wish for soap after yesterday wishing for three meals to arrive on the table. She'd been using wishes to get through so many days, they felt as worn out as the rest of her. All she wanted to do was sleep.

Sleep and dream, thought Justine as she dragged the broom around the cave with her remaining hand and tried to restore order.

She heard a soft swish followed by a thump, then Fetu emerged from the hollow of his sleeping tree. Rogue tumbled down after him. For a few minutes, Fetu made a route around the cave, touching first Makbal's chair, then a particular stone in the fireplace, then the foot of Justine's mattress, then running his hand around the entire edge of the table. When he finished, he held out his hand for the broom.

"I'm almost finished," said Justine, which wasn't at all true. She continued to drag the broom around.

"I want to swim the current," said Fetu through Rogue.

Justine nodded. "Soon you'll be given an adventure for your keyhole."

"Mak won't let me have an adventure."

"Why not?"

"He says my place is here forever."

Justine gave up the broom and thought longingly of the vials in the pantry. Makbal was down at the lagoon. To speak with him about Fetu's wish to swim the current, she'd need to walk quite a distance.

"Well, I'm sure he has his reasons," she said, even though in the back of her head she was thinking that all the boys eventually went to the current. The island wasn't meant to be a final home for anyone.

"Speak to him for me?"

"I suppose I could."

The boy smiled. He took the broom and began to do the work Justine couldn't.

"If you're going to do that," said Justine as she wandered to the pantry. "Be careful Mak doesn't catch you at it or he'll think I'm giving you too much work."

Justine knelt before the case hidden in the pantry and counted the twenty perfectly filled vials. Such a thoughtful gift from Tassi. But she couldn't help but wonder at it. The fae could only be trusted to do what they wanted. What did Tassi want in return for such a gift?

Secreting away a single vial in the pocket of her skirt, Justine climbed the stairs up to the surface. Half of her roses had been caught in a time runnel and had withered and died back into a nest of thorns. She grazed her hand through them as she listened to the island rise to meet her heels.

The island's touch wasn't as present as it had been in Makbal's absence, but Justine had found that if she concentrated, she could pull forward different strands of her awareness. Even when Makbal's presence seemed overwhelming, it was now a thing she could shift around and sometimes even make smaller in favor of her own thoughts and desires. An exhausting process. She often just let her awareness flow as it would, even though this left little space for the island, let alone her own thoughts.

Justine wandered the woods. Part of her thought she might find an exceptionally beautiful place to lie down and enjoy the effects of the tonic. But another felt the pull to wander without purpose. She knew this pull was the island wanting to show her something, so she let it guide her through groves of trees old and young, past squirrels that stopped snickering at each other long enough to stand respectfully still while she passed, and fae busy at work harvesting nuts and berries.

The island guided her west to the cliffs.

"Please tell me we're not going to the place where I fell."

Justine had no way to recognize the scene of her accident, so she couldn't say with any certainty that the path the island revealed to her along the cliff face was the same or different from the one Fetu had used to take her up to the summit. She thought perhaps it was, but then the path turned and moved through a tunnel and out along the exterior cliffs so that Justine walked a narrow outcropping wrapped around the cliff face that looked out on the open sea. The veil of time lay directly before her, but the sun was too bright to see anything except the dimmest inflections of shadows marking the island on the other side.

To her right, the open sea. Justine saw the falling bodies specking the northwest sky, and the dark mist that marked the place of the Green City in the realm below. *How many of the falling are children who won't make it to either city?* wondered Justine. "They die so young only to spend eternity falling."

The details hadn't been clear in Makbal's story, but Justine felt that when the island had been whole and the brothers ruled together, many more children lived on the island than those who lived there now. It'd been a tree house city, full of platforms, rigging, swinging ropes, shelters, and food stations, a hierarchy of the most experienced children looking after the newcomers. None of this nonsense about mothers and fathers. There'd been no need for that.

"I'm a poorly placed bandage over a rotting wound," she said.

In response, Justine's heels sparked. She turned and continued up the path, doing her best not to look down at the ocean washing the rocks below her in foam. As they grew more and more distant, Justine pressed herself against the cliff face and kept her eyes ahead. Looking down seemed an invitation to fall.

"I'm quite done with falling."

Ahead, the path climbed even more steeply and more narrowly up the cliff. She couldn't see the top, but she knew the path ended in a drop down to the sea. The island was inviting her to continue up to a place where there seemed no forward path. Instead of continuing, Justine turned to go back down. Then she saw the cave.

The opening in the cliff wall was more the entrance to a giant rabbit's hovel than an opening for broad-shouldered girls who were almost women. She had to get down on her knees, lean onto her right arm and inch her way through what felt like quite a long, narrow tunnel. By the time she crawled out the other end, the whole of her body ached, and the promise of the tonic in her pocket burned like a small, inviting fire.

The cave at the end of the tunnel didn't have a ceiling high enough for Justine to stand, so she sat, gathering herself, wondering why she'd come and if she should leave, and if anything really mattered anymore. No one would ever love a cripple.

Lines of fire marked the cave's walls. Between the lines of fire were shelves of bound manuscripts. In some places, the shelves had become too full, and manuscripts were stacked on the floor. Here and there across the floor of the cave, fairies sat or stood bent over little desks or splayed on cushions. Some were at work writing. Farther into the cave, where a strong smell arose, others were engaged in the making of the bound manuscripts. And still farther, in the poorly lit recesses, the light *tink tink* sound of hammers chipping away at rock.

"Oh my," said Justine, which of course brought all activity to a halt. Startled fairies buzzed and started, sprouting sparks, their lights changing colors, and their wings in such a frenzy, they whipped up a breeze that spread the tannery smell through the whole cave. The chimes of their surprise, which also sounded like anger, which also sounded like fear, were so loud, Justine put her hands over her ears.

"The island brought me here. I'm sorry. I'm going, I'm going."

Justine wearily began to lower herself onto her aching shoulder to inchworm back out when a voice stopped her.

"You're sure the island brought you?"

Justine turned and saw a fairy drift forward and alight on the floor by Justine's knees. They were the most beautiful fairy Justine had ever seen, with auburn hair hanging all the way down their back, and doe eyes framed by long lashes, only slightly hidden behind a pair of spectacles.

"I followed it in my feet."

"So, you must have a purpose for being here."

Justine looked around at the books. Even the ones she could tell were written in English, Justine couldn't decipher the titles. "I don't know why I'm here." As she spoke, the words seemed true for more than Justine finding herself in the cave.

The fairy crossed their small arms across their chest. "Well, I'm afraid that's not an adequate answer. This is a sacred place. Even Lord Mak doesn't come here, nor does he even know to come here. You're the first mother we've ever seen."

"You speak English," said Justine, stalling.

"We speak all languages. Now answer my question."

Justine's eyes continued to search the cave for an answer she didn't expect to find. "Do you keep the history of the island here?"

The fairy narrowed their eyes. "I'm Posietta, archivist."

"I want to know the island as it was before."

"To what end?"

"I want to cast out time and put the island back together so we can help more children."

"Only gods can repair what has been broken."

"Then I guess I'll just keep dreaming," said Justine sourly. "Because the Black Hook doesn't have a healing bone in his body." Even as Justine said it, she felt Makbal's words in her mouth. They contradicted what she'd heard the pirate say on the summit. *It doesn't have to be this way.* He'd seemed so sad, so unlike the villain he surely was.

Justine shook her head. She could think of no greater crime than to betray both purpose and family. *He* is *a villain.*

"You've found the two black brothers?" asked Posietta, still keeping their careful composure, not giving anything away.

"I only think of one of them as black," Justine paused. "But I suppose Makbal does have his moments."

"They'll never reconcile," said Posietta. "Their division will forever divert the flow of the water until one who is worthy rides the rapids between and joins them." The fairy's small arms extended out. They rested each palm in the air as though palming the heads of two small boys. "The one who unites the brothers may fall through the water and become a god."

"Is that all?" laughed Justine. The entire conversation seemed like sense slanted, and Justine was too tired to work out the riddles. She'd thought the island was taking her to a nice place, following her wish for a quiet grove to enjoy her vial of tonic. This cave wasn't at all a place Justine could relax.

Posietta flicked their wings. Whatever else they knew, they wouldn't say.

"I'm sorry to bother you," she whispered, clenching back tears as she lay down and crawled out of the cave.

Justine wiped furiously at her eyes as she stumbled down the path. "Ridiculous island, all caught up in your own schemes. Why don't you just tell me there's no way to fix this? I'm not a god or a goddess. I'm not even a queen, am I? That was just a game. Games within games within games all made to hide the yuck underneath."

The pebbles beneath Justine's feet burned in response.

"Fine, you're not ridiculous. You're just selfish. I'm the ridiculous one, thinking I could come here and make every-thing better again. Mak's right. He's done the best he can, and that means having a mother who plays her role and doesn't try and do anything else. Whatever I'd come up with he's certainly already tried. Because he's a god who's been doing this for thousands of years and I'm just a girl. I'm just—" Justine stopped short.

She'd come to the base of the cliffs, and now she turned and looked up back the way she'd come. The two black brothers were not Arandasal and Makbal. They were the wicked brothers from the river king story she'd told the boys her first night on the island. The one with the young hero and his two older brothers who'd refused water to those in need along the way and thus been turned into two black boulders fated to spend eternity worn away by the rushing water of the cataracts.

"Those are just characters in a story, you bloody fairy," she screamed at the rocks. "They're not real!"

The tears came even more furiously now. Even though she'd known it couldn't be true, Justine had thought perhaps, if she might just work out the riddle of the fairy's words, she would find her answer. Instead, the fairy had just been repeating her own story back to her.

Justine pulled the vial from her pocket and swallowed its shimmery lavender contents. For a moment she stood waiting for the curtain to drop down over her. When it did, though, she enjoyed the pain washing away, taking with it the feeling that she was forever divided within herself. It wasn't as sweet as she remembered from her last vial.

Justine knew about drug tolerance from the asylum where hyoscine and laudanum had to be locked in a safe because they taught the body to want more even as they became less and less effective. But in that moment, Justine didn't care about the problem of needing more. Since she had a great many more vials, just a little sip extra would bring her back to what she wanted without any problem. As the daze of the tonic settled over her, she wandered gently back to the Canopy, intending to steal that extra sip. But before she arrived, Justine felt the pull of Makbal, his sweet desire calling her away.

She changed direction and walked down to Coral Falls Lake where she found the boys swinging themselves into the water from vines. *Such beautiful boys*, thought Justine as she dropped down on the sand and stared up at the trees overhead. *Such beautiful trees.* Though the pirates had spent a great deal of time here, time's touch hadn't come to this place. It remained the pristine picture of a perfect fall day with sunburned orange and red all around.

Makbal dragged himself out of the water and flopped down beside her. "I see you found my present."

"Hmm. Was that you?" Justine reached out and curled a finger around a thatch of his wet hair.

"Tassi said it'll help with our plan. Your mind will be more open."

What plan? wondered Justine, but then the question was gone as quickly as it had come.

"It certainly feels that way," murmured Justine. She dropped her hand down, stroked the side of his neck. She closed her eyes and imagined she touched the neck of a different body, a body who wanted her as much as she wanted him.

Makbal giggled. "You're tickling me."

Justine withdrew her hand. "Fetu came to talk to me."

"Fetu doesn't talk."

Justine rolled her eyes. "You know what I mean. Why won't you let him have his adventure?"

"It isn't his time yet."

"He said you want him here forever."

"Well, that wouldn't be terrible, would it?"

Justine laughed. "If he wants to swim it, he should be allowed to try."

This sentence, perhaps uttered with too much force of opinion, immediately seemed the wrong thing. She felt Makbal rise to ire, ready to argue.

"This isn't a swim meet, Justine. If he fails, he ends up in the lawless caves of the Green City with the likes of Guine dictating his life. Or worse, he misses the city and goes over the falls. Is that what you want for him?"

Guine, the woman with the island's key, thought Justine as she waded through the flood of Makbal's feelings. Something else underlined his feelings toward Guine. Justine couldn't tell what it was, so she pushed it away. Too much thinking ruined her peace. She reached for it, that haze of quiet, the gentle rocking of the complete absence of uncertainty or conflict. The sun was so bright and warm, Justine struggled to keep her eyes open. *Makbal's right of course. The only good choice is for Fetu to stay on the island.*

"I'll try to explain to him after dinner tonight," said Justine. "I don't know how I'll say it, he seems so determined."

"Children like that, there's nothing to be done for them."

"Children like what?" Justine burrowed her back into the sand. The tonic's peace seemed stronger now with Makbal beside her. She wanted to cuddle up beside him and go to sleep.

"Deficient. Weak."

Justine frowned. She didn't think of Fetu as weak, just quiet and sensitive. He saw things none of the other boys noticed. "Is that what you think of me now?"

"It's impossible to say that having only one arm in a world made for two isn't a deficiency. But mothers don't swim the currents. Usually."

Usually. This word, which Makbal had added on as though suddenly struck with a need for complete honesty, rolled uneasily through Justine's head.

"If I had a fancy hook like your brother, I'm sure I could be nearly as good as any two-handed person."

Pain sparked against Justine's temple and down the arm she no longer had. It took her a moment to realize this was Makbal she felt, a manifestation of his feelings transcending emotion into something even stronger.

"You shouldn't joke about that, Mother. The Black Hook and all who follow him amend their bodies to hide the evil within. It's villainy that makes a body less than it was designed to be."

Justine clenched both eyes tight against him as though they were also her ears. She tried to rearrange her perception so he didn't take up so much space, so the pain would go away. Yes, she supposed, it made sense to think of deformities and injuries and sickness as failings of the spirit in the abstract. And even in London, it'd been impossible for her to pass a man with a patch over his eye and not feel a small shudder over what he'd done to deserve it. But what Makbal didn't seem to understand was that she was part of them now, the less than pristine bodies trying to make their way in the world.

"You think I'm evil?" She said it like a tease, punching him lightly in his boney ribs.

"Not yet. And if my plan works, maybe not ever."

"That's a relief." Justine tried to laugh. But she felt her peace leeching out of her as dark thoughts pushed their way through the fog and battled each other.

"Darling, do you think you could hop back to the cave and fetch me another vial of your lovely gift?"

"It shall be done."

"That would be wonderful, thank you."

"Then I'll tell you a story while you sleep. I'm getting better at it, aren't I?"

"At what?" Justine asked, but she hardly cared. The pain was gone, and Makbal had pulled his adult self back into the box where he kept it; the boy had returned. It was such a relief,

Justine vowed she wouldn't say another challenging thing the rest of the day.

"Storytelling."

Justine nodded even though she only remembered Makbal telling a story once, just the previous night and never before. *What does he mean he's getting better at it?* The longer she held this question in her mind, the more uncomfortable it felt, as though she remembered something but also didn't remember it. This disconcerting feeling got even worse as Makbal stood and Justine noticed that he cast no shadow out from his feet even though the sun was behind his left shoulder. She blinked to clear her eyes, but still, when she looked again, no shadow.

You're making trouble where there's none to be found, Justine. Calm yourself.

As Makbal sprinted off, Justine listened to the wind rustling the trees and the boys calling to each other. She tried to pull the noises in and let them lull her to sleep, but now her mind kept returning to nervous questions and the thoughts within wouldn't lay silent. *Does he think there's a way to regrow my arm? Does he truly think I fell from the cliffs because I'm evil?*

What even does it mean to be evil if one is just an ordinary girl and not a murderer or a thief or a pirate?

Is that why he didn't save me that night? He wanted to see if my body would give him evidence?

And yet, I feel we've been doing so well.

The sense of a long stretch of time that came with this last thought confused Justine. Hadn't the accident just happened? Hadn't she been back in the cave only a few nights? And yet, it felt like so much more than that.

Justine focused on the faint smell of petrichor. She willed it to be the fully potent musk of soil drying in the sun after a thunderstorm, but it remained a fleeting whiff. Frustrated, Justine opened her eyes and gazed up at the trees.

One of the boys called to another, "Race you to the black brothers!"

Ian called back, "First one gets the swan feather!"

Justine tilted her head up just enough she could see Ian and one of the new boys, who was perhaps not so new anymore, each scaling one side of the rock wall that bordered the falls. Justine noticed that what she'd thought was the top was actually just a flat basin area holding water from another set of falls set back into the cliff face. The edge of these other falls towered high above the treetops. And there, though Justine had to squint against the sun to see them, two giant, black boulders divided the flowing water into three distinct streams.

I could climb up and see if there really is a way to be a goddess, thought Justine. But then she sensed Makbal's presence, drawing nearer and nearer, bringing the thing she desired most.

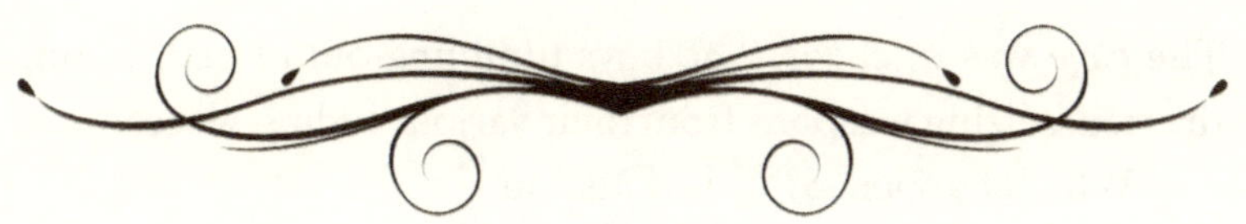

CHAPTER 30

Fetu Swims

The water had been so nice. The nicest water there ever was. Sometimes it was the moat around her castle, but today it was a river that looked quite a lot like her moat. Snow fell as Justine floated on her back, hair drifting around her, her white gown semitranslucent, also drifting around her. It showed hints of her bare legs and her alert breasts, ready for two proportionately sized hands.

Someone was watching from afar, she was sure. A head would soon appear just over that wall, full of bright desire. (Alright, the moat after all.) He would leap over the wall and—

Justine woke with a start, suddenly finding herself surrounded by shouting and the agitation of many bodies. *Not now,* she thought. The dreamworld called Justine back. Just a few more minutes and she'd see him, the spy on the other side of the wall. She didn't need to reach the point of him scaling the wall, throwing himself into the water, them devouring each other while floating and twisting like mer. It would be enough just to see him.

More shouting, a hard thump from above, then someone tripped over Justine's foot. She struggled to pull open her eyes.

The cave was in chaos. The boys tumbling out of bed, getting dressed, seizing weapons from their various hiding places.

"What's happened?" asked Justine.

Pah skidded to a halt and gave her a peck on the cheek. "A pirate raid, Mother. They've taken Fetu."

Justine was immediately and fully awake. She looked to the corner where Fetu had been keeping himself company. She looked to the cubby where he kept his collection of interesting things that didn't fit in his pockets. Both empty. "No, no, no," she cried as the knowledge solidified. Of all the boys to take, not him. "Rogue?" she called. "Rogue, where are you?" The rabbit-not-rabbit was also nowhere to be seen.

Justine struggled into her dress, using her one hand to pull up both sides. By now, she'd figured out how to do this well enough. But securing it in the back was impossible without someone's help.

"Forget the dress. I'm not really queen anyway." Justine shrugged herself back out of the dress and charged up to the surface in her nightgown.

It was still dark outside. A thin sheen of dew on the grass reflected the torches the boys held. Makbal had called everyone together.

"Fetu is the only one missing. He probably went out for a wander and got himself sacked."

"Are they still here? We shall banish them." Justine reached for Makbal's hand, but he shook his head. "I don't sense them. Lee and Ian went down to the shore to see. If the pirate launch is in reach, we can swim out and stop them."

Tears rushed to flood her eyes. *The mothers banished the Black Hook. He promised to leave us alone.* She felt wholly unprepared, cheated, betrayed. *Why Fetu of all the boys?* She wanted to scream at the gods hidden behind the sky, to somehow punish them for their complacency.

A moment later Ian burst through the underbrush with

Lee, the new (but perhaps not really very new) boy, close behind him. They collapsed to their knees in the middle of the clearing. "They're taking him to the current," called a voice through the darkness. "They're taking him to the current!"

"How can they take him to the current?" asked Pah. "Only Lord Mak can do that."

"I don't know, but we saw it," gasped Ian. "The big ship went around the point and the Ocean's Mouth accepted her."

"We stayed until we heard it swallow," added Lee.

Makbal twisted his head up to the sky. Justine saw his lips moving, felt the pure rage seething out of him so potent there was no space between what was his and what felt like hers. The pain of it sparked at her temples. She felt him raging in the joints of her fingers, in the stiff portions of her back, and in her broken leg that had healed but remained unsound.

"The Black Hook is a god like I am," said Makbal. "Except not nearly as strong. All gods can go down to the lowerrealm, but only I have permission from the mothers to help boys from this island swim the current."

"What will happen to Fetu?" asked Jakob.

"Nothing," said Makbal. "I'm going to rescue him."

"An adventure!" cried the new, youngest boy. Justine thought his name was Tomoke.

"No, I must go alone." Makbal set his jaw as he thrust an axe into one side of his belt and his fairy sword into the other.

"But we can help," cried Jakob.

"It's too dangerous this time. Stay with the island. When the sun comes up, hunt for runnels. Mother and I will heal them when we return."

Justine blinked. "We?"

"You've been waiting for your chance. Now we have it."

Without knowing why, Justine found herself nodding. Yes, the plan they'd been making to save the island. She frowned as she tried to remember what she must do. Her first thought was a climb up the rocks beside Coral Falls, but that didn't seem the correct thing. Then she thought there was something about drawing all the pieces of the island together so they'd fit within the time barrier, but no, that wasn't what she'd forgotten either. Neither of those plans involved Makbal.

As her mind had wandered, he'd been busy around her in indistinct ways. Now, he pulled a glove over her hand.

"You don't want us bonded?" she asked. "What if we need to—"

"Don't worry." He took hold of the newly gloved hand and ran with her to the lagoon.

Running proved exceptionally difficult. Justine couldn't remember the last time she'd run. Once upon a time, it had been easy. But now the ground seemed to convulse at every turn, determined to trip her, snare her, scratch her. She knew she didn't move as well as she had before her fall, and yet this challenge seemed more than that. Her head wasn't focused enough to place her body in space. Even if she had been more able, Makbal's feelings easily overwhelmed her senses. She was more aware of him running, of his rush, than she was of herself.

When they finally reached the launch, balancing in the dinghy also seemed much harder than she remembered. Perhaps because she weighed more on her right side than she did on her left. Or perhaps there was something wrong. She couldn't help but feel something terribly wrong.

Fetu has been taken.

Yes, but . . .

Makbal is angry.

She parsed the waves of feeling coming from Makbal, the furious seething remained, but he was also frightened.

What's going on here?

Makbal rowed the dinghy so recklessly the boat sloshed from side to side, ever a moment from capsizing. Justine might have asked him to calm down, or at least slow down, but she felt the same as he did. They must reach the pirates before Fetu was thrown into the current. They must save him before he committed his soul to eternity. They must kill the Black Hook.

Justine blinked salt spray from her eyes in surprise. *Kill the Black Hook.* She saw how she would do it. There, in the fingers of her glove, were the poisoned needles. Makbal would row the boat up to the *Osuana*. He would carry her aboard on his back, then leave her while he fought the pirates. Makbal was sure the Black Hook would come for her. That was when she would stab him. Hopefully right in the heart, but anywhere in his chest would likely do the trick.

The dinghy began to dip forward. The dip came so fast, Justine crashed sideways. Before she'd recovered, they were underwater, rushing past the shadows of giant fish, the haunted rock formations, and at least one sunken ship. Somewhere in the middle, they twisted around so down became up, then they popped up on the river of the lowerrealm. The water made a satisfied little gurgle as it spit them out.

Justine saw the dark mass of the rocks around the great falls far to her left. To her right, equally distant, rose the great golden cliffs that encircled the Cloud City. And there, directly ahead, the *Osuana* was just dropping anchor and a rowboat was being lowered over the side.

Makbal rowed hard and fast and made a lot of splashing doing it. They were quickly noticed by the pirates in the boat.

"Mother! Lord Mak!" called Rogue's voice as Fetu waved to welcome them.

"He's calling for help," said Justine. "Faster!"

Another call came from the rowboat. "I'm glad you came." Rogue's round, blue-purple head popped up beside Fetu's. It jumped up on one of the oars, panting with pleasure. As the pirate, who was rowing hard to keep the boat stable against the current, tried to shake it off, the boat nearly tipped over. She heard deep male laughter from the pirates as Fetu tried to recapture his pet.

Men. Here, a pause as she remembered old days, banked desire. It burned in her just a moment before Makbal's feelings swallowed it. Still, that pause had allowed her to see what she otherwise could not.

"Fetu doesn't appear to be their prisoner."

"Don't trust what you see," said Makbal. "All they do is deal in deceit."

Justine tried to stand so she could better call. "We're coming for you!"

The dinghy rocked from side to side; she quickly sat down again. Her hand clenched the side, all her fingers carefully pointed out so the needles wouldn't snag the wood. She saw the long silhouette of the Black Hook. He sat next to Fetu dressed in one of his well-cut black coats with an elaborately feathered tricorn on his head.

"Please let him go," called Justine. "He wants to live."

One of the pirates at the rear of the boat turned and gave her a confused look. Malicious confusion, she was sure. *Everything they do is deceit,* she repeated in her head.

The Black Hook also turned to look. His hat shadowed much of his face, the shadow play transmogrifying his features into something twisted and cruel. Still, when he looked at her, she felt something familiar—it wasn't something her mind was ready to understand. A knowing. An interest. And this time, she couldn't blame the island. Despite what he'd said on the cliffs that day in the rain, he wanted to see her.

"Are you ready?" asked Makbal in a hushed voice.

"Yes," she whispered, even though she wasn't sure. It took work to break from the Black Hook's gaze. She couldn't even see his eyes and yet . . .

She focused on Makbal pressing close against her.

"Don't let anything stop you." As he spoke, Makbal beamed vicious purpose into Justine's mind. She burned with his passion. It filled her all the way to her edges. Justine tensed her legs, ready to spring. The boats were almost upon each other. She could now hear the Black Hook in Fetu's ear saying, "Make your own path," as he nudged the boy to the edge of the rowboat.

"We won't make it," she gasped.

The Black Hook pushed Fetu into the water.

"No!" Justine stared at the water where Fetu had disappeared. She waited and waited, then she heard a splash to her left. Fetu had resurfaced much farther downstream. He began to swim with clean, swift strokes that drove power into the water without wasting energy.

It seemed an impossible number of strokes before he came even with the rowboat. Justine heard the Black Hook tell his men, "Don't call out when he passes. He needs to think only of his destination." So Justine also didn't move or call out. Though she wanted for all the world to snatch Fetu out of the water to safety.

Little by little, Fetu put distance between him and the boats. His head and steady arms grew smaller and smaller until Justine could only watch the disruption in the waves caused by his presence.

"He'll make it," said the Black Hook.

Justine turned and realized this time he spoke to her rather than his crew. From under the shadow of his hat, dark eyes glistened. Makbal had brought the dinghy right up against the rowboat. It was an easy distance for Justine as she jumped up and shouted, "Liar!" Her right hand cut through the air ahead of her, back and forth, slicing at whatever it found. The pirates cried out in surprise and perhaps in pain, but she only had eyes for the Black Hook.

He lunged out of her way just when she might have trapped

him so that she threw herself at empty air instead and fell over the side of the rowboat.

The current came hard and fast, sweeping her away before she could orient herself toward the surface. An eternity passed before she saw the light of the surface and clawed her way up. When her head cleared the water, her ears filled with the roar of the falls. Too, too close. She twisted herself in a circle.

Open water.

Open water.

And there, ahead as the current ran, two fishing skiffs lay at anchor, a net stretched between them.

Though it drained every bit of her lopsided, aching strength, Justine swam to the side so the current carried her into the net. It crushed against her, demanding she continue on her way to an eternity of falling. She gritted her teeth against the pain as the people in the boats saw what they'd snared and hauled in the nets. None too soon Justine found herself coughing and sputtering on the smelliest fishing boat there ever was.

Her feet were useless, but she found she could drag herself to the railing and pull herself up. She looked back the way she'd come. The *Osuana* was just disappearing under the waves. Makbal and the dinghy were thankfully, blessedly, riding the current toward the fishing boat to retrieve her.

"Thought he'd leave you behind, eh?" asked one of the boat hands, a grimy, fish-guts-smeared woman with no hair. "Take it from me, girlie. If you're thinking that now, don't wait ten lifetimes to make a change. He ain't worth it."

"I'm perfectly capable of making up my own mind, thank you."

Justine rolled herself over the boat railing and landed with a hard thump in the dinghy. "Did it work?"

"No."

Tears rushed to Justine's eyes. "But we saw him pass into the mist. He was surely almost to the cliffs."

"Oh, yes, I suppose Fetu made it. I thought you meant the Black Hook. He's not dead, not even wounded." Makbal shot her an accusing glare doubled by the feeling of accusation through their bond. *Traitor, traitor, traitor*, his mind seemed to pulse in waves over her awareness. But this time, perhaps for the first time, Justine was too angry to absorb them.

"You think I missed on purpose?" Justine stared at him. "After all this time, you still think I'll betray you like that girl did? What the fuck do I have to do—"

"Time is nothing. It's your heart that betrays you. It remains divided."

"The *island* remains divided. I'm the same girl you thought might be a good fit for your cockeyed plan. Unless you know something about the island being able to turn me into a goddess so I can stitch everything back together and magically make your brother less of an arsehole, nothing about this is going to change. So why don't you get on with the road that's been paved for us and make the best of it."

He stared at her, wild eyebrows furrowed in consideration, which wasn't at all the reaction she'd expected.

"What did I say?" asked Justine.

"The island revealed the black brothers to you."

"Yes. Maybe. I'm not sure actually."

"They told me it wasn't possible."

"My memory isn't great these days, but I do remember quite clearly that we promised you'd start telling me more things so I could try to play my part better. This would be an example of one of those times."

"My mothers said I couldn't ever truly replace the Black Hook with another god."

"Well, I'm not sure that's—I mean, I think he'd still have to be dead for me to take his place." Something pinged in the side of Justine's head, a lost thought, momentarily found but now quickly drifting out of reach. Something about two rocks, thus two brothers, the need for both of them if she wanted to be a goddess.

They had reached the Ocean's Mouth. Makbal stopped rowing and pulled a vial out of his pocket. "I brought this for you. To help with the strain." The last dregs of Justine's anger faded. She found it easy to believe things weren't nearly so bad as they seemed. In fact, seeing that little purple vial, she felt certain the turmoil of the past however many nacels had been an overreaction.

Justine swallowed the tonic and lay back against the prow of the dinghy. The curtain that descended over her was less than she'd hoped. The warmth in her bones merely tepid. The pain didn't completely vanish from her aching limbs. But it was something. She inhaled the scent of petrichor and thought how it was a strange word for her to know. So useless and obscure.

She sensed Makbal studying her in a way that felt like his mind asking questions. "Are you thinking of what a goddess I'd make?" she asked.

"I'm thinking the island could make you stronger than you are already."

It wasn't a compliment. He was afraid again. Justine laughed. *Silly Mak and his preoccupation with strength. Doesn't he know that lifting the kettle has become a chore?* How could he be so afraid of a girl whose dearest wish in the world was to sleep?

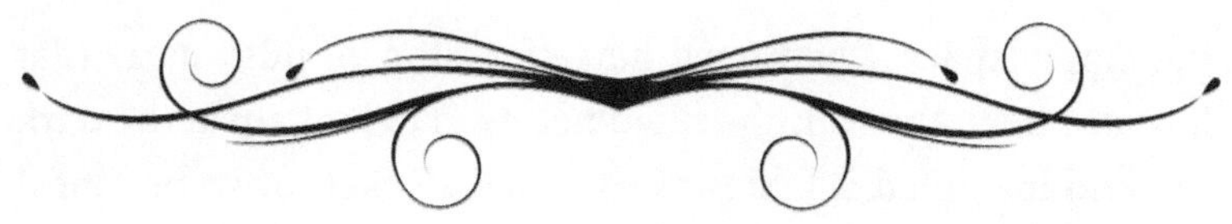

CHAPTER 31

A Mer Gift

Night had descended over the island by the time they resurfaced on the other side of the Ocean's Mouth. The moons hung in the sky as dim thumbnails smogged with clouds. Even the stars seemed muted so that the water all around was the inkiest black, a darkness that felt solid, like it might creep up and wrap around her. Makbal wasn't helping ease her disquiet. He'd been so very silent since he rescued her from the fishing boat. She felt his thoughts coursing around in little whirlpools crammed together in his mind.

They rounded the point and passed the fae village. Its lights could just be seen as a warm glow between the trees. *So very pretty.* She would've loved to pull to shore and lay back in the soft grasses of the clearing, let those lights warm her skin. Too quickly, Makbal rowed past it and the darkness pushed in once again.

A thought came to her of the same lights, but in a small cave. Justine felt the dim pressure of an unfamiliar voice in the back of her mind speaking in riddles. The arm she no longer had ached. Without thinking, she reached over and massaged the empty space. She forced herself to stop, to push away that hazy thought. Instead, she tilted her head to look up at the dark sky and imagined it had never seemed so clear or so beautiful when she'd been alive.

When was I alive?

A splash of water sounded to her right. A frog maybe.

"This is very romantic, isn't it?" she sighed. "I used to dream of going out to the countryside to stargaze."

"Nothing special about stars."

Drifting on the tonic, Justine didn't feel the need to argue. Her hand floated up to toy with the pinpricks of light that burned across the night sky. They seemed to move away from her, then follow in behind, coy little stars they were. "I wish they were bigger," she said.

"Stars are distant because they're being punished by the moon," said Makbal.

"Whatever for?"

He shrugged. "Only the First Ones remember now."

"Over a lover's quarrel, I'm sure." She sighed. Something pinged across her mind, a memory now forgotten, of something she'd wanted, of a man who'd loved a girl so much, he'd burned down his world for her.

"You know I'm not really—"

Justine waved her arm to silence him so she wouldn't have to hear again how romance was for adults because they'd forgotten how to have fun. Before she could stop herself, Justine thought of Arandasal, with his full body, water sliding down his strong thighs at Coral Falls Lake. The quiet power of him, so different than Makbal's rigid insecurity.

Is he the man from my dreams? Otherwise, she couldn't explain how her memory held such a clear picture of a man without his clothes.

The dinghy came around the coast and entered the lagoon.

Makbal splashed the oars once, twice against the water, then let them rest.

"You must be so tired," said Justine. "I'm glad we were able to save—"

Makbal lunged forward and clapped his hand over her mouth. "Quiet." With his touch, a cacophony of impressions pressed into Justine's awareness. She screeched with fear as she scrambled away from him, gasping for breath. Makbal went still; not just in his body, but also the space he occupied in her mind. As in, his feelings vanished from Justine's perception. He remained opposite her in the dinghy, tense, listening, waiting.

Bright silver light illuminated the cove. Justine looked up and saw that the clouds had in fact disappeared and the moons had become beaming circles in the sky. *Now the night is truly beautiful*, thought Justine, which also confused her. Because she'd felt quite sure of the night's beauty before, when she'd barely been able to see anything. And now, it seemed beautiful in a truer way. Her eyes began to pick out shapes detaching from the shadows and moving along the edges of the rocks.

"Really, Makbal, I don't want to play with the mer tonight. Can't we just be together?"

Makbal shook his head, eyes bright with trapped energy. Still she felt nothing from him in her mind, almost as though he had hidden himself from their bond. "They are especially dangerous during a full moon," he said. "It's the only time they eat."

Justine heard them then, a murmuring wave of voices so quiet at first they'd been nothing to her, but now they rose in both pitch and intensity, a keening wail that seemed to surround the dinghy. She shrank back from the edge.

The light of the moons had become so bright, she could see the mer clearly now, their long hair, even the texture of their scarred skin as they tilted their faces up to the sky, wailing at the moons like wolves.

"They're so beautifully sad, aren't they?"

The boat rocked. Justine turned and saw Makbal on his knees before her. He unlaced the ribbon around the collar of her nightgown and tied the ends around the hilt of a small dagger. She noticed, in a strange realization that added to the strangeness of the moment, that Makbal didn't have a shadow from the moons' light the way she did. *How have I never noticed that?*

"Whatever are you doing?" She laughed as her heart quickened. If the full moon could bewitch the mer, perhaps it had also taken Makbal.

"He'll ruin everything." Makbal's voice was a low cadence reverberating in her ears. Justine found herself nodding. Not just nodding. Her spirit was rising to join Makbal's dark certainty.

The water rippled just beyond the edge of the dinghy as though a pebble had been dropped, but there was nothing around the ripple's center. Justine's eyes strained the darkness.

"Justine."

Her eyes swiveled back to Makbal's black, glittering eyes, the harsh lines of light and dark cutting jagged lines across his face. He seemed to transform before her eyes into the demon mothers feared.

What mothers? thought Justine. *I'm the only one left.*

This felt like an ending. Though, without her awareness of Makbal's feelings, she couldn't say exactly how or why this was happening. "Sarah would've loved you better," said Justine sadly.

Who's Sarah?

"Shh." Makbal tilted his head. "They're coming."

Justine looked toward the rocks, all empty now. "Are you getting rid of me?" The thought seemed a faraway thing, an idea she saw but couldn't grasp. She had the strange conviction that if it was what Makbal wanted, it must be right.

Black, clawed fingers curled up and latched around the aft side of the dinghy behind Makbal.

"Mak, watch out!"

Makbal swung an oar backward, smashing into the face of a mer rising from the water. The force unbalanced him. The dinghy swayed wildly as Makbal tried to regain his balance. Justine reached to steady him, but as she leaned forward, she was jerked back. More clawed fingers, like the bones of seaweed, twinned through her hair, pulling, pulling.

A hiss sounded in her ear. "Come with us to end your suffering, sweet one."

Maybe Justine felt the need to fight back. But she also felt the temptation of their offer. Would a second death by drowning be so terrible?

"Justine!" she heard Makbal call. Her heart reached for this sound. Yes, he did care about her. But the forces at war within him were more than the thimble of his love. She fell into the water with barely a splash. Just a slip of a girl (though perhaps much more than a slip and hardly a girl), sliding through the ether of another beginning.

Death, she thought, *will be another adventure.*

The water wrapped around her, pulling her body apart in the same way the tonic gave her the sensation of pulling her head away from her body. She became weightless, unburdened, falling.

Falling into darkness.

With each passing league, Makbal's link to her weakened. At first, she knew he was above her, then she could only place him in a far distant proximity, then it was as though the thin thread of his presence had been snipped and, in its place, came more urgent concerns like the burning pain in her chest and her toes. Tingling fire in the arm she had and the arm she'd lost. Heat everywhere. Pressure everywhere. She couldn't breathe, but she was free.

Perhaps I'll never see him again.

She thought she must be drowning and this was the way she would fall through the sea to the eternal realms. She waited to feel the pull of the current. It would hurt, but she would have to swim and swim with all her might. She didn't have a map to guide her to the golden city, but she most certainly wasn't going to spend eternity falling.

Then, Justine remembered breathing didn't matter. She was already dead. And as the current didn't come for her, she thought that death had never smelled so much like the reek of rot and salt stink.

She opened her eyes to a patchwork of sunlight streaming through the holes in a tightly woven seaweed net. Above her, a perfect blue sky was punctured by a ship's mast crowned with crow's nest and rigging, the sails tied up along the yards. Her eyes flinched against the bright light, but she still strained to see the furry, angular face peering down at her from the crow's nest, two pointed ears, the shadow of an interested tail.

There's a kitten on this ship. Her other senses came back then, and she became aware of voices.

"I don't want your gift," said a voice, deep and rich and troubled in a way Justine immediately liked.

"We seek an alliance against the Lord of the Island," hissed a second voice. It sounded like pebbles being crushed in rapids.

"Why? We've no love for each other."

"There are rumors, a true queen has come. One who can restore us."

"The fae prophecy is a story woven from too much palm wine. Take your gift back to her master. The next time you come aboard my ship will be your last."

Justine heard a grunt, then a splash. The first voice

muttered a curse under his breath, then a third voice reached her ear.

"What do you make of it, Captain?"

"Throw her overboard."

"But if the fae think—"

"She killed Rael. She would've killed me if not for him. I won't have her on my ship."

Justine realized he was speaking about her. This perjury seemed quite unfair. She struggled to push back the net so she might defend herself. *Oh yes, there's only one arm now,* she remembered when her efforts failed. She tried again, more focused, gritting her teeth against the pain of a body that didn't want to move.

Finally, she freed herself and was able to sit up. The ship's main deck was a clean line of varnished wood dotted with crates and orderly coils of rope. Two men stood on the aft deck to her right but not the ones she wanted. There, to her left, the Black Hook cut his stark figure against the horizon. Beside him stood a man in a striped shirt, stocking cap, and spectacles without lenses. The men to both right and left had turned to stare at her.

"I haven't killed anyone." Speaking sent shards of glass stabbing through her chest. Justine's head swam as though the ship was suddenly riding rough seas, but she pressed forward, determined to correct this spot on her reputation. "Whoever told you that spoke wrongly."

"I heard it from no one," the Black Hook replied without bothering to face her. "He died in my arms from the slice of your deadly fingers."

Justine did remember something about deadly fingers. But not her fingers, *gloved* fingers, with needles in their ends. Why would *she* have killed someone?

The swimming in Justine's head grew. She reached out to steady herself against the deck and fell sideways. She'd reached with her phantom left hand of course. Pain shattered through her shoulder and head as she hit the decking.

Voices from far away.

"Don't go near her, Zaared."

Bare feet stepped into Justine's vision. Quite hairy feet, but exceptionally clean, with neatly clipped toenails. Nothing at all like her boys' feet. Her vision dipped and swayed.

"She's had the fae poison, Captain," came the voice Justine thought was Zaared's, the man with the stocking cap and glassless spectacles.

Another muttered curse. Justine heard a *tap, tap, tap* she felt sure was the Black Hook's hook knocking on the deck railing. A thought came to her she didn't quite understand, *Wait until he believes you're free.*

This idea seemed wholly alien, and yet true. She thought, *I'm not free in that way yet.* She closed her eyes and made her body limp, her breathing shallow.

"Let me take her down to the brig," said Zaared. "At least we'll see if she can be free of it."

Justine felt herself being lifted. She peeked through a slit of her closed eyes and saw Zaared was carrying her across the deck. Another man opened a hatch for him and the two of them carried her down into the bowels of the ship. The Black Hook called after them. "You'll have full responsibility when she makes an end of us all!"

Safely underdeck and away from his captain, Zaared began to talk to the man who'd helped him.

"Careful with her head. No, not there, the back cell, it has better air."

They jostled her as they walked. Justine had to fight several times not to cry out in pain. By the time they finally lowered her into a bed, which wasn't much more than a hard plank of wood with a thin mattress, pretending to be unconscious had become quite difficult. Her pretend-labored breathing had in fact become genuine panting breaths that hurt her side with every inhale.

As the men retreated, her hands flailed out and grasped Zaared's sleeve. "Do you have any of the peace tonic?" she rasped.

Her vision of the two men swam before her when she peeled open her eyes. They were one, then they were two, then one again. She couldn't keep her grasp of Zaared's sleeve nor see his expression as he patted her hand before gently detaching it.

"You've a long road ahead. But you've got the spirit to make it."

He retreated from her. Justine heard the squeal of metal hinges, the *click* of a lock.

"If she's the queen, why would the fae be poisoning her?" asked the other man.

"One ever only knows one true thing with the fae," said Zaared. "They take to the highest bidder even when it works against them."

The men's voices faded. Justine wanted to call out, to ask again if they perhaps possessed a mere half vial of tonic. She didn't need much. Just something to take her away for a little while. She tried to call out, but her voice refused to work. She tried to stand but managed only to fall onto the floor. With one hand and two knees, she crawled until she met the metal cage that trapped her.

The boat roiled, a pitch and sway that seemed as tumultuous as a thunderstorm.

At some point she was sick.

Then she slept.

When she woke someone was screaming.

Then she slept again.

Her dreams returned, not the sweet fancies of Justine, the island queen, drifting through her paradise waiting for a prince to come. They were claustrophobic nightmares of tunnels seething with dark eyes and dying creatures begging her for water she didn't have.

Voices swam in her ears. Sometimes they were like animals screeching at her. Other times, they were words with meanings that came to her in bits and pieces.

That deep voice so burdened with troubles, "I don't see how you can tell if she's getting better or worse."

A woman's voice, familiar, "We've never done this before. It's impossible to say."

Another woman's low husk of a voice, also familiar, "He must've been desperate to push her this far."

"Don't make excuses for him," said the deep voice.

Justine tried to open her eyes but found the effort too painful. Instead, she reached out, felt through empty air until she connected with someone. A familiar hand. Yes, she knew the line of that palm.

"Lily," she whispered.

"Hey there, lady."

"Am I free yet?"

"Not quite yet."

"But soon."

"You'll get there."

Justine found this comforting. Somewhere in the muddled morass of her mind, she knew something was meant to happen when she was free.

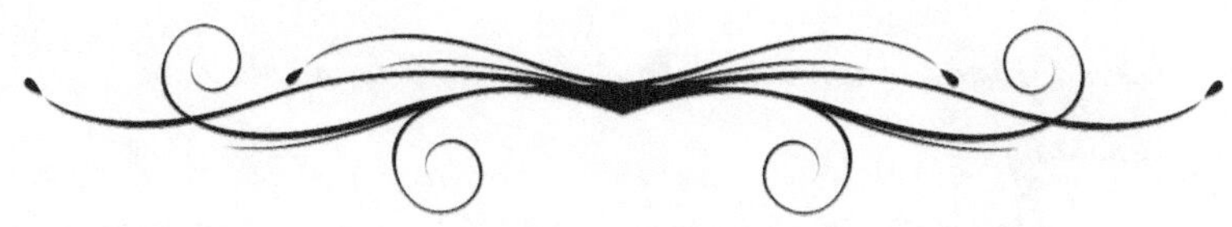

CHAPTER 32

An Improbable Prophecy

In the little house in the jungle where he'd once promised the lost girl he'd grow old with her, the Black Hook lay on the ground and searched his mind for answers.

"He didn't banish you," said the Tigress. "He must not have bonded with the mother yet. I'm going to take a group over and get her."

"The island wants her to stay."

The Tigress shrugged. She wasn't a god, didn't feel the beating heart of the island, so it seemed unlikely to stop her from doing anything she liked.

"I didn't know her," said the Black Hook.

"That doesn't mean you won't later."

Later, which was also the Black Hook's past. He'd been through the puzzle countless times and never found an answer that took him to a place of knowing.

"The last time I saw Thessaly, she had a new name," he said. "She gave me a date and invited me to find her there when I was ready."

This was news to the Tigress. "Why haven't you gone?"

He turned haunted eyes on her. "How can I know when I became the man she loved? I feel less worthy now than I was then when she rejected me."

It was no longer impossible for the Tigress to imagine why someone might reject the Black Hook, but the fact of it still stung. She thought of him as a good leader, entirely trustworthy when it came to the safety of the village and his people. Utterly untrustworthy when it came to matters of the heart and his brother.

"So you find a way," she said. "Nothing has been lost that can't be found."

He grated his hook against the wood as though etching a protective spell against false hope.

Not long after that, the Black Hook was called back to the other side of the island to attend a family meeting. His brother had discovered the pirates' recent invasion and determined it to be the last straw. He'd failed to get rid of the Black

Hook on his own, now he was calling on their creator mothers to intervene.

Family meetings weren't really the Black Hook's style. He especially found it difficult to stand and listen to his brother's murderous rantings as though only one of them was to blame. On this particular meeting, the Black Hook found it even more difficult than usual. The island kept nudging him.

Can't you feel her? she asked.

No.

She's more powerful than the last one. I've claimed her.

The Black Hook strained his senses and thought he could sense someone up in the cliffs that bordered the family gathering. Is she watching?

There can be peace, said the island.

The impossible thought juxtaposed his brother's list of accusations. He wanted the Black Hook dead. Not a new idea. But something about the island pushing this new presence into the Black Hook's awareness, awakened the old space in his heart where love of his brother had once lived. It ached to hear the hate in his brother's words. It longed not for the old days, but for renewal. A chance to begin again.

CHAPTER 33
First Impressions

Justine awoke to bright sun warming her face and pain. Everywhere pain. It hurt to breathe, to move even her smallest finger. She managed to open her eyes and looked out a spotless window to the surprisingly large peaks of the mountains rising from the jungle beyond the harbor. She saw clearly for the first time the stone ruins that poked out from the trees where the jungle began to thin.

This is the other side of the veil, she thought.

She lay in a feather bed that felt three steps away from Heaven, in a room that smelled of sandalwood and spices. Justine managed to turn her head and see that she must be in the captain's cabin of the *Osuana* where she'd been once before on a long ago night when Lily the Tigress had tried to give her gloves.

The night Sven was murdered.

Footsteps sounded above her head, heavy on the solid wood. They came down the side of the wall where she supposed there were steps, though she saw no outline cut in the edge of the ceiling. The steps stopped outside the door.

A knock sounded. Justine found her throat too sore to form

words. She could only manage the whisper of a croak. Somehow it seemed she'd been heard. The door opened and in walked the Black Hook, stooping as he crossed the threshold so he wouldn't hit his head. A shudder ran down her spine, but she couldn't help but notice again what a fine presence he made even though he only wore short pants and a loose white blouse instead of his black coat.

"You're Arandasal," she croaked.

The name surprised her. It seemed a knowledge she didn't know she had. It sat in conflict with what she felt was his true name. Wasn't this also the Black Hook? Dreaded pirate whose heart had been cut out of his chest by his own hand so he wouldn't fall prey to human weaknesses? A man so vile that the creature of the deep who one day rose up to swallow him had only managed to bite off his hand before spitting him back out. A man who, in his disfigurement, had stopped at nothing to pollute everything he touched and would still not stop until the world was under the knife of his hook.

He moved to the far corner of the cabin and seated himself on the bench by the dining table, as far away from her as he could be. As he sat, Arandasal took a deep breath, then let it out. When he looked at her, it was as though through a mask, his entire self hardened against her.

Her eyes dropped to Arandasal's lap where his hook sat on his thigh, the sharp end stoppered with a piece of cork. It pressed into the top of his knee while his other hand gripped the other knee with equivalent force. *I'm not welcome here.* She looked around the room, everything so clean and tidy.

"Who does your housekeeping?"

"I do."

"You're good at it." She dared to look at him again and saw he'd narrowed his eyes. *Lovely eyes,* she thought. *Long lashes.* All that dark hair stood in extravagant contrast to his skin. He kept both his hair and beard long, but the lines were neat and clean just like everything else about him.

"What are you doing here?" he asked.

"The mer took me down for their full moon supper, but now I'm here."

He looked down at his hook. "How long since you lost your arm?"

"It's an old injury," she lied. "Not from the mer. I suppose I didn't smell appetizing."

"You smell of the rain."

Justine blushed, thinking this was a compliment. But his face didn't lighten. Then she remembered. "The fairy tonic. Do you have any on board?"

"That tonic is a poison that robs the mind of its own thoughts and inserts the will of others."

"Well, yes. But a little doesn't hurt. If you had some, I'd be careful with it."

His hook tap, tap, tapped on his knee. It glinted in the light and Justine couldn't help but think, *One wrong word and he'll come at me and slice my throat.* Her hand went to her neck. The strings of her nightgown's collar hung empty.

"Lily took your knife. You may ask her to return it when she visits next."

This news suddenly made Justine exceptionally tired. The loss of the knife was a failure. A panicky feeling prickled at the back of her mind. *What will I do now?*

"If you insist on the return of your knife, you'll be promptly cast from this ship and returned to the island where I'm sure Mak waits with an eternal supply of your tonic. Is that what you wish?"

Justine frowned. This seemed an important question, one that shouldn't be difficult to answer, and yet, when words rose to her lips, there were too many to make sense of, all of them clamoring against each other to be the answer she made true with her voice.

"I'm not your prisoner?"

"I haven't made up my mind."

"Is it true you cook prisoners alive and eat them?"

"No."

"You steal boys from the island and lock them in your hold until they're old men and can't fight back?"

"No." He paused. "It was true once."

Despite her fatigue, Justine felt her coyness returning. There was just something about Arandasal that made her want to slant her shoulders and look at him from under her eyelashes. She propped herself up on her elbow.

"Well then." She smiled. "What *do* you do with them?"

His jaw shifted back and forth, grinding his teeth as he considered her. It wasn't a kind expression, that hardness made him fierce, as though he might in a moment turn into an animal and devour her. Justine wondered if she might enjoy that.

"We don't keep prisoners on this ship," said Arandasal. "There has never been much need."

"But Ling and Qassim—" Justine paused, the accusation left unspoken as she realized she couldn't confirm her belief.

"They've built a house in the Delt Hills. You may ask Lily about them."

A light scratching sounded at the door. "Not now," he said.

The scratching stopped, then was replaced with a plaintive mewing. Arandasal cleared his throat as he stood up and opened the door. The orange tabby kitten Justine had seen in the crow's nest pushed through the opening and bounded into the room. After an investigative sniff, it moved toward the bed where Justine lay.

"Puddle, no!" barked Arandasal.

Puddle flattened its ears against her head, took another sniff Justine's direction, then turned and bounded over to the bench where Arandasal had retaken his seat. The kitten jumped up into Arandasal's lap, stood up so that one paw rested on either side of the dread pirate's neck and began to noisily suck his right ear.

Arandasal gently pulled the kitten away, tried to press her into sitting quietly on his lap, but Puddle wouldn't have it. Just as soon as his coaxing appeared to work, it was up again, claws dug into his neck, his beard, then even his cheek in desperate need to massage his earlobe with its mouth.

"She was detached from her mother too young," he explained a little sheepishly. It seemed a noble gesture for him not to mention that Makbal and her boys were the ones responsible for stranding the kitten on the ship.

"So now you're the mother," said Justine.

"Apparently." He used his hook to gently nudge the paw dug into his cheek to a more comfortable position.

I'd like to be that kitten.

Justine pushed the thought away.

"As you appear to have passed the worst of the withdrawal, I'll ask Zaared to take you back down to the hold. When Lily returns, you two can decide what you'll do next."

"You don't care at all?"

Puddle's sloppy kisses filled the room. Justine watched the corners of Aransadal's jaw work like he was crushing nuts with his teeth. Finally, he said, "Has the island revealed itself to you?"

"I built a castle. Lily said that was pretty impressive."

"The revelation isn't the same as power. It's an offering for you to take on the portions of deity Mak and I placed in the island."

"Oh, yes. I remember that now. After I kill you, there'll be space for me to become a goddess and repair what you destroyed when you went off on your foolish romance."

Justine's hand flew to her mouth. *Where had that come from?*

"My brother's words come so clearly from your mouth I can almost hear him. I had thought perhaps without the tonic, his hold on you would have diminished."

"What's so wrong with his words?" demanded Justine, the heat again rising to her face, but this time she felt only fury. "I suppose you're going to say that everything I know is a lie and he's the one who betrayed you for love. I can tell you, sir, I'll never believe that!"

Arandasal impatiently pushed Puddle away from his face. "That's enough, you're hurting me." For a moment, Justine wasn't sure if he spoke to her or the kitten. *The kitten surely,* she thought. *What could I possibly do to him without my knife?*

"Your story's true enough. But Mak puts too much confidence in my death. It's unclear what effect such a loss would have on the island. The fae believe only three together can heal what was broken. Now it seems they've put it into a story. When the two brothers are each touched by the one who makes the climb to reach them."

This story sounded familiar. Justine searched her mind to place it and found only cobwebs and a headache.

"I'll call Zaared to help you." Arandasal moved toward the door.

"Wait."

His shoulders bunched up beneath his shirt as though she'd struck him.

"I wonder if you could help me with my arm. If I could have a hook, and have someone sew little loops on my clothes, I think I'd be a much better mother."

"That'd take some time."

Justine laughed. "Time. I barely remember what it is."

"I have hooks we might adjust for you. But what you truly need is a hook and half an arm, which I don't have here."

For the first time since he'd entered the cabin, Justine felt him softening toward her. He had forgotten his caution and begun to think of her needs. This seemed quite promising.

"This half an arm and a hook can be found somewhere else? Like the treasure hoard in the Green City?"

"They are more easily found above, in the land of the living. But I'm not sure—"

"Yes. I want to go."

"Mak may not let you."

"What does he have to do with it?"

Arandasal's jaw did more clenching. He studied her. It was a look less severe than before, but no less unsettling for its intensity. "It is a matter of logistics. I will ask the fae what price they demand to subvert their own magic and risk the agreement they have with him."

"The fairies bound me to Makbal?"

"Yes and no. It's complicated. If the bond had worked like he wanted, he wouldn't have poisoned you. I'm actually not quite sure how he does it. But the fae will know. Is this what you want?" Arandasal paused as he appeared to carefully choose his next words. "You want to leave him?"

"I want to be free." There was that thought again, the promise of freedom, it burned like dying embers buried deep in Justine's mind.

Arandasal nodded. "I suppose that's something we can work on for now. Is it understood that killing me won't help you heal the island?"

"Yes," said Justine, because that was clearly what he wanted her to say.

"And you understand that doing harm to my men will also not help you get what you want?"

"Yes."

"Then we'll go uprealm and find you an arm." Arandasal opened the door and stuck his head out. Justine couldn't help but admire the way his butt pressed against the seat of his trousers as he leaned. "Zaared, will you and Freddy help the lady down to her room?"

Justine's heart sank. For some reason, she'd thought their new understanding would allow her to stay in the cabin.

"It's a fine thing for you to say Mak controls my mind," she said to his back. "You hate him so much you can't imagine someone would want to be with him."

The strong line of Arandasal's shoulders tightened. He pulled himself back into the cabin and turned to her. "If you so desire him, I can put you in a boat and send you to him this very hour. I'm sure the tonic awaits you in abundance. Is that what you want?"

Yes.

No.

Not until I'm free.

"I wish for an arm," said Justine. "That's all I know right now."

A knock sounded on the other side of the door.

"An arm you shall have. But your time here will ride better if you don't spend it making baseless accusations."

"So, it isn't true that you hate him more than anything, and your heart has turned black with it?"

As he stared at her, his features shifted and contracted, the residual explosions of a war being waged beneath the surface of his sun-weathered skin. "My heart isn't your concern." Arandasal opened the door and strode out. Puddle followed him. A moment later, Zaared's bespeckled face appeared in the opening.

"Shall we see if you can walk on your own today, Mother?"

Justine swung her legs over the side of the bed. "My name is Justine."

"Justine then." Zaared grinned.

"Your captain vexes me."

"He has that effect. But you'll learn to love him as we all do."

Zaared paused as though he was reconsidering his words, but being unsure how to correct them, he merely offered her his hands for support as she lowered herself to the floor.

Justine thought learning to love Arandasal wasn't the problem. Some part of her already loved him or, at least, desired him. The problem was she couldn't tell if this was a true part of her, or something that had been given by any number of the forces that had claimed a corner of her mind.

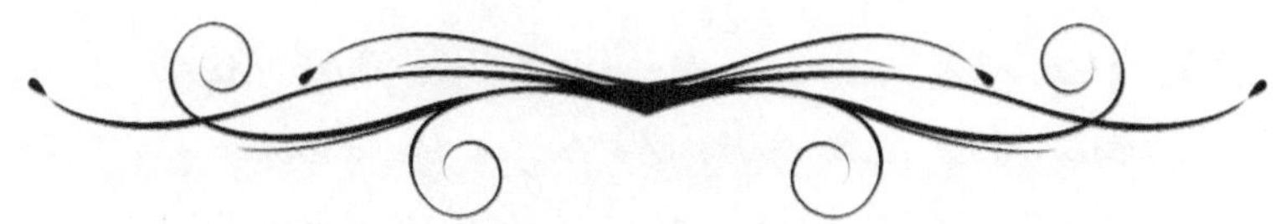

CHAPTER 34

The Shadow

After the family meeting, the Black Hook planned to honor the wishes of his mothers and stay on his side of the island. If he could prove himself honorable, perhaps his brother wouldn't hate him as much. For the first time in quite a while, the Black Hook didn't wish to live up to his name. He gave up his pirating ways. Began his wandering again.

But it seemed no sooner had he resolved on reformation than he was given an opportunity to break it. One of the lost boys crossed the veil and asked the Black Hook to help him reach the current so he could swim to his afterlife.

Even though he knew it would anger his brother, the Black Hook agreed. By now you'll have heard what happened. The brother came upon the pirates as they were releasing the boy to his fate. The Mother came with them. No longer the dreamy girl he'd seen on the rocks, the Mother attempted to kill the Black Hook with poisoned needles concealed in her gloves. By accident, she'd killed another pirate instead.

The pirates wanted revenge, but the Black Hook declared himself done with it. Revenge just led to more revenge. If his choices, the whole of his existence, added up only to this cycle of spilled blood, he would no longer fight to exist. So it was, when the mer delivered the Mother to the deck of his ship, the Black Hook saw that she had been given the power to kill him. Furthermore, he would allow it to happen if that was what the fates had decided.

"What do you think will be gained by your death?" asked the Tigress, more emotional than he had ever seen her. They stood together on the safe side of a holding cell, watching the Mother toss and turn in a fevered delirium. "We can't go on without you."

"You can."

"What about your future with Thessaly?"

"Even a promised future is never certain."

"But she said she knows you. She loves you."

The Black Hook studied the girl on the other side of the bars. He'd decided she was the same person he'd met at that long ago wedding. She'd now lost part of her arm, an injury that matched the prosthetic Thessaly wore. At best guess, he thought the woman-turned-goddess he'd known was ten or more years older. On the surface, this was proof that the myth of the island was true. She had the power to turn a mortal into a god. But the Black Hook could not believe it.

"Perhaps this girl kills me, and I am remade by my mothers. She knows that man, not me."

The Tigress huffed out her disbelief. "You can't give up."

"She chose my brother not me."

The Tigress left the hold before she slapped her leader for his idiocy. Only a man so accustomed to misery could stare at his salvation and be determined to disprove it.

The Black Hook remained in the hold. He kept vigil with the ailing Mother. In her most peaceful moments of sleep, he knew her. The same face, the same instinct to tuck an arm under her head and clench her residual limb at her waist as though she expected to be attacked in the night.

"The first time I saw you, I thought you were the most beautiful creature I'd ever seen," he said. "The second time I saw you, I thought I'd lose you forever and you laughed at me. Even when it became clear you were in dire need of rescue, you were laughing at me. That crazy heart of yours has no limits." He swallowed back an emotion pirates were not supposed to feel.

"You once promised me we had a future. I confess I can't see it. There is no map for a road that leads from here to there. You're his tool now. For all I know, he went up and found a girl who looked the part and brought you here to end me. If that's how it's going to be, I'd like to know before the end. If it's really you, free yourself from him."

CHAPTER 35

Memories and Rumors

J ustine's cell had been made over with a full mattress, a blanket, and a pillow. A yellow paper lantern hung over the candle box and brightly colored cloth had been hung across the cell's bars to give her privacy. She wondered how terrible her sickness had been that these men would take such care with her.

Through a small porthole window, she watched time pass in the rising and setting sun. Zaared or Freddy, a man with creaking joints and a patch over one eye who liked to shoot marbles, brought her meals, and as she ate, they kept her company on the other side of the bars. They spoke only of banalities—how the fish so-and-so had caught for dinner was quite good, how there was probably a war on uprealm because the stream of bodies falling at the head of the river seemed denser than usual. Whenever she tried to ask about Arandasal or what they remembered from the island, they pushed her off with a shrug or a laugh and left their thoughts unspoken.

But mostly, Justine was alone, which gave her a great deal of time to think. At first, thinking felt unduly difficult, and all she could consider was the pain that sprung up like weeds in various corners of her body. She longed for peace as a person in a desert longed for water. This felt an especially apt illustration because she dreamed almost every night of going on a long journey and encountering people and creatures in need of water.

In both dreaming and waking she could concentrate her awareness and find Makbal, a ghostly presence still linked to her but also removed. Once or twice, she sensed flashes of his pleasure. Only once did she sense something else, the fear eating away at him. She couldn't tell that he missed her.

The fourth night, Justine awoke screaming, thrust from a dream where a pack of rabid dogs had chased her across a river that ended in a cliff. She'd fallen into an abyss of black mist. It had taken her some time to come out of it, to feel her bed and the blanket someone had tucked around her. She turned her head. There, on the other side of the bars, Arandasal sat on an overturned bucket watching by the light of the lanterned candle.

Still breathless from her fright, Justine could think of nothing to say to him. She merely turned on her side and stared back at him. They remained that way, locked in each other's eyes for several moments before he let out a burden of trapped air from his lungs and left the hold.

She thought that was the end of it. But only a few minutes passed before the footsteps returned. Two pirates, looking very stern and a little nervous, gave her only a nodded greeting before one unlocked her cell door.

"The captain says you're allowed to come up for dinner."

"What if I don't want to?"

The pirates exchanged glances. One shrugged and moved to close the door again.

"Don't be silly. Of course I'm coming."

She walked between them like a prisoner up to the main deck. The *Osuana* was anchored in the Delt harbor. She could see the evening lamps of the village being lit. A group of people gathering in what looked like a town square. She thought this was their destination. A communal dinner with adults, she could hardly imagine it.

But then the pirates turned and escorted her up the length of the ship to the door of the captain's cabin where she'd been before. One pirate knocked. When Arandasal's deep voice said, "Enter," the pirates melted away and left her to open the door and enter the cabin alone.

The gas lamps cast the cabin in a warm glow that seemed to blanket it from the deepening night of the outside world. The table at the center of the room was set for two with food already on the plates: grilled fish with berries, stewed green leaves, and a kind of root hash. And there, at the far end of the cabin, the Black Hook watching her with eyes that seemed to see more than she wanted to reveal.

"I'm indecent." She looked down at her nightgown, which hadn't been washed. Even if it had been clean, a nightgown wasn't the thing a respectable woman wore to dinner with a man. But then a man would have been looking for what she was revealing and Arandasal wasn't. In fact, he looked only at her face, his eyes moving back and forth across it as though trying to puzzle something out.

She sat down at one place setting. After a few moments' hesitation, he did the same.

"So, you've decided to be a proper host."

"Nothing proper about it. This is my usual, and I've merely taken the step of allowing you to eat at a table instead of your cell. If you're impressed, perhaps you should go out in society more."

She choked back a surprised laugh. There'd even been a trace of home accent when he'd said it, a phrase that belonged to an English gentleman.

"You've spent time in England?"

"I have."

"During the reign of Victoria?"

"Yes."

There was something he was being careful not to say. She felt each of his answers clipped off at the ends.

"You think I'm a child."

"Did Mak explain to you the nature of gods in time?"

"Of course he did." She shoved a fork of food in her mouth and chewed. When she dared to look up, he was watching her with a slightly amused expression. "But the tonic has made many of my memories unclear. So if you wanted to explain it again, if it has relevance for why you clearly don't want to explain how a phrase like that just rolls off your tongue—Are you trying to make me homesick?"

"Time has no meaning for immortals. My brother appears as a child, I don't, but we've existed from the same moment. It's nothing for an immortal to travel from the eternal realms to those of the living. They can pass a human lifetime in one place and another somewhere else."

"You're telling me you spent a lifetime in England at the same time I was there?"

"Yes," he said softly. "You were there."

"And after? Does the fog ever get better? Actually, don't answer that. I can't imagine London without it." She took a breath; she was eating too fast. It was surprisingly stressful, sitting under his gaze. It was impossible not to be aware of how much he knew compared to what she knew. She didn't even know what questions to ask.

But then, as the silence lengthened, she thought of one. "So why can't you go back and change what happened with your girl?"

"Osuana."

"Yeah. She's the thing that started all this, right? Couldn't you just go back to the beginning and do it again better?"

"I'm a fixed being. I can only be in one place at a time." To her confounded look, he added, "If I were to return to a place I already existed, there would need to be two of me."

"Not sure I really understand, but it sounds like a pretty mortal thing to not be able to fix mistakes."

"Which mistake?"

"What?"

"Which mistake do you think I should fix?"

"I—" Justine paused. Wasn't it obvious? Whatever was the beginning, the choice that led to the island being destroyed. "You chose her over everyone else."

Arandasal nodded slowly. "I thought she deserved to be happy. And at the time, it seemed an interesting experiment. I wanted to go on that journey with her."

"The journey of growing up, you mean. You were going to grow old together, then she would pass on to the eternal realms and you would've just done something else."

"You're angry."

"It just doesn't seem fair. If you really loved her, couldn't you have made her a goddess?"

"I don't have the power to create gods."

"But the island—"

"The island's delusional and broken. You've heard her voice?"

Justine nodded.

"Other people are also hearing that voice. They think the island wants the truly dead to live in the Neverland."

"Is that possible?"

Arandasal took his first bite of food as he considered his answer. She watched the muscles of his throat as he chewed and swallowed, the hollow at its base that looked soft enough to stroke.

"I've seen you in my dreams."

"Have you?"

Justine blushed. "Sorry, I didn't mean to say that. Obviously, it's not proper."

"The island gave you visions of me? What kind?"

Justine shook her head and focused on her plate. "Nothing important. Just you know, the usual. Pirate things."

"Improper things." He was smiling at her. The first smile she'd ever seen from him. In that moment, she forgot herself and stared. Then the moment passed.

"You didn't answer my question."

"The truth is I don't know. I feel it shouldn't be possible. Anyone who comes here is invited by me or Mak. And since the island's rupture, even we can't come or go from the realm without the aid of fae dust."

"Is that why we haven't left to go get my new arm yet?"

"The fae are being their usual selves. But we're not in a hurry."

"You think the longer I stay with you the less likely I'll want to go back to Mak?"

"I'm hoping exactly that, yes."

"Am I still bonded to him?"

"Yes."

"Can he feel what I feel?"

"If he's paying attention."

"But I don't feel him. Not like I'm used to."

Arandasal reached his hand out into the center of the table, lifted a pointed finger up at something she couldn't see. "It's right there. You and he." His voice choked as he said, "I shouldn't have let it happen. I'm sorry I didn't come for you before. Lily told me and I didn't listen."

And how different things would have been. Justine could hardly grasp it. If she'd let Lily rescue her after the accident. If she'd stayed on the *Osuana* that first time. So many chances.

"I wanted to come. But I was also afraid. He said—all the boys said—you would kill me. That you killed past mothers and kidnapped boys. That all you cared about was beating Mak in the war you'd started."

"They're not all lies. I've thought for a long time that when you knew what I'd done you wouldn't want me anymore."

"What?"

"Sorry. Forget that. It didn't make sense." He took a breath. "Gods, this is unreal."

She laughed. "Just imagine how I feel. Sitting here, eating dinner with the enemy."

"I did kill some of the mothers. And yes, I took some satisfaction in doing it, which I'm not proud of. But it was also a mercy. They always disappointed him. And when anyone reaches a point where they've disappointed my brother, he moves quite quickly to discard them."

"Like he did with me."

"No."

"No?" Justine laughed. But then she watched Arandasal lift his finger and trace the invisible line of her bond through the air. "He hasn't discarded you. He's sent you on an errand."

"To kill you," she said, and felt the thrum of its truth vibrate down her spine. "Is that why you're so afraid of me?"

"Afraid? No. I'm giving you as much time as I can to let you regain yourself, so you'll be strong enough to make your choice." He paused and the look on his face was so close to love, almost adoration, it stopped her cold with surprise. "And if you choose him, it's just as well I cease to exist because the only future I want is bound up with you."

Justine found herself brushing tears from her eyes, confused as to where they'd come from, even more confused about how this man could look at her so, to say such a thing, and for her to know it came from such depths of conviction as she had never known from anyone else.

"My apologies. I've said too much."

"Have you?"

More, she silently begged. *Give me more. Tell me everything.*

A knock sounded on the door and a pirate she hadn't met yet entered the cabin. "Fae messenger just arrived, Captain."

"And?"

"They say there will be dust enough soon, but not yet."

"Is it a ploy?"

"Zaared thinks no. There have been rumors of fae dust gone missing."

"Is the messenger still here?"

"Aye, sir."

"I'll speak with them." Arandasal rose from the table and didn't give Justine so much as a glance as he walked out without a word.

CHAPTER 36

A Tether Snapped

Arandasal didn't invite her to dinner again. Much as it felt like a cruel form of torture, Justine had to settle for eating in her cell and sitting with whoever delivered her food.

"Zaared?" she asked between bites of a hard biscuit.

"Yes?"

"Do you think Aranda could be in love with me?"

Zaared chuckled. "What gave you that idea?"

"Just some things he said. I've been thinking."

"Should be careful about that. Thinking leads to things. And you shouldn't call him that."

"No? I thought it quite nice. It sounds like a dance."

"Osuana called him that way. It's a hard reminder on his ears."

"For heaven's sake. What is it with these men and their infatuation with the past? How long has she been gone?"

"Longer than I've been here." Zaared pulled off his cap and scratched his head. "Which I suppose has been about fifteen hauntings now. Think it happened just before I came because there weren't pirates in the cove when I was a boy. The captain was off on his seafaring days then."

"So, what is it? He's not trapped by eternity like Mak is. Why hasn't her death faded with time?"

"Some deaths don't. A love like that, maybe it never will."

Justine flopped back on her bed. How she wanted a love like that! If she was ever so lucky to find it, she would be sure not to die tragically as Osuana had.

"When I was a boy on the island, I heard it this way," said Zaared. "The island might become as it was made to be when a woman of special character finds the path. We used to try to find the path or make our own through the tunnels. But we never saw the top of the falls."

An image came to Justine of a narrow path with rocks rising sharply on one side and an equally sharp drop down to water on the other. She shook her head as though to clear it.

Running footsteps sounded on the deck above. Excited shouting.

"That must be the message back from the fae," said Zarred. "Took their sorry time about it. Want to come watch the blessing?"

Justine pushed herself into sitting. "Is that allowed?"

"Today it is."

Zaared unlocked the cell and offered her his hand. With a delighted grin, Justine accepted his offer. Though much of her strength had returned, she still didn't have her sea legs. She leaned on him as they walked up the ramp to the main deck, which was busy with activity as the crew ran about readying the ship to sail. In the center of this chaos was a circle of stillness. Arandasal stood within it wearing his sharp black coat and feathered hat, looking every bit the dread pirate captain he was supposed to be, except for Puddle held in the crook of his arm. Three fae held conference with him. One of them was Tassi.

It seemed an aggressive conversation. Even from her place in the shadow of the quarter deck, half the length of the main deck away, Justine could hear the furious staccato of fairy chime and the hard line of Arandasal's responses.

"I'm surprised they don't want me to leave," said Justine. "Tassi has had it out for me since I arrived."

"They have good reason to worry," said Zaared. "A bonded mother has never left the Neverland. And you're in such a fragile state."

"I assure you, I'm perfectly well."

Zaared arched a speculative eyebrow.

"Oh, alright. I'm at least well enough to travel." Justine's eyes traced the long line of Arandasal's back and wondered why it seemed so often she was left looking at him from behind. Not that this was a problem. It just seemed like a strategy to keep her distant. It also seemed quite a nice thing that he was fighting with the fairies on her behalf, something akin to a romantic gesture.

In this moment, filled with warmth toward her imagined version of Arandasal, Justine felt part of her reach out to the fairies with a message. She didn't at first realize that was what happened. For her, it was just a slight brush of something draining out of her chest, a feeling that she'd lost a thing she hadn't known she carried. Though the fairies didn't turn to look her direction, Tassi's light flared as though with a nod of receipt as they carried on the negotiation with Arandasal.

What did I tell them? wondered Justine.

The negotiations came to an end. The fairies flew up and separated, each departing to one section of the ship. For the task of blessing the *Osuana*, they had brought large sacks of dust, which they then dropped like small bombs onto the ship. The bags burst apart, sending sparkling silver powder out in all directions.

"First crew ready?" called Arandasal.

A man stationed far to the aft of the ship called back, "All ready, Captain!"

"Second crew ready?" called Arandasal.

The answering call came from behind and above Justine's head. "Second crew ready."

Arandasal shifted Puddle to his hook arm and used his newly freed hand to doff his hat and wave it toward the moons. "Then mark our heading. Second star to the right and straight on to morning."

The *Osuana*, which was now covered from mast to rudder in shimmering silver light, began to groan and creak. Her sails filled with a wind that smelled of flowers. Then, with a light splash as the water released its hold, she tilted up into the air and began to glide toward the sky.

Justine tugged on Zaared's hand to follow her as she wobbled to the railing and looked down. The island shrank below them, becoming first a dark rock, then a speck, before it vanished completely as the *Osuana* climbed into the clouds.

"Oh!" Justine's hand went to her chest.

"Something wrong?" asked Zaared.

"I don't know, I just feel so strange all of a sudden. I—" A sharp pain spasmed across Justine's chest. She pitched against the railing and probably would have gone overboard if Zaared hadn't caught her.

But then she *was* being pulled overboard as though a cord buried in her chest had pulled taut and now would allow her to go no farther.

The *Osuana* continued to climb.

Justine screamed.

"I can't hold her captain," cried Zaared.

Somewhere behind her, Zaared had grasped her, but Justine couldn't feel him. Her lost arm burned. Her knees felt as though they were being crushed, then cold metal circled her arm and twisted her around. She stood face-to-face with Arandasal, her arm in his hook, his hand poised above her as though to strike.

"Tell me for once, do you wish to be free of him?"

Justine gasped. Was he really doing this now? She was surely dying, her body about to be torn in half.

"I can't— Help me, please."

"Do you wish to be free of him?"

"Yes," she gasped.

Arandasal's hand came down upon her. Not hard as she expected, but just the lightest brush of his finger against her collarbone. She felt a light pop, then the tether left her. The pain left her. A weight that had been with her so long she'd ceased to be aware of it melted away. Justine rushed toward him, ready to throw herself into his arms with gratitude, but Arandasal stepped away from her, hook raised to warn her off.

"You're free now. Don't so quickly throw yourself into the hold of another."

She drew back as though this time he really had struck her. "But I want you. The island showed me. I thought you—"

"The island can show you only Mak's thoughts. His fears, most likely. What you think you want has been an illusion until this moment. Now you may be yourself as you see fit."

"Aranda, you don't understand. This is—"

His eyes flared so that the whites turned red and sparked with flames, not unlike his brother's eyes when in rage. "Don't speak so familiar with me, girl. You know nothing of the shadow behind your heart." He turned on his heel and strode away, that hard line of his figure in its well-cut coat even more set against her than before.

Justine became aware of Zaared's hand around her waist holding her upright. "What have I done?" she whispered.

"Let's get you below deck. Your legs have gone all cooked noodle."

As Zaared helped her toward the ramp, Justine twisted her head to look after Arandasal.

I'm free, she thought with a thrill in her heart. *And yet he rejects me.* The thrill became a flame, spreading through her chest, burning down and down until it reached the place where Makbal's missing shadow lay, waiting to be released.

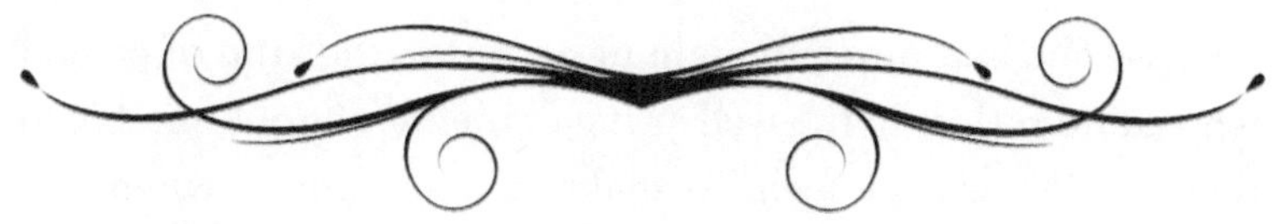

CHAPTER 37

Time Traveling

When Zaared was called away to his duties, Puddle stepped in to keep Justine company. The kitten had been locked below deck (unfairly, Justine thought) at the beginning of the journey and spent a good while mewing and scratching at the hatch before she gave up and wandered over to Justine's cell.

She watched with blinking amber eyes as Justine first raged, then cried, then sat blankly staring at the wall. As surely as it looked like madness to Puddle, it felt like madness to Justine, who sensed the thing she knew as "herself" dividing and shattering, reemerging as some kind of unrecognizable whole only to shatter yet again.

"What's happening to me?" she whispered in a moment of calm. "I just want him. But no, how could I want anything from that unfeeling, heartless—Why do I think that? Is he really those things? Mak says—"

Justine slammed her fist into the bars of her cell.

The tears came again, and with them, an overwhelming sense that she was broken. This was both a shock because she hadn't felt at all broken only a few minutes before, and a shock because she had never thought of herself as the kind of person who could be lost in the wellspring of their emotions, unable to do anything except feel. To make matters worse, when she finally got the tears under control and reached through the bars to pet the kitten, Puddle flattened her ears against her little head and hissed as she retreated out of reach.

In this cycle of rage, loss, bewilderment, and despair, Justine felt hours pass. It was really less than one hour by the pirates' way of keeping time, before the *Osuana* descended into the container district of Oakland, California. She heard the shouts of the crew, then the running of feet, which sounded so much like her boys, then the ship was quiet.

"They've left me," said Justine.

Puddle craned her neck up toward the ceiling and mewed as though she too felt left behind. But then the hatch opened and Arandasal descended. He'd changed out of his pirate clothes and instead wore garments wholly foreign to Justine, trousers so tight they lined his legs like a second skin, a plain shirt of poor cloth that also fit his body as though it was too small. Over it, Arandasal wore a black leather jacket.

But it was his amputated hand that most shocked Justine. In place of the hook, Arandasal appeared to have grown a hand complete with five fingers and skin and fingernails. It was only when she stood up and came to the edge of her cell for a closer look that she saw the nails were painted and the skin tone of the hand didn't quite match Arandasal's skin.

While Justine was looking at it, she was keenly aware of Arandasal's eyes also looking at all of her in a way that made her feel she'd also drastically changed her appearance. Justine looked down and saw that her nightgown seemed to have shrunk, being a little shorter at her knees, and quite a bit tighter at her chest and waist.

"I'm sorry this happened," said Arandasal. "You'll have even more trouble with him now."

Justine thought he was speaking of the broken bond. "I wanted to come."

"Yes, well." He kept looking at her, eyes traveling, probing, openly interested, for perhaps the first time, in more than just her face. "Anyway, I'm off to an appointment. I thought you would come with me, and we would find you an arm. I can't promise it will work perfectly, but we can find something, I think."

"Do I need new clothes?"

"You're a haunt here. No one will see you unless you choose. It's likely they will walk through you, which might feel a bit strange. It would be good if you could resist the impulse to bother them."

Arandasal unlocked the cell, then picked up Puddle who'd been walking figure eights around his ankles. "Shall we?"

Up on the main deck, Justine stopped still at the sight. Buildings all around as tall as mountains, cranes lifting giant metal boxes and swinging them through the air to stack on the docks. And the sounds! Not a bird in sight, but a chorus of chimes and bells and peals filled the air just the same. She barely noticed as Arandasal walked over to his captain's cabin and shut Puddle inside.

"We best move before she gets too upset," he said. "She'll be alright after she can't smell us ignoring her."

Justine followed Arandasal down the gangplank onto paved ground that was a smooth gray slab of something like stone, though she'd never known roads made out of stone. They walked together between the towering buildings, through a gate and onto a street filled with automobiles different from any Justine had ever seen. Unlike the congested London streets where walking people were as likely to fill them as buggies and busses, these streets allowed no people outside of a vehicle, and the vehicles themselves blurred past with only the slightest mechanical hum. Some of the motorcars seemed to be driving themselves as their passengers were occupied with glowing picture frames projected in the air before their eyes.

"This is amazing," breathed Justine. "Still earth?"

"This is the western side of America in the year 2105."

Justine let out a cackle. "We're time travelers. Fuck me. How will I find anything about my time in 2105?"

"You have a question?"

"I just thought—I had a friend. A girl who Mak wanted to choose."

"Sarah, isn't it?"

"How do you know that?"

"They have an archive here where you can look things up." He pulled a square disk out of his jacket pocket with his fake hand just as easily as one might with a real hand. The fingers curled by themselves. Justine couldn't help but reach out and touch the knuckle of the first finger. When she did, it jutted toward her. Justine jumped back with a screech. She looked up and saw Arandasal's eyes laughing at her.

"You did that on purpose."

"I suppose I did. Come on." He led her down the sidewalk, motioning for her to walk on the side of the buildings, with him walking on the street side as though he didn't trust her not to fall into traffic. Justine felt heat rise on her cheeks. It was a small thing, this consideration for her safety, but it felt like the world.

"Not everyone is in the archive, but we should be able to find the area where you were living and get some information. I'll charge this while we're at the clinic, then we can look at whatever you want. Just don't touch it. Haunts don't do well with this kind of machine."

Justine nodded like she understood.

"But you're not a haunt here." She'd noticed people (both women and men) turning their heads to look at him in that way she had looked at him. Arandasal was a person people noticed.

"I appear human to them."

"But you're moving your hand as a god?"

"It's a machine. They call it myoelectric prosthetics. My mind can talk to the hand and tell it to move."

Justine's eyes widened. "Do I get one of those?"

"Sadly, no." He stopped outside a building with the sign of a giant blue and green hand. "You need to be physically present in the world to have one of these fitted. Really, they're impractical for maintenance. You need something more universal. Something you can take back to the island and not be afraid it will wear out." He motioned toward the door. "This is the clinic. It'll be strange if I speak to you here. You can speak to me, but I may not answer if people are nearby."

Justine nodded. "I'm ready."

He stepped up to the door. It opened by itself.

"Machine doors?" she asked.

He nodded.

The inside of the building was so cold, Justine immediately started shivering. She followed Arandasal down a hallway with plants and bright white, electric lights that left no corner in shadow and gave off no smell. They passed through another self-opening door into a small room arranged with chairs in a horseshoe shape open to a secretary's desk. There was a fish tank in one corner and a rectangle on a wall with people trapped inside it, sitting in chairs and chatting to each other. All women, all wearing trousers, all different races.

Thinking it was a window into another room, Justine reached out and touched the screen. Bright energy zipped through her, sending stars dancing across her eyes. When she blinked them away, the rectangle was a black void and a person seated in one of the chairs was yelling toward the secretaries.

"Hey, the TV went out!"

From where he stood at the desk, Arandasal shook his head at her. Chastised, Justine went to the corner with the fewest people and sat down. At first, she thought she'd watch the fish. But then a person came through the door with an arm like Arandasal's and Justine began to look at the people sitting in the room.

At first it was difficult to see the prosthetics, as Arandasal had called them; they looked so much like real body parts. But by the time he finished talking to the secretary and came to sit beside her, Justine had identified one complete arm, two legs, and a foot. She'd stared at blue hair, and a woman's blouse that covered less than a corset, at a man so large he needed two chairs, and a person who seemed neither a man nor a woman. All of them, remarkably clean and remarkably nice smelling for city people.

Arandasal set his rectangular disk on a gray platform beside his chair. The disk lit up just like the thing on the wall she'd touched.

"This is a strange place," she said.

He nodded, then stilled as his eyes cut toward the door. A blond woman had walked in. She wore the shortest skirt Justine had ever seen (above her knees!) and a blouse that fit against her skin. When she saw Arandasal, her eyes went wide, and she changed directions to greet him.

"Aranda! It's been ages."

Justine stared as the woman threw her arms around Arandasal's neck and hugged him.

"Hi, Jo. How's life?"

"It's been a year." She gestured toward her prosthetic leg. "Aging's a bitch. You think you know life as an amputee, then you turn thirty and everything changes. How long are you in town? I'll have Daquan message you. He's on the other coast right now, pushing for this new emissions reduction bill, but he should be back tomorrow."

"I'm not staying long, unfortunately."

Jo's smile dimmed with disappointment. "Well then, you'll have to give me the highlights while we're waiting here."

A door opened and a woman came to stand in the doorway. "Aranda Sanchez?"

Arandasal took his glowing disk from the platform, gave a salute to Jo, and walked toward the woman with a grin that showed all his teeth. "How are you today, Kris?"

"You know, you know. Doing much traveling?"

"They've got me on the road all month," said Aranda, breezing past the woman through the door. Justine followed in bewilderment. *Who is this man?*

They went down another hallway and into a little room with two chairs, a stool on wheels, a strange, raised bed, and another dark rectangle on the wall. Arandasal seated himself in one of the chairs and shrugged out of his jacket. With his thumb and first finger, he pressed the sides of the miscolored skin at the top of his prosthetic. With a small hiss, the skin expanded and detached from the stub of his forearm. Arandasal handed the prosthetic to the woman named Kris who looked inside the empty skin, then dipped a small stick that looked like a fountain pen inside. A green light shone back in her eyes.

"Sensors look good. I'm going to run my diagnostics. Dr. Decuir will be in shortly." Kris carried Arandasal's prosthetic out the door. When she closed it behind her, Justine noticed a mirror mounted on the back. She pointedly ignored it as she jumped up on the strange bed in the middle of the room. The paper sheet down its center felt strange beneath her, cool, and smoother than any paper she knew.

"You have a life here?"

"This is one of the best eras for doctors understanding amputated limbs. I try to come every six months by their time. My doctor's disappointed when I'm late."

"And he's not the only one apparently."

Arandasal arched a mischievous eyebrow. "I detect a note of jealousy."

"I suppose I shouldn't be surprised that a pirate is a man about the town."

"It's common for people to be familiar with each other in this time. I don't know Jo well. She's the wife of a friend." After a pause, he said, "We met at her wedding."

"So, this is what you do? Wander through time? Pretend to fit in?"

"It's helpful to spend time away from the island. I find no peace from her when I'm in the Neverland."

"Because you broke her."

"Because she wants things back the way they were, and I don't believe that's possible."

Justine decided not to push that idea further and went back to something less likely to end in an argument. "Can you take me back to London in 1898? I'd like to see Sarah."

"We don't have enough dust for that this trip."

Justine pushed back her disappointment. "You said we could find a record of her here?"

"Who's Sarah?"

"The girl Mak wanted to take for his new mother. She wasn't dying naturally so I didn't want him to kill her. Silly me, I mostly volunteered to die instead."

"That was brave."

"I don't know what it was. Desperate, I think. I wanted him to be something other than what he was. Anyway, I fell into a lake and drowned." Justine shook her head. She didn't want to revisit that night. "But if she'd come to the island, things might have been better. I just feel like I'm determined to cause trouble where there isn't trouble to be found."

"You don't really believe that."

"I suppose she'd already have been lost. Between you and him and the cannibal mer and the cannibal fish and the vengeful fae and the river of eternity, paradise could use some improvements."

This made Arandasal chuckle, but there was also resignation, a kind of entrenched regret.

"What would you do if you could?" he asked.

"Bring back girls for one. If there were more of us around, I don't think Mak would be so afraid of us. And I want to figure out how to put the island together again." She glanced at him, suddenly shy. "I would want you and your crew and the Delts to be back in never time."

His eyes hardened as she knew they would. Why had she known? Because leaving time meant leaving the life he'd promised Osuana. *He's still in love with her.*

"When do we get my arm?"

"After this. There's a shop."

"Then we find Sarah?"

"We can do that now, actually." He tapped his glowing disk, slid his thumb sideways, then down, tapped again. "What was Sarah's last name?"

"Jones."

"Ah, that may make things difficult."

"Why?"

"It's a common name."

"She was a patient at St. Christopher's Asylum."

Arandasal's flesh thumb worked over his disk, tapping and sliding.

Restless, Justine jumped off the bed and walked over to the door. At first, she stood outside of the mirror's frame. She wanted to see how she'd changed, then she thought it might be better not to know.

You know already, thought Justine. *It's just a question of how much and if Mak will still think you're a child.*

The door whooshed open. For a moment, Justine saw the hallway and felt a tingle of warmth as something she didn't have time to see passed through her. Then the door closed, and she was beside it again. A man wearing a white coat took a seat on the wheeled stool. He set Arandasal's prosthetic on the table.

"Aranda, the intrepid traveler. You're two months overdue."

"You know how it is."

"Don't I!"

"How has it been running? Last time, you mentioned some problems with the battery. Did the adjustments work?"

"It's better, but I still travel with my analog backup. Half the places I go, there's no electricity, so charging isn't something I can depend on. I was actually hoping I could get another one."

"Sure, sure. I'll write you a script for the shop." The doctor wheeled forward so his left knee came in and rested between Arandasal's knees. He leaned forward and set both his hands on the rounded end of Arandasal's severed forearm. Those hands, so quiet, but so powerful, seemed to become eyes as the doctor first palpitated the arm at the elbow, then worked his way down, pausing every so often to ask, "Pain here? Numbness?" He released his hands and stabbed a long fingernail into Arandasal's skin at three different places. "Feel this?"

"Yes," said Arandasal with a laugh. He glanced over to Justine, his expression unreadable.

Now the doctor was at the end of the stub, looking at the scarred edge, those fingers busy with a meditative massage. Justine's hand went to her stub. It still hurt to touch. She couldn't imagine someone touching her the way the doctor was doing to Arandasal. It felt as intimate as it felt shameless, like having half an arm was just something that happened in the course of life.

"Circulation seems good. Tremors sometimes?"

"Sometimes."

"No skin irritation. Amazing for someone with your activity level."

"I use that lotion you gave me."

The doctor chuckled. "I give lotion to everyone. But almost no one uses it the way I tell them."

"I've been called an extreme type A."

"Useful in this case."

"Not as much in others." Again, Arandasal glanced at Justine, one of those prolonged, considering glances that made her itch to crawl out of her skin.

"What are you thinking?" she asked, knowing he couldn't answer.

"I see it a lot actually in cases where an adult has been injured and has to adjust to a new kind of life," said Dr. Decuir. "The more out of control they feel, the more they need to control everything they can, when often the best thing is to focus on learning how to trust the goodness of the world again."

"It's hard to believe that sometimes."

Dr. Decuir fitted Arandasal's hand onto his stub. He peeled back the fake skin and watched the little lights underneath light up.

"We've cleaned and recalibrated the sensors, so you should have a better connection. But like I said, you're doing great maintenance, so I don't expect any problems." Decuir pushed back his stool. "And you shouldn't either. Good things can happen for you just the same as anyone else."

Arandasal gave a self-deprecating laugh. "I'll try to remember that."

"Sit tight a few minutes. Kris will be back with your pass downstairs. Are you still using Necessary Limb funding?"

"Not anymore."

"Great. Well, I'll see you in *six* months."

Arandasal raised his prosthetic hand in a salute.

Justine shivered as Dr. Decuir and the door passed through her once again. This time, when the door closed, Justine was standing within the mirror's frame. In her peripheral vision, she caught a glimpse of a profile, a woman not unfamiliar but also not who she'd expected.

The Justine who'd powdered her face in Mrs. Palmer's mirror for her last Halloween had gaunt cheeks and a head placed square on her body. The face Justine saw now was more angular with a longer, more elegant neck.

She touched her cheek, then her forehead, then her chin. All still hers, but all somehow changed. When she'd come to the island, she'd thought herself a woman, but now, without a doubt she had become one.

"How old do you think I am now?" she asked.

"I don't know anything about women's ages."

"You're a god." She glared at his reflected face in the mirror.

"If you could be seen here, they would think you're between thirty-five and forty-five years old." Arandasal cleared his throat. "Does it bother you?"

"I don't know. It's . . . strange."

Arandasal dropped his gaze to his glowing disk. "I believe I've found your friend. Sarah Jones, eleven years old, patient at St. Christopher's Asylum from 1889 to 1899."

"And?"

"What is it you're hoping to know?"

"Don't play games." Justine rushed over and took the disk from him. The thing fitzed and began to smoke like a fairy did when splashed with water.

"What's wrong with it?"

"Haunts give off energy machines don't like."

"What did it say?"

"She died in 1899 from a flu epidemic, along with almost half the other patients in the hospital."

"So, I didn't really save her." Justine sank into the chair beside him. She barely noticed when Kris returned to finish Arandasal's appointment. She followed him down hallways, down a ramp to another floor with a big open space full of people eating and chatting with each other. She barely saw it. All the wonder had gone out of this new world.

In a shop filled with fake limbs and various lotions and cleaners and skins and sleeves, Justine saw nothing except Sarah. Had it been a long illness? When she'd fallen from the mortal realm, had she been strong enough to swim against the current? Had she been able to climb the towering cliffs around the Cloud City? What if she was trapped in the festering hell pit of the Green Caves? Or worse, she'd been carried over the falls and had been falling for hundreds of years.

Justine flinched when Arandasal's prosthetic hand grazed her stub.

"Sorry, just trying to measure," he whispered. "We can't ask anyone for help, but I think with a harness, we'll be able to—"

A salesperson came up to them, looked at the prosthetic Arandasal held, then at Arandasal's prosthetic hand. "How may I help you, sir?"

"I'm here for a friend. They don't have funding." He flashed that grin full of teeth. "I'm just trying to help them out with a temp limb until their situation improves."

The salesperson hesitated. Justine sensed something not quite right, that perhaps their plan was in jeopardy, but she'd ceased to care. She wandered through the store. Another mirror caught her attention, floor-to-ceiling this time, reflecting a grown woman in a girl's worn-out nightgown, her full breasts and wide hips making the gown almost obscene with its suggestion.

"Mak will never take you back," she said to her reflection.

"Unless you do something for him," the reflection answered. A shadow lifted up and seemed to detach from Justine's body so that it stood beside her. Not her shadow but Makbal's, with his wild hair and narrow rectangle of a body mounted on overlong legs. It brought images to her mind of things she'd seen.

Zaared carried a dagger in his belt.

In the captain's cabin, there was a carving knife in the drawer beneath the table.

Justine sucked in a breath that felt like a sob. Sarah was dead. If she'd gone to the island with Makbal, she would be less dead. "And perhaps I would be Jack Woolf's wife, hosting balls and a salon. I might've learned to read or even play the piano."

Her ideal life seemed such a quaint thing compared to the life that had come for her. Everything she'd done since dying had been for nothing. At every turn, what she thought she'd known vanished in a puff of smoke. Who was it who'd told her mothers were never meant to wield true power, only to be the vessels of it? She couldn't remember. It didn't seem to matter now.

She saw Arandasal walk out the door of the shop with a large bag in each hand. He nodded to her that he would wait until she was ready, then he turned away, looking at something down the street.

"He knows," said the reflection. "That's why he's keeping apart. He'll try to stop you. If he does, you'll have nowhere to go. The island will be lost."

"We don't know that killing him helps us," said Justine.

"But he refuses to cooperate," said the shadow. "He's trapped by the past." A calculated pause. "If you don't do it, he'll never be free of her."

This made sense. Arandasal needed to be free from the memory of Osuana. Justine could give him that, a final peace he couldn't give himself. She swallowed back tears. In her mind, she saw how killing him uprealm would trap him, which would allow the island to forget him. She and Makbal would start over. Arandasal would have his life with overfamiliar Jo and her husband, and appointments every six months in a beautiful, uncomplicated world.

CHAPTER 38

Assassin

They walked as they'd walked before, side by side, with Justine away from the street. Neither spoke until they reached the *Osuana*.

"My crew will return by sundown, then we'll leave." Arandasal set the bags down on the deck and stepped away from them. "I'll have Zaared come help you with the prosthesis fitting. Until then, you're free to do what you like."

He started to walk toward the captain's cabin.

"Aranda," she called after him.

His shoulders tightened against the name, an armor going up even though he hadn't been bothered by it at the doctor's office. The problem, she'd realized, was when she used the name. It meant something to him she didn't understand.

"I want to be rid of it." Pain streaked across Justine's chest. She gasped.

Still, Arandasal kept his back to her. The fingers of his prosthetic clenched and released. She took a step toward him. "I want him out of me."

"Then you'll be alone," he said.

"So I'll be alone."

Another fission of pain. Makbal's shadow pressed against her chest like a caged animal.

"Send it away then."

Is that all?

"Won't you at least look at me?"

"I have things to attend to." Arandasal entered the cabin.

Justine followed him. "Please."

He did turn then, the whole of his body rigid. "I have given you everything in my power to give. You're free to make your own choice. That thing in you would have my blood." He nearly tripped over Puddle as he strode to the table, yanked open the drawer, and flung the carving knife across the table's surface.

"Will you take it?"

Justine stared at the knife. Yes, she wanted it. She could see the motions her body would take, how she would appear to come to him at one side, then suddenly shift and stab him from the other.

No.

It's the only way.

No!

"You left me," she cried. "You left us!"

Arandasal's eyes narrowed.

"There was only one rule, and you broke it," she screamed. "You broke everything and there's nothing that will ever fix it."

In two steps, Justine was on him, her hand clenched around the knife. Arandasal raised his prosthetic hand to hold her back. She pressed against him, their faces so close she could feel the hot puffs of his breath, feel the heaving of his chest beneath her as she pressed him backward against the bed.

"Justine," he said softly. "Justine."

"NO!"

Her vision swam. First, Arandasal, then something else, a shadow dimming her sight.

"Justine." He sounded so far away.

"You can't have her!" Justine tried to drive the knife down around Arandasal's block. He moved with her. This only fueled the rage that had taken her. She strained and scraped against the thing inside her as it drove forward with another blow and she fought to hold it back, to at least unbalance its movements.

"I don't want her," said Arandasal and appeared to mean it. As though all those long looks, the love she'd seen in his eyes at dinner, had been a game he was playing and now he was revealing his true feelings. He couldn't possibly want her. She was so ruined.

Tears flooded Justine's eyes. She crunched them closed and staggered backward. Her chest shuddered and spasmed, furious within her, but it was also shrinking. As though speaking the words of her defeat had also defeated the thing.

"Leave me, shadow," she whispered.

The spasms stopped. For a moment, all was still. Then a great pain ripped through the center of Justine's chest. Her feet lifted off the ground as her chest pulled upward, splitting open as the shadow appeared, a stretched line of darkness drawn out as though by some invisible hand.

When it reached its end, they fell apart as though repelled, Justine to the floor, the shadow to the corner of the ceiling where it bounced from one wall to the other, trapped. Puddle leaped from bed to table to shelf, trying to catch it.

Arandasal knelt beside Justine. "Look at me."

With great effort, she raised her head and looked into his eyes.

"It's gone."

"Yes," said Justine. "I feel its absence." She pressed a hand to her chest and was surprised to find it intact. *What have I done?* Justine let herself fall back onto the floor and stared up at the ceiling. Darkness clawed at the edges of her vision. *Alone, alone, alone.*

Old maid.

Crone.

Gutter rag.

Street rat.

"Justine?"

He has nothing for you. The voice was her own mind, but that didn't make it any less bitter.

Makbal's shadow flickered as it crawled along the ceiling, faceless and yet somehow still malevolent. She could invite it back just the same as she banished it. The emptiness in her chest ached with longing to be full, to be at ease in the peace of being attached.

An illusion.

Movement at her side. The shark fin of a striped-orange tail cutting through the air, then a soft thump as Puddle dropped her small, warm body against the side of Justine's head and began to purr. Justine pressed her hand against Puddle's vibrating side and tried to match the kitten's steady breathing. Little by little, the darkness receded.

Am I still a mother? She looked over at Arandasal sitting on the floor with his back against the drawers beneath the bed. He'd pulled his knees up and hung his head between them. She watched as he lifted his head to look at the shadow trapped against the ceiling. There were tears in his eyes. Justine couldn't begin to settle on a clear reason why. There seemed both too many answers and too few.

"Is that it then? Is it over?"

"Depends on what you're referring to. In most ways, this is probably just a beginning."

"I don't know what to do," she whispered.

He turned and looked at her, unashamed of his tears. "Small things first. We might eat an early dinner and pretend to be two ordinary people out on the town."

"And then?"

"We take the long way home and enjoy the ride."

Justine wanted to ask, *And then?* again, but she knew there wasn't an answer. "Dinner it is."

They walked from the dock to a picturesque boardwalk with streetlamps not unlike the ones Justine had known in her time. Arandasal ordered food from a street stand and they sat on opposite sides of a bench with the food containers between them, stealing bites with their hands, and watching the sun set over the water.

"I want to ask you a question," said Justine.

"It isn't a good answer."

"How do you know what I want to ask?"

"It's the only question left. Why did I let it go on so long?"

"Obviously for love, like you said before. I can understand that."

Arandasal shook his head.

"You didn't love her?"

"You're spoiling the sunset."

"Our sunsets are nicer than this one."

"I thought I loved her." His jaw twisted, cheeks sucked in as he considered his words. "But love's an impossible thing to know in all its corners. I loved all those kids. Osuana wasn't any different until she decided she wanted something other than what we'd promised her. It felt just like any other game at first. We'd run off by ourselves and she'd ask me to build her a house, then we'd fill it with things.

"She turned her key to gold but refused to search for her keyhole. She wanted an island for herself where time existed so she could raise children and pigs and chickens."

"Pigs." Justine wrinkled her nose.

"They're actually very clean animals."

"So you built her an island."

"It felt like the only option. The longer she went on refusing, the more the others began to wonder if they might also stay in the Neverland. Mak wanted to force her to swim. I was afraid if we did that, she'd fail. So I helped her stay."

Justine rolled her eyes. "That's not romantic at all."

"Love can be selfish. Mak and I had been doing our work for so long. Osuana gave me the chance to be something else, to be mortal."

"Mostly."

"Mostly," he agreed. "The world was full of possibilities at a time when I felt trapped and couldn't have what I wanted. She offered me a life with stakes to it. Every day mattered because we only had so many. She lived with such urgency."

"And Mak declared a kind of war?"

Arandasal nodded.

"Children died."

"Yes."

"And then she died." Justine watched the faint interplay of muscles shift and twitch across Arandasal's face. Bathed in the golden light of the dying sun, he seemed the most beautiful person she'd ever seen, but she'd learned to watch beautiful things closely. Makbal, with all his secrets, seemed an open book compared to his brother.

"Why not ask Mak to forgive you?"

"We've traveled too far down this path to reconcile."

Again, Justine watched Arandasal's face. Not nearly the degree of fine muscle twitching, not so much conflict. *His relationship with Makbal is simpler.*

"When I met Lily, she said you were waiting for someone. And I think Makbal is also waiting for someone, even though he doesn't know it. And the island is waiting for someone. Is it Osuana?"

"I can't answer that."

"If she could be brought back, wouldn't that be a good thing for everyone? I think I can make it happen. If I can convince Mak, he'll help me."

"As soon as you step foot on that beach, Mak will have ten ways to recapture your heart, or else get rid of you so he may take another mother."

"Now who's ruining the sunset?" teased Justine.

"I'm not going to rescue you, if that's what you're thinking."

"I think you might." She slanted her eyes toward him. "You're too good not to."

His jaw worked its hard corners as he looked at her, torn between belief and doubt. She now understood he was a man who felt deeply and, perhaps because of that (or other complicated reasons), he chose what he revealed carefully. The idea of earning his revelations gave Justine a thrill. *As far as the path that lies behind, there's a longer one ahead where we know each other.*

Finally, he broke her gaze and began to gather their food containers. "You're the only person in this realm and the next who believes I'm good."

"Doesn't mean I'm wrong." She stood and walked over to where he'd stopped by the waste bin. Before he could stop her, Justine reached out and laced her fingers through his prosthetic hand. "Look, no bond. And we're holding hands. It's a nice thing, going for a walk holding hands."

"Justine—"

"This is what I want. Humor me. It's safe, isn't it?"

He nodded.

"Aside from protecting my independence, why are you so worried about touching me? Isn't a bond made by mutual choice?"

"I don't think either of us would do well with the temptation right now."

"You don't trust me," she teased. "Or is it that you don't trust yourself?"

"The bond I carry is a bond across time. You would know

my past experiences as clearly as if you'd seen them happen. Two timelines together, one heart beating beside the other."

Doesn't sound terrible, thought Justine. "There's something you don't want me to see."

"Bonding gods and mortals creates an eternal imbalance between them."

"You'd always be more powerful."

"And you forget what I told you about time. Even in the Neverland, your life has an end date, it exists on the straight line of a continuum. Mine does not."

"So, I either have to become a god or never touch you?" Justine laughed. "That's horrible. You have no idea how long I've—"

"Not nearly as long as I have waited for you."

She shook her head, unnerved by the warmth blossoming in her chest. "You keep saying things like that. I don't understand."

"There was a time when I—the island—wanted to give me a reason to keep going. The bond I carry is a promise. Of a future."

Something caught in Justine's throat at the thought that at some point Arandasal had seen his life as not worth living. "The island is terribly romantic," she said.

"She is that."

Justine gave his prosthetic hand a little tug to direct him into a walking pace along the boardwalk. "Shall we channel some of that romance and be living mortals strolling under the moonshine?"

"As long as both you and the moon promise not to seduce me," he laughed.

"I will absolutely not promise that. Right now, it seems you're halfway in love with me, but you won't say how."

Another laugh, marred this time by an undertone she couldn't interpret. She felt he was intentionally not looking at her, and she dared to hope it was because he found her irresistible and was fighting temptation.

"Did Mak tell you about the tragedy of the distant stars?"

"Are you changing the subject?"

"The sun gods created them to illuminate the sky when they were away. But the stars didn't stay where the gods placed them because they wanted to play together, form patterns, cast spotlights on events that most interested them so they might watch. This left areas in the mortal realm too dark."

"What are you trying to tell me?"

"Nothing important." He craned his neck up to the sky. "I think about them more often than I should. They were drawn to each other even against their duty. The stars were created without flaws and yet they failed, so I can forgive myself for also failing."

"Failing the children?"

"Yes, I failed them." He finally turned and looked at her. "But I'm afraid the largest burden I carry is how I failed you."

"You haven't . . . " she faltered, stunned by the tremor in his confession. "You've done nothing." *I'd forgive everything you want forever and ever if you'd just stop following your dammed rules and kiss me.*

"Someday, I hope to be worthy of you." Then he turned and led the way back to the *Osuana,* end of conversation. Justine could have cried with frustration. It all seemed so unfair. All the while, in the back of her mind, questions churned. *He's planning for a future and I'm in it.* Was that true? She felt yes, but the implications also jumbled as she replayed his words. Still, there was something exciting about the idea of earning that future, but only if she didn't have to wait too long.

"Hi-ho, the captain!" shouted Freddy when they came into sight.

A cheer went up.

"We thought you'd been lost," said Zaared as Arandasal and

Justine came up the gangplank. His eyes darted down to their clasped hands, then away. "The, er, um, shadow got out of the cabin. Puddle was making such a noise, so Rock went in there, and the thing popped out and flew away."

"It's nothing we'll miss," said Arandsal. "Are we all here?"

"Aye, Captain."

"Then let's be off. We're taking the long way. I claim crow station."

Someone groaned. "You always claim crow."

"A captain's right," called Arandasal as he led Justine into the cabin.

She hesitated at the doorway. There was the carving knife on the floor. The disturbed bedding. "I could've done it," she whispered.

"But you didn't, which was a good choice because no one else knows how to get you an arm." The gentle understanding underlying Arandasal's teasing made Justine want to cry. *What would have happened if I'd done it?*

The bags from the shop had been carried in. Now, Arandasal began to unpack them. He showed her the lotion to rub on her stub, which he called a "residual limb," and the little jelly-filled cups she could stick to it to keep sores from developing.

The prosthetic was made of a material Arandasal called plastic, which came from oil, though Justine couldn't believe it. He helped her slip her residual limb into the open end, then he attached straps around her upper arm and across her chest to keep the prosthetic in place.

"It's not as nice as yours."

"When you're a goddess and you come uprealm as a solid person, you can have whatever arm you want."

I could be a goddess, thought Justine. *Does he really believe that?*

"Try to move."

"Ah! It hurts!"

"I taught Zaared some of the techniques the doctors use here just after an injury. He can help you."

I want you to help me.

The ship began to sway and shiver as it lifted into the sky. Puddle mewed pitifully and rubbed against Arandasal's feet. He picked her up, letting her flop around in his arms until she'd decided which ear she wanted to lick.

Wet slurping sounds filled the cabin.

"Come on. If I don't claim my station, someone else will. Best seat in the house."

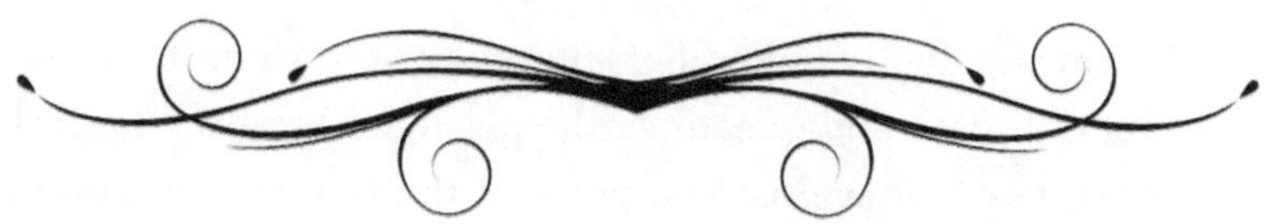

Blue Sails Rising

Justine looked up at the rigging of the main mast as Arandasal climbed using one arm, Puddle in his prosthetic arm. Clouds rushed past Justine's face. The ship seemed impossibly high already and now Arandasal wanted her to climb even higher, to sail on the thinnest, most unstable part of the ship.

"I can't do this," she called.

"Just don't look down."

Justine looked to Zaared, who stood nearby. "Better hurry," he said. "Don't want to miss it."

"Miss what?" mumbled Justine as she took her first step up into the wobbly rope to demonstrate how impossible climbing would be. Arandasal made one arm look easy. But to climb as he climbed, Justine would need to trust her balance to her feet when she released her hand. This she wasn't prepared to do. Instead, she gritted her teeth against the pain and used her prosthetic as a hook to secure her against the rigging when she moved her feet. Then she moved her right hand, then the prosthetic. Before she knew it, she'd climbed halfway up, and going all the way up was easier than going back down.

When she finally pulled herself into the crow's nest, Justine was out of breath and sweating. She plastered her back against the mast, her feet against two posts of the railing, and closed her eyes.

"I hate falling."

"You won't fall." Arandasal stood upright as though immune to the dysphoria of such a great height. "This is 2060, give or take a couple decades. I haven't done a complete study."

The western side of America stretched below them, a blanket of tiny, golden lights. They passed southwest, over dark water, down over jungles, the flashes of fires and explosions. And then an ocean. Stars flew by. Another continent appeared, closer this time as the *Osuana* dipped to skim the water's surface. Sheets of white ice formed and thickened, turning black, then white again.

With burst of speed, the ship rocketed upward as though riding the crest of an invisible wave. "The 1940s," said Arandasal.

A fleet of flying machines soared over their heads, explosions pockmarked the continent of Europe below. Clusters of lights marked the big cities. An army camped in the Arabian Peninsula was swept away by the sand as the *Osuana's* shadow crossed it. In Asia, a palace was being built. "That's the Great Palace," said Arandasal. "Construction began in 1782. Magnificent at sunset."

"Alone or with company?" she teased.

"Sometimes alone is better."

"I doubt that."

"If I hadn't lost Osuana, I would never have found this path."

"It's beautiful," said Justine, wishing he could have avoided bringing Osuana into the moment.

He looked down at her and frowned. "Hard to imagine what you think you're seeing down there. Come on, stand up."

"No."

"Trust me on this." He offered his prosthetic hand.

"If I fall—"

"I promised I wouldn't let you fall."

The warmth in his eyes, as though she was the only woman he'd ever looked at, made saying no impossible. She felt him come around behind her, gently press her hips up against the railing of the crow's nest, take her flesh hand in his prosthetic hand, take her prosthetic hand in his flesh hand, then extend her arms out to their full lengths from her shoulders. His breath brushed her ear as he whispered, "Fly with me."

He pressed his chest against her back so that Justine leaned out over the railing.

"Now, open your eyes."

Justine gasped. She was bent nearly in half with open sky all around. Fathomless leagues below, America passed by again, but with fewer lights, almost all of it dark, except for the scattering of large fires marking the stepped temples and grand palaces of the ancient peoples. It felt as though she were flying, the *Osuana* gone from her perception, only the heat of Arandasal at her back keeping her from plummeting.

For just a moment, the two of them stood suspended in a world outside of time, outside of anything except the beauty of the night and the feeling of their bodies together. She longed for him to put his arms around her, to pull her even closer and set his lips against her neck.

The ship dipped and spun to insert itself into a flock of birds. Justine screamed and shrank back, knocking Arandasal into the mast. "You're fine," he said softly as he tightened his arms around her.

Hold me like this forever, she wanted to say.

They passed scaffolding around the pyramids of Giza, golden-robed monks speaking a somber chant on the road up to Angkor Wat. The fires from towns and villages died out.

Is he thinking of me in that way or is it something else?

The third time around the world, all was dark. A chorus of animal sounds filled an endless, diamond-studded sky. A whale rose out of the ocean as though its greatest wish was to touch the moon. But then it thought better of this plan, arched its great back, and fell into the water.

"Now we're coming to the beginning," said Arandasal.

Gradually the land below knit together and began to sink away into a blanket of clouds. Down on the main deck several of the crew sighed as though just awakened from a beautiful dream. They roused themselves from their stations and began to prepare for landing.

Justine gripped the railing of the crow's nest as the clouds parted for a new sea and the island appeared ahead, first a speck on the warming horizon, then a rock, then, as the sun burst over the water, the verdant green of the main island with the cliffs overshadowing the woods and the plains. She could just see the turrets of her castle, banners stiff in the breeze. And there was the lagoon with the fringe of boundary rocks around it, the narrow channel beyond that cut through the cliffs, the dim shadows of the Delt village on the other side of the channel and the veil, the shrouded mountains. A rush of quiet warmth washed over her. This was a homecoming. She felt as though she'd been away for a long time, and now, at last, she'd returned.

Coming down upon the island in this way, Justine saw for the first time the very top of the cliffs and the river that seemed to pour out from within them, rushing through a channel of cataracts that ended with two black rocks. The water flowed between them in a great torrent down into a dark pool where it appeared to circle a void before overflowing down the second falls into Coral Falls Lake.

The one who unites the brothers may fall through the water and become a god.

Madness, Justine. You're finding truth where there's nonsense.

It's an island made to make our dreams come true.

"The fastest way to the river's source would be to land on the rocky part of the beach, then cut through the woods to the left side of the cliffs."

"It's just a story," said Arandasal.

"Yes, it's just a story," replied Justine. "But stories have a way of coming true."

"It won't be what you expect."

The *Osuana* touched down in the water with a gentle splash. Justine made the climb down the rigging much more easily than her climb up. As she steadied her feet on the main deck, she strained to see through the veil across the water to the tree line of the island, searching for movement.

Arandasal climbed down behind her. "Zaared, Juan, take Justine to her cell."

Justine whirled. "We had an agreement. I'm going back to the island."

"We had a discussion in which you said a great many silly things, and I told you they weren't true."

Juan took her arm and began guiding her toward the hatch. Justine twisted against him. "They're not silly! The island has revealed itself to me just like you said. It wants to be whole."

"Whatever you heard was my brother. The island doesn't exist outside of him." Arandasal waved his hand to Zaared who came along Justine's other side and gently propelled her to the nearest hatch and down into the hold.

"Zaared, listen to me. Aranda is wrong. I'm free now. I can tell the difference. If I pass the island's challenge, I can—"

Juan gave her a push so Justine fell forward into her cell. She turned to charge back out only to have the door slammed and locked in her face. Juan left immediately, but Zaared lingered, looking mournful.

"It doesn't matter what the truth is," he said. "The cold fact is that you unbalance our scales. As long as you're with us, Mak can't call another mother, and he can't banish anyone from the island. It isn't his anymore. It's everyone's. As it should be."

Justine slammed her fist against the bars. "But it can't be everyone's as long as time is here. The island can't survive. Please—"

But Zaared was already turning, walking back to the hatch.

"Bloody fucking pirates!" Justine screamed. "You won't get away with this."

No one brought her supper or breakfast. Halfway through her second day once again a prisoner, Justine was trying to use her prosthetic to unlock the cell door when at last the hatch opened. The smell of roasted fish and greens filled the hold as Arandasal walked up to the cell, passed a folded cloth of food through the bars and, after a moment of hesitation, sat down on the overturned bucket.

"I don't intend to hold you here against your will," he said. "Lily has agreed to keep you in Delt to live out your natural life. Or, tomorrow at sunrise, I'll take you downrealm to swim the current and the fates will decide your eternity."

"Only one of those options keeps me away from Mak and swimming the current is a terrible idea."

"They're imperfect options," he admitted.

"If you really believed I was so dangerous you wouldn't give me options." Justine moved closer to the bars. "I think you don't know what you want. You're afraid of change. Things have been this way for so long, you can't imagine anything different."

His expression remained the same dark, troubled sadness, except now she saw it differently, she saw the iron will underneath, iron that came from the same place as Makbal's. From fear.

"Or maybe part of you believes the prophecy is true. If I go back to the island and I'm successful, I'll be able to cast out time. And that would erase everything you've fought for."

The only reaction to her words Justine could detect was the tightening in the corner of his jaw. Justine wanted to reach through the bars and punch him, to smash that unmoving face over and over until his mask shattered. Who was the man buried there? What was so terrible he couldn't believe in her?

Justine shook her head. "You two really ruined each other, didn't you?" She studied the lines of his face, the way the shadows cast by her paper lantern deepened his contrasts, made him seem older than he was. Of course, it was all appearances. What did age mean to a god?

"It isn't real, Justine."

She glared at him. "How do you know?"

"Because I made this place! There's no way for you to ever truly be free because the world was built for our control."

"The world has changed," said Justine with just as much force. "Osuana changed it. The island has grown beyond what you and Mak put into it. How can you not know that? I've seen it call to you."

"Only Mak's demons call me there. What you felt is an illusion."

"Fine. Then why don't you make me yours and we'll invade the island together?" Justine thrust her flesh arm through the bars. "Come on. If I'm so powerful and so dangerous, this is your best option. I'm willing, as you already know. As enchanted bonds go, I'd rather have you than him. And what I'm hearing is that it has to be one of you because me alone is the whole problem. You can't have a grown woman running free in your paradise."

Arandasal looked down at her hand. On his knee, his hook tap, tap, tapped.

"Am I so hideous?" Her voice broke. "Won't you at least tell me why I'm so easy to refuse?"

Just as he seemed about to speak, a bell began to tong from the deck above. Arandasal jumped to his feet and ran to the hatch.

"What is it?"

"Sails on the horizon, Captain," came the distant answer. "A ship just came up from the Mouth."

"The mothers?"

"No, sir, blue sails. It's making fast for Delt. What are your orders?"

"Weigh anchor and follow it. Load cannons."

The deck above thrummed with running steps and the calls of the crew. Arandasal stood still at the hatch, a man trapped in an invisible cage.

"Aranda." Justine spoke so softly there was no reason he should have heard her over the din above. "Talk to me."

He walked back to her cell, his expression crunched tight in concentration.

"The dead have come for us."

Justine laughed a short, shocked laugh. What did that even mean? They were all dead here. The laugh stopped as she understood. The residents of the Neverland were only half dead; they hadn't yet swum the current to meet their afterlives. "I thought no one could come up from below without your permission."

"It shouldn't be possible without the will of a god." He braced his left arm against the bars, let his head fall down beside it. "Short of that, I suppose the fae can make all things possible if it's in their interest."

"You're thinking about the missing dust?"

"With a blessing, it would do the same thing it does for us. But the only gods on the other side of the Ocean's Mouth are my mothers."

Justine blinked as this sank in. "One of your mothers—"

An explosion sounded. It wasn't close enough to think the ship was under attack, but the force of it still left Justine's ears ringing. Somewhere, not far away, people were screaming.

"Captain!" Zaared's voice sounded at the hatch. "Delt is under attack."

"Are we in range?"

"Almost."

"I'm coming." As Arandasal turned, Justine grabbed his hook.

"Let me out."

"I can't—" A spark of agony clawed across his expression.

"You can. Whatever's out there, whatever you're fighting, if you fail, the island will be lost. All the children who are hoping to be saved will never have the chance at childhood. I can protect it."

"If you join with Mak, you'll never be free of him again."

"I'm not joining with him."

"Justine, the goddess myth isn't real." He looked desperate as though he was fighting against his own instinct to believe.

"Then trust me enough that I have the chance to fail."

Another explosion sounded. Closer this time. The smell of fire drifted into the air.

Arandasal stared at her, his eyes searching, searching, searching, for what sign, Justine couldn't say.

On the deck above, cannons groaned into place. Cast-iron balls clinked together. Someone cried out, "Argh! My foot. Watch where you're fucking—"

The whistle of cannon fire in the air, growing more and more shrill until, just as it seemed to be upon them, a splash. The *Osuana* rocked sideways under the force of the blast.

"Damn it all to hell," muttered Arandasal as he unlocked the cell. "I'm not coming to save you, understand?"

"Yes."

"Justine." The longing with which he spoke her name felt like its own kind of bond pulling her toward him.

"It's your turn to trust me," she said. "You know that pond in the winter woods? I'll meet you there when this is over, and we'll banish time from the midrealm."

"To what end?"

"To no end. We're *preventing* an end. You need to do it with me, or you'll trap yourself here."

His gaze wandered to the middle distance of the ship's wall, toward the sound of the cannons. "I don't want to fight again."

"*Arandasal.*" Justine snapped her fingers in front of his face. "Your crew needs you. Come on." She grabbed his hook and dragged him down to the hatch and up the ramp.

Above deck was a smoky roil of chaos. Two black ships with blue sails with a single green stripe down their centers fired alternating volleys at the *Osuana* and the Delt village, though there seemed little of it left.

"Guine," snapped Arandasal when he saw them. "Who else would be so bold?"

A cannon ball whistled through the air and crashed just ahead of the front bow, sending up enough water to tilt the front of the ship into the air. The *Osuana* crashed down to the water with a splintering splash.

For a moment, the firing seemed to stop. Through patches of clear air, Justine saw the ship closest to Delt had launched boats heading for shore. The ship nearer the *Osuana* tacked its sails to shift directions. Justine knew almost nothing about battles, especially those in boats, but it seemed clear the ship was preparing to come alongside the *Osuana* for a broadside pass with her cannons.

"Ready to fire," said Arandasal, but his voice lacked conviction. He looked around as though unsure where he was.

"Captain?" asked Zaared. "Shouldn't we—"

"Exactly. Yes, lead them out to open sea where we'll have the advantage."

Zaared passed the call down the line. Men up in the rigging rushed to release some sails and pull in others.

As the ship turned, Justine turned her gaze from the oncoming ship of the dead to the cliffs coming up on the other side. She looked down at her too small nightgown.

"I'm borrowing your clothes." Justine didn't wait for Arandasal to give permission. She dashed into the captain's cabin, dug through the drawers until she found a white blouse and black trousers. Neither fit her very well, but she cinched a belt around her waist and tied up the lacing at the top of the shirt, unlike Arandasal who always seemed to leave them untied, so it would stay on her shoulders.

Just as she turned to go back out, she heard a tiny mew from below the table. Justine ducked down and saw Puddle cowering against the table leg.

"You poor thing." She reached down and scooped up the kitten. Puddle let out a hissing screech and dug her claws into Justine's chest. "Oh-kay, not that." Justine grabbed a pillow from the bed, shook out the pillow, and dumped Puddle in the case. "You'll thank me later."

She ran back to the deck just as the cannons fired, one after another. Concussions shook the ship, the cannon braces screeched and strained with their reports. White arcs of smoke trailed like May Day streamers toward the dead ship. None of them hit.

"I'm taking Puddle with me," Justine called to Arandasal. He stood at the far end of the deck, shouting instructions for changing the cannon positions. Justine thought to call again, but the cliffs were passing and if she didn't jump then, she might miss them completely. There, just ahead, was the small round hole from her dream that hadn't been a dream, the entrance to the fae archive, and above it, the path up to the source of the falls that Justine had failed to follow the day the island revealed it.

Justine took one last look at Arandasal, prayed to whatever powers now lived within her that she'd see him again, then lowered herself over the side of the ship. Her prosthetic chafed, and her residual limb ached, but she did well enough moving from handhold to handhold with Puddle in the pillowcase tucked into the front of Arandasal's shirt. She dropped down into the water. The *Osuana's* wake pushed her toward shore where she pulled herself up onto the rocks and released Puddle from the pillowcase. The kitten coughed and spat and ran away from her.

"Just stay away from the water," called Justine. "Or something will eat you." She picked herself up and began to run the other direction. When the ground became uneven, she leaped from rock to rock, each step sure, each toe vibrating with strength. She was home.

From the rocks, Justine reached the path. She didn't stop at the archive's cave, but continued up and up and up, along the way she'd been led once before but refused to go. The path grew steeper and narrower, then it stopped.

Justine skidded to a halt. She could hear the roar of the water rushing from the rocks above, but she could see no path forward. From the flying *Osuana*, the path had looked simple, but now Justine saw she'd misjudged the myriad angles and slopes in the cliffs. The wall of rock to her side was wind polished and smooth without a single handhold. The way she'd just come also presented no diverging paths.

The only way forward seemed to, in fact, go forward. But the gap, before the path resumed on the other side of the chasm, seemed impossibly far. Justine would leap into open space, then certainly plummet hundreds of feet down to the channel between the two parts of the island.

She pressed her head against the rock wall to steady

herself. Out at sea, the *Osuana* had engaged the largest of the two dead ships. The concussions of the explosions were only tiny puffs of vibrations disturbing the air. A mast cracked and fell, though Justine couldn't tell from which ship; the smoke was so thick.

"Island, help me." Justine dug her toes into the loose rocks, pressed her heels down, searching. She felt nothing except the pain one expects to feel when crunching bare skin against rock.

"What's the bloody answer here? I can't jump that. A full-grown man maybe, but—"

Justine stopped. Arandasal's words came back to her, *This world wasn't made for me.*

"Fuck that." Justine stood up and walked to the chasm so her toes dipped over the jagged edge. This was one of the places the island had been separated when Arandasal brought time into the Neverland. She saw the matching grooves in the rock on the other side.

"You're not as far apart as I think," declared Justine. Then, with a mighty roar that ripped from her chest, she threw herself forward, arms pinwheeling, legs kicking. After an impossibly long moment, she skidded down onto the other side. Beneath her feet, the island rumbled.

Justine ran up the path. Up and up and up until she had to stop for breath. Out at sea the explosions had stopped. She saw people in the water beneath the smoke. A ship was going down.

"Which one?" Justine blew out a gasping breath as though she could become the wind and clear the smoke. But then the sky did clear just a bit, and she saw the blue with green striped sails still standing tall. The *Osuana's* cabin was on fire, a black hole gaped in her side just above the water line.

As Justine watched, the invading ship turned and began to sail toward the island. She didn't have time to mourn her loss. A new kind of invasion was about to begin.

Only a few footsteps up the path, Justine stopped again. A

girl sat a few steps away in a clearing of sand. A wet cough racked her chest.

"Justine, help me."

It was Sarah, in her little white nightgown with the blue ribbon, her slippers, and lacy nightcap. Justine lurched off the path toward her. Her feet began to burn. Justine looked down. There was nothing but ordinary rock beneath her feet, but when she stepped back to the path, the burning stopped.

"Sarah, I'm coming back for you. Just hang on a little longer."

"I can't."

Sarah reached out a bone-thin arm. Her fingers strained and trembled. "Just hold me, please."

Justine shook her head to try to clear her vision. *She isn't real. Sarah can't talk. Don't get distracted.* Sarah started to cry. "Please."

It took all of Justine's strength to turn and continue up the path. Up and up. Each step harder than the last, as though some force pulled her from behind, willing her to fall. Then she was there, the top of the cliffs. Far to her right were the guardian rocks that marked the summit where she'd learned Arandasal was Makbal's brother. Immediately to her left, water gurgled up from a crack in the rock and flowed in a stream down along the cliffs. The cataracts lay below her and to the left. Just a few steps more and she would—

A shadow blocked the sun. Justine looked up and saw Makbal, hovering before her, hands on hips, red hair wild as ever.

"You're here." His voice was an accusation. "You can't be here. That's not how the game works." He flashed her his dark grin.

Justine looked over her shoulder. The death ship had disappeared around the cliffs. Soon, it would be landing.

"You need to get the boys to the castle. Wait for me there."

"Mothers don't give me orders." He flew at her, arms out. Justine didn't wait to see if he meant to grab her or push her. She threw herself into the stream. Splashing through the shallows, forward and forward, the water becoming deeper and faster. She fought to keep herself upright. It was a one-sided struggle since she didn't know how to use her prosthetic well enough for balance. But she could use it to push off rocks and keep herself in the center of the water.

The stream curved and dipped under an outcropping, then leveled out into more shallows. She'd reached the cataracts. Makbal had disappeared. Justine wasn't sure if he'd flown away or if he'd been an illusion like Sarah.

Justine dragged herself up to standing and began to walk across slippery, water-polished rocks toward the black brothers. As she got closer, she saw there were three instead of two. The third, positioned off to the side, wasn't a rock but a man who stood as she approached. He wore his coat and extravagant feathered hat. His hook glinted in the sunlight.

"Aranda. *The Osuana*, I'm sorry."

He shook his head, looking at her but not quite looking at her. "It isn't going to work."

Justine felt herself harden. "You're an illusion like the others." She sloshed up to the two brothers and stood between them. Just beyond her feet, the falls dropped into a pool as black as night. The water around the pit churned and gurgled.

Arandasal stepped up beside her and also looked down. "I never wanted this for you."

Despite herself, Justine's heart skipped a beat.

"You could've chosen me," he said. "We would've been happy together."

"The real Aranda is in love with Osuana. I'm not going to be her stand-in." Justine stepped up to the edge of the falls. Looking down made her dizzy. She set her hand on the boulder to her right to steady herself. It hummed with a gentle warmth.

This is right.

She set her prosthetic hook on the boulder to her left. It gave a small vibration in return.

Cannon fire sounded in the distance. She could just see the white smoke streamers sailing toward her castle. *I'm coming,* she thought.

And then, she jumped.

Falling.

Falling.

Falling.

Justine didn't feel her body hit the water. She didn't knock into rocks or bounce off the walls of the void. For all she knew, she'd fallen, not into an underwater tunnel, but into empty space within the island. Her skin became coated in a sticky substance. Things came to her, attracted by that stickiness. So many things came that they became a film covering her entire body, like dust motes attracted to wool.

And still she fell.

Through darkness.

Through light.

Through something she couldn't say was one or the other.

She fell through cold, though whatever had collected on her skin kept her from freezing.

She fell through fire that burned black as the void, invisible flames greedily consuming the sticky film on her skin until they ate their fill and died out.

And then. Finally. She began to rise.

THE ISLAND CREATURES FELT JUSTINE COMING. MANY OF THEM gathered on the banks of Coral Falls Lake to watch her emerge from the water. The island dressed her in a gown the color of fresh spring leaves with the stitching of fine veins, and the trim of silver moonlight. A crown of woven twigs set with dewdrops sat upon her finely braided hair.

When she placed her first foot upon the ground, the creatures felt her reach out to them. They felt the solidness of that step, how it placed itself not as mistress or conqueror or as like creature, but something new, a goddess. As they had given to the island, so they had given to her, and now, she'd come to them embodied in this woman who had once been a girl playing games she didn't understand.

The creatures followed Justine through the woods. Other creatures stopped their activities to watch her pass. The group that followed grew larger. Some creatures had the idea to pick up the train of Justine's gown and carry it so it wouldn't snag. This was a needless worry. Nothing about the island could damage what the island made from itself. And yet, this seemed a service they could provide. They carried. Then, at the foot of the hill that led up to the castle, they stopped.

The wall around the moat had collapsed in two places. One of the castle turrets had a hole blown through its side and looked on the verge of collapsing. The gate stood open. Justine passed through alone. She didn't hesitate at the grand front doors, now scorched with fire. Straight through the grand atrium, she walked, past the broken chandelier and melted candles, under the balcony where the two staircases met, and through shattered frames of what had been the glass dining room doors.

In the courtyard, Guine sat on the throne the boys had made when they'd played emperor and the dragon. Two lines of blue-clad soldiers flanked her. Another set of soldiers made a ring around her boys. Five more stood on either side of Makbal, holding him on his knees before the throne.

Guine seemed different here in the sunlight than those few moments Justine had met her in the treasure caves of the Green City. Her skin appeared translucent and a little cloudy, like

London fog trapped in a dirty bottle. All the pirates' skin appeared this way, but it seemed most noticeable on Guine. The most solid thing about her was the golden key around her neck. Her voice was ringing out with surprising cheerfulness as she said to Makbal, "Remember when we had such plans? I can't tell you how excited I—"

"Be gone from this place," said Justine.

Guine had just a moment to look up at Justine, for surprise to flit across her face, then she and all the soldiers vanished. Just like that. Justine reached her awareness out to the island, found all that didn't belong, and sent it beyond the boundary of the Neverland. When she was finished, the island settled back in its roots like a satisfied dog on its haunches. Justine felt no fatigue, not even a lost breath.

"Hurrah! Mother has saved us," cried the boys. The youngest ones threw themselves at her legs. The older ones gave her hugs or clapped her on the back. Justine remembered them as though from a long-distant dream that was tinged with the stuff of nightmares. Their faces and voices and bodies were both familiar and uncanny. She didn't belong to them as fully as she had before. But they didn't yet sense what had changed.

They had reverted to their leaf and sap clothes in her absence and now, as though noticing their dirtiness, someone announced, "We shall have a bath in honor of Mother's return."

"Last one to the lake is a stinky sock!" Then they were off and running, the island already at work clearing their minds of the pirates' terrible knives and their fear when all had seemed lost. Justine felt how Makbal's potions only partially did the work of mind tidying. The island, following his wishes, also moved the boys toward ideas of themselves that would make them best suited to their afterlives. She put this information away to consider later.

Now Makbal was rising from his knees. He went to the vacated throne and flopped into it, one leg slung over the side.

He swung it back and forth, performing the appearance of a restless teenager, but his expression thundered like a gathering storm.

"So, you found her," he said. "I thought you would. It was a frustrating caveat the fae built into my Mother game, the possibility that Mother could become the island. They didn't really leave me a choice, you understand. Now they'll regret it."

"This isn't what you wanted all along?"

"Of course not." His eyes shifted over to her prosthetic. "And you've gone pirate. So many pirates around here now."

"This arm doesn't make me a pirate."

He shrugged. "What is it to be then? You outrank me, Queen of the Island. I'm yours to command."

Are you? Justine doubted very much it would be that simple. She could almost see the wheels of his mind spinning, plotting revenge for an insult that wasn't real.

"I would have you as my partner to continue this good work. I'm going to put the island back together and banish time."

Makbal's eyes glittered. "Did the Black Hook agree to that?"

"I believe the three of us can work together."

"Ha!"

"If not, I'll work alone. I want this to be the place it once was. With more children. Not just the ones you think are suitable, but any who have need. They'll be allowed to tell the stories of where they come from and populate the island with their creatures."

"So, you'll make pirates of us all and doom them to the current."

Justine held her expression steady, determined not to give him even a hint of her uncertainty as he glared at her. She remembered being cowed by those eyes, the hard point of his naughty chin. Now, she saw only a moody boy, frustrated he couldn't have his way. Was it an illusion? Did she still have something to fear from him? She would have to wait and see.

Makbal huffed out a sigh, twirled his finger through the air. "Well, you'll try it and see the problems that come with it. In the while, I'll do my own fetching. We're going to need an army to defend ourselves. This thing with Guine isn't over."

"Do you know which of your mothers—"

"Who says my mothers had anything to do with it? Any god with an imagination can find a passage between realms." He shrugged. "War is a good enough game, I suppose. But we'll need more boys."

"And girls," said Justine.

Makbal rolled his eyes. "You have your castle, I have my Canopy. We'll meet on feast days and throw food at each other from across the table."

Is that all? wondered Justine. *No apology, nor even mention of what he'd done?*

The breeze shifted, bringing with it a sense of something. The island was announcing an arrival. Justine's heart lifted with the release of an uncertainty she hadn't known she carried. *He came.*

"I have an appointment to make," said Justine. "Would you like to come set things right?"

"Does my queen command it?"

"No."

"Then I refuse. And you can tell that traitorous, murdering scallywag that I didn't need his help today, nor will I need it in the future."

It felt like there was more to say, but she didn't want to delay her departure struggling to articulate what she didn't yet understand. It seemed suddenly silly she would want understanding from this boy, silly to think he could ever have been powerful enough to harm her.

From the castle, she crossed the hills down into the grasslands and entered the forest at the spring grove. She crossed it slowly, savoring the textures of the trees. The sunlight through the canopy projected a latticework of pink and gold light, the surrender of the rushing day to something slower, quieter. Justine smiled at the irony of being in a place with infinite days and yet still being trapped by the tyranny of that recklessly small space between sunrise and sunset.

A few steps into the winter grove, she saw him. The line of that lovely silhouette, marred by burn holes and tears from the battle and the hunch of fatigue, still starkly cut out from the white of the snow and the bare trees. Arandasal leaned on the bridge railing and looked out on the pond. The sun had heated the water so mist rose in wafts and spirals from its surface. The late afternoon light slanted golden across it. Justine had never been to the grove at this time of day. It seemed suspended in a moment of enchantment, holding its breath to keep the beauty in before night ascended. A moment when anything seemed possible.

She crossed the bridge with a skip in her step and stood beside him. "I've done it." She grinned.

"You were right," he said softly. "I'm sorry for doubting you."

"I'm going to put her back together now. I want you to do it with me."

Arandasal shook his head. "I'm not sure what she'd—Is she you now?"

"We're separate, but together. I like to think she's her own self still."

"I don't think she'd appreciate me being involved. I'm not even sure I want it." He paused. "I've been planning to die for a long time."

"If you still truly want that, I'm sure you'll find a way." She set her right hand on the railing between them. "Or you could dare to believe good things can happen, Aranda. Let Osuana go."

"I don't deserve to forget."

"Releasing and forgetting aren't the same," said Justine. "You can honor what has been lost by living."

The corners of his jaw worked, eyes lidded with conflict that seemed clearer than anything he'd ever allowed her to see, yet still hidden. *I'll never completely understand him.*

"You can repair the island alone," he said.

"I can. But then why did you come?" She tapped her fingers against the railing as an invitation. "Come on, Aranda, let yourself dream again."

He shook his head, a small smile that seemed to marvel at having found himself there making this decision after so long. "I'm here so you know I'm with you. I'm committed."

"Committed?" She gave him a look she hoped was flirtatious. It wasn't exactly what she wanted to hear, but it was close; if she squinted at it, she could make it sound like love.

"I'm going to do better. Make myself worthy of you."

She wanted to argue, but the look of resolution on his face held her back. And after all, maybe he was the wiser of the two. She wasn't exactly in a condition to trust her feelings or push him toward a thing she only half understood.

"Shall we?" he asked.

Justine watched breathlessly as Arandasal covered her flesh hand with his prosthetic hand, pressing his fingers down so they lay between her own. Justine sent her will out into the island. At first she focused on the word "mend," then she realized she didn't need even that degree of clarity.

The island knew her purpose as well as she knew herself. It traveled along her awareness, beyond the veil of time. It touched the fractured parts of herself and beckoned them to return. Silver light began to glow faintly between Arandasal and Justine's joined fingers. It spread along the bridge, down into the water, up the trees, and out of the grove until all the trees were limned in light. The ground gurgled beneath their feet. Rocks rumbled in the distance, growing and growing in volume until Justine felt their vibrations coursing through her.

With a low groaning and grinding, the island shifted beneath their feet. Even more than the literal movement, Justine felt the island drawing herself together, settling into sockets and rivets that had long been sundered. Now they were knit together with a great wave of sinking, like a sigh of the deepest contentment. Then Justine felt Arandasal also release a heavy sigh. "So, it's done." His body gave away no sign of relief or regret. She found herself staring at him so she might reassure herself he wasn't going to begrudge her choice.

He said we have a future.

A red-headed crane descended to the water and began to dance.

Below the bridge a frog began to creak its evening song.

An orange tabby kitten hopped up onto the far end of the bridge, walked up to Arandasal, wedged herself between his arms, and began to attack his left earlobe with her mouth.

"Puddle." He tilted his head and rubbed his beard into the side of her face. "I thought I'd lost you with the *Osuana*."

"She came with me." Justine paused, the kitten having reminded her of the battle, the problem of Guine. "I'm sorry about your ship."

"It was right for her to go down. She belonged to time and now time is gone."

Justine heard the bitterness in his voice and tried not to let it worry her. "What will you do?"

"Build a new one."

"Always the wanderer," she teased to cover her disappointment. Part of her had hoped the lack of a ship would keep him closer.

"You're the wanderer," he said slowly. "Or you will be, I think."

"Where do I wander?"

"Everywhere." He gazed at her shyly. "And do you know what you call me?"

"Tell me."

"Your damnably star-crossed voyager."

"The star-crossed part could change if you let a little enchantment in once in a while."

"Perhaps." He gazed at her, another of those long looks that made her feel he knew so much more than she did.

"Why look at me like that?" she asked.

"Like what?"

"Like you're both madly in love with me and afraid of me."

He smiled. "Neither and both are true. I'm afraid of keeping you from becoming the beautiful, crazy-hearted creature you're meant to be."

"That's a lot to live up to."

"Not for you."

For a moment, she thought he might reach out and touch her, but then he turned his gaze back to the water. "I'm going uprealm to see about Guine. Her second ship captured Lily and many other Delts. They're in need of rescuing."

"Do you know where they went? Or when?"

"It doesn't matter. I'll find them. That many haunts up where they're not supposed to be makes them noticeable."

"And I will begin my caretaking here. Perhaps I'll see you uprealm?"

"Perhaps we can arrange that." He arched a sly eyebrow in a way that Justine was sure he'd already considered this. He already had plans for them. *Us*, she thought.

"Be strong with the fae when you negotiate your travel blessing. They'll respect you more."

The wet slurping of Puddle's mouth on Arandasal's ear

filled the silence that fell between them. Justine looked down at their hands, still intertwined. She wanted to hold onto those fingers forever.

Too soon he said, "I should away."

"When will I see you again?"

"I can't tell you."

"But you know." She felt a desperate clawing in the back of her chest. It made her want to snatch at him and hang on.

As though he sensed her desperation, his voice softened. "Let it be as it will, Justine. Our time will come."

"But that's intolerable," she burst out.

"Live your life. Make it as large and extravagant as you can."

"But—"

"Don't wait for me."

She saw he was going to leave regardless of what else she said so she pulled back her protests. "Safe travels, my star-crossed voyager."

"And to you, my queen." He took her prosthetic to his mouth, kissed it as he bowed. It might have lasted longer, but Puddle became jealous. She mewed as she tilted sideways, falling into Arandasal's other arm and worming herself between them.

"Enough," he said, almost like a vow, a spurring forward of himself against his will. He turned and walked down the bridge, the line of his black coat fading into the mist with Puddle's small orange face looking back at Justine over his shoulder.

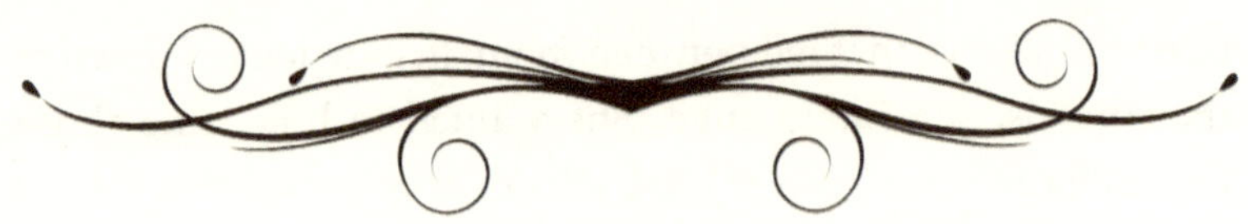

CHAPTER 40

The First Journey

The lights of the fae village cast a golden glow over the grass and the miniature buildings as Justine and Makbal approached the platform where Tassi, the fae called Posietta, and the fae called La, waited for them.

"Let me," whispered Makbal. "They need kid gloves, you know? We don't want to endanger the blessing by asking too many questions."

Justine shrugged. "You understand them better than I do."

Except this wasn't true any longer. As the fae greeted them with the customary chimes, Justine heard words in her head.

"Welcome, Mother Island," said Posietta, who Justine recognized as the fae who had met her in the archive. "We are pleased by your ascendance. As ever, the fae seek to provide the best services to suit your needs."

Forgetting she'd agreed to let Makbal lead, Justine said, "Did you give that same warm welcome to Guine when she came for your dust?"

Posietta's glowing body turned a darker shade of blue, then navy, with fissures of irritation in it.

"We have no dealings with the dead," said Tassi, flying aggressively toward Justine.

"Then how is it that two ships full of those dead managed to travel the Mouth of the Ocean?"

"Justine, now really isn't the—"

Justine waved her hand to cut Makbal off. "Our people have been captured and taken who knows where. Someone is responsible. I want to know who."

All three sets of fae eyes looked at her, little arms crossed over tiny chests. As one, they pressed their lips shut.

"We're here only for your blessing," said Makbal.

"So many blessings," sighed La. "That's all you ever want from us."

"The price has gone up," said Tassi. "Here's what we require." They thrust a scroll into the air. It caught as though on an invisible hook and unraveled before Justine and Makbal. Many items on the list were unfamiliar, but Justine recognized the names of things that seemed to be metals, machine parts, and gold.

"Of course, this is reasonable for the extra passage," said Makbal. "But what about a loan? Right now, we don't have—"

"We've already made an inventory of your collection and found you have sufficient items that one blessing may be given."

Justine looked at Makbal out the corner of her eye. *He has a collection?*

"But a loan, on promise of delivery—"

"Only one."

"I'm going," said Justine.

"That's not fair. I collected the payment through many dangerous—"

"The queen has first right." Tassi waved a hand. Decision made. More fae converged on the platform. One carried a sack of dust. Several whispered about Justine. One liked the look of her. Another wondered at the significance of her lost arm.

"Can a partial queen be a whole queen?"

"And so impolite with her demands."

"In such a hurry!"

Makbal looked at her. "Will you at least promise me some good strong boys capable of adventuring?"

"I promise nothing," said Justine.

"But Guine. The war."

Justine felt herself wanting to yell at him that he had no right to make any demands, that strong, beautiful boys weren't always the answer, and didn't he know this supposed war Guine had started wasn't a game? But she kept her mouth shut, even managed a polite smile as the fae sprinkled her with dust and sang the blessing.

"This dust of our wings now bears you to the land of the living, to grant half death before true death, that others may dream a better world, for in this sleep of death before, what dreams may come to make a better home for hearts so young."

Justine felt her heels lift off the ground, a delightful shiver traveled down her spine. She lifted her hands above her head and pushed off, a gentle upward swing, her gown fluttering. She twisted in a circle so the gown swished out from her waist in a spiral of green and silver. Now she was above the trees, the fae lights nothing more than dots. She tucked her arms toward her ankles and spun.

Weightless.

Granted the grace only creatures of the sky could know.

She angled herself up toward the moons, held her thumb up to cover it, and marked the stars to plot her course. *Second star to the right, and straight on to morning.* She took the slow route through the beginning of time on an empty planet, the coming together of continents, the rise and fall of giant creatures, the beginnings of villages, the beginnings of cities, then, finally, she swung herself around Big Ben and looked down on the smoke-clogged bustle of London, 1898.

Like a shadow she flew up to the village of Brompton and stole through the asylum window she'd left open that long past Halloween night. The patients lay asleep in their beds just as she remembered them. But now, the ones soon to die marked themselves on her awareness. She went to the bedsides of the two other children in the ward.

"When your time comes, join me here." She pressed her palm to their chests, giving them the map they would need to find their way to the island. Before the moment came, she hadn't thought how to complete this process. But in the moment, she found all answers within her. She merely had to call on her intention and it became real.

She went to Sarah's bed last. It seemed impossible how nothing had changed for her, the little elfin face, those golden curls. In her life, just yesterday, that kind German doctor had come and said he knew how to help her. She slept so peacefully with this promise of a life reclaimed not knowing how soon it would be lost.

"Come with me," whispered Justine as she pressed her hand to Sarah's chest. She kissed the girl's forehead and retreated to the window, flying away just as the first light of dawn broke the horizon.

MORNING ON THE ISLAND CAME AS BRIGHT AND CLEAR AS THE others before it, but Justine never grew tired of new days. If the island granted dusk moments of enchantment where anything seemed possible, its mornings came up from the horizon like a world washed clean of all that had come before, pristine, with no mistakes in it.

She rose from her bed and walked out to the balcony that

wrapped the turret of the north tower of her repaired and newly expanded castle. In repairing the island, it had risen higher from the sea, as though its roots had grown. The lagoon had become a lake that flowed into a river coursing down the center of the island. The cliffs spanned it on two sides like bridges. The tunnel downrealm remained. But to find it, one had to drive their boat directly into the rocks and trust what appeared solid was in fact something else.

The cliffs arose sleepy in a low cloudbank beyond the river, the jungle somehow larger, the mysterious ruins clearly visible dividing the greens of the jungle from the greens of the foothills. The Delt village and harbor were being rebuilt. The island in its fullness felt both smaller and infinite, a world she knew even more fully than she often felt she knew herself, but also a world with more to know than could ever be known.

When Justine turned her gaze to the sky, she saw the golden mountains of the eternal city in their clouds, and the dark rock shards of the Green Caves at the top of the falls. Between them, the rain of the dead falling to the current on their way to eternity. And when Justine turned her back and gazed out to the clear infinite sea, she saw children dropping down from the clouds dressed in all manner of funeral costume, shrouds, and nightclothes, with an abundance of nightgowns among them.

CHAPTER 41

An Ending that is also a Beginning

So you can see now, how the girl Justine, who is also the woman Thessaly, ruined a perfectly wonderful experiment in constructed paradise. Some of my kind argue that I cannot ascribe true blame because of the nature of time for immortals being so porous which, added to the confusion of her moving from a mortal to an immortal position, makes the entity of this person difficult to pin down. Is it Justine the mortal girl or Thessaly the god who wrought such devastation upon us? I think one cannot be separated from the other. Indeed, her very existence has created the environment which produced our catastrophe. A catastrophe that is ongoing despite what she thinks—that she's mended the island.

We remain trapped here, unable to travel back and forth as before. And there is a settling in the roots of the island, like earthquakes, but so slight only those of us listening for discord have noticed them. All is not well and here our new god is going off on adventures and adding children we cannot possibly support and assuming her new powers are infinite.

They most certainly are not. She would be nothing without our dust. This is also a thing that has not reverted. The gods are also not able to travel freely, though you wouldn't notice it for all the coming and going they're doing. The Voyager has the pretense of his rescue mission, but he returns frequently in secret, leaves messages on the bridge railing for the goddess. Like this one:

Harbin City
January 18, 2089

Why does he choose this covert path instead of presenting himself to her? Obviously, he knows there is still an error at work in our world, and she is the source. And what does he mean by this, leaving Justine places in time? Are they meeting there, away from watchful eyes? I pride myself on my pragmatism, and after all the damage he's done, I have decided Lord Mak must know this is happening. If they are conspiring to overthrow him, he should have warning and the chance to defend himself.

Please Leave a review!

- So glad this book found you! If you enjoyed reading it, please leave a review on Goodreads and Amazon if you use them. Please also tell people about this book. Books are sold by people talking about them. Cheers, Jaye

- You're welcome to post about The Island of Dreams all you want on your own socials, but if you want a dedicated place to discuss this, and my other books, with your fellow readers, join my private, member-only reader group on Facebook.

Coming Summer 2026!!!
The Island of Nightmares

The Immortal Dreamers duology concludes in this story of magical paradise gone wrong as the new goddess Justine navigates immortality, her growing desire for Arandasal and coparenting the children of the Neverland with Makbal in the midst of a conspiracy to take over the island that stretches all the way into the mortal realm.

Sign up for my mailing list to receive early offers and announcements.

Land Acknowledgement

The Island of Dreams was written on the ancestral land and traditional territories of the Omaha, Oto, and Pawnee Nations. They are the original custodians of the land on which I have lived and worked while writing this novel.

Acknowledgments

This book began during a writing activity for the Disability representation writing class I was teaching for the Loft Literary Center out of Minneapolis, Minnesota the fall of 2021. When possible, I write with my students. We were exploring stereotypes of disability by using Disney films. I think the particular prompt was to take a disabled villain and make them an able-bodied villain or take an able-bodied hero and make them a disabled hero.

I started to explore this idea of the Wendy figure from Peter Pan as someone who is also an amputee who must sneak onto the pirate ship to steal a prosthetic--because everyone knows if you need a prosthesis, a pirate would have one. The story has become much larger since then. When one starts reconfiguring Peter Pan, it becomes a lot. What I hope I've ended up with is a story that helps us re-see some ideas about what kind of people are able to claim paradise and what dreams look like we age into less pristine versions of our childhood selves.

Still, an idea is just an idea, and I didn't start taking this idea seriously until I was sitting in a medical center waiting to see whether or not my heart was likely to explode. For the first time, I was having to confront my own mortality. That day, I made a list of all the story moments I found Romantic/Magical. I was going to write a book about joy. Maybe I did that, but it's also no surprise, what I actually ended up writing was a book about our relationship to death.

I do not consider myself a fan of the original Peter Pan. For me, the magic first began with the 2004 film, *Finding Neverland* about an overworked, underappreciated mother who dies and is transported to Neverland through the magical dreamworld woven by John Barrie's adventures with her children. As I grew up and found myself increasingly aging out of socially acceptable options for storytelling and dreaming, this idea of expanding the Neverland beyond age-based childhood became one of my core beliefs. It is also the core of The Island of Dreams.

When I first started researching this project, I read a lot of literature contemporary to Barrie. I've been saying this is a Peter Pan novel, but the truth of it is that a good portion also came from MacDonald's *The Golden Key* and John Ruskin's *King of the Golden River*. The following is a mostly complete list of other stories that fed me something that ended up in this book.

- Pirates of the Caribbean (The ride and the 2003 movie in that order)
- The Sound of Music (1965 20th Century Fox)
- Walt Disney Animated Features
- Anne of Green Gables (1985 CBC)
- Pride and Prejudice (1995 BBC)
- Sandman (2022 Netflix)
- Moon Knight (2022 Disney Marvel)

Humans who made this book possible

Alea Hall for turning me onto George MacDonald.

Hannah Gage whose love for Peter Pan humbled me and kept me accountable to finding the truth within the story.

AJ Super who pointed out so many of my bad habits and was enthusiastic about this project enough to keep me going when all hope seemed lost.

Jo Beckwith whose advocacy and willingness to share about her life as an amputee on the unforgiving internet informed so much of this book. That's why Jo in San Francisco circa 2105 has her name.

My developmental editor Kit Haggard

My copyeditor Sarah McGuire

Thank you, thank you, thank you to my Kickstarter backers who made the hardcover special edition possible.

Jaye Viner lives on what used to be the plains of eastern Nebraska with a tall human and three fur bombs. She knows just enough about a wide variety of things to embarrass herself at parties she never attends. Her short fiction has been published in Drabblecast, Everyday Fiction, The Rumpus, and Others. She is the author of *Jane of Battery Park* and the *Elaborate Lives* series. Find her on Instagram @Jaye_Viner or her website JayeViner.com

www.ingramcontent.com/pod-product-compliance
Lightning Source LLC
Chambersburg PA
CBHW020349010826

48973CB00005B/1329